By Josh Aterovis

CAV CRAWFORD MYSTERIES
A Kind of Death

Published by DSP Publications
www.dsppublications.com

A KIND OF
DEATH

JOSH ATEROVIS

DSP PUBLICATIONS

Published by

DSP PUBLICATIONS

5032 Capital Circle SW, Suite 2, PMB# 279, Tallahassee, FL 32305-7886 USA
www.dsppublications.com

A Kind of Death
© 2023 Josh Aterovis

Cover Art
© 2023 Kris Norris
https://krisnorris.com
coverrequest@krisnorris.com
Cover content is for illustrative purposes only and any person depicted on the cover is a model.

Trade Paperback ISBN: 978-1-64108-436-9
Digital ISBN: 978-1-64108-435-2
Trade Paperback published April 2023
v. 1.0

Printed in the United States of America

Thanks to James Cavanaugh, Anthony Carter, and Berlin Kofoed for their all their help and advice while writing *A Kind of Death*.

A KIND OF DEATH

JOSH ATEROVIS

WADE RUSHED to catch up to the others, but the ground was uneven, and he kept tripping. They'd almost been to the house when Kyle realized they'd forgotten the EMF meter. They'd all forgotten it, but of course Kyle sent him back to the car to get it. It sucked being the youngest. Kyle liked to think he was the leader of their group. Technically he was the club president, but only because the school required that they have officers in order to be recognized. Kyle was the bossiest, but everyone in the group liked to order Wade around.

Sometimes he wondered why he put up with it. Did he even like them? But then he remembered sitting at home alone in his room trying to avoid his jerk of a father or his overbearing mother, and he knew, whether he liked them or not, it was better than being lonely.

Why had they parked so far away? Why was this field so big? And where were they? He was almost to the spot where he'd left them. They'd promised to wait for him, but he didn't see them anywhere.

He followed the tree line, figuring he'd catch up eventually. He almost rushed past it—a break in the trees that allowed a brief glimpse of a roofline. Was that where they were going?

As he fought his way through the underbrush toward the house, he noticed a second house a little farther into the woods. And was that a third one beyond that? He stopped in his tracks and looked around. How was he supposed to know which house they were investigating?

He pulled out his phone and shot the guys a text: *Where are you?*

He waited but got no reply. After a minute, he took a deep breath and yelled, "Where did you go? Which house?"

Still nothing.

They were probably hiding somewhere, waiting to jump out and scare him. They'd done it before. They thought it was hilarious.

With a heavy sigh, he continued to the first house. The porch was long gone, now just a pile of disintegrating rubble. The front door hung askew, clinging to the frame by one hinge. This place looked in much worse condition than the places they usually explored.

He clambered over the timbers, trying to avoid nails and sharp edges, until he made it to the door. He pushed it a little farther open and peered inside.

The back half of the house had caved in. Vines and small trees grew up through gaping holes in the floor. He was pretty sure the guys hadn't gone into this house.

Just to be sure, though, he called softly, "Guys? Are you in here?"

No answer.

He backed out just as carefully. Even if they were in there, he wasn't going in.

He glanced over at the next house. It looked a lot sturdier than the first ruin. The windows on the first floor were all boarded up. The porch was still standing. Just as he started to approach, he thought he heard a noise from inside. Was it a muffled scream?

The hair on the back on his neck stood up. Was something wrong? He almost turned back to the car, but he took a deep breath and stood his ground. It was probably just the guys messing with him. Or maybe someone was hurt. Either way, he couldn't just run away like a little kid. He'd never hear the end of it.

He took a deep breath and started toward the front of the second house again. When he reached the porch, he realized part of the floor had rotted away. The edges of one of the holes looked fresh, as if someone had put their foot through it. It made him more confident that the guys were inside.

He cautiously made his way across the porch, testing the floor with each step to make sure it was solid before he put his full weight on it. The front door had also been boarded up, but someone had pried enough boards away to allow them to squeeze through. The door stood ajar on the other side.

He pushed in and found himself in a very dark house. The only light came from the front door and the little that filtered down the wide staircase from the second floor. It smelled sour, like mildew and dust. As his eyes adjusted, he realized the house was still basically furnished, although it had clearly been vandalized at some point. All the furniture was flipped over, the stuffing pulled out of some of the pieces. Paper, debris, and broken knickknacks were scattered around the floor.

This place gave him the creeps. He was too nervous to call out for the others. He pulled out his phone and turned on the flashlight. Somehow the illumination made it worse. Where were they? Between the uneasy feeling the house gave him and waiting for the guys to jump out, he was crazy tense.

He took a step into what he assumed used to the living room and scanned the light around. Broken glass twinkled in the beam, but the light wasn't strong enough to pierce the darkness deeper into the house. The others had the strong flashlights with them. If they were back there, they'd have to wait a long time before he'd venture farther.

A loud thump from the second floor made him jump. His heart raced, but at least he knew where they were. He turned and headed for the staircase. He paused at the bottom and looked up. The stairs looked sturdy enough. Still, he gripped the banister and started a careful ascent.

The farther he went, the more his sense of dread grew. He wasn't even sure it had anything to do with being scared by the boys anymore. Something was wrong. Every fiber of his being was telling him to turn around and get out of the house. But if his friends were in trouble, he couldn't just leave them. He'd never forgive himself.

He reached the top of the stairs. The hallway was open to the staircase, separated only by the wooden handrail. Several doors opened off the hall. As he approached the first door, his terror grew.

The room came into view, and he stopped in his tracks.

Two bodies lay on the floor next to each other, facedown. He recognized both of them. He prayed the guys were pranking him, but it wasn't funny. He'd never been so scared. He edged closer but stopped outside the door.

Then he noticed the blood. A puddle of it. Too much. He gasped, frozen in place.

Before he could run, a figure leaped out from the doorway, swinging something toward him. He didn't even have time to scream.

Chapter 1

"ARE GHOSTS real?"

My attention snapped back to my professor as she paced the front of the room. My mind had wandered to the big break in the case I was working, but her words cut through. What had I missed? Why were we talking about ghosts?

World Religions was a recommended elective, and I had to admit, I wasn't taking it that seriously. In fact, the only reason I was there that morning was because Professor Lawson had told me that if I missed any more classes, I'd drop a letter grade, and my grade was already perilously low. I was a criminal justice major with a human services specialty, at the urging of my boss, and in my senior year. I wasn't interested in debating the existence of ghosts or talking about folklore and mythology.

"No, ghosts aren't real," said a guy in the front row of the class. "There's no empirical evidence that they exist."

"There's plenty of firsthand accounts," another girl spoke up.

"Sure, and there's plenty of people who claim they were abducted and probed by aliens too," the guy responded.

"We're not talking about your personal fantasies," the girl shot back.

"Has anyone here ever had an experience with a ghost?" Professor Lawson interrupted. I could have sworn she looked right at me.

I stayed quiet. It just so happened that I did see ghosts—I had as long as I could remember—but I'd be damned if I was going to admit that in class. I'd learned early on that it was better not to talk about it, especially with strangers. I was the weird kid who talked to himself for the first few years of school, and I still got teased about it even in high school whenever someone remembered. Eventually, I learned to ignore most of the spirits.

I'd tuned out again, lost in my own thoughts, when Professor Lawson's voice broke through once more.

"Cavanaugh?"

I jumped. Hardly anyone ever called me by my full name. I went by Cav almost exclusively.

"What about you?" she said, her eyes boring into mine. "Do you think ghosts are real?"

"What's real?" I countered. "If someone believes they have experienced a ghost, then it's more real to them than a—" I paused while I fished for an example. "—Komodo dragon."

Professor Lawson gave me an amused look. "A Komodo dragon?"

"Yeah, because they believe they've seen a ghost in person, but I bet they've never seen a Komodo dragon in person."

"But Komodo dragons *are* real," front row guy practically shouted. "Even if you've never seen one in person, they've been observed, they are at zoos, you can see them on TV."

"And we all know everything you see on TV is real," someone else said, and the class laughed.

The debate—argument, really—continued as I zoned out again.

This was my last class of the day, and I was eager to escape and get on the road. I had to drive to Philadelphia, and I wanted to get there while it was still light out.

A week ago, I'd been hired to find a fifteen-year-old kid. A distraught mother had shown up at our office door looking for help. My boss, private investigator Sutton Walker, assigned the case to me. He'd been giving me more of the missing people cases, especially if they involved teens. He said that at twenty-one, I had a better grasp on how teenagers thought than he did. I was new to investigating without his direct supervision, so it was still exciting to get a case of my own.

This particular case was challenging. Summer, the missing kid, was nonbinary, used they/them pronouns, and was having a rough time. While the mother was clearly struggling to understand and tripping over the correct terminology, the father was having an even harder time accepting it all and had been verbal with his disapproval. When school started and some of their classmates at their rural high school started giving them a hard time, the kid took off.

There wasn't much to go on. Summer was something of a loner at school, and their blog was mostly shared memes and vague text posts about not being understood—no clues as to where they might have gone or if they'd even had a destination in mind.

After asking around and showing photos everywhere I could think of, I'd finally gotten lucky and found my first clue. "Yeah, I remember that baby," the woman in the ticket counter at the bus station told me the day before. "Bought a ticket to Philly."

"You're sure it's them?"

"Yeah. I mean, I can't be one hundred, but I'm pretty sure. I only remember because she was alone."

"They."

"It was just her."

"I know, but they use they/them pronouns."

"Oh honey, I don't know nothing about all that. I just thought she—"

"They."

She scrunched up her face. "I just thought *they* looked so lost and little and scared, and she… they were clearly all alone, and I said, 'Baby, where you going all by yourself?' And they just slid the cash to me and said, 'Away.' Stood out to me, you know?"

It was something.

When Summer finally posted a selfie with an overpass in the background, Walker sent it to a PI he knew who worked in the Philadelphia area. The PI recognized the location, which meant I was going to the city. I had no idea if Summer was still there, but it was my best shot at finding them.

Finally, after what seemed like forever, the class ended. I grabbed my bag and started for the door, but Professor Lawson called my name.

I stifled a sigh and turned in her direction. She beckoned me closer, so I made my way to the front of the class against the flow of students pouring out of the room.

While it probably didn't sound like it, I actually liked Professor Lawson. She seemed cool. One of the first things she told us as she introduced herself on day one was that she was a practicing witch. She was a willowy white woman in her midforties with black hair cut in a sharp bob.

"Cavanaugh," she started as I approached.

"You can call me Cav, Professor Lawson," I said, cutting her off. "Sorry. It's just that only my grandmother calls me by my full name."

She peered at me over her black-framed glasses, her silvery-blue eyes measuring me up. "It's a good name."

I shrugged. "You wanted to see me?" I wasn't trying to be rude, but I was itching to get on the road. It was already midafternoon, and it was a two-hour drive from Baltimore to Philadelphia with no delays.

"Yes. While I appreciate your corporeal form being present in class, I'd love if your mind joined you now and then. I have a sense about you. I feel like you have a lot to offer."

"Sorry, Professor Lawson. I'm working on a case right now, and I've just been distracted lately."

"Yes, you've mentioned a few times that you work for a private investigator. I appreciate how working a job while going to school can be difficult, but when you're in my class, I'd like to ask you to at least try to be a little more attentive. I can't help but feel you don't take me or this course very seriously."

"Oh! I never meant to make you feel that way."

She cocked her head to one side. "I notice you didn't jump to say that you do take this class seriously."

My cheeks warmed. "I, um… I think it's an interesting class, and you seem especially interesting, but I guess I don't really see how this class contributes to my major."

"So you think that only classes that contribute to your ultimate goal have value?"

"I, uh—"

"What is your major, Cavanaugh?"

I noted the use of my full name, but it wasn't the time to press the point. "Criminal justice with a human services specialty."

"And you don't see how understanding what other people believe might be useful?"

"I mean, when you put it like that…."

"You seem like a very focused young man. You already have your career path chosen, and you're working to achieve those goals. That's very admirable. But I think it would be good for you to expand your horizons a little."

I nodded. "Yes, Professor Lawson."

She sighed. "Have you heard a word I've said?"

"Yes. I promise I'll pay more attention in class."

"That's great, and I hope you do, but if you want to bring your grade up, you'll need to do more than just pay attention."

"Like what?"

"Participate in discussions more, for one thing."

"I can do that." I would have agreed to about anything at that point just to end the conversation so I could leave.

"Are you interested in some extra credit?"

"Uh…. Sure, why not?"

She looked like she was holding back a smile, but she simply nodded. "Great. I liked what you said today about ghosts being real to people who have seen them. If you write a paper expanding on that idea, I'll give you some bonus grade points. The better it's written, the more points you get. Throw in some interviews with people who have seen ghosts and cite your sources and you might even salvage this class."

The last thing I wanted was another paper to write, but it was a fair bargain. "When is it due?"

"Midterms are coming up and I don't want to overburden you, so let's say before winter break. Does that seem doable?"

"Yes, ma'am. Very doable. Thank you. But if you'll excuse me, I have to drive to Philadelphia now, and I really need to get on the road."

She studied me silently for a moment, then waved me off. "Drive safe. I'll see you next week… Cav."

I broke into a smile. "See you next week!" As I spun around to leave, I was surprised to see one of the other students waiting by the door. I had a momentary flash of embarrassment, wondering how much of our conversation he'd overheard, but then I brushed it off. What did it matter?

I'd noticed him in class—he was gorgeous, so hard to miss—but we'd never spoken, and I didn't know his name. He was tall, close to six feet, with a narrow waist, broad shoulders, and muscles in all the right places. He wore his hair in shoulder-length dreads, and his honey-brown eyes held a warm intelligence. He didn't speak much more than I did in class.

"Were you waiting to see me, Kyreh?" Professor Lawson asked.

"Yes, if you have a minute," he said. He flashed me a smile and a nod as I passed him, and I returned the gesture on my way out the door.

I PARKED my car and took a deep breath. If I'd hoped to arrive with plenty of daylight left, I had failed miserably. An accident on I-95 had caused a traffic backup, and driving in an unfamiliar city had eaten up more time than I'd anticipated. So there I was, parked in a neglected lot just off a busy highway as the sun sank below the horizon and the streetlights flickered to life. Not an ideal situation when looking for a missing person in a potentially dangerous location you've never been to before.

I leaned over, popped open my glove box, and rummaged through it until I found the canister of pepper spray I kept in the car for dicey situations. If looking for a teenage runaway in a homeless encampment in Philadelphia after dark didn't qualify as dicey, I don't know what would. My boss had a strict no-gun policy that I was more than happy to abide by, but I was on the small side, and my mama didn't raise a dummy.

I flipped the safety switch back and forth a couple of times, slid the pepper spray into my pocket, climbed out of the car, and headed toward the tent city set up under the overpass. In the twilight, with the added sickly orange light cast by the sodium lamps, it looked especially unwelcoming.

As I neared the campsite, I noticed that in addition to the tents, there were quite a few people lying on the ground, some wrapped up in blankets but some directly on the pavement or on pieces of cardboard. There were at least a dozen people that I could see, and possibly more in the darker areas away from the lights.

I was being watched. A woman in a faded floral dress worn over a pair of jeans stared at me warily as I approached. She was standing protectively in front of a blue tent, feet apart, arms crossed over her chest.

I smiled at her and hoped it translated as friendly and not nervous. I'd been going to school in Baltimore for the past four years, but sometimes I still felt like a country bumpkin.

"Hi," I greeted her.

She didn't smile back. Or respond in any way, for that matter.

"I'm looking for someone," I said as if she had replied. "Maybe you can help me?"

Her eyes narrowed. Up close, I could see the dirt on her face. She was very tan under the grime, and her face was creased. Her hair was dark, though. It was impossible to guess her age, but she looked as if she'd lived a rough life.

I pulled my phone out of my pocket and opened a photo of Summer. I held it up for her to see. I belatedly realized flashing my phone around here probably wasn't my smartest move.

The woman still didn't speak, but our one-sided conversation had caught the attention of a nearby tent owner. The gray-haired Black man sitting in the tent crawled out and shambled over. He glanced at the picture on my phone, then at me.

"You might want to put that away."

I smiled uneasily and slid the phone back into my pocket. At least he'd spoken to me. I shifted my attention to him. "Thanks. Have you seen the person I'm looking for?"

"Ain't nobody here wants to be found."

I reached back into my pocket and pulled out a twenty-dollar bill. "I know. And probably for good reason, but I really need to find them."

He glanced at the bill in my hand. "They a friend of yours?"

"Yeah." It was a fib. I was a good liar. I lied a lot in my line of work. I had to. "I just want to help."

He shrugged. "That's what they all say."

"Please. It's important that I find them."

He held out his hand. I debated with myself for a second, then gave him the twenty. He quickly shoved it into his pocket. "I guess you don't look like too much of a threat."

Once again, my boyish stature worked to my advantage. No one was ever intimidated by me. Most of the time that was a good thing, though not always. I felt particularly vulnerable under that overpass, for instance.

He jerked his head toward the darkest part of the lot, deep in the shadows of the overpass. I could make out a few people huddled against the concrete wall. "Over there." Then he turned and crawled back into his tent.

I turned back to the woman. She hadn't moved a muscle. She was still glaring at me. I smiled again. "Have a good night."

I quickly made my way across the camp, weaving through the tents and sleeping areas, trying to be as sensitive to their space as possible. A few people watched me—some with wary expressions, some curious, some impassive—but most ignored me or were in their own little worlds.

As I approached the three figures against the wall, I immediately ruled out one of them. She was far too old and the wrong race. She was also unconscious, legs sprawled akimbo, head rolled back. At least I hoped she was only unconscious.

The other two would take a closer inspection. One lay on their side, face turned away from me, wrapped tightly in a grubby blanket. The other sat with their back against the concrete, knees pulled up to their chest, head down in their arms. They wore a knit cap over their hair, but now that

I was just a few feet away, I thought I could see a few pale wisps curling around the edges. Something about the body type and hair made me think I'd found Summer.

I walked over and crouched down by the sitting figure. "Summer?"

The head snapped up and a pair of huge round eyes met mine, theirs filled with fear.

"Hey, it's okay. My name is Cav. I'm here to help."

Summer looked around frantically, as if searching for an escape route.

"Your mom really wants you to come home."

Their eyes found mine again. "Yeah, right."

"No, really. She hired me to find you. She's really worried."

"And Dad?"

"Honestly, I don't know. I haven't met him. He's writing my check, though, so that has to count for something, right? And trust me, I'm not cheap." I laughed, but Summer didn't crack a smile.

"Who are you?" they asked.

"Cav Crawford. I'm a private investigator."

"How did you find me?"

"A bit of luck and a lot of work."

"I'm not going home. Not with my dad."

"Has he hurt you?"

Summer rolled their eyes. "Not physically, if that's what you mean. But he's sure made it clear how little he cares about my feelings or who I am."

"I'm really sorry to hear that. Your mom seems to be trying, though. She really wants to know you're okay."

"What… what did she say?" Summer was looking anywhere but at me.

"She told me she was worried sick. She hasn't been sleeping—"

"I mean about me. What did she say about me?"

"Oh. She said that you told them that you're nonbinary a couple months ago, and that you asked them to call you Summer and use they/them pronouns. She said your dad was kind of a jerk about it."

"She said that?"

"Maybe not in those exact words, but yeah. She also said school was really rough for you this year."

"Understatement."

"She wants to help with that, though. She said you wouldn't have to go back to school until you were ready. She's already talked to the school. Apparently they're doing some sensitivity training about what being nonbinary means and stressing their zero-tolerance bullying policy. You'll be protected if... *when* you go back."

Summer looked surprised. "Are you serious? They're actually doing all that?"

"That's what your mom said."

"Huh."

"So what do you think? You ready to leave this luxury resort and head back with me?"

Summer glanced around. "They've been nice to me here. Mostly. Some of them watch out for me."

"Your mom would like to watch out for you too."

They avoided eye contact.

"Look, if you don't feel safe at home—"

"It's not that."

"Okay, then I think you've made your point, don't you? Let's go home."

I stood up and held out a hand. After a moment's hesitation, they slid their small hand into mine, and I pulled them to their feet.

IT WAS almost midnight when I got back to the office. I'd dropped Summer off at home to a very relieved mother and a surprisingly emotional father. I had a feeling he'd be making more of an effort going forward. I could have gone home, but I wanted to get my notes typed up while they were fresh on my mind. That way our office manager, Jordan Fisher, would be able to submit the final report and billing to our satisfied clients as quickly as possible. Besides, I was keyed up and excited from such a happy ending. Most of our cases involved cheating spouses or insurance fraud, so this was a cause for celebration.

Our office was located in a slightly run-down 1980s-era strip mall on the outskirts of Baltimore City. Our neighbors included a Mexican restaurant, a cell phone store, a thrift shop, a sad little pet store, and a space that seemed to change at least once a year but was currently serving as a Korean church.

The restaurant was going strong, the sound of lively Tejano music spilling out into the parking lot, but the rest of the storefronts were locked up and dark. I let myself into our office and flipped on the light before locking the door behind me, then went directly to the security panel to disable the alarm.

If the alarm was armed, I knew I was alone in the building. It wasn't uncommon for Walker to work late nights, something I often gave him a hard time about. It wasn't lost on me that I was apparently falling into the same bad habits.

I crossed the reception area and paused by Jordan's desk, checking to make sure there was nothing in my inbox. His desk stretched across the far end of the room, with a door to one side that led to a long hallway. Three doors opened off the hallway—the bathroom, my office, and Walker's office.

When I'd started at the agency as an intern in my sophomore year, I'd mostly worked the front desk. I quickly showed an aptitude for investigation, though, and Walker found my knowledge of technology and social media especially helpful, so when my internship ended, he'd offered to keep me on—on the condition that I got my private investigator's license. I did, and my reward was my own office. I loved it, even if it was basically a glorified broom closet.

I unlocked my office and turned on the tarnished brass architect's lamp that had belonged to my father. I sat down at the desk, opened my case notes, filled in the night's happenings, then shot the finished product off to Jordan in an email. I was just locking up when my phone vibrated. It was a text from my friend and roommate, Haniah.

Are you coming home tonight? She worried about me when she knew I was out working a case.

Leaving the office. On my way home now, I texted.

Are you seriously at work right now?

I laughed and shot back a quick reply. *Yes, I wanted to type up my notes. Another successful conclusion to a case.*

You're ridiculous. Are you hungry?

I realized that I was, in fact, starving. I hadn't eaten since lunch. *So hungry.*

Come home. I'll order pizza.

Be right there.

I locked up and headed home. Haniah and I rented a two-bedroom apartment on the second floor of an old Victorian in Lauraville, a neighborhood in the northeast corner of Baltimore. It was convenient, being equidistant from my office and Waring University, but also cheap for how nice it was.

As I opened our door, Haniah was waiting for me with a disapproving scowl, arms crossed under her generous bosom in an oversize orange tee that she would never be caught dead in outside of our apartment. Even dressed down, she was stunning—taller than me and curvaceous, with dark skin, upturned catlike eyes, and a cloud of dark natural hair.

"Uh, hi," I greeted her.

"Only you would be working at midnight on a Wednesday night," she said in a mock-scolding tone. "And forget to eat." Haniah had grown up in Ghana, and while she spoke fluent English—along with at least three other languages—her accent added a lyrical cadence to everything she said.

"You don't know that I forgot to eat," I said as I hung my keys on the rack.

She raised an eyebrow as I closed and locked the door.

"Okay, I forgot to eat."

"The pizza should be here soon," she said with a chuckle as she headed into the living room.

I followed her and dropped onto the sofa as she curled into one of the big, comfy chairs by the window.

"How was your day?" I asked.

"It was fine. Just class and homework. You closed your case?"

"Yeah, a happy ending for a change."

Before I could elaborate, her phone buzzed.

"Pizza's here!" She jumped up to answer the door. Moments later, she returned carrying a large pizza box. She popped it open and offered it to me first, so I grabbed a piece and started eating. Haniah took a slice for herself and then set the box on the coffee table before she reclaimed her place in her favorite chair.

"So you said your case had a happy ending?"

"Yep. Best-case scenario," I said with my mouth full.

"So which case was this?"

"The runaway teen," I explained.

"Ah. You didn't tell me much about that one. Why did they run away?"

"They were misunderstood at home."

"What teen isn't?" Haniah came to America for college partly because she was bisexual and could be more open here.

"Well, they're nonbinary, so it's a whole other can of worms."

Haniah made a face. "Ew. Why would you have a can of worms?"

"It's just a saying," I explained. "It means that something is a lot more complicated or unpleasant than you might think."

"But why worms?" Haniah insisted.

"It doesn't matter!" I said, exasperated. "The important part is that I found them."

"Where were they?"

"In a homeless camp in Philly. That's why I was working so late. But they're home safe and sound now."

"Good," Haniah cooed, the worms forgotten. "Poor baby. I'm so glad you found them."

"Me too. The place where I found them…. It was awful. I know we have plenty of homeless camps here in Baltimore, but it was so intimidating. I can't imagine being out there on my own at Summer's age. They're so tiny. It could have been really bad for them."

"But you found them and they're back home," she said. "Happily ever after."

I sighed. "There's no such thing. Life isn't a Disney movie. Their dad sounds like a dick."

She frowned. "Is he abusive?"

"I don't know. Maybe emotionally. But he seemed really relieved that Summer was home, so who knows. Maybe he'll come around."

She nodded. "Either way, the case is over. You have to let go."

"Intellectually, I know you're right. Family stuff just gets to me, you know."

Her face softened. "You've got a great family."

"Oh, I know. But family means a lot to me."

"Of course. You experienced a lot of loss," she said.

"That's an understatement," I muttered.

When I was a baby, most of my family died in a tragic multi-car accident caused by a drunk driver. My father, his parents, and my maternal grandfather all died. Only my mom, her mother, and I survived, although my grandmother was paralyzed from the waist down.

If that wasn't enough, when I was fifteen, my mom was diagnosed with an aggressive form of breast cancer. She was dead within a year.

"But you still have your nana," Haniah said. "And Jason and Eli. And best of all, you have me!"

I rolled my eyes and laughed. "Lucky me."

Jason and Eli were my adopted dads. Jason was my mom's best friend since grade school, so I'd known him my whole life. He and Eli were a huge support when Mom got sick. There was never any question about where I'd go when she passed.

I shook off those memories. "But enough of that. Let's change the subject."

"Of course." She stood up. "I'll get us some drinks. Any preference?"

I shook my head as I shoveled in more pizza. She handed me an ice-cold can of Natty Boh beer on her return.

We chewed and drank for a moment before Haniah asked with exaggerated casualness, "So… how's your love life?"

"That wasn't what I had in mind when I said to change the subject." My love life was a bit of a sore subject since the death of my last boyfriend.

"You can't stay alone forever," she said.

I opened my mouth, showing off my chewed pizza, then swallowed. "I can if I want to."

"Is that what you really want? That's not healthy. You've got to get back out there eventually, Cav," she scolded.

"Oh my God, I will. When I'm ready."

"It's been a year."

"So?"

"So that's a long time to be alone and sad. You're still seeing your therapist, right?"

"Duh." I reached for another slice of pizza.

"What does she say?"

"She says you should stay out of my business."

"All you do is work, go to school, and hang out with me. You should be dating and having fun."

"We have fun."

"That's not what I mean, and you know it."

I threw my hands up. "When am I supposed to even have time to meet guys? I've got work and school."

Haniah huffed. "That's just an excuse. You had time for Mason."

I tried not to flinch at his name. "And how would I meet these hypothetical guys?"

"It's the twenty-first century," she said with exaggerated patience. "There are dating apps."

"Yeah, I've been on them," I snapped. It was how I'd met Mason. I'd deleted all of the apps when we started dating and hadn't re-downloaded them since he disappeared. It felt unfaithful, somehow, as if I'd be defiling his memory. "I'm not looking for a hookup."

"Who said anything about a hookup?" she said. "But while we are on the subject, maybe that is exactly what you need."

"What I need is more time."

"How much more time? Don't you think Mason would want you to move on?"

I stopped chewing and stared.

"What?" she asked.

"You don't know what he would want," I said quietly.

"I know he wouldn't want you to be sad and miserable forever. He would want you to love and be loved again. You deserve that."

"Haniah, I love you and I appreciate that you're worried about me, but I'm not a project."

"Well...." She drew out the word dramatically.

"Shut it." I yawned suddenly. "Sorry, psychoanalyzing me has been a blast and all, but it's getting late, and I have work and class tomorrow. Can we just drop it for now so I can get to bed?"

"Of course," she said. She was still watching me carefully, so I knew this wouldn't be the last I heard of the subject. Haniah had always been the protective type, but after Mason disappeared, it was like she saw herself as my caretaker. It was very sweet, and I knew it came from a good place, but it could be a little suffocating at times. Still, I adored her.

I stood up and held my hand out for her. "Thanks for feeding me," I said. She took my hand, and I pulled her up and into a hug. "And thank you for caring about me."

Haniah hugged me back, then gently pushed me away, holding on to my shoulders. "Somebody has to make sure you aren't wasting away. I know I'm a pain sometimes, but it's only because I worry about you."

I gave her a half smile. "I know. But I'm okay. I promise. You don't have to always be poking around in my private life."

She didn't look fully convinced, but she let go of my shoulders and patted me on the cheek. "Yes, I do." She picked up the pizza box and started down the hall to the small kitchen. "I'll stick the leftovers in the fridge."

I collected the spent beer cans to recycle and followed her.

WITH OUR conversation still running through my head, I got ready for bed and turned off the light. Once under the covers, though, I couldn't turn off my brain. Maybe Haniah was right. Maybe it was time to get back out there. My therapist kept telling me I'd know when I was ready, but *how* would I know? Certainly no one had caught my eye in a long time. I mean, I noticed guys I found attractive, but I didn't have any interest in actually approaching them or going on a date.

I grabbed my phone from next to my bed and downloaded one of the apps. When I logged in, it immediately connected to my old profile. I briefly wondered if that meant my conversation with Mason was still in my chats but resisted the urge to look. Instead, I closed the app and returned my phone to the bedside table. I was pretty sure I still wasn't ready, and I didn't know when I would be.

I tried to fall asleep, but my mind refused to cooperate, and my body was still buzzing from the excitement of my day. After tossing and turning for a while, I gave up and slipped out of my bed. I needed to clear my mind. I wasn't much into meditation, but I remembered a ritual my mom used to do when she was stressed. She said my nana had taught her when she was little.

I slid out from under my blanket and grabbed a candle and a box of matches off my dresser. My mom had given me the candle when she got sick. I rarely lit it because I didn't want it to melt away, but Mom was on my mind tonight, and it seemed appropriate.

I placed the candle on the floor and sat in front of it, closed my eyes, and took a deep, calming breath. After a few moments, I opened my eyes, grabbed a box of matches, and lit the wick.

I hadn't said the prayer in years, so it took a few seconds to remember how it started. Then it came to me.

"Tonight, I honor my ancestors. Spirits of my fathers and mothers, I call to you and welcome you to join me for this night. You watch over me always, protecting and guiding me, and tonight I thank you. Your blood runs in my veins, your spirit is in my heart, your memories are in my soul."

There was more, but I couldn't remember it. I hadn't said it since before my mom died. Tears pricked my eyes just thinking about her, and suddenly, I was hit with a wave of grief. I still missed her. That thread of grief led to one much more recent, one still raw and painful where my grief for my mother had softened over the years.

A little over a year ago, my boyfriend Mason didn't show up for our one-year anniversary dinner. It turned out he'd vanished entirely. His parents were frantic. I was panicked. Needless to say, it was very triggering for me.

For months no one knew what happened to him. Then a hiker found his body off a trail in a state park, miles away. He was so badly decomposed that the police weren't even sure about his cause of death. The medical examiner found a fracture in his skull, but there was no way to tell if he'd fallen and hit his head or if he'd been attacked. In the end, they called it an accident and that was the end of it—officially, at least.

None of it made sense. Why had he gone to that park that day? What was he doing? Why didn't he mention it to me? Was he hiding something? Was he with someone? If so, why didn't they help him when he fell? *If* he fell.

I had so many unanswered questions, but these thoughts weren't helping. I was supposed to be clearing my mind so I could relax.

I refocused on the candle flame and started again, hoping more of the words would come back to me this time. "Tonight, I honor my ancestors. Spirits of my fathers and mothers, loved ones who have gone before, I call to you and welcome you to join me for this night…." I paused again, then sighed. "Oh, Mason McKibben, what happened to you? I wish I could see you again."

I leaned forward and blew out the candle. This was a waste of time.

Suddenly there was another presence in the room. My eyes hadn't adjusted to the dark, so I was as good as blind, but I knew someone else was there. I scrambled backward, reaching for my phone, but froze as my eyes fell on a figure standing by my window. I recognized him immediately.

"Mason."

As soon as I spoke his name, Mason—if that's really who it was—vanished, leaving me even more unsettled than I was before I'd lit the candle. Questions flew through my mind.

Despite the fact that I'd seen ghosts as long as I could remember, I'd never seen anyone I knew—not after my father and grandparents died, not after my mom died. It was decidedly more upsetting when you knew them, when you'd slept with them and loved them. Why had Mason appeared? Did I summon him somehow? And more importantly, why did he vanish?

A visit with my grandmother was in order, but I couldn't very well just show up at her facility in the middle of the night. Reluctantly, I crawled back into bed, pulled the blankets over my head, and willed myself to sleep. It took a while, but eventually I drifted off.

Chapter 2

UNDERSTANDABLY, I was dragging the next morning. My classes were in the afternoon, so after a shower, I went to the office.

"What are you doing here?" Jordan asked when I came through the door.

"I work here," I shot back.

"I figured you'd take the morning off after your late night. Congrats on wrapping up that case, though."

"Thanks. I still have some paperwork to catch up on. You know Walker."

Jordan nodded knowingly. He was a few years older than me, midtwenties, and mixed race, with curly brown hair and big hazel eyes. He was quite the looker, but I had no idea how he identified, and I wouldn't want to get involved with a coworker even if he were into guys.

I passed the desk and let myself into my office. Since I'd wrapped up Summer's case, I was technically between jobs, but, as I'd said to Jordan, that didn't mean there wasn't paperwork and other stuff to work on. Walker was a stickler for a paper trail. During my internship, I'd done a lot to move Walker in more of a digital direction—most of our reports and stuff like our travel logs were now online—and Jordan had continued in that vein after he was hired, but Walker still insisted we print everything out and keep a hard copy as backup. I spent a little time updating my logs, but I couldn't keep my mind off Mason.

When he'd vanished, there'd been a massive search for him, followed by months of not knowing anything. Then, when his body was found, I thought I'd finally get some answers, but no. Only more questions.

I was startled from my thoughts when Walker appeared in the doorway. "Knock-knock."

My boss was retired CIA, and he looked the part. He had a sort of everyman look that had served him well in both of his chosen careers. Tall

and trim, he kept his salt-and-pepper hair short and perfectly parted and
had a well-groomed mustache that was still dark brown. His icy blue eyes
had a way of looking right through you.

He raised an eyebrow. "You're awfully jumpy this morning."

"Just a lot on my mind," I replied with a sigh.

"Anything to do with your last case?"

"No, that's all wrapped up."

He nodded. "You did a good job on that."

"Thank you."

"Think you're ready for another case?"

I was surprised. "What do you mean?"

"I just got a call about a possible new case."

"For me?"

"That's up to you. Have you heard about those missing kids in
Baltimore County? The four boys?"

"Yeah, it's been all over the news. Didn't they find one of them?"

"They did, and it's his parents who want to hire you."

"They want to hire me?"

"Well, I suggested you for the case. I have plenty on my plate right
now, and you're free after wrapping up that runaway case. Besides, you're
closer to the boys' age and you've proven you have a knack for finding
missing people lately."

Everyone except Mason, I thought. Out loud, though, I simply said,
"Ah. If their kid is the only one who's been found, then why do they want
to hire us?"

"They'll explain everything. It's better you hear it directly from
them. But let's just say that, as the only one who has turned up so far, their
son is obviously a person of interest with the police."

"So they want me to find out what happened and prove their kid
innocent. But if the police think he did it…."

"I don't know what the police think. I only said he's a person of
interest."

"Okay, so what do I have to do, call them?"

"They're coming in to meet with you."

"What? When?"

"Now."

"As in right now?"

"Yep. Your calendar said you were free."

"I mean, I am, but you couldn't have warned me?"

"What do you think I'm doing?"

"I'm not dressed to meet with clients—"

"You look like a college student."

"I *am* a college student!"

"That's the point."

I looked down at my stretched-out secondhand sweater and jeans. They would have to do. The only clothes I kept in my car were what I thought of as my skulking outfit—black jeans, a black T-shirt, and a black sweatshirt. Maybe I should start keeping a change of nicer clothes in my office.

"Trust me," Walker said. "You're fine. They'll be here in fifteen or twenty minutes. It should give you plenty of time to meet with them and still make it to class on time. It's up to you whether you take the case or not." He disappeared from my doorway and returned to his office.

I quickly looked up an article about the missing kids to refresh my memory. The four boys, all students at the same high school in northern Baltimore County, had vanished over a week ago. They left together the previous weekend to go ghost hunting and never came home. There was a manhunt, but it was difficult since no one knew where they were going.

Four photos of the boys accompanied the article, very obviously school pictures. Kyle Itoh stared stoically into the camera. He looked younger than his reported age of sixteen. Thin, with a baby face, straight black hair, and serious dark eyes behind glasses. DJ Juarez also had black hair, though his was a mass of unruly curls, and dark eyes, but even though he was a year younger, he looked more solid than Kyle. He wore a big smile. Wade Smith was fourteen, a chubby boy with a round face, reddish-brown hair in a bowl cut, and blue eyes that looked sad despite his polite smile. Last was Gareth Miller. He was a cute sixteen-year-old with curly brown hair, big brown eyes, and a goofy smile.

According to the article, Gareth Miller was found two days ago wandering on the side of the road, dazed, dirty, bloody, and dehydrated. There was no sign of the other three boys. There was no question that it was an intriguing puzzle.

My desk phone chirped. It was Jordan.

"The Millers are here to see you," he said.

"I'll be right out."

I found a couple waiting in the lobby area, standing nervously a few feet from the desk. The man was tall and fit, white, probably in his early forties, with brown hair graying at the temples. The woman was roughly my height, also white, with warm brown eyes and a mass of curls. She looked a little younger than her husband. They both tried to smile, but behind their polite expressions, I could read the stress and exhaustion in their eyes.

"Hello, I'm Cav Crawford," I said, extending my hand.

"I'm Iwan Miller," he replied, pumping just a little too hard. "This is my wife, Robin."

She nodded but didn't offer her hand.

"It's nice to meet you, but I'm sorry for the circumstances," I said. "Why don't you come into my office?" I led them down the hall and indicated the chairs in front of my desk. Once we were seated, I jumped right into it. "I know you've got to be tired of talking about it, and you probably just went over it all with Mr. Walker, but why don't you tell me what's going on and why you want to hire me."

"What do you know already?" Mr. Miller asked.

"I only know what's been reported in the news, but assume I know nothing. I want to hear it from you."

He drew in a deep breath. "Two Saturdays ago, our son, Gareth, told us he was going out with his friends Kyle, Wade, and DJ. They formed some sort of ghost-hunting club at school. They were always off investigating something or other. To be honest, I didn't pay as much attention as I probably should have. Gareth is a good kid, never caused us any trouble. His friends seemed like good kids. We just didn't worry about them."

"How long had they been doing their ghost hunting?" I asked.

He turned to his wife. "A few months?"

"They started getting into it about a year ago," she said. "Kyle and Gareth have been watching those ghost-hunting shows on TV for years. Then they suddenly decided they wanted to do it. All Gareth wanted for Christmas last year was ghost-hunting equipment."

"Equipment?"

"Meters and digital recorders, that sort of thing."

"And did the boys know each other before they started the club?"

Mrs. Miller answered again. "Just Gareth and Kyle. The club was their idea. The other boys were the only ones who joined."

"Okay, so they left to go ghost hunting. Do you know where?"

They both looked slightly guilty. "No," Mrs. Miller answered.

"Tell me what happened."

"He never came home." Mr. Miller resumed his narrative. "None of them did. By nightfall, we were all panicking. The parents of the boys, I mean. It was so out of character for all of them. We knew something was wrong. None of them were answering their phones. We tried to use Gareth's phone tracker, but he must have turned it off at some point or turned off his cloud access, I don't know. It couldn't be located."

"None of their phones could be traced?"

"Only three of them, Gareth and Kyle and Wade, had phones with them. DJ doesn't have a phone."

"What about the other phones?"

"Neither had the trackers activated."

"Got it. What did you do next?"

"We called the police. There was a search, but none of us had asked where they were going, so no one knew where to start. We're just not helicopter parents, you know?"

"No one is blaming you."

"Oh yes, they are," Mrs. Miller said sharply. "You'd better believe plenty of people are judging us. I've seen the comments online. 'What kind of parent doesn't know where their kids are?' And worse. People are saying this is our fault. Maybe they're right."

"You can't be with them every second of the day," I tried to assure them.

"Still—"

"Blaming ourselves isn't going to change what happened," Mr. Miller cut in.

"Right," I agreed. "Let's get back to what did happen. The police searched but obviously didn't find anything. What happened next?"

Mr. Miller continued, "Nothing happened until two days ago. It was the longest eight days of my life. We talked to the police every day, several times a day. We went on the news. We begged and pleaded that if anyone knew something, to contact the police."

"And no one did?"

"There were a few calls, but they were all cranks or dead ends. Nothing that amounted to anything. Then on Tuesday, we got a call from the police. We were expecting the worst, but… they said they'd found him, found Gareth." Mr. Miller's voice broke, but he held himself together.

Mrs. Miller picked up the story. "We'd hoped, you know, but every day that went by it just seemed less likely." She shook her head. "But they found him."

"Alone?"

"Yes, no sign of the other boys." Mrs. Miller looked guilty again. "I feel bad being so relieved when I know what the other parents are still going through."

"It's only natural to feel relieved. What did the police tell you when they called?"

Mr. Miller had composed himself enough to continue. "Not much at first, just that they'd found him on the side of the road and he was in rough shape. They were taking him to the hospital."

"We rushed right there," Mrs. Miller said. "They wouldn't let us see him for a while. They wouldn't tell us anything either, just that he was being stabilized."

"Eventually they told us that he was severely dehydrated. A while later, they allowed us to see him. There was a police officer in the room with him. They still wouldn't say why. We didn't know if something was wrong, if they still thought he was in danger or what. Gareth was on an IV and looked…." Mr. Miller faltered again.

"He looked terrible," Mrs. Miller said softly. "They didn't warn us. He was… gray and covered in cuts and scratches. And so skinny. He looked so tiny in that hospital bed. Plus, he was confused. The doctors said that was because he was so dehydrated. They were worried his organs might shut down. It was horrible. We'd just gotten him back only to find out we still might lose him."

"What do you mean by confused?"

"He couldn't remember anything that happened while he was missing."

"Nothing at all?"

"Nothing. And he also seemed to sort of go in and out about other things. He kept forgetting where he was, he asked what year it was, and it was almost like he didn't recognize us at first."

"The doctor said that was all pretty normal for someone as dehydrated as he was," Mr. Miller said. "They thought he would be okay once he rehydrated."

"But he wasn't?"

"He… looks better. They're not worried about his organs. But he still doesn't remember anything. It's like he has amnesia. And he's still not himself…."

"He's been through a lot," Mrs. Miller said. "We can't expect him to be back to himself already."

"I know, but he almost seems like a different person sometimes."

"What are the police saying?" I interrupted gently.

Both of their heads swiveled toward me. "What do you mean?" Mrs. Miller asked, an edge to her voice.

"Do they have any theories about what might have happened?"

Mrs. Miller's lips tightened. Mr. Miller spoke up after a long, uncomfortable pause. "The police are considering Gareth a person of interest."

I could almost hear air quotes around the phrase "person of interest." "Do you know what that means?"

"It means they think my son had something to do with the disappearance of his friends," Mrs. Miller said tightly.

"We don't know that," Mr. Miller said quickly, laying a calming hand on his wife's arm. He turned back to me. "They haven't told us anything directly, but from the questions they've been asking, it sounds like at the very least, they think Gareth is lying about his memory or hiding something."

"What kinds of questions have they been asking?"

"Was he having any problems with any of the other boys? Had he ever lied to us? Had he seemed different lately?"

"They thought it was suspicious that he had turned off his phone's tracker," Mrs. Miller said. "They kept asking why he would do that. How the hell am I supposed to know?"

Mr. Miller took her hand. "Hon…."

"It's okay," I said. "This is a hard time." I gave them a moment to pull themselves together. "So what exactly do you want to hire me to do?"

Mr. Miller took over again. "We want you to find out what happened."

"Isn't that what the police are trying to do?"

"They couldn't even find Gareth and the boys. All they're doing now is trying to pin it on him so they don't look like complete fools. They want to make him a scapegoat."

I couldn't deny that stuff like that happened, even if it did seem far-fetched in this case. Even just hearing their side, the whole thing sounded fishy. Still, I had to admit I was intrigued. "Who is the officer in charge of this case?" I asked.

"Detective Gibson," Mr. Miller said.

I knew a few cops in the area, but I didn't recognize that name. If I took the case, I'd have to check in with my contacts there. Walker and I tried to keep a cordial relationship with the police. Sometimes they'd cooperate with us as long as we promised to keep them informed on what we discovered in our own investigation.

"Will you help us?" Mrs. Miller asked.

"I'd like to talk to Gareth before I make a decision. Is that possible?"

They looked at each other. "We'll find out and get back to you," Mr. Miller said, turning back to me.

I glanced at the clock. I needed to leave soon to get to my class on time, but I still had a ton of questions running through my mind. "Tell me more about Gareth," I said.

"Like what?" Mrs. Miller asked.

"Anything you think of. I want to get a feel for him before I meet him."

"He's a good kid. Never been in trouble. Not real trouble. There's normal teenage boy stuff, but nothing serious. Straight As at school. Always the teacher's pet. A little bit of a… a geek, I guess you'd say."

"I wouldn't say a geek," Mr. Miller said. "Just… studious."

Mrs. Miller smiled a little. "He's a big old nerd, and you know it. Just like his daddy. He's sixteen, wants to be a scientist one day and a paranormal investigator the next."

"I told him that's not even a real job," Mr. Miller said, almost under his breath.

"He reads a lot. Likes video games. He's a normal kid."

"Any siblings?"

"No, he's our only child."

"What about his friends?"

"Kyle is his best friend," Mr. Miller took over. "They've been friends since they started school. Another good kid. We know his family well since they've practically grown up together. They're good people, Hiro and Marta. We don't really know the other boys that well, Wade and DJ. They're a little younger, in a different grade."

"What are their last names?"

"Kyle Itoh," Mr. Miller said confidently, then faltered.

"Wade Smith and DJ Juarez," Mrs. Miller provided.

I glanced at the clock again. "I'm afraid I have to go, but I do want to talk to Gareth as soon as possible. I'll give you my cell number so you can let me know when you find out if I can get in to see him. The sooner the better." I handed them my card. "Thank you so much for coming in."

I walked them out, then quickly stuck my head into Walker's office. "I have to get to class."

"How'd the meeting go?"

"Fine, I guess."

"You guess? Are you taking the case?"

"I haven't decided yet. I want to talk to the kid first, get a feel for him. If the police suspect him and my gut says he did it, then I don't want to get involved."

"Did what? Murdered all his friends and hid in the woods for over a week?"

"I don't know. I just have a weird feeling. I want to get a read on him before I make up my mind."

Walker looked at me appraisingly.

"What?" I asked.

"I'm just surprised you aren't jumping at the chance to take a case like this."

I shrugged. "Hopefully his parents will get me in to see him today and I'll know more. Gotta go. I'll let you know when I decide."

MY FIRST two classes were back-to-back, and in different buildings halfway across campus. Since I hated being late, that usually meant I single-mindedly power walked between them. I was crossing the quad, thinking about the Miller kid's case, when someone called my name. I stopped and looked around, expecting to see Haniah. Much to my surprise, it was the guy from my World Religions class. I knew Professor Lawson said his name the other day, but for the life of me I couldn't remember it.

He jogged up to me with a grin. "Hey! I don't think we've really met." He thrust out his hand. "I'm Kyreh Chambers. I'm in your—"

"World Religions class," I finished as we shook. "Yeah. I'm Cav Crawford, but I guess you knew that since you were just yelling my name across the quad."

"Sorry about that. I wanted to catch you after class, but I keep missing you. Man, you move fast." He laughed.

"Uh, sorry?" I offered, unsure of what exactly I was apologizing for, but it seemed like the correct response.

"No, it's cool. And I swear I wasn't trying to eavesdrop the other day, but I could use some extra credit in that class too, so when Professor Lawson said you could write a paper, I thought maybe I could do the same thing. Except when I asked her, she suggested we work on the paper together."

I frowned. "Like a group project?"

"Are two people really a group?"

He had a point. "I guess not."

"So… what do you think?"

I started to say no, but then my self-preservation kicked in as I realized that two people on a project meant doing half the work. In theory, anyway, assuming everyone pulled their weight. Besides, Kyreh was very attractive. I was pretty sure he was straight, but spending time with him outside of class seemed like a win-win.

"Sure. Sounds good."

"Sweet." He pulled out his phone. "What's your number?"

I gave it to him as he punched it in. "I'll shoot you a text so you have mine."

"Cool. I'll look for it, but my next class starts in five minutes, so I have to run. See you around."

He glanced up from his phone and flashed me a smile that made my heart skip a beat. "See you soon."

WHEN MY last class of the day ended, I pulled my phone out to see I had missed a call from Iwan Miller, but fortunately he'd left a message. He'd cleared it with the hospital and police for me to get in to talk to Gareth that night. I took a minute before my last class to call him back and thank him and tell him I'd be by that evening. He gave me the floor and room number.

A few hours later, I was walking through the hospital. I hated hospitals. They reminded me of the hours spent at my mother's bedside while she faded before my eyes. Then there was the inundation of emotions. And did I mention all the confused, angry and/or scared spirits wandering the halls? I pushed the memories, feelings, and ghosts aside and tried to focus on work. I found Gareth's room and knocked on the frame of the open door.

"Come in," a young male voice called.

I stepped in and found a thin boy in a gown sitting propped up on the bed. There were cartoons playing on the TV. He picked up the remote and muted the sound as I entered. It was a private room, so I didn't have to guess. "Hi, you must be Gareth. I'm Cavanaugh Crawford. You can call me Cav."

He nodded. "Dad said you were coming."

"Is it okay if we talk?"

Gareth nodded again, so I came farther into the room. His mom had mentioned he was covered in scratches, and he was. Some looked fresher than others. He was pale, with an unhealthy undertone to his skin, and he looked gaunt. His brown hair was cut short, curling close to his scalp.

He wouldn't quite make eye contact with me. His eyes would dart in my direction, and then he'd quickly look away.

The hair on the back of my neck prickled. Something was wrong, but I couldn't put my finger on what.

"How are you feeling?"

He shrugged, staring down at his hands clenched together on his lap. "Still pretty weak."

"You know why I'm here, right?"

"You're a private investigator. Mom and Dad want to hire you to find out… what happened to me."

"Yeah. And to your friends."

His face clouded over. "I… I don't remember."

"You don't remember what happened?"

He shook his head, still not looking up.

"I'm sure you're tired of talking about this, but what's the last thing you remember?"

"I remember waking up that morning—"

"The Saturday you disappeared?"

"Yeah. I was excited because Kyle said he'd found a really cool place for us to investigate."

"Do you remember where it was?"

"No. Only Kyle knew where it was. He'd been researching places for us to go."

"Okay, so you remember waking up, and then what?"

"Nothing. It's like I blinked and the next thing I knew, I'm on the side of the road, covered in blood and scratches." Frustration—and a tinge of anger—filled his voice.

His emotions rang true, but something still seemed wrong. It was almost like I was being watched, or like there was someone else in the room with us. I glanced around but didn't see anything out of place. Of course, it was possible the police had a hidden camera somewhere. I tried to shrug it off and concentrate on Gareth.

"Tell me about ghost hunting. How'd you get into it?"

Gareth seemed surprised by the question. He glanced up at me and then quickly away. "Kyle and I used to watch all the TV shows. We thought it would be cool to do our own investigations. We started an after-school club, but only two guys joined, Wade and DJ."

"Did you get along with them?"

"Yeah, they're cool."

"And none of you ever fought?"

He scrunched his face up. "No. I mean, maybe we argued about where to go next, but we never fought."

"What were some of the places you investigated?"

"A few graveyards, an old church out in the middle of nowhere, an abandoned house we found while driving around."

"Did you encounter anything?"

His eyes flicked in my direction again. "What do you mean?"

"You're ghost hunting, right? Did you meet any ghosts?"

"We got a few readings in the graveyards and at the church. Nothing at the old house."

"What kind of readings?"

"On the EMF meter. And some EVP and temperature fluctuations."

"I've never watched those shows, so I don't really know what an EMF meter is. Or an EVP."

"An EMF meter detects changes in the electromagnetic field so you know when ghosts are around. EVP stands for electronic voice phenomenon. It's catching voices on recordings."

"You can do that?"

He shrugged. "Sometimes."

"What kinds of things did you record?"

"Once, at one of the graveyards, we could hear something say, 'Get out,'" he said, excitement creeping into his voice. "And at the church, we heard a voice saying, 'Pray for me.'"

I'd talked to many ghosts over the years but never encountered anything like that. It gave me the creeps. "And you... like that?"

"Yeah, it's cool."

"Have you ever seen a ghost?"

"No." He sounded disappointed. Maybe I could use my experience to bond with him.

"I have."

"You have?" He looked up at me, his eyes locking with mine for a second before he looked away. In that split second, though, that feeling of wrongness hit me again. What was going on with this kid? His eyes darted toward me again.

"Yeah. All the time. All my life."

"More than one?"

"Lots."

"Are they scary?"

"Not really, at least not the ones I've seen. Most of the time they just seem... lonely."

He frowned. "You're making that up."

"No, really. I swear. My grandmother says it runs in our family."

"Wow." He stole another glance at me. I couldn't figure out if he was shy or if he was avoiding eye contact for a reason.

It was time to bring it back to the case. "Do you remember anything at all about where you were going last Saturday?"

His face fell. "No. I told you. All I remember is that Kyle was super excited. He said we were going to love it."

"Gareth, your parents want me to try to help you, but if I take the case, I need something to go on, somewhere to start. Right now, I got nothing."

His hands balled into fists. "Don't you think I wish I could remember? Don't you think I want to help Kyle and Wade and DJ? I.... There's just nothing. It's like I fell asleep and woke up a week later." He looked up at me and his eyes locked with mine. "I'm scared."

He looked scared. But there was something else. Something behind the fear, behind his eyes. It was almost like someone—or something—else was looking at me through his eyes. Every hair on my body stood up, and fear gripped me.

Gareth looked away, breaking the spell, but the sense of fear lingered.

"Please help me," he said in a small voice.

"Gareth...." Thankfully my voice sounded steadier than I felt. "Can you look at me again?"

He hesitated for a second, but then his eyes met mine again.

I stared into his eyes, but whatever I thought I'd seen before was gone. All I saw now was a scared kid.

"Thanks. I should probably get going."

"Are you going to help me?" he asked. He sounded more drained than he had just a few minutes ago.

"I'm not sure. I need to think on it."

He closed his eyes and rubbed his face, then opened them and looked at me again. "If not for me, then for Kyle, Wade, and DJ?"

I had to admit that whatever was going on, this didn't sound like a kid who was guilty of something. He sounded scared, confused, and worried about his friends. I sighed. Who was I kidding? I was already hooked.

"Okay."

He glanced at me again. "Okay?"

"I'll take the case."

He closed his eyes again and nodded. "Thanks. I'm really tired...."

"No problem. I need to go anyway. I'll talk to you again soon, though."

As I was leaving the room, he laid his head back on the pillow. I stopped in the hall outside the door to gather my thoughts. Something very strange was going on, but I didn't know what. Had I really seen something else looking at me through his eyes, or was it just my imagination? My instincts told me something was wrong, but at the same time, Gareth seemed sincere. His fear was real; I was sure of that.

While I was standing there, the elevator doors opened and Iwan and Robin Miller stepped out. They looked relieved when they saw me.

"Cav! I was hoping we wouldn't miss you. Have you talked to Gareth yet?" Mr. Miller asked as they approached.

"Yeah, we just finished. I think it wore him out."

Mrs. Miller shook her head with a worried expression. "Everything wears him out. But what about you? Are you going to take the case?"

I nodded. "Yes, I'll take it. Jordan will send you over a contract in the morning."

I shook their hands and left, but I couldn't shake the eerie feeling. I thought about it all the way to my car. I checked the time. I needed to talk to somebody about what I'd seen—or thought I'd seen—and I knew just where to go.

Chapter 3

I KNOCKED on the doorframe and waited.

"Come in," a voice called.

As I entered the room, my grandmother's face broke into a wide smile. "Cav! I didn't know you were coming to visit tonight! You were just here this weekend."

Sometimes when I came to visit, the staff would have her in a wheelchair. She still had use of her arms and could steer her electric chair around, terrorizing the staff and other residents alike. That night, however, she was already tucked into bed. She looked so tiny under the blankets.

"Hi, Nana. Just thought I'd stop by."

My grandmother was in her mid-seventies, but she looked older. I'd seen photos of her before the accident, and she'd been striking—petite but feisty, with long, flowing dark hair, rosy cheeks, and eyes filled with fire. Now her body was frail and birdlike, and her steely-gray hair was cropped short, but her cheeks were still rosy, and her silver eyes sparked with sharp intelligence. Those eyes were currently narrowed.

"Something has happened," she said. It was a statement, not a question.

I smiled. There was never any point in trying to fool my grandmother.

"A few things, actually. I thought you might be able to help." I pulled a chair closer to her bed.

"I'm always here for you." She took my hand in hers. "We're all we have left."

I leaned forward and gave her a kiss on the cheek.

"So what's going on?"

"I saw Mason last night."

I'd come out to my mom when I was fourteen, and she was completely accepting, as I knew she would be. I'd told my grandmother not long after. She'd simply said, "It's about time you admitted it." She swore she'd known even before I did. And she probably had. I'd brought Mason to meet her a few times, and she'd liked him from the start. Mason was handsome and charming; it seemed like everybody liked him.

"Saw him how? In a dream, or...."

"He was in my room. But only for a second, and then he was gone."

"He didn't say anything?"

"No. Nothing."

"And you didn't say anything to him?"

"I didn't have time. By the time it registered who it was, he disappeared. And to be honest, it kind of freaked me out. I wasn't thinking too clearly."

"Why would it freak you out? You've seen ghosts before."

"Yes, but not the ghost of a loved one. It... hit different. Have... have you?"

"Seen my loved ones after they passed? Yes. After the accident, your grandfather came to me in the hospital. He told me I needed to fight, that it wasn't my time and that you and Deirdre needed me." Deirdre was my mother.

I smiled and squeezed her hand. "He was right."

"But Mason. You're sure it wasn't a dream?"

"I was wide-awake."

"I wonder what took him so long."

"What do you mean?"

"It's been, what? A year since he died?"

"About that, yeah."

"Usually if someone is going to seek you out, they would do so quickly, soon after they died, while the bonds are still strong. How would he even find you after all this time?"

"I, uh, may have summoned him. Maybe?"

"What do you mean?"

"I was trying to remember the ancestor prayer."

"Which ancestor prayer?"

"The one that starts 'Tonight, I honor my ancestors. Spirits of my fathers and mothers, loved ones who have gone before, I call to you and welcome you to join me for this night.' I couldn't remember the rest, and I got distracted and started thinking about Mason—"

"That's not just an ancestor prayer. It's a Samhain prayer. You're literally calling their spirits to you."

"So I did summon him?"

"Possibly. The prayer is most powerful on Samhain, but that's still weeks away. Your gifts have always been strong, though, maybe strong enough to call out to him even when the veil isn't at its thinnest. I blame the Malleys."

"What? Why the Malleys? You have the Sight too."

The Sight, as our family called it, was a nebulous set of gifts that seemed to change from person to person and, much to my mother's chagrin, occasionally skipped a generation. Nana had dreams. I saw ghosts. The Malleys were my paternal grandmother's family, but I wasn't sure what they had to do with anything.

"I do, but my gifts are nowhere near as strong as yours. The Malleys, though, their gifts were something else. They swore up and down that they were direct descendants of Biddy Early, and who knows, maybe they were, though every Irish family with a touch of the Sight tries to claim her."

"Biddy who?"

She sighed. "I have so much to teach you. Biddy Early is perhaps Ireland's most famous witch, though she wouldn't have considered herself a witch. She would have said she was a *bean feasa*, a woman of knowledge. She was an herbalist, a healer and diviner, who was said to talk to the faeries."

"Like, actual faeries?"

"I don't know. Perhaps, or simply one way of saying they were steeped in the old ways."

"So you're saying faeries are real? Wait. Scratch that. We're getting sidetracked. If I did summon Mason, then why did he vanish?"

"Maybe because you weren't doing it with intention. Or perhaps he sensed your fear."

"Should I try again?"

"Why would you?"

"I don't know. To say goodbye, find out what happened to him, get some closure."

"Sometimes it's better to not know."

"What's the rest of the prayer? That's all I could remember."

She took a deep breath, then, in a soft, lyrical voice, began. "Tonight, I honor my ancestors. Spirits of my fathers and mothers, loved ones who have gone before, I call to you and welcome you to join me for this night.

"You watch over me always, protecting and guiding me, and tonight I thank you. Your blood runs in my veins, your spirit is in my heart, your memories are in my soul. With the gift of remembrance, I remember all of you. You are dead but never forgotten, and you live on within me and within those who are yet to come."

The room was quiet after she finished. Then she took another deep breath. "My grandmother taught me that prayer." Her grandmother—my great-great grandmother—had emigrated directly from Ireland. "We used to light a candle and say it every Samhain. I tried to teach it to your mother, but she was always too pragmatic for the old ways. It didn't help that she didn't have the Sight. I think she half believed I was crazy and making it all up. How do you know it?"

"From Mom. She taught me the prayer when I was little. She said it brought it her a lot of comfort after Dad and Grandpa died."

"She never told me."

"I think she thought of it as more of, like, a meditation."

"That sounds more like your mother." She eyed me for a second, then said with a wry smile, "You know my thoughts on the subject, but be careful if you try to call him again. If an untethered spirit becomes attached to you, they're hard to get rid of."

"Attached?"

"Spirits that are adrift can attach themselves to people or places that held significance to them while they were alive."

"And then what happens?"

"Let's just hope we don't have to worry about that. Now, you said a few things happened. What else?"

It took me a moment to shift gears, my mind still on Mason. "Oh. Um, I started a new case today. Have you heard about those boys who went missing last week?"

"It's all over the news. They found one of them, right?"

"Yes. And it's his parents who are hiring me. I went to talk to him—he's still in the hospital—and something weird happened."

"Weird?" she asked.

"As soon as I entered his room, something felt… off. I can't even describe it, but I just knew something was wrong, like we weren't alone, even though as far as I could tell, it was just the two of us in the room. He wouldn't make eye contact with me, and then when he finally did, it was like there was someone else looking at me through his eyes."

Nana frowned. "What do you mean?"

I shook my head. "The kid was there, but it was like something else was there too."

"Something or someone?"

"I don't know."

"And whatever it was, you felt like it was inside him? Or just looking through him?"

"There's a difference?"

"Obviously."

"Right. Obviously. I don't know. It happened so quickly, and then it was gone."

"Gone?"

"Yeah, I asked him to look at me again, and whatever it was didn't seem to be there the second time."

"Hmm…." Nana stared over my shoulder, lost in thought.

"What do you think it was?"

"The most likely answer is nothing."

"Nothing?"

"Maybe your imagination. Or your intuition warning you that the boy is hiding something."

"Oh, he's definitely hiding something. I just can't figure out if he's doing it on purpose or if it's out of his control."

"What do you mean?"

"Something happened to him and his friends. He says he doesn't remember, that it's like an entire week is just missing from his memory."

"Then maybe he's repressing something he can't process yet. The brain is capable of doing some amazing things in order to protect itself. Maybe what you saw was his suppressed memories."

That was certainly an interesting possibility. I hadn't thought about that. "What are some less likely answers?"

She arched an eyebrow. "How would I know? You haven't given me much to go on."

"You always know more than you say."

She chuckled. "What about split personality?"

"I don't think it's called that anymore."

"Whatever. You know what I mean. That's another survival strategy the brain employs in extreme circumstances."

"Maybe."

"It's obvious you have your own theory, so spit it out. What are you thinking?"

"Well, could it be… possession?"

She frowned. "You'd better hope not."

"But possession is possible?"

"You should know better than to discount the power of the spirit world."

"So… it could be possession?" I asked.

"I didn't say that. I just said you'd better hope it's not."

"But it could be?"

"If I've learned anything in my years on this earth, it's that anything is possible. Could this child be possessed? I suppose, but it seems unlikely. Your Sight is strong, especially when dealing with the spirit world, so I feel like you'd know if that's what you were dealing with. As I said, though, I think the most likely answer is that you were just sensing his hidden memories."

"If it is possession, what do I do?"

"Stay away? I don't know much about possession except that I don't ever want to mess with it."

"Okay, well, if it's his memories, is there some way I can access them?"

"You're not a mind reader."

"Then what do I do?"

"What would you have done if you hadn't sensed anything amiss? You conduct your investigation the old-fashioned way."

I laughed. "Point made."

She gave my hand another squeeze. "Just promise me you'll be careful."

"Aren't I always?"

She gave me a look, and we laughed. I stayed with her a while longer, just chatting, but then I got a text.

Dinner plans? It was from Jason, my adopted dad.

Nada. I'm just visiting Nana, I replied.

Why don't you come over? I'm making your favorite. It should be ready in about an hour.

On my way. If Jason was making crab cakes, I wasn't missing it.

THE HOUR-LONG drive out to my adopted parents' farm in rural Harford County gave me plenty of time to think about my conversations with Gareth and Nana. Something weird was going on with Gareth, and it was setting off all my internal alarm bells.

Was I just seeing repressed memories? That didn't explain the feeling of being watched. Memories weren't sentient, were they? Or maybe it was a combination of memories and police surveillance. Then again, maybe it was just my overactive imagination.

Perhaps more concerning, what was I supposed to do about Mason? Had I accidentally summoned him? If so, could I do it again? Did I want to do it again?

Yes. I definitely wanted to do it again. I knew that with dead certainty. I just wasn't sure if I should. On one hand, the idea of getting answers after all this time was unbelievably tempting. But what about Nana's warning about untethered spirits becoming attached?

As I turned off the road onto the long tree-lined gravel drive that led back to the farmhouse, I tried my best to shake off all these thoughts. Jason and Eli were supportive of my work, and they put up with my weird quirks, like talking to invisible dead people, but they both worried about me—especially Jason—so it was better not to give them extra things to fret over.

I parked next to Eli's truck and hopped out. A black horse on the far side of the field gave a high-pitched whinny and charged toward me. Cormac was my horse, given to me by Jason and Eli when my adoption was final. I met him at the fence and gave him scratches while he alternated between nuzzling me aggressively and nipping at me as punishment for not visiting more often.

"Give him this and he might forgive you," Eli said, appearing at my side with an apple in hand.

Elias "Eli" Benson was in his late forties, with wavy auburn hair and a bushy beard that was just a shade darker. At well over six feet tall with a sturdy, stocky frame, he looked like he could toss a bale of hay like it was nothing—and he could.

"Thanks," I said with a laugh as I accepted the apple. "But do you have a peace offering for Jason?"

It had been a couple of weeks since I'd been out to the farm. Between school and work, time just got away from me. I felt guilty but also knew Jason and Eli understood, even if Cormac didn't.

I offered the horse the apple, which he begrudgingly accepted, then gave him a final scratch between his ears. As Eli and I started back toward the house, Cormac tossed his head and stamped his hoof as if to demand I stay longer.

"You might want to come out and take him for a ride soon," Eli said. "He misses you."

I knew that was his way of saying he missed me too. Of my two adopted dads, Eli was more of the strong, silent type. He rarely said much, but when he did speak up, people tended to listen.

"Oh hey, I thought you were dead and nobody thought to tell us," Jason boomed as Eli and I came inside. He was standing in the door between the mudroom and the kitchen, hands on his hips. I briefly wondered if he'd been waiting the entire time I was with Cormac just to deliver that line, but I broke into a grin and gave him a big hug. I was used to his theatrics.

Jason Kofoed was a few years younger than Eli and was all bubbling energy and bustling charm. He was a drag performer in his younger years, and as Eli often said, once a drag queen, always a drag queen. He was a big teddy bear—average height, dark brown hair and beard, covered in fur, round and cuddly.

"I know, I know," I said with my face mashed into his shoulder. "I'm sorry. I'll try to do better."

He playfully pushed me away. "It's okay. I understand. You're all grown up and don't need your daddies anymore." He gave a dramatic sniff and turned back to the stove.

I rolled my eyes at Eli, who was smirking, before once more wrapping my arms around Jason from behind. "You know I'll always need you guys, no matter how old I get. Now, admit you only made crab cakes tonight to lure me back."

"Psh. Crab meat was on sale, that's all," he said as he stirred a pot of what looked like creamy grits.

I snorted.

"But speaking of crab cakes," he continued, ignoring my snort, "dinner is almost ready. Could one of you set the table?"

Eli and I set the table together and finished just as Jason started plating.

Dinner was amazing as always. I caught them up on school and work, though I left out some of the more worrisome details about my case. Jason told me all about the fall-themed wedding come up in a few weeks. Eli just chewed and listened, occasionally adding a quiet thought or comment.

Shortly before he and Jason got married, Eli had taken over his parents' farm after they retired and moved to Florida. Jason took to farm life surprisingly well but had big ideas for the rural estate. They fixed up the old farmhouse, sold off most of the crop fields, and started boarding horses. Then they converted one of the old barns into a wedding venue. Within a few years, it became a very sought-after location for exchanging vows, and as a bonus, Jason often got to play bartender, which he loved. Eli mostly stayed out of the way.

We'd barely taken our last bite before Jason started clearing plates. "I made dessert," he informed us. "Apple Brown Betty."

Eli's eyes lit up. That was his favorite. One of mine too, for that matter.

"Can I help?" I offered.

"No, I've got it. Stay where you are."

While Jason was dishing up dessert, I asked Eli about the horses, and he gave me a rundown on all of their current boarders. He cut off when Jason reappeared with the bowls of apple-y goodness.

As soon as everyone dug in, Jason set down his fork and looked at Eli. Eli purposefully shoved a giant forkful into his mouth. Jason sighed.

"What's going on?" I asked.

"We, uh, have something we wanted to talk to you about," Jason said, still staring at Eli. Eli refused to look up from his bowl.

Nervously, I looked back and forth between them. What was going on? Were they splitting up?

Jason cleared his throat, but Eli just kept eating. Finally Jason sighed again and gave up.

"Fine. You know, Eli and I never talked about having kids. I think it just never crossed our minds. I know I never saw myself as the paternal type. I was a rowdy, loudmouthed drag queen who loved to drink and dance around in a dress. But when Dierdre called me and asked if I would take you in after she...." He stopped as his eyes filled up. I knew he still missed Mom almost as much as I did. "She'd just found out about the cancer, and her first thought was you. Who would take care of you? And she chose me, of all people. Of course I knew right away what the answer would be, but I talked it over with Eli, and he agreed without hesitation. We had no idea what we were getting ourselves into. It was harder than we ever imagined. But it was also the most rewarding thing either of us has ever done."

Eli nodded, and Jason continued, "We love you like you are our own son."

"Guys, I am your son. Where is this going?" They were definitely making me nervous.

"Well, it's just that since you left for college, and then got your own place with Haniah, it's been... a little too quiet around here. We miss you, obviously, but you're an adult now. You have a career. You're not moving back home."

"Okay. Are you trying to tell me you're pregnant?"

Jason threw back his head and laughed, and even Eli chuckled.

"Look, if Eli could get me pregnant, we'd have ten kids by now," Jason said.

"TMI, Jason," I said quickly as Eli blushed.

Jason waved away my protest. "Oh please. You're old enough to know your dads have a healthy sex life. But no, I'm not knocked up. But we are thinking about becoming foster parents."

"Oh wow!"

"How would you feel about that?" Eli asked.

"Um, I'm thrilled for you. And for whatever lucky kid who ends up with you. You guys have been great dads. I'd be a selfish asshole to want to keep you all to myself."

Jason beamed with relief. "So you wouldn't feel displaced or anything?"

"Displaced? Not at all. I'm out of the house. And besides, you'll never find someone as wonderful as me."

Jason rolled his eyes and Eli just smirked.

"How does all this work? Do you get a say in who you get?"

"We just started looking into it, and there's a whole process to be approved, but we do get some say. We're thinking we'd want to request a queer kid specifically. They tend to be harder to place and have a rough go of it even if they are."

"I think that's great. I am totally supportive. I've always been an only child, so I'm really looking forward to being a big brother."

Jason slid his hand into Eli's as he finally set down his fork. "We really lucked out with you."

"Nah, I lucked out with you guys."

"Or maybe it wasn't luck at all and we were just meant to be a family," Eli said softly. "Now, is there any more Apple Brown Betty left?"

Chapter 4

I ONLY had two morning classes on Fridays, so afterward, I went right to the office. I'd emailed Jordan asking him to send a contract to the Millers first thing. I was hoping they'd already sent it back so I could get right to work.

Sure enough, Jordan greeted me with good news as I walked through the door.

"You're official." He handed me a file.

"Great. I want to get started right away."

"I figured you would. I included the contact info for the other parents of the missing boys and the name of the detective in charge of the original missing person's case."

"Damn, you're good."

He winked. "I know."

"I'll give Mead a call. He can also give me the skinny on this other detective…." I opened the file. "Travis Gibson. Never heard of him."

Detective Sergeant Zebulon Mead was an investigator with the Maryland State Police. Walker had been working with him for years. He was usually willing to cooperate with us, and he'd proven especially useful when I was working missing person cases outside the city. I ducked into my office and called him on my cell.

He didn't answer, so I left him a message asking him to call me when he got the chance. Then I tried looking up the social media accounts for each kid to see if there'd been any activity at all in the time since they disappeared, or maybe a clue about where they were going. I figured the police would have done that already, but you never know.

I couldn't find anything on any platform for DJ, at least not under his real name. Wade had an account on Instagram but hadn't updated it in months. Both Gareth and Kyle had accounts on various platforms, but there'd been no posts since they vanished, and there were no clues to where they might have been going.

Next, I flipped through the rest of the file. As promised, there was a fact sheet with contact information for everyone involved.

I called all the parents. Perhaps not surprisingly, everyone was home and quickly agreed to meet with me.

I started with the parents of Kyle Itoh, Gareth Miller's best friend. The Itohs lived in a quiet neighborhood with modest two-story houses in neat rows, each with an attached garage. The houses weren't cookie-cutter exactly, but there wasn't much variation. The trees in the yards were mature, so I figured the development was about twenty or thirty years old. Many of the homes were decorated for Halloween—ghosts hanging from trees, gravestones on the lawn, skeletons hanging limply on front doors.

I parked on the street and walked up the concrete path to the front door. There were no Halloween decorations here. I knocked and didn't have to wait long before the door swung open to reveal an Asian man in his early forties. He would have been handsome if he didn't look so tired. His face was tight with worry, and dark circles surrounded his eyes. He was just a little taller than me and thin. He tried to smile welcomingly.

"You must be Cav," he said.

"Yes, I am." I held out my hand and he shook it. "And you must be Mr. Itoh?"

He nodded. "Yes. Hiroshi Itoh. Please come in."

I followed him into a living room. The furniture was very formal, but the room was still inviting. Family photos were everywhere, showing Mr. Itoh, a woman I assumed was his wife, and two children—a son and a daughter.

"Have a seat," Mr. Itoh said. "I'll get my wife. She had a headache so went to lie down."

He left me in the room alone, and I wandered around looking at the pictures. The Itohs looked like an ad for the perfect family. I picked up a frame that held a photo of Kyle. It was taken outdoors, the sky a deep blue behind him. He was staring into the camera with a wide smile. His eyes sparkled mischievously, his teeth slightly uneven.

"He looks so happy there, doesn't he?" a woman said from behind me.

I sat the frame down and turned to face Mr. Itoh and the woman I assumed to be his wife.

I nodded. "He does."

Mrs. Itoh was several inches shorter than her husband. Her curly hair was a little messy, as if she hadn't brushed it today. Pain emanated from her in almost visible waves. I felt an empathetic stabbing behind my eyes.

"That's my favorite picture of him. He doesn't like to smile for pictures. He's self-conscious about his teeth." She sat in one of the armchairs. She had a slight accent and an olive skin tone but didn't look Asian.

I took a seat on the couch, and Mr. Itoh took the other armchair.

"He's supposed to get braces in the spring," Mr. Itoh said. "Cav, this is my wife, Maryam."

I nodded in her direction. "Like I said on the phone, I'm a private investigator. I've been hired by the Millers."

"We were so relieved when the police found Gareth. We thought that meant we'd find Kyle, but it's been two days since...." Mrs. Itoh's voice faded out.

"There's still hope," Mr. Itoh said softly.

Mrs. Itoh closed her eyes.

"If this is a bad time, I can come back," I said gently.

Her eyes opened again. "There is no good time these days," she said. Her words were blunt, but she softened it with a sad smile. "It's just so hard...."

"I'm sorry. I can't even imagine."

"It's the not knowing. Teenage boys don't just disappear here. Where I come from, people go missing, but not here."

"Maryam is Palestinian," Mr. Itoh explained.

"I came here for university, Johns Hopkins. Then I met Hiro and fell in love. We had Mira and then Kyle and everything seemed so perfect. I became complacent—"

"This isn't your fault," Mr. Itoh interrupted. I had a feeling they'd had this conversation a lot in the last week.

"Tell me about Kyle," I suggested.

"He's such a good son. Straight As at school. So curious."

"What's his personality like?"

"He's quiet," Mr. Itoh said. "He can be a little too serious sometimes. He takes after me."

Mrs. Itoh nodded. "He's just like his father. Scientific mind."

"We're both scientists," Mr. Itoh said. "We both work in biology research."

I didn't know quite what that meant, but it didn't seem relevant to my case, so I didn't delve deeper. "Does Kyle want to be a scientist too?"

Mr. Itoh shrugged. "Kyle doesn't talk about the future much. He's more interested in his hobbies."

"Like ghost hunting?"

He nodded. "Yes."

"Do you approve of his hobby?"

"We don't approve or disapprove. It's just something he and Gareth do together, a phase."

"They started a school club, didn't they?"

"Yes. Children are like that. When Mira was his age, she wanted to be an NFL cheerleader. Now she's taking college entrance exams to be a teacher."

Mrs. Itoh spoke up. "It seemed like harmless make-believe. We.... We never thought it would be dangerous. It never occurred to us that anything could happen."

"Do you believe in ghosts?"

"Of course not. That's not what I meant by dangerous."

"Ah, sorry. What did you mean?"

"Breaking into places, exploring abandoned buildings alone. That's not safe."

"And is that what you think happened?"

"I don't know what to think. They found Gareth. Why can't they find Kyle?"

I wasn't sure if I was supposed to talk about Gareth's memory loss or not. As much as I wanted to offer something—anything—to the Itohs, I decided to err on the side of caution. "I haven't met with the police yet, but I'm sure they're doing everything they can with what they have to go on. You don't know where the boys were going that day?"

"No, Kyle never told us what they were doing. If he had, we wouldn't have let him go."

Which is probably why he didn't tell you, I thought. "But you said the boys were breaking into places and exploring abandoned buildings. If he didn't tell, how did you know that?"

"Mira told us," Mr. Itoh explained, "after they didn't come home."

"Mira is your daughter, Kyle's sister?"

"Yes."

"But she didn't know where they were going that day?"

"No."

"Is Mira home? I'd like to talk to her as well."

"She's at school. We're trying to keep her life as normal as possible through all of this."

I nodded. "Could you ask her to call me? I'd like to find a time to speak with her."

"Of course," Mr. Itoh said.

I asked a few more routine questions but didn't learn anything useful. "Would you mind if I took a look at Kyle's room?"

Mrs. Itoh frowned. "The police already went through his room. So did we."

"We might be looking for different things. Plus, it'll give me more of a feel for him."

She still looked concerned. "He's so private. He'd hate to know all these strangers have been looking through his things."

"It can't hurt at this point," Mr. Itoh said. "Follow me."

As I followed him up the flight of stairs, I glanced back at Mrs. Itoh, who hadn't moved from her chair. Her eyes were closed again.

Mr. Itoh led me into a small bedroom that clearly belonged to a teenage boy. It had been empty for over a week and it still had that distinctive smell, half locker room and half feet. The pile of sneakers by the closet door probably explained the scent. The bed was made; I wondered if Kyle had made it before heading out or if Mrs. Itoh had done it after he disappeared.

A desk by the window had a few books piled up, a cup filled with pencils and pens, a calculator, and not much else. A dresser next to it held a TV. Directly opposite was a bed and bedside table with a lamp.

Mr. Itoh stayed in the doorway, watching as I walked around the room. I didn't touch anything. I stopped in front of the closet. "May I?"

He nodded an affirmative, and I opened the closet door. Clothes hung on hangers from a rod. A backpack sat on the floor. It was open, and I could see schoolbooks inside. I knelt and looked through the bag, but there was nothing of interest. I stood up and closed the door.

I looked around again. I was itching to do a real search, but I couldn't exactly tear the room apart with Mr. Itoh watching me. "Kyle is very neat," I said finally.

Mr. Itoh smiled sadly. "Not this neat. His mother cleaned the room after the police finished. They left it very messy. She didn't want Kyle to come home to that...." His smile faded with his voice.

"Did he have a laptop?"

"Yes, but the police took it."

"Ah. Then I think I'm done."

Mr. Itoh turned without a word and led me back downstairs. Mrs. Itoh still hadn't moved; her eyes remained closed.

I thanked Mr. Itoh for their time and left.

I sat in the car for a few minutes before I started it. I needed to regroup. I hadn't learned much, but their fear and anxiety were overwhelming. I took a deep breath and checked the file. Daniel and Olivia Juarez were next—DJ's parents. I entered their address into my GPS and headed off.

The Juarezes' neighborhood was similar to the Itohs' but older. The houses seemed to be mostly from the late seventies and early eighties. It was more organic and less planned. Fewer houses were decorated for Halloween.

The Juarez family lived in a white split-level that could have used a fresh coat of paint, or at least a good power washing. The lawn was a little overgrown, but that made sense under the circumstances.

I parked on the street and approached the front door. Mr. and Mrs. Juarez answered my knock together, Mr. Juarez with his hand protectively on his wife's shoulder. Like the Itohs, their living room was filled with family photos. It was much more lived-in, though, and much less formal.

"Thank you for meeting with me on such short notice," I said once we were seated. I was on a chair, and they were seated next to each other on the sofa.

"Of course," Mr. Juarez said. "We'd do anything to help find DJ."

Mrs. Juarez's hands knotted anxiously in her lap. "We've just been so worried," she said in a soft, heavily accented voice. "We feel so powerless."

"I can't even imagine," I found myself saying again. The words felt empty. I took a deep breath and tried to block out some of the painful emotions washing against me like relentless waves. "As I mentioned on the phone, the Millers have hired me. I'm looking into... the disappearances."

"I don't know what we can tell you," Mr. Juarez said, a note of helplessness in his voice. "We don't know anything. We talked to the police."

"You never know what might help. I haven't talked to the police yet, so this is all new to me. Can you start by telling me about DJ?"

"He's a good boy," Mrs. Juarez said. "Never any trouble. Works hard at school."

"Is he an only child?"

"He has an older brother," Mr. Juarez said. "Manuel. He's in his first year of college."

"What school does he go to?"

"Harvard. He's premed."

"You must be proud."

"We are, of both of the boys."

"Are DJ and Manuel close?"

"Very," Mr. Juarez said. "DJ was so lost when Manny left for school."

"Did he have any close friends?"

Mrs. Juarez shook her head no. "He was kind of a loner. We tried to get him into football—soccer—but he wasn't a physical boy. He preferred his video games and movies."

"That's why we were so relieved when he said he wanted to join a school club," Mr. Juarez broke in. "We thought it would be good for him, help him meet new people."

"Was this the ghost-hunting club?" I asked.

Mr. Juarez frowned. "Yes, but we didn't know that's what it was."

"What do you mean?"

"He just told us it was a club for people who liked a TV show."

"But he didn't tell you what TV show?"

"No."

"Why do you think he didn't tell you?"

The two exchanged a glance. Mrs. Juarez answered. "He probably knew we wouldn't approve."

"Why not?"

"We're very religious," she said.

"Catholic," Mr. Juarez supplied before I could ask.

"So you believe in the supernatural?"

"Of course," Mrs. Juarez responded with no hesitation.

Mr. Juarez's frown deepened. "I don't know if I believe in haunted houses and ghost hunting, but I do believe there are spirits and demons, and it's best if we stay away from them."

"Where did DJ say he was going when he left that morning?"

"He just said he was hanging out with his friends from school."

"Have you met them?"

Mrs. Juarez shook her head again. "We saw them when they picked him up, but that's all—two white boys and an Asian boy. We should have known nothing good would come out of him hanging out with white boys."

"Olivia!" Mr. Juarez said.

"It's true."

Mr. Juarez gave me an embarrassed look. "We weren't exactly welcomed when we moved to this neighborhood," he offered by way of explanation.

"They called us dirty Mexicans," Mrs. Juarez said angrily. "Told us to go back to where we came from. They would say awful things to DJ, like his mom scrubbed their toilets. Not that there's anything wrong with work like that, but it was racist and cruel. We're bakers. We own our own bakery. We work hard."

"I'm sorry you had to deal with that."

"Have to deal with it. We've lived here for seven years, and people still treat us like dirt."

"It's gotten better," Mr. Juarez said weakly, as if trying to convince himself.

"Has it? Maybe they don't spray paint things on the garage anymore, but most of the neighbors still won't speak to us."

"But some do. It has gotten better."

"Why do you stay?" I asked.

Mrs. Juarez shrugged. "It would be the same anywhere. And if we leave, they win."

"Do you think that's why DJ stayed to himself so much?"

Mrs. Juarez looked sad again, her anger draining away. "Probably. Part of it, anyway. When DJ was little, we lived in a mostly Hispanic neighborhood. He had friends then. But the school was bad. Manny was so smart, we wanted him to have a better chance. I know we made the right decision, at least for Manny. Maybe… maybe not for DJ."

"We don't know that, Olivia," Mr. Juarez said. "We did what we thought was best."

It was time to steer the conversation back to my investigation. "Did Manny and DJ stay close after Manny went to college?"

"For a while," Mr. Juarez said, "but Manny was busy with classes and homework. And once DJ joined the club, he was very involved with that."

"He wouldn't have confided in Manny about the club?"

"We asked that," said Mrs. Juarez. "Manny didn't know what the club was either. He's feeling very guilty. He wanted to come home, but we insisted he stay at school. He can't afford to miss classes."

I wasn't learning anything useful here. DJ kept his family in the dark about his supernatural interests.

"Did the police search DJ's room?" I asked.

Mr. Juarez nodded. "Yes. And his locker at school. They even took his laptop."

"And they didn't find anything useful?"

"If they did, they didn't tell us."

"Would you mind if I took a look around his room?"

"Of course," he said. They both stood up, but just then, Mr. Juarez's phone rang. He glanced at it. "It's the bakery."

"You should answer it," Mrs. Juarez said. "I'll show Cav DJ's room."

He excused himself as Mrs. Juarez led me down the hall to a closed door. She swung it open and moved aside, carefully averting her gaze as if she couldn't bear to look in.

I stepped into the room. It was decorated in dark blues and warm grays, giving it a homey, cozy feel. There were a couple of video game posters on the wall—one of a popular first-person shooter and the other from a creepy, atmospheric game about ghosts.

The room was neat. Too neat. Which, since the police had searched the room, I assumed meant Mr. or Mrs. Juarez had cleaned it up, just like the Itohs. I knew I wouldn't learn much from the room, but I'd hoped to get a feel for the missing boy.

"Is DJ neat?" I asked, just for something to say.

Mrs. Juarez chuckled. "No, he's very messy. There's usually clothes everywhere. I... I cleaned up after the police left. He'll be so mad when...."

I turned to face her. "You seem close to him."

She paused. "Not as close as I'd like. I'm not his mother, you know. I mean, I'm not his birth mother. She ran off when he was just a baby. Moved back to Mexico, we think. She got in trouble with the law. Daniel says she was always wild. We got married when DJ was two, so I raised him. I love him like he's my own, but he's always been distant. Manny was more affectionate. He was easier in some ways than DJ. Not that DJ was difficult. Like I said, he was a good boy, always treated me with respect, did as he was told, but he was never… warm with me. Even when he was a baby, he always wanted Daniel when he was tired or when he got hurt. It was like he never trusted that I was there to stay, even as a little thing."

She stopped and took a shaky breath. "I wish I could do more to help find him, anything. It's killing Daniel. He's not sleeping, barely eating. Sometimes he just gets in the car and drives around looking for him."

She paused again and looked up, making eye contact as a single tear rolled down her cheek. "I light a candle for him every night and I pray that he'll be returned safely, but I'm scared. I'm so scared. I have a bad feeling, right here." She laid a hand over her stomach.

I wanted to reach out to her, to hug her, but I didn't know her well enough and didn't have any words of comfort to offer, so I stood there awkwardly. "I'm so sorry. I'm going to do everything I can to find them."

She wiped away the tear and nodded. "I know. Thank you."

I glanced around the room again and wondered why I was there. I walked over to the bed and laid my hand on his pillow, hoping it would trigger some psychic revelation, but of course my gifts didn't work like that. I smoothed a wrinkle in the bedspread and then walked to the door.

"I've been enough of a bother. I should probably go."

Her eyes widened. "You've not been any bother. At least this feels like something concrete we can do to help." She stopped, and the corners of her mouth tugged down. "Not that I guess we've been much help."

"You never know what will help…." I was just repeating myself at this point. "But I have one more stop for the day, so I should get going. If I have any more questions, is it okay to contact you?"

"Please do."

As we were coming down the hall, Mr. Juarez met us.

"Is everything okay at the bakery?" Mrs. Juarez asked.

He nodded. "Maria just had some questions about the oven. And I might run over later to help with the deposit." He turned to me. "Are you all finished?"

"Yes. Thank you both for taking the time to talk to me."

"Of course. It was nice meeting you," he said politely.

I shook his hand. "You too. Both of you. I only wish it was under better circumstances."

They stood in the door watching as I made my way to my car, Mr. Juarez with his arms around his wife. They were such kind people. My heart ached for them. Much like Mrs. Juarez, I had a bad feeling growing in the pit of my stomach. If I didn't find DJ, they would both crumble apart.

A nagging little voice in the back of my head suggested that they might be broken even if I did find him.

The last neighborhood was nicer than the first two. The yards were larger and meticulously manicured, and the huge houses sat far back from the road and were faced with brick or stone. This wasn't the sort of neighborhood that decorated for Halloween, aside from a tasteful, black-bowed wreath here and there or some fall pumpkin displays.

This also wasn't the sort of neighborhood where you parked on the street. I pulled into the paved driveway of the address Jordan had provided for the Smiths. The front door opened before I was even out of my car.

A short, dark-haired woman stepped out, her arms crossed over her chest and an anxious expression on her pretty face. She looked young—too young to be Wade's mother. A sister maybe?

"Hello," I said as I approached. "I'm Cav Crawford. I spoke to Mr. Smith earlier."

She nodded. "Yes, we've been expecting you," she said with a heavy Latin inflection. "I'm Yara." She held out a delicate hand, and I shook it. "Please come in."

She led me into an ostentatious entrance hall. The walls were paneled and hung with gilt-framed paintings. "Patrick," she said, stepping to a doorway, "the private investigator is here."

"Come in," a man's voice said from inside.

Yara gestured for me to follow her, and we entered an office. The room was devoid of personal touches aside from an array of framed certificates on the walls. An ornate fireplace filled the far wall, but the mantel was empty. Two large windows overlooked the front lawn. In the center of the room sat an enormous, highly polished dark wood desk.

The man sitting at the desk stood and came around to shake my hand. "Patrick Smith," he said gruffly. Patrick Smith was tall and veering toward overweight. His fleshy face was clean-shaven, his brown eyes stern behind his glasses. His dark hair was cut short and carefully parted and combed.

He gestured to the two chairs facing his desk. "Have a seat."

He returned to the chair behind his desk, and Yara and I each took one of the other chairs. He stared expectantly at me.

I cleared my throat. "Thank you for meeting with me, Mr. Smith."

"Dr. Smith," he corrected me.

"I'm sorry, Dr. Smith. I'm sure this is a very hard time for you."

Dr. Smith blinked at me. "It's been very stressful."

"I'm sure. I appreciate your time. What can you tell me about Wade?"

Dr. Smith frowned. "He's… a good kid."

I waited for more, but nothing came. "Ah. Okay, how would you describe him?"

Dr. Smith looked to Yara. She spoke up. "Wade is very quiet," she said in her thick accent. "He doesn't cause much problems, does okay in school." She paused. "He keeps to himself, in his room a lot, reading or playing video games."

"Does he have many friends?"

Dr. Smith snorted, but it was Yara who continued. "No. Wade has always had trouble making friends."

"What about the ghost-hunting club?" I asked.

Dr. Smith snorted again. "Ghost-hunting club," he muttered derisively.

"You didn't approve?" I asked him.

"No, I didn't. I told him it was a stupid waste of time, searching for imaginary spirits with a tape recorder and a magnetic meter. He might as well be chasing leprechauns."

"But you allowed him to join the club anyway?"

He waved in Yara's direction. Her eyes were glued to the beige carpet. "My wife insisted we should let him, said it would get him out of the house."

"I thought maybe he'd make some friends," she said quietly. "Boys his age need friends."

"Did he tell you where they were going that day?" I asked, even though I suspected I knew the answer.

"No," Dr. Smith responded curtly. "As we've told the police, he only said he was going out with his club."

"You hadn't met the other boys?"

"No."

I didn't like Dr. Smith. "Did Wade have anybody he confided in, someone who might know something more?"

Dr. Smith pressed his fingertips together. "If he did, I wouldn't know. We didn't talk much about personal matters."

Personal matters? This was a father talking about his missing son. How could he be so cold? I glanced at Yara again, but she was still staring at the floor.

"Is Wade an only child?"

"No, Yara and I have a daughter, Célia."

"Are they close?"

"No, there's too much of an age gap. She's only seven."

I felt like I was wasting my time. All the boys were good boys. Nobody knew anything about their club or where they were going. And Dr. Smith seemed to resent my presence. How was I supposed to find them? Maybe I'd have better luck in Wade's bedroom than I had in the other boys'.

"Would it be possible to see Wade's bedroom?" I asked.

Dr. Smith frowned. "What for? The police already searched it."

"It just helps me get a feel for him."

He waved dismissively. "Yara, show Mr. Crawford Wade's room."

She nodded and stood. "Follow me."

We went up a broad staircase and then down a long hall. Wade's room was at the far end. She opened the door and stepped in. The room wasn't trashed, but it clearly hadn't been neatened up the way the others had. The bedspread and pillows were askew on the bed, dresser drawers slightly open, the closet door ajar.

To my surprise, Yara closed the door when I'd stepped in behind her.

"I apologize for my husband," she said in a hushed tone.

"Oh, uh, there's no need to apologize," I said awkwardly, matching her tone.

"He's not good with emotional…" She paused as if searching for the right word. "…emotions," she finished with a rueful shrug. "He and Wade weren't close. They argued a lot. I think they were too much alike."

"You keep using the past tense for Wade," I said gently. "Do you think he's dead?"

She gasped and covered her mouth. "I don't… I mean, I didn't mean…. I'm not very good with English sometimes." Tears welled up in her eyes. "I hope he's okay. He really is a good boy. His father is so hard on him. I do what I can to make it better, but he's not close to me either. He's always resented me. He thinks I replaced his mother."

"What happened to his mother?"

"Patrick divorced her when Wade was young."

"What's her name?"

"Vanessa, Vanessa Watson."

"Does Wade see her or stay in contact with her?"

"Yes, he visits her for holidays and some weekends. She's remarried now, has a new family. I don't think he fits in there either."

"Do you know how to contact her?"

Yara shook her head. "She doesn't like me very much. Patrick would know."

"When did you marry Dr. Smith?"

"Wade was Célia's age when we got married, so about eight years ago."

"Do you mind if I ask where you're from?"

"Brazil."

"How did you meet Dr. Smith?"

"I was in a university study abroad program. We met while I was taking a tour of the hospital. He took to me right away, showed me lots of extra attention. He was… very persistent. It was flattering, this older successful man being interested in me." Her eyes glazed over. "When my visa ran out, he asked me to marry him. I was already pregnant with Célia, so I said yes. He insisted I drop out of school to raise our daughter." She suddenly blinked and focused on me again. "I love Célia. He adores her. He gives us a good life."

"And what about Wade?"

She frowned slightly. "After Célia was born, it was almost like he no longer wanted Wade around. I think… maybe he reminded him of his first wife? I don't know. I tried to make up for it, but Wade never let me in. He just pulled into himself, spent more time alone. He was always a chubby boy. The other kids teased him. That's why I was so happy when he wanted to join this club."

"The ghost-hunting club."

"Yes, even though I was a little worried."

"Worried?"

She glanced nervously at the door. "My husband doesn't believe in ghosts, but I do. I've seen them. It's not good to go looking for them."

"You've… seen ghosts?" She was one of the few other people I'd ever met who claimed to see ghosts.

She nodded. "You probably don't believe me, but in Brazil, everybody believes. We know."

"Why do you say it's not good to go looking for them?"

"If they stay here, they are unhappy. They either had a tragic death or they are seeking something. Or they are bad spirits. Either way, it's better to keep your distance."

"Then why did you let him join the club?"

She shrugged. "He was so lonely. He needed to make friends. And they're just kids. I told myself, 'Yara, how much trouble can they get into?'" Her eyes filled with tears. "And now look. Something bad has happened to him."

"It's not your fault, Yara."

"Isn't it?"

"No, you were doing what you thought was best for him. And we might still find him."

"I know." She placed a fist over her heart. "Right here. I know it in my heart. Something bad has happened."

I hoped she was wrong.

I turned to take in the room. Aside from the general disorder, I noted several gaming systems and an enormous TV. There was a movie poster tacked to the wall, but not much else to give me any indication of Wade's personality. I walked around, but I wasn't sure what I was looking for, and I didn't pick up on anything.

"You didn't clean up after the police searched the room," I commented idly.

Yara shook her head. "My husband would not let the cleaning lady go in there. He shut the door and forbid anyone from coming in." She looked around, her face drawn. "But he's not coming back."

"You seem so sure."

She looked at me, her eyes filled with unshed tears. "I am sure."

I stopped back by the office when we returned to the first floor. Dr. Smith was typing away on a laptop. "Excuse me, Dr. Smith. I was wondering about Wade's mother."

He looked up at me with an annoyed expression. "What about her?"

"I was hoping you could tell me how to get in touch with her."

He looked past me at Yara. He looked pissed. I hoped I hadn't gotten her into trouble. "Why do you need to talk to her? Wade was here the weekend he disappeared."

"I like to be thorough in my investigations. It's possible he told her something."

"I doubt that."

"Still, I like to cover all my bases."

Dr. Smith frowned but pulled over a notepad and jotted something down on it, ripped off the top page, and held it out to me.

"Thank you," I said as I took it. I glanced down. He'd scribbled her name and a phone number in a typical doctor's scrawl. It was almost illegible. I repeated the number just to be sure I had it right. He nodded, and I thanked him for his time. He didn't look up.

Yara saw me to the door. "Thank you," she said softly after we'd stepped outside.

"For what?"

"For trying to help. For caring. You're a kind man, I can tell."

I didn't know what to say, so I simply nodded and turned toward my car.

I was glad Wade had her in his life. She at least seemed to care about the boy. His own father seemed oddly unconcerned about his missing son. From everything I'd seen and learned, it almost felt like he was a little relieved Wade was gone.

In the car, I called Wade's mother, Vanessa. She didn't answer, so I left a message telling her who I was, why I was calling, and asking her to call me at her earliest convenience, then headed back to my office to type up my notes. I didn't feel like I'd learned much, but as I'd kept telling the Juarez family, you never knew what might help.

Chapter 5

WHEN I walked into our apartment, I immediately knew Haniah was cooking. The air was filled with the smell of spices.

I stuck my head in the kitchen door. "Smells good."

Haniah jumped. "You scared me!"

"Sorry. I thought you heard me come in."

"Well, I didn't." She was standing at the stove with a skillet sizzling on the front burner.

"So I see. What are you making?"

"Kelewele," she said and plucked a piece out of the bowl on the counter, then popped it in my mouth.

"Hot! Hot!"

"It just came out of the skillet," she said as if I were particularly dense.

"Then why did you put it my mouth?"

"So you could taste it."

"I can't taste anything because my tongue is burned. What is it anyway?"

"Plantains. It's a Ghanaian dish."

"Okay, well I'll try it again when it's not the same temperature as the surface of the sun."

"I'm frying fish too. You can have some if you're nice."

"I'm always nice."

Haniah rolled her eyes and turned back to the skillet.

The kelewele turned out to be delicious, and the fish too. Both were spicy with a warm heat that was pleasant rather than overwhelming, and the fish was crispy outside and succulent on the inside.

Later that night, alone in my room, my thoughts returned to Mason. I eyed the candle and wondered if I should try to summon him again, assuming that was even what I had done. I didn't debate long. I wanted to know what had happened to him, and this seemed like my only chance.

I grabbed the candle, sat down on the floor, and lit it.

"Now what?" I mused aloud.

Maybe I should just do what I did before. It couldn't hurt to ask for my ancestors' protection before summoning a spirit, even if he was my ex.

With the prayer fresh in my mind thanks to Nana, I started. "Tonight, I honor my ancestors. Spirits of my fathers and mothers, loved ones who have gone before, I call to you and welcome you to join me for this night. You watch over me always, protecting and guiding me, and tonight I thank you. Your blood runs in my veins, your spirit is in my heart, your memories are in my soul. With the gift of remembrance, I remember all of you. You are dead but never forgotten, and you live on within me and within those who are yet to come."

I took a deep breath, then said, "Mason, if you can hear me...."

What? What exactly was I asking for? Maybe I should have thought this out a little more before starting.

"Mason, it's Cav. If you can hear me, come back."

Nothing happened. What was different? Then I remembered that I'd used his full name last time. It was worth a try. I repeated the prayer and ended with, "Mason McKibben, if you can hear me, come back to me."

The words hadn't even left my mouth before the candle flame flickered so violently I thought it would sputter out. The fire returned to normal just as suddenly as it had started its wild dance. My attempt hadn't worked. Maybe it had just been my imagination after all, just seeing what I wanted to see.

"Cav?"

I knew that voice anywhere. I spun around and gasped. Mason stood behind me, looking every bit as alive as the last time I'd seen him... well, alive. Mason was about five ten and was very handsome—or, as Nana once described him, quite dashing. He had a lithe build and big, soulful brown eyes with floppy brown hair that tended to fall over his forehead. He had a habit of pushing it back with one hand when he was excited or flustered or upset. He was doing it now.

I scrambled to my feet.

"You're here," I said, my voice suddenly hoarse. "You're really here."

"What's going on?" he asked. He had a sort of half smile and an uncertain look, as if he thought I was playing some sort of elaborate prank and he wasn't sure he liked it. "Why am I in your bedroom? How did I get here?"

"I... think I summoned you?"

"Summoned me? What's that supposed to mean?"

My heart sank. Did he even know he was dead?

"What's the last thing you remember?"

His face screwed up in a familiar expression that meant he was thinking hard. "I don't know. It's all... dark. I... I remember... it's our anniversary, right? Wait.... Is this some sort of surprise party?" He paused and gave me an incredulous look. "Did you drug me?"

"No! Of course not." I sat down heavily on my bed. He didn't know he was dead. And if he didn't know he was dead, he almost certainly wouldn't remember how he died.

"Then why is my head so fuzzy? What's going on, Cav?"

Was I going to have to be the one to break it to him that he was dead? How did one even do that? Was there a protocol?

"I don't know how to tell you this."

"Are you breaking up with me? On our anniversary?"

"No! I mean... it's not our anniversary."

"What do you mean? Why are you acting so strange?"

"Mason, our anniversary was over a year ago."

"That's not possible. Is this some sort of sick joke? If so, it's not funny."

"I wish it was a joke. You.... You were...." I couldn't force the words out.

"I'm what? Just spit it out."

I shook my head. This wasn't turning out the way I'd thought it would at all.

"Are you mad at me? Did I do something? Whatever it is you think I did, I promise I'll make it better."

"Mason, you're dead."

He stared at me with almost no expression. "What did you say?"

"You're dead. You disappeared on our anniversary over a year ago. Nobody knew where you were. We were all so worried. Then they found your body in a park months later." Once I started talking, it was like a dam had burst. The words kept tumbling out. "I was devastated. We all were. Nothing made sense. Why did you go to a park? Were you killed? Did you fall?"

"Cav," he said softly, but I couldn't stop.

"It's been tearing me up inside. I accidentally called you a few nights ago, and I tried it again tonight. I don't even know how it worked."

"Cav."

"I just needed answers. I wanted to know what happened to you."

"Cav!" he shouted.

My verbal torrent finally stopped with a shuddering breath.

"What the fuck are you talking about?" Mason said, an edge to his voice.

"You're dead."

"Stop saying that!" he roared.

The candle flickered again.

This was new territory for me. Every ghost I'd encountered in the past knew they were dead. Some were melancholy about it, but most seemed to have accepted it. They were just happy to have someone who could see and talk to them again. Some of them faded away after a while, lost their connection with the living world. Some lingered longer, but I'd never encountered one who didn't know they were deceased.

"I'm sorry," I said finally. I felt a tear spill over and run down my cheek.

This had been a mistake. I could see that now. I was being selfish. I had no idea where Mason's spirit had been for the past year, but I'd yanked him from whatever state he'd been in and forced him back into our plane. Maybe it wasn't too late to send him back.

I slid off the bed and reached for the candle.

"The joke has gone far enough, Cav."

"I wish it was a joke," I mumbled.

I leaned in to blow out the candle, but just as I did, Mason closed the distance between us. I paused and looked up at him. He crouched down next to me and studied my face.

"You're crying," he said softly.

"Yeah." I didn't know what else to say.

"Cav...." His gaze shifted to the candle. He reached out as if to take it from me, but his hand passed through it. His eyes grew wide as they returned to my face.

"Cav?" He sounded scared now.

"I'm sorry," I said again.

Suddenly the room grew cold and darker, as if all the light and warmth were being sucked out, the circle of illumination shrinking until all I could see was the candle and Mason's terrified face. The hair stood up on my arms, and the candle flame jumped in a wind that seemed to spring up out of nowhere.

"No," Mason said hoarsely, almost to himself. "I can't be dead."

The wind swirled around us with increasing speed. I tried to shelter the candle with my hand.

"Mason, I'm sorry. I shouldn't have called you. I didn't know what I was doing. I'm so sorry."

His eyes never left my face. "Why? Why would you do this?"

"This isn't.... I didn't...."

The wind was growing even stronger. I pulled the candle in closer to my body. Its feeble light wasn't much, but it was all I had.

"Mason, listen. Maybe I can help. Maybe I can find out—"

"Can you bring me back to life?"

My breath caught in my throat. "No."

"Then what *can* you do?"

The wind kicked up until it was howling around us. There was a crash, and the candle went out, leaving me in pitch black with only the sound of wind rushing in my ears.

And then it was over. The wind didn't die down. It was just gone, along with the utter darkness. A streetlight outside my window lit the room. Someone was banging on my door.

"Cav, are you okay?" It was Haniah. "I heard a crash."

"I'm... I'm fine," I managed, even if my voice was a little shaky. "I just knocked something over."

"Okay, well, keep it down. I'm going to bed."

"I will. Sorry."

Had that really happened? I looked down at the candle in my hand. In the dim light, I could just make out a splatter of wax across my fingers. I set the candle down and pulled myself up using the bed. My bedside lamp had fallen over. I stood it up and turned it on, revealing that my room was a mess. Anything paper on my desk had been scattered, my rolling chair was on its side against the wall, and the framed poster over my desk hung askew. My curtain rod dangled drunkenly from one bracket. Mason was nowhere to be seen.

What had I done?

IT TOOK forever to fall asleep, and once I did, I had a series of nightmares back-to-back, mostly starring Mason, but Gareth made an appearance as well. The details were lost as soon as I surfaced into consciousness, but the emotions lingered.

Once the sun rose, I gave up any hope of sleeping in. I got up, took a quick shower, and straightened up my room the best I could before forcing down a light breakfast.

It was Saturday, but there was no way I was sitting around worrying about Mason all day. I had no idea what to do or even if there was anything *to* do. I probably needed to talk to Nana again, but I wasn't ready to admit how much I'd messed up.

I needed to focus on something else—something productive—so I drove to the hospital. I was relieved to find Gareth alone in his room again.

"Hey," he said when I knocked on the doorframe. "Come on in." He didn't sound particularly enthused to see me.

"Hey, Gareth. How are you feeling?"

"About the same."

"No memories have returned?"

"No."

"How about physically? No improvement there either?"

He shook his head no.

"I'm sorry. I guess this stuff just takes time. Do you know how much longer you'll be in the hospital?"

"Not really. They're worried about my memory loss and the fact that I keep getting confused about stuff."

"Confused?"

"Yeah, and I keep losing time, like I'm blacking out, but sometimes it's when a nurse or a doctor is in here and I'm talking to them and stuff, but then I don't remember it later." He rubbed his eyes. "It's freaking me out."

"Yeah, I'm sure. And they don't know what's causing it?"

"No. They did some scans of my brain, and they said there's nothing wrong that they can see. They want to keep observing me, but I just want to go home."

"You've been through a lot."

He frowned. "I don't even know what I've been through. Everybody keeps saying that, but you don't know either."

He wasn't wrong, but that was what I'd been hired to find out. Part of me felt bad for the kid, but some part of me was still on high alert. That sense of being watched was still there.

"I talked to some of the parents of your friends yesterday. I didn't learn much. I'm kind of running out of leads. Is it okay if I search your room?"

He shrugged. "I don't care. I doubt it'll help much, though."

"Why do you say that?"

"Because I didn't know where we were going that day. That's what you need, right? So you can find Kyle and DJ and Wade. But if only Kyle knew where we were going, then it's not like I wrote it down in my room."

I hated to admit he was right, but he most likely was. Still, I needed to do it anyway, just to be thorough.

"Okay, well, if you think of anything else that might help, let me know."

He nodded. We said goodbye and I left. I really felt like I was spinning my wheels with this case. I had zero leads and no idea where to go next. Maybe if I finished interviewing the rest of the family, that would give me some direction.

Outside, I called the Millers to see if I could search Gareth's room. Mrs. Miller was home and agreed, so I headed directly there.

As I pulled up to their address, I was struck by how nice their house was. It wasn't quite the McMansion that Wade's father owned, but it was a beautiful older brick home. The yard was meticulously landscaped, with fall mums in bloom everywhere.

Robin Miller answered the door. "Please come in. How's the investigation going? Have you learned anything?"

"The investigation is off to a slow start. I still have a few more people to interview, though. That's also why I wanted to take a look at Gareth's room."

"Right. I can show you where it is."

She led me upstairs and down a hall, then opened a door and stepped back.

I entered the room and looked around. Like Wade's parents, the Millers hadn't cleaned up after the police search. The bed was unmade, dresser drawers stood open with clothes hanging over the edge, a bookshelf was literally overflowing with books, his closet door stood open with a landslide of clothes, shoes, games, and more books spilling out, and his desk looked like a tornado had struck it.

I realized Mrs. Miller was still in the doorway.

"I'd really like to do this alone, if that's okay."

"Oh, of course. Sorry. I'll be downstairs if you need me."

"Before you go, how much of this is what the police left and how much is normal?"

She laughed. "His room always looks like this. Our arrangement with him is that his room is his space, and we don't enter without his permission. He's responsible for cleaning it, and as long as it doesn't smell and he doesn't leave food sitting around, we stay out."

"Okay, but the police did search it, right?"

"They did, although how they could find anything in this mess, I don't know."

I had to agree with her, but they were trained for this stuff.

After Mrs. Miller left, I got to work. First I dug through his dresser drawers—just a quick scan—then felt under each drawer. I even pulled the dresser out and checked behind it. Nothing except a few hopeful condoms in his underwear drawer.

Then I rifled through his desk, checking each of those drawers inside, back, and underneath as well. The sheer number of papers on his desk took a while since I had to check each one to make sure he hadn't jotted anything important on his schoolwork, but I found nothing out of the ordinary there either.

I checked his bedside table next. Nada. Same with his bed. I even looked between the mattress and the box spring and under the bed.

The bookshelf was filled with an interesting mix of novels—Harry Potter had a place of prominence on the top shelf—and books about the occult and ghost hunting. I found the occult books interesting. I'd been under the impression that the boys went into the ghost hunting with a more pseudoscientific approach, but the occult books implied that Gareth, at least, had some more spiritual leanings. It wasn't exactly a clue, but I filed it away as an interesting fact to maybe bring up with him at some point.

Finally I tackled the closet. He had some clothes hanging up, but most of them were on the floor. There was no way to do it in a neat and orderly fashion, so I just started pulling things out and putting them behind me. As far as I could tell, there wasn't any order to anything, so I'd just toss it all back in when I was finished.

It took a while, but I finally had the closet floor cleared. I was disappointed to not find anything of interest. The kid seemed remarkably normal. I shoved everything back into the closet and took a final look around the room. It hadn't given me a single lead, which, with the way this case was going, didn't really surprise me. I went back downstairs to find Mrs. Miller. I thanked her for letting me search the room, then said goodbye.

On my way to the car, I checked my phone and saw I had two missed calls and two voicemail messages. I kept my phone on silent whenever I was out on a case. You never knew when you'd need to hide, and the last thing you want when you're hiding is your phone buzzing in your pocket or, worse, the ringer going off.

I got in the car and listened to the messages. The first was from Detective Sergeant Mead. He said he'd be at his office all afternoon and to swing by the barracks if I wanted to talk. The next was Vanessa Watson, Wade's mother. She said she was willing to talk to me and asked me to call her back.

I quickly returned Mrs. Watson's call.

"Thank you so much for calling back. Of course I'll talk to you. I'm glad someone is looking for Wade!" she said after I'd introduced myself and explained why I was calling.

"To be fair, the police are looking too."

"And look what good that's done," she snapped. "And my asshole of an ex-husband refuses to tell me anything."

"Well, I'll be happy to tell you what I know, but I'm afraid that's not much. That's why I need to talk to you. Are you free this afternoon, by any chance?"

"I am, but not until, like, two."

I checked the time. It was a little before noon. "That works. Can you give me your address?"

I scribbled the address down on a notepad and told her I'd see her in a few hours.

It was getting close to lunchtime, but I wasn't hungry. Instead I dropped by Mead's office.

I checked in at the front desk of the state police barracks and had a seat while they called the detective and told him I was there to see him. I didn't have to wait long before the inner door buzzed and swung open to reveal Mead. He was a tall, burly, serious-faced man who looked like he'd seen too much. He wore a fitted blue two-piece suit, his jacket open, the top button of his white shirt undone, and his tie askew. His black hair was buzzed close to his scalp, and his dark brown eyes looked as tired as I felt. His closely trimmed pencil mustache quirked to one side in a proximation of a smile as he waved me in without a word.

I followed him back to his office, decorated only with the accolades and honors he'd received over the years and a smattering of sports memorabilia. I took a seat in the black faux-leather chair facing him while he settled behind his desk.

He stared at me for a few second before saying, "You're on this Miller case, huh?"

"Yeah, Gareth Miller's parents hired me."

"Sounds about right. They've got their hackles up. How's your investigation going?"

"It's not. I have zero leads so far."

"Join the club. I've never seen so many people know so little."

"Are you on the case?"

"I wasn't, but I am now."

"Then you think it's homicide?"

"Honestly, yes, but I doubt we know much more than you do."

"What can you tell me?"

He stood up. "Follow me."

He led me back into the central common area set up with tables and chairs. On one wall was a huge map of the county and the surrounding areas. He jabbed at a spot on the map with a long finger. "This is where we found the Miller kid."

I took a closer look. He'd indicated a rural road on the edge of Carroll and Frederick counties.

"A motorist called it in," he continued. "Said a boy was stumbling on the side of the road, looked injured, covered in blood. The responding officer recognized him immediately. Said he was confused. Knew his name but not how he got there. Didn't know what day it was. The officer called in an ambulance. Drugs were suspected, but blood tests showed he was clean. He was also extremely dehydrated and probably hadn't eaten since he vanished. Barely alive, barely coherent."

With his finger, he drew a big circle around where Gareth had been found. "We've searched this entire area. Brought in dogs and everything. Nothing. No sign of the others or even the car."

"What about the blood on his clothes? Was it his?"

Mead jerked his head back toward his office. Once we were seated again, he rubbed his forehead and sighed. "This isn't public knowledge, but no. We tested it, and none of it was his. So the lab checked it against the other parents. We got two conclusive matches."

"Meaning that the blood belonged to two of the boys?"

He nodded.

"What about the third?"

"They're still running tests. There was a lot of blood."

I shuddered. "Was it fresh?"

"No, it was dry. Looked like maybe he'd been rained on or something but didn't seem like there was any attempt to wash it off."

"You think the other boys are dead?"

"That's our best guess. They've been missing too long. And did I mention that there was a lot of blood?"

"And Gareth is your suspect?"

"The most obvious answer is usually the right one in my line of work. He's the only one who has turned up. He's covered in the other boys' blood. He refuses to tell us what happened."

"Then you think he's lying about not remembering?"

"Most likely. True amnesia is incredibly rare."

"He was pretty convincing to me."

"Liars often are."

"Has he been seen by a therapist or anything?"

"Not yet. We're more focused on finding the other boys right now."

"Understandably. Do you have a case if you don't find them?"

"Who knows? Having the bodies would obviously be a lot stronger. The blood on his clothes is pretty damning if they never resurface, though. He was the last person to see them alive. Still, a good lawyer would probably get him off. You never know how these things will go."

"So... what's next? How do you find them?"

He raised his hands in an elaborate shrug. "You got me. That's one of the reasons I agreed to meet with you. We're just spinning our wheels at this point until we find the boys or the Miller kid decides to talk. I was hoping you might have something more than we do."

"Sorry to disappoint. Are you keeping Gareth at the hospital because you suspect him?"

"Not really, although it is nice to know where he is. But he's not exactly a flight risk. The hospital is still running tests and keeping an eye on him. He really was in bad shape when we found him. No faking that."

I cocked my head to the side. "Doesn't that make it more likely that something bad happened to all of them and he just escaped somehow?"

"Not necessarily. Maybe he just got scared after he killed them and hid out until he started getting loopy from dehydration. Or he thought he'd been gone long enough to reappear without suspicion. What's the alternative? That we have some crazy serial killer hiding out somewhere murdering teenage boys? This isn't a slasher movie."

"I mean, that stuff does happen."

"Perhaps, but that's not the most likely scenario, so until we find the boys or prove that Miller didn't do it, that's all I have to go on."

I frowned. "I thought we were innocent until proven guilty, not assumed guilty until proven innocent."

"Sure, and that's why he hasn't been arrested. Personally, I still think he's guilty."

"Are there any photos of him when he was found?"

Mead gave me a look, and for a second, I thought he was going to refuse, but then he flipped open his laptop and clicked away for a while. Then he turned it so I could see the photo of Gareth that filled the screen. He was leaning against a police cruiser, staring down at the ground, and looked extremely ill: gray skin, dark circles around his eyes, sunken cheeks. He was wearing a pair of jeans, high-top sneakers, and a gray athletic-brand T-shirt. The shirt and jeans were crusted with dark rust-colored stains. My stomach clenched.

Mead hit the Forward key, and a series of close-up shots paraded across the screen, including several scratches and cuts on his arms and face.

"Are any of those scratches defensive wounds?" I asked.

"They don't seem to be. More like what you'd expect to find on someone who stumbled through thorns and branches."

"Were there any defensive wounds?"

"Not that we found."

"Doesn't that poke a hole in your theory? How would he brutally murder three boys without any of them fighting back?"

"Caught them by surprise?"

"All three? And what's his motive? He doesn't have any history of violence, does he?"

Mead sighed and closed the laptop. "I didn't say the case was closed. It's an active investigation. I don't have any idea why he'd kill his friends. People snap. It happens all the time."

I shook my head. "Something doesn't feel right."

"Three boys are missing, probably dead, and you think something doesn't feel right?"

"You know what I mean. What about the room searches? Or their laptops?"

"Nada."

"Did you search their lockers at school?"

"Yep."

"And still nothing?"

"Like I said, we've got nothing. Look, we need a break in this case, and soon. I'm hoping you can help us out. I've been very forthcoming with you, but whatever you find, I expect you to let us know right away. Deal?"

"Deal."

"Even if it implicates your client."

"Of course."

"Good. That's everything I know. Any more questions?"

"Yeah. What can you tell me about the officer who was in charge of the case when it was just missing persons?"

"Gibson? He's a good cop. It's not his fault we haven't found them. Technically he's still in charge of the case."

"I'd like to talk to him."

"He can't tell you anything I haven't."

"I know, but still. He's been working on the case longer."

Mead rolled his eyes but picked up his desk phone and hit some buttons. "Gibson, it's Zeb. I've got a private eye who's working the Gareth Miller case. He wants to meet you." A pause and a frown. "Well, he's your problem now. I'm sending him over." He hung up, then gestured toward the door. "Across the bullpen. Name's on the wall."

I stood up. "Thanks, Detective Mead."

He shook my outstretched hand. "No problem. Just don't forget your promise to let us know if you find anything."

"I won't." I paused in the doorway and looked back. "Scout's honor."

I turned around and almost ran into an officer in full uniform.

"Oh! Sorry," I said as my cheeks heated up.

The officer looked me up and down. "I'll forgive a fellow scout… this time. You must be the kid PI. Figured I'd come get you so you weren't wandering all over the barracks."

My face was burning. I didn't like being called a kid. That meant this must be Gibson. I nodded and stuck out my hand. "Cav Crawford."

Gibson shook my hand. "I'm Detective Gibson. What can I do for you?"

Gibson was fairly attractive. He was tall, though not quite as tall as Mead. He was white, early- to mid-thirties, dark brown hair cut short, and brown eyes that seemed very amused at that moment.

I was flustered but tried to pull myself together. "I was hoping we could talk about the Miller case. I've been hired by Iwan and Robin Miller. Thanks for talking to me."

He nodded and started walking away. "I wasn't given a choice. Come on into my office."

He led me across the room to a door with two names next to it, his and a Det. Michael Farmer. There were two desks in a room too small for two desks. There was barely room for a single chair between them. Gibson slid behind one, but there was no one at the other desk.

"Have a seat," he said, gesturing to the lone chair in the middle of the room.

"What happens if you and Detective Farmer both need to talk to someone in your office at the same time?" I asked as I sat.

He chuckled. "We make sure that never happens. We're rarely on duty at the same time, so it's usually not an issue."

"Gotcha."

He leaned forward with his elbows on the desk, a smile playing around his full lips.

What exactly did he find so amusing? Was he not taking me seriously? That happened sometimes with law-enforcement types. I was small and looked young.

"How can I help you?" he asked.

"Well, Mead gave me the overall details of the case as it stands now."

"Then I guess he told you we're pretty much at a standstill."

"He did."

"Not sure what I can add to that."

"You were on the case for a week before it became a possible homicide investigation. You're more familiar with the details."

"Unfortunately, there aren't any details. Not a single person in any of the families seemed to know anything about where those boys were going that day. We searched all their rooms and their computers, checked their social media accounts, talked to the school, interviewed their school club advisor... and nothing. We got nothing. Not even a rough idea to start narrowing it down. Until we picked up Gareth Miller, we didn't even have a geographical area to start looking. And even after we found him, we've turned up nothing. We still haven't even found the damn car." The frustration was clear in his voice.

"Mead is pretty convinced the boys are dead. Do you agree?"

"I work missing persons, so I always try to hold out hope until we know for sure. Mead works homicide. He has a less optimistic outlook. Unfortunately, at least statistically speaking, that's certainly the most probable outcome. When it comes to teens, most missing person cases are either runaways, accidents, or murders."

"I just tracked down a runaway for a different case."

"That's great. They're back home now?"

I nodded.

"A success case, then. Congrats. I don't think these boys are runaways, though."

"I don't think so either. What about an accident? Maybe something happened while they were exploring an abandoned building—the floor caved in or something."

"I was investigating the case under that assumption up until we found the Miller kid. Now... it seems less likely."

"What about an abduction? Is that possible?"

"Anything is possible, but then where did all that blood on Gareth Miller come from? And how did he get away? And why can't he remember anything?"

"Do you think his memory loss is real?"

He shrugged. "I'm not a shrink. Can't say."

"Did you talk to him after he was picked up?"

"Yeah."

"Then you must have an impression, at least."

Gibson thought for a moment. "He's a hard nut to crack. He seemed genuinely confused and scared, but he was also in very bad shape physically, and his fear might have had more to do with being caught. You've talked to him?"

I nodded again.

"And what was your impression?"

"I don't think he's lying.... Or at least I don't think he thinks he's lying."

"An important—and interesting—distinction. Does that mean you have a theory?"

I shook my head. "Not yet. I don't know enough to have a theory yet. I'm just hoping the boys are still alive."

"Me too, man. Me too. Anything else?"

"No. Oh, wait. Yes. Are you guys surveilling Gareth?"

He looked a little confused by the question. "We had an officer stationed at the hospital for a while, but we decided he was too weak to be a flight risk and it was a waste of money."

"No, I mean, do you have a camera in his room?"

"No. Nothing like that. Why?"

"Just a weird feeling I get when I'm in his room. I guess that's it. Thanks for taking the time to talk to me." I stood up, and he did too.

"No problem. I'll walk you out."

"Oh, that's okay. I can find my way."

"Department policy." He gestured grandly toward the door. "After you."

He trailed me to the door to the lobby and held it open for me. To my surprise, he followed me out.

"You really don't have to—" I started.

"I'm just stepping out for some fresh air," he said, cutting me off. "I can only sit cooped up in that office for so long before I start feeling like one of our prisoners." He held open the door to the parking lot.

"Where's your car?" he asked when we were outside.

This was getting a little weird. I pointed out my car, an older model nondescript black Honda. It wasn't impressive or flashy, but that made it the perfect car for a private investigator. It wasn't the sort of car you noticed.

"Nice."

"Yeah, so… thanks again," I said awkwardly.

"Hey, look, if I'm out of line, just say so, no problem, but I was thinking we could get dinner sometime."

I blinked. "Like… to talk about the case?"

He grinned. "I was thinking more like a date."

"A date," I repeated.

"You know, dinner, drinks, that sort of thing."

My mind raced. He was probably twice my age, or close to it. Did that matter? More importantly, did I want to go on a date? All I'd been saying lately was that I wasn't ready, and after my disastrous encounter with Mason the night before, my mind was more muddled than ever.

"I don't know," I said. "Wouldn't that be, like, a conflict of interest or something?"

"I'm not investigating you, so no. How about dinner Monday night?"

Tell him you're not interested. "Um, maybe?" Where had that come from?

"Great. How about La Régal Bohème?"

I hesitated. That was the most expensive restaurant in town. Besides, I hadn't even agreed yet. Not really. Maybe wasn't a firm commitment.

"My treat," he added quickly.

"Oh no, I couldn't—"

"Really, I'd like to."

This guy was a little pushy. I was growing even more uncomfortable.

Meanwhile, Gibson seemed to be having the time of his life. His grin was back. "Come on. Let me take the cutest PI in town out for a nice dinner."

"My boss is going to be really surprised when you take him out to dinner."

He laughed. "Ha. Cute and funny. Are we good, then?"

"I never said yes."

"But you want to. I can tell."

"Look," I said a bit more sharply than intended, "I didn't even know you were gay—or bi or whatever—one minute ago, and now you're pressuring me to go out with you."

"Hey," he said, holding his hands out in front of him, "no pressure. Really. And I'm gay, out and proud. My husband even comes to work socials sometimes."

"Husband?" I took a step back.

"Oh, don't worry. We're open."

"I mean, that great and all, but I'm not interested in being your side piece."

"It's not like that—"

"Save it. Let's keep this professional. Thanks for the information. Have a good day."

I turned and walked away, trying to keep my pace even. I could feel his eyes following me all the way to my car. I hoped that would be the end of it, but I had a bad feeling about Detective Gibson.

Chapter 6

VANESSA WATSON wasn't anything like I expected. Having met her ex-husband, I figured she'd be something like him. Or maybe like Yara, his second wife. She wasn't remotely like either of them. She was around my height and plump, with dyed-red hair—two inches of silver-shot dark roots showing—and heavy makeup. She wore an oversized Halloween-themed sweater dress over orange-and-black striped tights and strappy silver high-heeled shoes with her toes spilling over the edge.

She started talking as soon as she opened the door. "Oh, I'm so glad you're here. Anything we can do to help find Wade. I've been worried sick. Haven't I, Thomas?" She directed that last bit over her shoulder as she stepped aside to let me in.

The man I assumed to be Thomas nodded and looked as if he was accustomed to agreeing with whatever Vanessa said. He was older than she was, potbellied and slope-shouldered. He looked tired. His hair was graying, cut short and combed to the side. When he turned to lead us into a room that opened off the hallway, I noticed a perfectly round bald spot on the back of his head like a pink yarmulke.

Vanessa kept up a constant stream of chatter as we filed into the living room. "I don't even know what to do with myself. I thought about just driving around looking for him, but I don't even know where to start, you know? But it's terrible just sitting around doing nothing and feeling helpless. A mother wants to help her baby, you know? I mean, I know he's not a baby. He's fifteen. But he'll always be my baby. You know?"

"When was the last time you saw Wade?" I interrupted. Sometimes it helped to let someone ramble on. You never knew what they might give away without realizing it. This was not one of those times. As much as I hated to cut someone off, I had a sneaking suspicion that if I didn't, I'd never get a word in edgewise.

She paused and glanced at Thomas. "I don't know. Maybe a month ago? I used to get him on weekends, but then he thought he was getting too old for that. Things were never easy on him, especially after his father and I split up. He was quiet, a shy kid. Never had many friends. I sometimes wonder if all our fighting affected him, you know? His father and me, I mean. Not Thomas and me. We've never had a fight in our entire relationship, right, honey?"

Thomas nodded. I suspected they never fought because he let her do all the talking.

"Did you know about his ghost-hunting club?"

"Yes. We were just happy he was getting involved in something outside the house. Of course, his father disapproved. Thought it was a waste of time. Have you met Patrick?"

"Yes. I talked to him yesterday."

She nodded as if I'd said something profound. "Then you know."

"Know what?"

"How he is. A miserable son of a bitch. I was married to him for an entire decade. Put him through medical school. Gave birth to his son. Then he couldn't dump me fast enough to marry that girl from South America. She wasn't his first whore either, you know. Just the one he married. Probably because he got her pregnant. I bet he figured he could control her. He could never control me. He always said I had too many opinions."

"What did you think about the ghost-hunting club?" I asked, trying to steer the conversation back to Wade. I felt even worse for this kid after meeting Mrs. Watson. As if an uncaring, distant father wasn't bad enough, he also had to deal with a self-obsessed mother.

"What do you mean?"

"It didn't bother you that he was exploring abandoned buildings looking for ghosts?"

"We don't believe in ghosts, do we, Thomas?" Thomas gave a halfhearted shake of his head to indicate the negative. "But kids have imaginations, you know? I didn't see any harm in it." She paused, and her face fell. "I guess there was. Harm in it, I mean. I just didn't think.... I didn't know they were going in empty buildings. Kids explore. That's what they do. But I didn't know. Maybe if I'd known.... But he never mentioned that."

I wondered how much he didn't mention because she wasn't listening. I glanced at Thomas, and he gave me another almost imperceptible head shake, as if to confirm that Wade never mentioned it. I'd yet to hear his voice.

"What do you do for a living, Thomas?" I asked, more to give him an opportunity to speak than because it mattered.

"I run an appliance repair shop," he said in a quiet voice.

"He owns it," Vanessa corrected. "Best one in town. I keep books for him. And I help around the shop."

Thomas nodded.

"You mentioned earlier that you didn't know where to start looking for Wade, so can I assume you didn't know where they were going that day?"

She shook her head vigorously. "No! Like I said, I didn't even know they were exploring these old tumble-down buildings. So dangerous! Those babies probably fell through a floor, or a ceiling caved in on them."

"Is that what you think happened?"

She looked confused. "Of course. What else could it be?"

I thought it best not to bring up the police's suspicion of murder. "What about Gareth Miller?"

"He obviously escaped. Probably got hit on the head and just doesn't remember anything."

As far as theories went, it seemed as plausible as any of the others I'd heard.

"Do you have any other children?" I asked.

"Wade is my only child, but Thomas has a son."

I looked at Thomas, and he nodded. "Benji," he supplied.

"How old is Benji?"

"Sixteen," Vanessa answered.

"Does he live with you?"

"Yes."

"Is he home now?"

"He's in his room," Vanessa said, "but he doesn't know anything either. We asked."

"Would it be possible for me to talk to him alone for a few minutes?"

She looked to Thomas, who nodded. "Okay. Let me check with him."

Vanessa got up and left the room, and I found myself alone with Thomas.

"Do Wade and his mother have a good relationship?" I asked.

Thomas thought for a moment, then said, "She loves him. Like she said, he's a quiet boy. Didn't have much to say. He's a good boy."

It didn't quite answer my question but spoke volumes nonetheless.

Vanessa appeared in the doorway. "I'll show you to Benji's room."

I followed her down a hall to a room that unmistakably belonged to a teenager. Clothes covered almost every flat surface, and dozens of posters papered the walls, overlapping to create a dizzying wallpaper effect. There were band posters, movie posters, video game posters, and the perennial women in bikinis. Heavy curtains covered the windows, giving the room a cave-like effect.

A long-haired blond boy sat on the edge of the bed, looking nervous. He relaxed visibly when he saw me. He was wearing an oversize death-metal band shirt over a pair of brown corduroy pants, with bare feet. He was skinny and looked like he could use a shower.

"Benji, this is Cav Crawford. He just has a few questions for you," Vanessa said, then left us alone.

"Okay if I come in?" I asked.

Benji nodded, and I stepped into the room. It smelled like sweat and teenage boy, with a faint undertone of stale marijuana.

"I'm looking for your stepbrother," I told him.

"Vanessa said you're a private investigator. I was expecting someone a lot older."

I smiled. "I get that a lot. Are you and Wade close?"

He pushed his hair out of his face. "No. Wade isn't really close to anybody."

"What about his ghost-hunters club?"

Benji rolled his eyes. "That club is a joke at school. People call them the Spook Patrol. I guess he's friends with the other guys in the club, kind of."

"What do you mean 'kind of'?"

"I don't think they're tight or anything. They just go on their little adventures and meet after school once a week."

"They have an advisor from the faculty, right?"

"Every club has to have a teacher sponsor, but they don't have to attend the meetings or anything."

"Do you know who their sponsor was?"

"I don't really pay much attention to it. I mean, if I'm being honest, I mostly try to act like I don't know Wade. He's such a loser." He blushed. "Sorry. That was kind of shitty, I guess. He's just really… nerdy. We're not exactly in the same circles. And he's younger."

"Do you know any of the other guys in the club?"

"Kyle and Gareth are in my grade, so I've had classes with them, but we're not friends."

"Then I guess you don't have any ideas about where they could have gone that day."

He shook his head. "I mean, I wish I did. Maybe we aren't close, but I didn't want anything bad to happen to him. He's harmless."

I looked around the room. "Where did Wade sleep when he was here? Does he have his own room?"

Benji's eyes widened. "Oh yeah. We definitely couldn't share a room."

"Did the police search it, do you know?"

"I think they came. I wasn't home, so I don't know what they did while they were here."

"Do you think I could see it?"

"I guess. Maybe you should check with Dad and Vanessa?"

He was probably right. "Thanks, I will." I pulled out my wallet, fished out a business card, and held it out to him. "If you think of anything that might help, will you let me know?"

He took the card and stared at it. "Yeah, sure," he mumbled, distracted. Then he looked up and shook his hair out of his eyes. "How'd you become a private investigator? How old are you, anyway?"

"I'm twenty-one. I interned for a private investigator, and I've been working for him ever since. At first I was just his assistant, but I'm fully licensed now."

"Cool. Do you have a gun?"

I frowned. "No."

He rolled his eyes. "Lame."

"I should probably go find Vanessa and your dad," I said and left the room.

Vanessa was midrant when I appeared in the doorway. "I'm just saying, I feel like you'd be a lot more concerned if it was Benji—" Thomas nodded in my direction, and Vanessa cut off and turned around. "You all done talking to Benji?" she asked, her tone suddenly sticky sweet.

"Yes, but I was wondering if I could see Wade's room before I leave."

"Of course. Anything to help."

She led me back down the hall, past Benji's room, where he was now sprawled across the bed wearing headphones, staring at the ceiling and pointing a finger gun at the light fixture. She threw open a door at the end of the hall and turned on the overhead light. Wade's room was half the size of Benji's. Barely room for a bed and a dresser. There was literally nothing in the room to show that a teenaged boy sometimes lived here—no personal touches, no posters, no books. It was completely bare, aside from a Pokémon bedspread that he'd probably outgrown years ago.

I walked in and looked around. Everything about this kid made me sad. No wonder he'd stopped coming every weekend. Or maybe it had felt more lived-in when he did. I opened the top drawer of the dresser to find it empty.

"He stopped keeping clothes here when he stopped staying every weekend," Vanessa explained. There was a note of sadness, or maybe regret, in her voice. "He never seemed to feel at home here. Not that he feels at home with his father either."

I quickly checked the other drawers, but they were all empty as well. I noticed a closet door and opened it next. There were some winter coats hanging and a few boxes sealed up on the floor. Nothing that looked like it belonged to Wade. I got down and looked under the bed. Nothing there either. I ran a hand over the bedspread and sighed.

"All done?" Vanessa asked.

"I guess I am," I said, feeling dejected. I'd really hoped this last interview would turn up a lead, but I was out of luck again. I just hoped this didn't mean my entire investigation was done too.

As I sat in my car outside the Watson house, I realized I was officially out of ideas, and so far the only thing that had come out of my investigation was an invitation to a date I didn't want. I had no idea how to move forward with no leads.

A conversation with Walker was in my future. When I got stuck, he usually had some insight or suggestion about an angle I'd missed, but that would have to wait until Monday. In the meantime, I wasn't sure how to proceed. Not knowing where to go with my case meant I was running out of diversions, which meant my mind went back to Mason.

I rested my forehead on my steering wheel. I'd really fucked things up there. I needed to talk to Nana. I'd put it off as long as possible. I knew she wouldn't be angry, just disappointed. Which was worse.

Nana was in her wheelchair when I knocked on her doorframe. She looked surprised to see me. "Twice in one week? To what do I owe the pleasure?"

"I, uh, need to talk to you."

Something in my voice must have given me away. "Oh dear," she said. "You'd better come in and shut the door."

I did as she directed, then sat down in the chair by her bed.

"What happened?"

"I tried to summon Mason again."

Her eyes widened. "Oh, Cavanaugh. Oh no," she said softly. She took a deep breath. "How? What did you do to summon him?" Her voice was hard and brittle. She'd never used that tone with me before. It was almost as devastating as my experience with Mason.

"I used the prayer with a candle, and then I asked him to come back."

"What candle?"

"The one Mom gave me when I was fifteen."

"I don't remember it. What does it look like?"

"I think it's maybe beeswax. It's kind of like honeycomb, and it's black and purple and orange."

She nodded. "That sounds like a Samhain candle. It would be especially powerful for contacting the dead, and it would be even more powerful as you get closer to Samhain. Not that your mother would have known all that. She probably just remembered the ones I used when she was growing up."

"You've mentioned Samhain a few times now, and I only have a vague idea of what it is exactly. It's another name for Halloween, right?"

"Not exactly. It's far older than our modern idea of Halloween. Samhain marks the Celtic new year, the end of summer and the beginning of winter. It begins at sundown on Halloween, and it's also the day when the veil between the living and the dead is at its thinnest."

She proceeded to give me a mini lecture about the history of Samhain and how it became Halloween. "But Samhain is still well over a week away," she said as she wound down the lesson. "Although as I said the other day, your gifts are strong, so that might not even matter. Did it work?"

"Oh, it worked."

Her eyes narrowed. "What happened, Cavanaugh?"

"I… I messed up. Nana, he didn't know he was dead. It was horrible."

Nana closed her eyes. "Tell me everything."

"He… he thought it was still the day of our anniversary, the day he died. But he didn't know he was dead. He said his memory was dark. I didn't know what to do. He was getting mad at me. He thought I was playing some sort of sick prank or something."

"You didn't tell him, did you?" Nana said, her eyes snapping open. She pinned me with her gaze. "Please say you didn't tell him he died."

"Why?" I tried to keep the panic out of my voice but failed miserably.

"Cavanaugh, did you tell him he was dead?"

"Yes," I admitted in a small voice.

She closed her eyes again. "Then what happened?"

"He didn't believe me at first. I was scared. I knew I'd messed up, so I tried to blow out the candle, thinking maybe that would send him back to… wherever he's been since he died. I don't know. I wasn't thinking clearly. He tried to grab the candle from me. His hand… his hand went through the candle. And then he knew. He knew I was telling the truth." I took a deep, shuddering breath. "Then… I don't know what happened. It was like all hell broke loose. The room went dark, and a wind started blowing, and it kept getting stronger, like a storm. I was so scared. Then the candle blew out, and when it did, everything stopped. The wind was gone instantly, and so was Mason."

I stopped talking and waited, but Nana didn't respond. Her eyes were still closed.

"Nana, what happened? How… how bad did I mess up?"

No response.

"Nana, I'm scared."

She sighed and opened her eyes. "You should be. You were playing with things beyond your knowledge. Beyond mine, for that matter. I was always taught that you never tell the departed that they are dead. You can't know how they will react, what they will do… what they will become."

"What do you mean, become?"

"The dead, they can be powerful. That storm was just a small taste of what a tormented soul can do. If Mason becomes twisted, corrupted, he could haunt you or even harm you. He might blame you for his death. You said he couldn't remember anything?"

My heart was racing. "Right. When I asked him what the last thing was that he could remember, he said it was all dark."

"That's not good. It implies he was in some sort of limbo, which would mean he was untethered. If you reawakened his consciousness, he might have attached to you."

"What does that mean?"

"It means he would use you as his anchor point in this world. As long as he remains on this side of the veil, the energy he needs to exist in this plane would come from you. He would be tied to you."

"Tied to me?"

"For better or worse. If he turns dark, it could be very bad for you. We'd have to find a way to cut him loose."

"Like an exorcism?"

She pursed her lips. "That's a very Catholic ideology, but more or less."

"And what if he doesn't turn dark?" I thought about the terrifying wind and darkness that had swirled around me.

"Then you'd still be stuck with a lost and confused ghost hovering around you. At the very least, it would probably put a damper on your dating life."

"What dating life?"

She gave me an understanding smile. "You need to get back out there eventually."

"That's what everyone keeps telling me, but I don't think I'm ready."

"You'll never be ready until you try."

"But what about Mason?"

"No matter what happens, you have to move on. You can't date a dead boy." I flinched slightly at her bluntness, and of course she didn't miss it. "But that's enough of me meddling in your love life. You're a grown man and you can make your own choices. Back to Mason—I can't lie, I'm very concerned. I wish you hadn't rushed headlong into things you know nothing about. But what's done is done. We don't know what way it will go just yet. Maybe you were lucky and Mason's spirit didn't attach to you. That would be the best-case scenario."

"But... what would happen to him? I mean if I awakened his consciousness and he's still untethered?"

She looked away. "I don't know."

"Nana...."

Her eyes met mine again. There was a sadness there. "He could be left to wander alone until he fades away."

My breath caught. "That sounds horrible," I managed around the lump in my throat.

She nodded once. "It is."

"How could that be the best-case scenario?"

"I meant the best for you. Not for him."

"I don't want that for him."

"You still love him."

"Of course."

"And he still loves you. Chances are, he attached to you. Only time will tell."

"Should I try to summon him again?"

"No. Leave him be. If he attached, he'll come to you. He may be working through all this new information. Summoning him before he's ready would only make things worse."

"Where is he?"

"I don't know. Maybe wherever he's been since his death."

"Which is where?"

"I don't know that either. I'm sorry, Cavanaugh. I know you wanted more answers. I wish I had them for you."

"Me too. But I understand. And I did this to myself."

"That you did, my dear grandson. That you did."

Chapter 7

WHEN I got home, I tried think about anything other than Mason. Of course, that only really left my case. What was going on with Gareth? Was he a cold-blooded killer? Was he the victim of an accident? Did he really have amnesia? What or who was watching me when I was with him? Or were they watching him?

That hadn't occurred to me before, and the thought stopped me in my tracks.

I made a mental note to search Gareth's hospital room the next time I was there, just to rule out a camera. If there was one and the police hadn't planted it, who had? And why were they watching? If there wasn't one, did that mean I was just imagining it? Or maybe Nana was right and Gareth did have split personalities, and the watchful feeling was one of his other ones.

I spent some time reading up on split personalities. A quick search revealed that it was now referred to as dissociative identity disorder, and while it was a real mental health condition, it was also extremely rare. I had to admit, some of the symptoms—memory loss, fugue states, confusion—sounded like Gareth. Another personality lurking beneath the surface would explain some of what I'd experienced.

Or maybe the kid was possessed, and a demon was watching my every move.

Too many questions. Too many possibilities. I needed a distraction or I was going to drive myself crazy. It was a Saturday night—I should be having fun.

I texted Haniah. *What's up?*

A minute later, I got a text from Haniah. *On a date. Why? Everything okay?*

Yeah, everything's fine. Talk to you later. Have fun. Don't do anything I wouldn't do.

That's very limiting. I'm going to do lots of things you wouldn't do. Bye.

With Haniah busy, I was acutely aware of how few other friends I had. That was the product of throwing myself so deeply into school and my job after Mason died. I'd lost touch with all my old friends from high school.

If I couldn't have fun, I could at least be productive. I did have midterms coming up, and I should probably study. I changed out of my Cavanaugh Crawford, PI outfit and into some comfy sweats and curled up on my bed with my books.

About an hour later, my phone buzzed. It was a text from a number not saved in my contacts.

Hey, what's up?

I was confused for a second until I opened it up and found one previous text: *This is Kyreh.*

I'd forgotten to save his number. I quickly texted back. *Hey, just doing some studying.*

Need a break?

From studying? Always.

LOL I thought maybe we could get together and talk about that paper.

So a break from studying to do more schoolwork?

How about if I promise you ice cream too?

Then you have yourself a deal.

Cool. Meet at my dorm?

That works. Which one?

I'm in the Fred.

Cool. See you soon.

I changed out of my sweats and into jeans and a super comfy cream-colored baggy thrift-store sweater and headed out the door.

Kyreh lived in Frederick Douglass Hall, or the Fred, as it was affectionately known. I'd lived in Thurgood Marshall Hall when I was on campus, but Haniah had been in the Fred, so I was familiar with it.

Kyreh was sitting outside waiting for me. He jumped up as I approached.

"Hey!" he said with a warm smile. He was wearing jeans and a tight blue T-shirt with a faded Doctor Who logo that looked like he might have owned it for years. The tightness showed off his muscles.

He's straight, I reminded myself.

"What?" he asked, catching me staring.

"Uh, nothing. Are you into Doctor Who?"

His face lit up. "Yeah? You?"

"I've seen a few episodes, but not like the whole show. Is it worth the deep dive?"

"Honestly, it's hit or miss. All depends on the show runner and the Doctor. Oh, and the companion. But you're not here to talk about nerdy sci-fi shows. Let's talk ghosties."

I laughed. "Sure. Where should we go? Your room, or…?"

"My roommate is studying in our room. Do you live on campus?"

"No, I live off campus with a friend."

"Nice. Next time, we meet at your place. For now, you good with pulling up some grass and talking out here?"

"That works."

We found a grassy area and sprawled out on the ground to plan out the paper and divide tasks, taking notes on our phones.

"So," I said as we wrapped up, "I was promised ice cream."

He grinned. "A deal's a deal. Come on." He jumped up and held out a hand for me. I took it and he pulled me to my feet like I weighed nothing.

"Where are we going?" I asked.

"Hooper's. Where else?" he said and jogged off.

I laughed. He was right. Where else would we go? Hooper's was the hands-down favorite ice cream parlor for students at Waring University—mostly because it was across the street from campus, but it didn't hurt that the ice cream was delicious.

I caught up to him in the ice cream parlor. He was leaning over the counter looking at the selections, and his T-shirt had ridden up while his jeans had slid down, showing off several inches of his striped underwear stretched tightly over his butt—his bubble butt.

"Hi!" I realized the girl behind the counter was waving at me. "Can I help you?" She had a little smirk on her face. How long had she been trying to get my attention?

I blushed as I joined Kyreh at the counter to check out the flavors. Fortunately he was too busy making his own selection to pay much attention to me.

Once we had our ice cream cones, we walked back to campus while we ate.

"So how come you were home studying on a Saturday night instead of partying or on a date or something?" he asked.

"I could ask the same of you. But I've never been much of a partier, and I work so much I sometimes forget to study, so when my friend was busy tonight, I figured it was a good time to catch up."

"And here you sit with me."

I laughed. "This is more fun than studying."

"Can't argue with that. You said your friend was busy. You only have one friend?"

"Pretty much. Her name is Haniah, and she's also my roommate. College changed a lot of things for me. I moved here, met Haniah, got a boyfriend, and just sort of... lost touch with my high school friends."

"Yeah, I can relate to that." He glanced over, his face unreadable. "So you have a boyfriend?"

"Had. Past tense. He, uh, died a little over a year ago."

"Oh wow. I'm so sorry."

"It's okay. How could you know?"

We sat in awkward silence for a moment, him staring down at his dripping cone; then he said, "I can't even imagine losing someone you're dating. Are you... okay?"

I shrugged. "I'm as okay I can be under the circumstances. I mean, it was really tough. I can't lie. But I had my dads, my grandmother, and Haniah for support."

He looked up at me again, this time with surprise. "Dads? Plural?"

"Yeah. My dad died when I was a baby and my mom died when I was sixteen, so my little orphan ass was adopted by this amazing gay couple, Jason and Eli."

"God. I keep putting my foot in it tonight."

I chuckled. "It's all good. Really."

"I'm sorry about your parents."

"Thanks."

"So, not to be rude or anything, but I have questions."

"Ask away."

"You said you lived with a gay couple, right? How'd that happen?"

"One of them was my mom's childhood friend, so I grew up with him around. He was sort of like an uncle. Then he and his husband became my dads."

"What was that like? Having gay dads, I mean."

"It was great. They're great. I love them to death. They own this huge horse farm in Harford County, so life with them was kind of idyllic in some ways."

"A horse farm? That's so cool. The only horses we see in the city are the ones that pull the Arabber carts. Do you have a horse?"

"Yeah, his name is Cormac. You'll have to meet him sometime."

"I'd love that."

"But what's an Arabber cart?"

"Horse-drawn carts selling fruits and vegetables. I think we're the only city left in the US that has them."

"Oh, cool. I haven't seen those."

"They don't make it up to this part of the city much."

"Got it. Enough about me. What about you? Why aren't *you* out partying on a Saturday night?"

"Same thing. No friends. I grew up here in Baltimore. It was kind of a rough neighborhood. School is my way out. Most of the people I grew up with—can't even call them friends really—are still out running the streets. I started out at Baltimore County Community College for a couple of years. I had a few people I was friendly with there, but I transferred here this semester and we didn't stay in touch. It's hard to make friends as an adult. Wait. Do I count as an adult?"

"Legally, at least."

"True. I guess I just haven't really met anyone here yet. Except you, I guess." He flashed me that grin that made my heart jump. "But hey, maybe we can hang out more."

"Tonight's been fun, so I guess I can give you another try."

"Gee, thanks," he said with a laugh. He popped the last of his cone in his mouth while I fished for another topic of conversation.

"So, what kind of name is Cavanaugh anyway?" he asked before I could come up with anything.

"Hey! What kind of name is Kyreh?"

"Touché. But really, is it, like, a family name or something?"

"Honestly, I'm not sure why my parents picked it. It's Irish, but it's usually a surname."

"You're Irish?"

"Yes. Why do you sound so surprised? Not all Irish people have red hair and freckles. You've never heard of the Black Irish?"

"Oh, so now you're Black?"

We both laughed.

"Do you know what it means?" he asked.

"What? Black Irish?"

"No, I mean your name."

"Oh, uh…." I tried to stall. "Not really. What about yours?"

He narrowed his eyes. "You do know."

"Fine. It means something like 'born handsome.'"

He cackled again. "Well, that's accurate at least."

I blushed and tried to divert the attention back to him. "Now it's your turn."

"Kyreh is a Jamaican name. My family is from there. I think it's African in origin, but I'm not sure what it means. I read somewhere that it meant 'teacher,' but I don't know if that was accurate. Next question: What are you studying?"

"Why does this suddenly feel like a job interview?"

"Do you want the job or not?"

"What's the position?"

"Friend. Just so happens I have an opening right now."

"Ah. In that case, I'm studying criminal justice," I told him. "With a human services specialty."

"What does that mean?"

"It means I work for a private investigator. Well, technically I'm a private investigator too. I got my license. So my major will make my job easier. In theory."

"Oh wow. So you've already got your career all planned out."

"More or less. But what about you? What are you studying?"

"Undeclared for now. No clue what I want to be when I grow up. You're lucky."

"How so?"

"You've got it all figured out."

I looked down at the last bite of my cone. It was mostly melted, dripping over my fingers, and it suddenly looked unappetizing. I tossed it into the bushes and looked up to find Kyreh studying me seriously.

I wiped my hands on the grass and looked away to avoid his gaze. "Sometimes I feel like I don't have anything figured out," I said finally.

"What do you mean?"

"When I interned for Walker at his agency, I really liked the work, and I seemed to have a knack for it. He offered me a permanent job and I took it. After that, I got licensed and everything just made sense."

"So what changed?"

I still wasn't ready to talk about Mason with someone I just met, so I shrugged. "Just life, I guess. Some things happened that have made me question things."

"What kind of things?"

"Things I'd really rather not talk about, if that's okay."

"Of course! Sorry, I didn't mean to pry."

I smiled. "Nothing to be sorry for. We're just getting to know each other. I'm sure I'll tell you all my deep, dark secrets eventually."

"Ha. Can't wait." His tone was joking, but his eyes were troubled.

I shook my head. "Damn. I really dragged the mood down. I should be the one apologizing."

"No, you shouldn't. It's okay, really. But... you can talk to me about anything. That's what friends are for, right?"

The intensity of his voice made me glance over at him. He was staring back at me, his eyes flashing. It was time to lighten things up.

"So," I said teasingly. "What about you? Are you dating anyone?"

"Nah. I'm chronically single. Guys on the apps are gross."

"No kidding," I said. Then the implications of what he'd just said hit me and my mouth dropped open. "You're gay?"

He shrugged. "Bi, maybe. I don't know. I don't really like labels."

"Gotcha." I fell silent, surprised by his admission. "So, like, you date guys and girls?"

"I date whoever I'm attracted to, and that doesn't seem to have much to do with gender. Although I think I form romantic relationships more with guys. What do they call that?"

"Homoromantic?"

"Yeah. That sounds right. But I've dated guys, gals, and nonbinary pals."

"You sound like Haniah. I think you two would get along."

He grinned. "Then maybe I'll have to meet her."

"I'll be sure to arrange it."

He narrowed his eyes. "Hold up. Are you trying to set me up with your roommate?"

I shrugged. "Maybe."

"Do I look like I need help?"

I gave him an exaggerated once-over. "You look like you'd do just fine on your own."

He seemed pleased with that answer. "Nah, I'm hopeless at dating. Like I said, chronically single. No game at all."

We fell into silence again. I broke it this time. "What about your family?"

"What about them?"

"Are you out to them?"

He made a face. "Sort of. They're not around much. My sister knows and doesn't care. My dad doesn't know. Or maybe he does and he just doesn't bring it up, but I haven't told him."

"Do you think he would be okay with it?"

"Honestly? I don't care. I know how that sounds, but to say we're not close would be an understatement. If he had a problem with it, oh well. It's not like he's putting me through college. I got a scholarship, and my grandma set up a fund to pay for the rest before she died."

"Sorry about your grandmother."

"It was a while ago."

I hesitated a moment, but my curiosity got the best of me. "And your mom?"

He looked away. "She's in prison."

"I'm sorry."

"Don't be. It's not your fault."

I didn't know what to say to that.

"Go ahead and ask," he said after a moment.

"Ask what?" I played dumb.

"I can tell you're dying to ask why my mom is locked up."

"It's none of my business."

"Your entire job is finding out stuff that isn't your business."

I snorted. "Fair. Okay. I mean, I have to admit I was curious."

"People always assume it was drugs because, you know, we're Black and from Baltimore. It wasn't, though. She killed a cop."

"Whoa!"

"Yeah. Shot him with his own gun. Claimed it was self-defense."

"Damn. What happened?"

"She got pulled over late at night coming home from work. She said he tried to rape her. She grabbed his gun and…." He made a finger gun and pulled the trigger. "Bang."

"That's horrible."

"Yeah. She panicked and left, but he'd already called in her tags and stuff, so they found her right away. Of course, there were no body cameras back then, so they had a dead cop and a Black woman who fled the scene. Nobody believed her story. She got life in prison. I don't even really remember her. My sister says everything changed after that. Dad never really got over it."

"I'm really sorry."

"It sucks, but it's the only life I've ever known."

"What a shitty cop."

He shot me a look out of the corner of his eye.

"What?" I asked.

"Let's just say you and I probably have very different experiences with cops."

I wasn't that naïve. I nodded. "Yeah, I'd imagine so."

"You probably think there are good cops."

I glanced over at him. "I mean, there are." I was thinking about Mead.

"You might know cops who are good people, especially to you, but all cops participate in a system of oppression."

"Systemic racism," I said. We'd talked about it in class. I knew what it was.

"Yeah. On a broad scale. But even smaller than that, how many good cops worked with that guy who tried to rape my mom?" He put air quotes around the word "good." "He'd probably done stuff like that before. He'd been written up a bunch of times for excessive force. And yet none of his fellow cops turned him in. Nobody held him accountable. Nobody believed my mom. They just… circled the wagons and tried to protect their own."

I shook my head. "That's really awful. I mean, I know there are corrupt cops. It's on the news all the time. I guess I've just never experienced it."

"Yeah, well, you might be Black Irish, but you're still a cute white boy. Of course you get the benefit of the doubt. Don't think for a second that if I was in your shoes, I'd get the same advantage."

I thought about what he'd said. My brain wanted to focus on the fact that he thought I was cute, but I brushed that aside and thought about what he was saying.

"White privilege," I said.

Kyreh smiled. "I promise I won't hold it against you."

My phone started buzzing in my pocket. Perfect timing to break the tension. I dug it out, expecting it to be Haniah, but I didn't recognize the number. I almost ignored it, but some instinct told me to answer.

"I should probably get this," I said to Kyreh as I accepted the call.

"Cav! It's Robin Miller," she shouted as soon as I said hello. She sounded frantic. "The hospital just called. Gareth is missing."

"What? For how long?"

"All I know is that they checked his room and he wasn't there. They've searched but can't find him. Iwan and I are on our way there now. I know it's late, but we were hoping you could meet us there."

I wasn't sure what I could do. "Did the hospital call the police?"

"Yes, that's why we want you there. Please!"

I sighed. "Okay, I'll meet you there."

I hung up and turned to Kyreh. "I have to go."

He sat up with a slight frown. "So I gathered. Is something wrong?"

"Kind of. I have to go to the hospital. It's the case I'm working on. Sorry."

"It's all good. It's getting chilly out here anyway."

I stood up. "Well, maybe if you were wearing more than a thin T-shirt…."

He jumped up too and flexed. "Are you trying to say there's something wrong with this shirt I've had since I was twelve?"

"No, nothing wrong at all," I mumbled, staring at his arms. I caught myself. "Maybe just not weather appropriate."

He laughed and shouldered me. "I thought we were just getting ice cream. I didn't know we were going to be stargazing over deep conversation."

I smiled. "It was a fun night. Sorry again to cut it short."

He shifted his weight, then lunged to give me an awkward hug. "No problem. Good night." He then turned on his heel and jogged off toward the dorms.

"Good night," I called after him. I watched him for a few more moments, then headed for my car.

WHEN THE elevator doors opened onto Gareth's floor, I found a chaotic scene. Nurses rushed about, and there were several uniformed police officers. I spotted Mr. and Mrs. Miller talking to Detective Gibson. He noticed me before they did.

"What are you doing here?" he asked, his eyebrows drawn together in obvious annoyance.

"We asked him to come," Mrs. Miller said quickly.

"Why?" His tone was sharp, very much in contrast with my last encounter with him.

Mrs. Miller seemed taken aback. "He's working for us."

"I'm aware."

"I can leave if it's a problem," I said, unsure what was going on.

A hand clamped down on my shoulder as Mead joined the conversation. "He's not hurting anything."

Gibson frowned but simply turned and stalked away.

"Sorry about that," Mead said to the Millers. "Detective Gibson is a little on edge. We just found your son, and now he's disappeared from under our noses. He takes it very personally."

Mr. Miller nodded. "I understand his frustration. We thought it best if Cav knew what was going on."

"Sure. Can't hurt to have another brain on this."

I cleared my throat. I wasn't sure what kind of good cop, bad cop thing Mead and Gibson were playing at, but if I was going to be there, someone needed to fill me in on what was going on. "What happened?"

"We just got here," Mr. Miller said. "All we know is a nurse went to check on Gareth about an hour ago and he wasn't in his bed. At first she thought he'd gotten out of bed to use the bathroom, even though he's supposed to call when he needs to do that, but then she realized the bathroom was empty. She alerted the desk, and they checked the entire floor. When they didn't find him, they alerted security. They did a sweep of the hospital, then called the police and us."

Mead nodded. "That's basically all we know at this point too."

"But how could he just walk out?" I asked. "How did nobody notice?"

"There's fewer staff at night," Mead explained. "Everyone was busy with other patients."

"But he's wearing a hospital gown. He couldn't have gotten far."

"And he's so weak," Mrs. Miller added. "He could barely stand up earlier today."

"We're counting on the fact that he couldn't have gotten far," Mead said.

Gibson reappeared just then. "Sergeant, could I have a word?"

They stepped aside and spoke in low voices.

I turned to the Millers. "When did you see Gareth last?"

"We were here around dinnertime," Mr. Miller answered. "We stayed for a while. He seemed fine when we went home."

"Are you sure he's not going home?"

They looked surprised, as if they hadn't thought about that. Before they could respond, though, Gibson and Mead rejoined us.

"We just learned that an orderly's clothes are missing from his locker and a balled-up hospital gown was found in the trash can in the same room. Security is checking surveillance footage now, but it seems like he left on his own," Mead told us. "We know he's wearing jeans, a green T-shirt, and a light jacket. Any ideas where he might be heading?"

"Cav just suggested that he might be going back to the house," Mrs. Miller said.

"I had the same thought," Gibson said. "Maybe one or both of you should head there just in case. Can you think of anywhere else he might be going? A friend's house? A relative he's close to?"

"All his friends are missing, remember?" Mr. Miller said sharply.

"What about relatives?" Mead asked gently as Gibson's lips pressed together tightly.

"My parents live in Connecticut," Mrs. Miller said. "Iwan's parents are gone."

"Then why don't you head home?" Mead suggested. "He's not likely to come back here. If we find him, we'll contact you right away." They nodded in unison. "Detective Gibson will walk you down."

When they were on the elevator, Mead turned to me and sighed. "Sorry about Gibson."

"Thanks. What's his problem, anyway?"

"He's feeling responsible for the kid getting away."

I raised an eyebrow. "Getting away? He wasn't under arrest, was he?"

"No, but he's the main suspect in the disappearance of three other boys."

"Okay, but how does that make Gibson responsible?"

He rubbed his eyes. "There was some discussion about keeping him under watch, and he argued against it. I gave in against my better judgment because he'd been on the case longer and I was still trying to let him lead the case at that point. Didn't want to pull rank. Maybe I should have." He noticed my frown. "Not to excuse his behavior. I have no idea why he was being so unprofessional toward you. Maybe he thinks you're encroaching on his turf."

I had a few theories about his attitude, but I didn't feel like telling Mead about Detective Gibson asking me out and me turning him down. "I'm just doing my job," I said instead.

"I know. Speaking of your job, there's no need for you to stick around. You heard me, the kid's not coming back here."

"Yeah, to be honest, I'm not sure why the Millers wanted me here."

"You don't? It's because they know that we suspect their precious little snowflake of committing multiple murders. They wanted a friendly face, someone who's on their side."

I frowned. "I'm not on anyone's side. I'm just trying to find out what happened."

"Don't tell them that. At least not until after the check is signed."

I HAD trouble falling asleep that night. My mind kept rotating between thinking about Gareth—wondering where he was and whether he was okay—to figuring out what I was going to do about this case, worrying about Mason, and thinking about Kyreh. The case in particular really weighed on me. I'd gained no traction at all, the police were convinced Gareth was a killer, and now their prime suspect had fled, which only gave weight to their theory.

Maybe they were right. If so, it might be better for me to cut my losses before I wasted too much time. I could either bill the Millers for my time so far or just write it off as a loss. I needed to talk to Walker soon.

I tossed and turned for what seemed like hours before I finally fell into a fitful sleep. I had nightmare after nightmare. I'd wake up from one, heart pounding, and drift back to sleep only to fall into another. Most I couldn't remember in the morning, but the last one stayed with me.

It was a disturbingly realistic nightmare where I somehow knew that
Gareth was being held hostage in a creepy old house. His captor lurked
just out of sight in the shadows, mocking me as I searched frantically for
him. I ran down endless hallways, opening door after door. At one point
Mason was there, following me silently, his lips moving but no sound
coming out. He kept plucking at my sleeve, but I ignored him until he
went away. Behind another door I found Kyreh… making out with Mason.
The last door I opened revealed a gory scene of blood-splattered walls of
a bedroom that looked an awful lot like mine. Gareth was sprawled across
the bed, his body riddled with stab wounds, his eyes open in a horrified
frozen gaze.

I cried out, and his head jerked around at the sound, his glassy eyes
staring through me.

"You're too late."

I WOKE up with a strangled cry, feeling very unsettled and thoroughly
unrested. I stayed in bed for a while, piecing together the dream in case it
held some important information, but it seemed like it was just a standard
nightmare—my subconscious working through everything going on—
and got up. I showered and found Haniah in the apartment kitchen.

"Hey," she said with a cheery smile. "How did you sleep?"

"Terribly." I grabbed the coffee pot and poured myself a cup.

I glanced up to see her smile had been replaced with a look of
concern. "What's wrong?"

I shook my head. "Just this case I'm working on."

"Well, I'll cook you some breakfast. That will cheer you up. We
haven't had brunch in forever. You work too much."

I almost said I wasn't in the mood, but my protest died in my throat.
Maybe some time with my roomie was just what I needed.

Haniah made pancakes—her favorite American breakfast food—and
they were light and fluffy perfection. After we ate, I insisted on cleaning
up. I had just put the last of the dishes in the dishwasher when my phone
started buzzing. It was Mead.

"Cav, this is Zeb Mead. We just picked up Gareth Miller."

"Where did you find him?"

"An officer found him sleeping on a bench in the park early this
morning."

"Did he say what he was thinking, leaving the hospital like that?"

"He hasn't said anything. He won't talk at all. To anyone. That's why I'm calling. We thought maybe he'd talk to you."

"Why me?"

"You're closer to his age, not a police officer, and you've established a level of trust as someone who is trying to help him."

"I don't know about that last one. What about his parents?"

"He wouldn't talk to them either. Just stared at them like he didn't even know them. So will you come down to the station?"

"Sure. I don't have any special bond with him or anything, but I guess it's worth a try."

"Thanks. See you soon."

I found Haniah in the living room, curled up in a chair positioned carefully in a ray of sunlight, a textbook open on her lap, though she was staring at her phone. "I have to head out for a while," I told her.

She glanced up. "Is it work-related? Because it's Sunday. You should relax."

"The police department called. They want me to come in to try to get this kid from my investigation to talk. I can't really say no."

"Sure you can. You just say no. It can wait until tomorrow."

"I don't think it can, actually. This case has been really demanding. He disappeared from the hospital last night and they found him this morning, but he won't talk to anybody. They're hoping I can get through to him."

She gave an extravagantly expressive shrug. "It's your life."

"I'll relax after this case is closed," I said as I headed back to my room to change.

She snorted.

I arrived at the barracks and was quickly whisked into the back, where Mead was waiting for me. Robin and Iwan Miller were there, Mrs. Miller seated in a chair. She looked as if she'd been crying. Mr. Miller was standing over her, saying something to her as she nodded.

"Thanks for coming in," Mead said. He looked tired.

"No problem. Have you slept at all since I last saw you?"

"I caught a few hours this morning before I got the call about finding the kid."

"Is he still not talking?"

"Not a word. You ready to give it a try?"

"As I'll ever be."

"He's in an interrogation room, so we'll be watching everything and listening in."

"Okay, but you don't think he's violent, do you?"

"He hasn't shown any signs of that, but he's acting very odd. Consider it a precaution."

"Odd how?"

"Just staring blankly at everybody who tries to talk to him. Frankly, it's creepy. He didn't even show any emotion when his parents went in."

I took a deep breath. "Okay. Let's get this over with."

Mead led me to a door and patted me on the back before he opened it. I'm sure the gesture was supposed to be comforting, but for some reason it made me more nervous.

Inside the room, Gareth sat impassively at a stainless-steel table, staring down at his hands resting limply on the tabletop. He didn't even look up as I entered.

I sat down across from him. "Hey, Gareth," I said softly.

His eyes darted in my direction and then quickly away. He didn't speak. I sensed the weird feeling of another presence in the room, but this time it wasn't so much that I was being watched—I knew I was—but more that someone else was there.

"You've really been through a lot lately," I said to fill the silence. "Are you okay?"

There was no response.

"Why did you leave the hospital, anyway? I mean, I know it's no fun there, but still."

Silence.

"Where were you going? Did you have somewhere in mind?" I sat in the quiet for a while, then said, "I guess you've already been asked all these questions, huh? Look, you need to say something. This silent treatment isn't helping. If anything, it just makes you look more guilty. I don't know what happened while you were missing. I don't know why you left the hospital last night. I don't know why you're not talking now. But I do know your parents are scared."

One of his fingers twitched. Maybe I was getting through to him. I remembered something I'd read the night before. If he did have multiple personalities, maybe one of the others was in charge right now, and that was why he was acting so weirdly. Or maybe he'd just shut off some part of his brain in order to protect himself. Either way, maybe I could reach him.

"Gareth, if you're in there, if you can hear me, it's Cav. I'm here to help you. I'd like to speak to you."

His finger twitched again, and he started blinking rapidly.

"Gareth? Can you hear me?"

Suddenly his eyes rolled up into his head and he started convulsing. I leaped to my feet.

"Somebody help!" I yelled. "He's having a seizure or something!"

The door flew open, and Mead and a uniformed officer rushed into the room. They gently lowered Gareth to the floor, where he continued to shake violently. Then they rolled him onto his side. From outside the room, Mrs. Miller asked what was going on, her voice panicked.

Then, just as abruptly as the seizure had started, it ended, and Gareth went limp.

"Get a medic," Mead told the other officer, who quickly left the room.

"What the hell was that about?" Mead growled.

"I don't know. He just started having a seizure."

"I know he had a seizure. I mean what was all that about asking if he was in there? What was that supposed to mean?"

Before I could answer, Gareth gasped loudly, and his eyes fluttered open.

Mead's attention snapped back to the boy on the floor. "Gareth, can you hear me?"

Gareth's eyes focused on Mead. Then he tried to push himself up as he looked around the room. His gaze locked on mine. "What?" he asked, his voice weak. "Where am I? What happened?"

"You had a seizure," Mead told him.

"I... what? I don't...." He looked around again. "Where.... Where am I?"

"You're at the police barracks." Mead narrowed his eyes. "Do you remember leaving the hospital?"

Gareth seemed more confused than ever, and more than a little scared. He glanced back at me. "I... I don't understand. What's going on?"

"What's the last thing you remember?" I asked.

"I was… in the hospital bed. Mom and Dad had left. I was watching TV. I guess… I guess I fell asleep?" It was more of a question than a statement. "But how…. How did I get here?"

Mead looked up at me, his expression grim. "We need to talk."

Chapter 8

MEAD SHUT his office door behind us and jerked his head at the chair by his desk. I sat as he collapsed into his own chair and rubbed his eyes. A medic was with Gareth, and he was almost definitely going back to the hospital for more tests. His parents said he didn't have a history of seizures.

"Start talking," he ordered without opening his eyes.

"About what?"

"What did you mean back there when you said 'if you're in there'?"

"I've been doing some reading. Something hasn't felt quite right about Gareth. Maybe it's just from a head injury or something, but it almost seems like sometimes he's not himself. Like, literally. But maybe whatever happened to him caused him to disassociate."

"You think he has multiple personalities?"

"I don't know. It's a possibility."

"A very remote one."

"It would explain a lot of what's going on. If whatever happened to him and the other boys was so awful, so traumatic that his brain couldn't deal with it—"

"I know what causes a personality dissociation. I also know that it's incredibly rare."

"But it does happen."

"Okay, sure, but I'm saying it's extremely unlikely."

"It sure seemed to trigger a reaction."

"I'll give you that. He could also be faking it."

"You really think so? He'd have to be a pretty good actor."

"I've seen some pretty good actors come through here."

"Well, those aren't the only two options. Don't head injuries also cause seizures sometimes?"

"Yes, but he's had an MRI, and there was no sign of any brain damage. Of course, those scans don't always find everything. The brain is weird."

There was a knock at the door.

"Come in," Mead called.

The officer from earlier opened the door. "Mr. and Mrs. Miller would like to speak—"

"We just spoke to Dr. Panwar," Mr. Miller said, cutting off the officer as he pushed into the office. "He wants to examine Gareth immediately. The seizure concerns him."

Mead sighed. "Let me see if—"

"You can't withhold medical treatment from him. I'll get a lawyer if I need to!"

"We're not going to withhold treatment," Mead said soothingly. "We just have to make sure we're handling things correctly. We need to keep him under observation, for his safety if nothing else."

"What do you mean by observation?"

"We'll have a twenty-four-hour watch on him."

"At the hospital?"

"Yes."

"Why? Are you charging him?"

"No, we just need to keep an eye on him, especially since he says he doesn't remember leaving the hospital. Until we know what is causing these memory lapses, it's not safe to leave him alone."

That answer seemed to mollify the Millers.

Mead spoke to the other officer about arranging transport back to the hospital. They were calling an ambulance in case Gareth had another seizure on the way.

"Can I speak with him before he leaves?" I asked.

Mead nodded. "Sure. He's still in the interrogation room. The medic is with him."

I squeezed out of the office and crossed the bullpen. The interrogation room was open, with another uniformed office standing guard by the door. I nodded to the officer and knocked on the doorframe. The medic glanced up but then went back to typing something on his phone. Gareth was sitting in a chair but looked very pale. He was holding an ice pack to his head.

"Hey, Gareth, how are you feeling?" I asked.

"My head is killing me. These lights hurt so much."

I looked at the officer. "Can these be dimmed?"

He shook his head no.

"Okay, well, could I have a minute alone with Gareth?" I said to the medic.

He looked like he was about to argue with me. "Sergeant Mead said it was okay. You can wait just outside the door in case anything happens."

He reluctantly stood up and moved out of the room. I took the chair he'd vacated.

"Have you remembered anything else?"

"No," he said, his voice almost inaudible. "I don't understand what's happening to me."

"I know it must be scary."

"You don't know anything," he snapped, his voice stronger. "You don't have any idea. I can't remember anything that happened last night. I don't remember leaving. I don't know where I was all night long. I don't remember coming here. It's like a huge blank spot between last night and waking up on the floor with you and that cop standing over me. You don't have any idea how scary that is."

"You're right, I don't. But I'm trying to find out what's going on. I'm trying to help."

"Do you know what's going to happen to me now?"

"I think you're going back to the hospital so they can run more tests."

"They've already done so many tests. They don't know what's happening either. I hear them talking. They say nothing is wrong, but something is."

"I'm sure they'll figure it out soon," I said, even though I wasn't. Nothing seemed sure with this case. "Gareth, how do you feel right now—other than the headache, I mean?"

He blinked. "I don't know. Kind of weak still, like my body is tired."

"What about mentally?"

"Freaked out?"

"Okay, but, like… do you ever feel like, I don't know, somebody is watching you?" He looked at me blankly. "Or like… there's somebody with you?"

"No."

"Okay, just checking."

"Why would you ask that?"

"No reason."

He frowned. "You must have had a reason."

"I'm just worried about you. I'm going to go check in with your parents."

I quickly left the room under his suspicious glare.

The Millers were still speaking intensely with Mead, but they'd moved into the bullpen. Just as I rejoined them, a young officer interrupted and asked to speak with the detective. Mead excused himself, leaving me with the concerned parents.

I looked them over as we sat at one of the tables in the room. They were visibly exhausted. They'd obviously rushed out of the house when they got the call from the police that morning. Mrs. Miller hadn't put on makeup, and they both looked disheveled.

The silence was heavy, but I didn't know what to say. I felt like I was letting them down. I reviewed my case notes while we waited for the ambulance.

I was reading back through my interviews when I realized I'd missed someone. Kyle Itoh had a sister I hadn't talked to yet. Her name was Mira. She would probably be as useless as everyone else, but it was a loose end I needed to tie up.

I told the Millers I'd be right back and walked a little distance away to call the Itohs. Mrs. Itoh answered.

"Hello, this is Cav Crawford. We spoke a few days ago."

"Yes, have you found Kyle?" Her voice was so full of hope, I felt instantly guilty again.

"No, I'm sorry. I was hoping I could talk to Mira. Is she home today?"

There was a deep sigh from the other end of the phone. "Yes. She is here. What time should we expect you?"

I had no clue how much longer it would be before the ambulance arrived. I told her probably an hour. She said she'd let Mira know. I hung up and rejoined the Millers.

The ambulance didn't show up for another twenty minutes. The crew took Gareth out on a gurney despite his protests that he was fine to walk, and his parents followed.

Mead joined me as soon as they were gone.

"You learn anything from your conversation with the kid?"

"No. Only that he's scared shitless."

"Or at least that's what he wants you to think," he said darkly.

"I'm pretty good at reading people. I think his fear is real."

"Then maybe he's just scared that he's going to get caught. And we're playing right into his hands. If he faked that seizure, the hospital is exactly where he wants to go. He's escaped once. He probably thinks he can do it again. But we have officers assigned to his room now. There will be someone outside at all times."

I shook my head. "I don't know what's fake and what's real anymore. This whole case is a mess. Did you interview Kyle Itoh's sister, Mira?"

"I'm sure we did. Why?"

"I just realized I haven't talked to her yet, so I'm heading over there when I leave here."

"As far as I know, we talked to all the family members of each boy. We didn't get anything from any of them."

"That checks out with my results so far as well," I said, sounding dejected even to myself.

"Good luck," Mead said, slapping me on the back.

MIRA ITOH was gorgeous. She looked far older than seventeen, with a curvy figure, long, thick dark hair, her mother's complexion, and her father's eyes. She also looked incredibly sad as she led me to her room to talk after greeting me at the door.

I sat on the desk chair as she perched on the edge of the bed.

"Thanks for talking to me," I started. "I know you've already talked to the police."

She nodded curtly. "Anything to help find Kyle."

"Are you guys close?"

"Kind of. It's not like we hung out or anything, but he's my little brother, you know?" Her eyes filled and she swiped at a tear.

"Sure. Did you talk much?"

"Some. Well, he talked and I listened. Or pretended to listen. I guess I tuned him out most of the time. He was just so dorky. He never really had a lot of friends, so he'd tell me all about whatever he was into at that moment, ever since he was little. First it was dinosaurs, then planets, then ghosts."

"He talked to you about ghost hunting?"

"Whenever he got the chance. I tried to be supportive, but…." Her tears spilled over as she choked back a sob. "I should have paid more attention. Maybe if I'd listened to him, we'd know where they are."

"You can't blame yourself. You couldn't know something was going to happen."

"I just didn't believe in all that stuff. He would go on and on about energies and readings, and I'd just… zone out."

"Did he tell you about where they were going that day?"

She buried her face in her hands. "I don't remember. The night before they disappeared, he came into my room while I was getting ready for a date. I wasn't listening to him at all. I think I told him to get lost." She broke down again.

"Okay, I know this is painful, but try to remember what he said. Anything at all."

"I've tried! Don't you think I've tried to remember? I wasn't paying attention. He said something about an abandoned neighborhood or something."

"Wait! A what?"

She blinked at the excitement in my voice. "An abandoned neighborhood? I think?"

"Not just an abandoned house?"

She thought hard, wiping her nose on the back of her hand. "I think he said neighborhood. Maybe town? Is that important? I wasn't listening…."

"It's a big difference. If he said neighborhood, that's the first real piece of information I've heard. Did you tell the police this?"

She shook her head. "No, I didn't remember until later, and then I didn't think it was significant enough to tell them. I don't know where the neighborhood is or anything."

"It could be very significant. There can't be that many abandoned neighborhoods or towns around here. It's not like we're in the Wild West."

She looked hopeful. "You mean I've helped?"

"Maybe. Is there anything else you can remember? Anything at all?"

"No. I've tried. I don't think he told me where the neighborhood was. I think I shooed him out before he got to that."

"Okay. It's still more than I had before. But if you think of anything else, no matter how small, please call me." I gave her my card, and she walked me out.

I could barely wait until I was in the car to call Mead. "Is Detective Gibson still there?" I asked as soon as he answered.

"I don't know. Why?"

"You might want to get him in your office and put him on speakerphone."

"Hold on," he said. He returned a minute later. "Okay, we're both here. What's going on?"

"I just spoke to Mira Itoh. She said that after you guys interviewed her, she remembered that Kyle had said something about an abandoned neighborhood or town, she wasn't totally sure. She didn't think it was enough to go on, so she didn't mention it to anyone."

"An abandoned neighborhood?" Gibson repeated.

"Or town. Do you know of anything like that?"

"There aren't any abandoned towns around here," he said.

"What about neighborhoods?"

"Not that I've ever heard of. We can ask around."

"Okay, I'll do some digging too. This is the closest thing I've found to a clue."

"Is she sure that's where the boys were going?" Mead asked.

"Well, no. She wasn't really paying attention when Kyle was trying to tell her."

"Got it. Try not to get your hopes up too high. It could be another dead end."

"Right. Or it could be the break we've been waiting for."

"Keep the faith, Crawford. Let us know if you find anything."

I agreed and hung up.

Who else might know about abandoned neighborhoods? Walker came to mind. He wasn't from around here originally, but I was always amazed at what he knew. I gave him a call.

"Are you working?" he barked instead of saying hello.

"Um, yes?"

"Have you been working all weekend?"

"I mean, here and there. Kind of. Yes."

"Cav...."

"I know! I know. But there are kids' lives on the line."

"It's been almost two weeks. The chances of those kids still being alive are next to none, especially in light of the shape the Miller boy was in when they found him."

"We don't know that."

"Why are you calling?"

"Do you know of any abandoned neighborhoods or towns around here?"

He took a deep breath. "Cav, why are you calling me on a Sunday to ask about abandoned neighborhoods?"

"The boys may have been going to explore one when they disappeared."

"May have?"

"It's the first real lead I've gotten."

"And it's barely a lead."

"It's something."

"Well, sorry to disappoint, but I don't know of any."

"Damn." I must have sounded as defeated as I felt, because Walker took pity on me.

"You could try contacting the historical society. Tomorrow. Because they're closed today. Because they took the day off to relax."

"Oh, that's a good idea. I'll do that."

"Cav, do not ignore my not-so-subtle hints. I want you to take the rest of the day off."

"In my defense, the police department called me in this morning to talk to Gareth. He ran away from the hospital last night, and they found him this morning. He was refusing to talk to anyone."

"Did he talk to you?"

"Eventually. Kind of. After he had some sort of a seizure."

"A what? No. Never mind. I'm not getting drawn into this. You can tell me tomorrow. For the rest of today, relax. Do something fun. That's an order."

"Fine. I can't really do anything else today anyway."

"Great. Now leave me alone. I'll talk to you at the office *tomorrow*."

"Sounds good. Enjoy the rest of your day."

As I disconnected the call, I was all smiles. I finally had a potential lead. It was about damn time.

I HEADED home. It was just as well that Walker ordered me to take the rest of the day off. I had household chores I'd been putting off and schoolwork I needed to do. I threw a load of laundry into the washer and then worked on a paper. I worked through the afternoon, only breaking to transfer my clothes to the dryer. I was just wrapping up the paper when I got a text from Kyreh.

Hey, what's up?

Not much, I replied. *Just finishing up a paper.*

Cool. No plans for the rest of your day?

Nope. Why? What's up?

Since you ran off last night, I thought maybe we could hang out.

I smiled. I'd had a great time the night before, so it was nice to know he had too. And the little flutter of excitement in my stomach was just the anticipation of making a new friend.

Sure, I sent back, trying not to sound too eager. *What do you want to do?*

I'm down for anything, he shot back. *But I bet I could whoop your ass at duckpin bowling.*

Duck what now?

You grew up around here and don't know about duckpin bowling?

I only know regular bowling.

Then it's settled. I'm teaching you some local history today. Prepare to get schooled.

I laughed. *Okay, but where are we going?*

I know of some lanes down in Fells Point, he said, referring to a historic neighborhood on the water near the Inner Harbor.

That works. I'll pick you up in half an hour?

Sounds good.

I ran upstairs to change. For some reason I wanted to look nice. I pulled on my tight jeans and a deep purple shirt. Then I second-guessed that and put a black hoodie on over it. Then I took the hoodie off because it wasn't quite that cool today. Then I put it back on. Then I stood in front of the mirror for five minutes, paralyzed by indecision.

Finally I snapped myself out of it and left to pick up Kyreh.

He was waiting in the parking lot when I arrived, so I pulled up next to him. He was also wearing jeans and a black hoodie. Great. I'd have to lose mine or we'd look like twins.

He opened the door and slid in. "I could get used to this curbside service," he said with a grin. Then he took in my outfit and raised an eyebrow. "Look, we've only hung out once. I think it's way too soon to start dressing alike."

I laughed. "Don't worry, I'll take off my hoodie."

"Nah, I got this." He unzipped his hoodie, pulled it off, and tossed it in the back seat. He was wearing a skin-tight gray thermal shirt under the hoodie. "Let's go."

"Right," I said as I tore my gaze away from his chest. "So where exactly are we going?"

He gave me the name of the bowling alley, I entered it into my GPS, and we set off.

We chatted all the way downtown. The conversation flowed as easily as it had the night before, which was a relief.

The sun was setting as we arrived in Fells Point. It took a few more minutes to find parking.

"So, what's this all about?" I asked as we walked down the sidewalk. "Is this anything like regular bowling?"

"In the sense that you're rolling balls down lanes to knock over pins, yes. But the balls and pins are a lot smaller. I can't believe you've never heard of duckpin bowling before. It's, like, a Baltimore tradition."

"Well, I didn't grow up in Baltimore. I only moved here for school."

"Sure, but it's not like you're from another state. You were only, what, an hour away?"

"About that. Fine. You have a point. I guess my family didn't really do a lot of stuff like this growing up. It was just me, my mom, and my grandmother, and my grandmother is paralyzed. Mom didn't have a lot of time for stuff like this. We didn't even go regular bowling. The first time I ever did that was with Jason and Eli. Besides, Mom's family isn't from here."

"Fair enough. Well, we're here, so you're about to see for yourself."

I looked up to see a sign declaring the Patterson Bowling Center, since 1927. The bowling alley was on two floors of an old building. We went up to the second floor, as the first floor was reserved for a private party. The room was fairly small, just seven lanes, and several of them were already taken. We claimed one of the empty ones, rented our shoes, and then Kyreh started explaining the rules, which differed a little from traditional ten-pin bowling.

"Because the balls are smaller and it's harder to get a strike, you get three balls per frame. If you knock them all down on the first ball, it's a strike. You get ten points plus however many pins you can knock down with your next two balls. If it takes two balls, it's a spare. You get ten points plus however many pins you knock down on your last ball. If you knock them all down with three balls, you just get ten points. If you don't knock them all down, you get one point for each pin you knocked down. Got it?"

While he was talking, I'd picked up one of the balls. It fit in the palm of my hand, maybe about five inches across. I turned it over but didn't see any holes.

"I think so, but how do you roll these things? They don't have any finger holes."

Kyreh grinned. "I'll leave that alone."

"What? Oh!" I laughed as a blush heated my cheeks. "But really…."

"You just kind of toss it underhand. Here, I'll go first and show you."

He proceeded to do exactly that. He knocked down all but two pins with his first ball, and the last two standing went down on his second ball.

In between balls, someone dropped down out of the ceiling to clear the fallen pins or reset them.

My mouth fell open. "It's not automated?"

He shrugged. "I think it used to be, but duckpin bowling isn't very popular these days. I don't think they make the parts for the machines anymore. Anyway, I get one more ball. These will be added to the ten points I got for the spare."

He got eight more pins on his final ball.

"That's eighteen points," he said. "You're up."

"Why do I feel like I'm getting hustled?" I asked as I stood up to take my turn.

He bumped me with his shoulder as he passed me. "You've got this. It's easy."

I don't know if I'd say it was easy, but I caught on after a few gutter balls, and it did turn out to be fun. In fact, by the time we reached the last frame, I was slightly ahead.

Kyreh was lining up his final ball when my stomach growled so loudly, he stopped and gave me a lopsided grin. "No fair trying to distract me," he said.

I laughed and clutched my belly. "Sorry! My stomach is reminding me that I skipped lunch today."

"Then we should go get something to eat. They have food here, but I'm sure we can find something better nearby. Right after I nail your ass on this last frame."

"You really shouldn't use the words 'nail' and 'my ass' in the same sentence," I said casually just as he released the ball, which went directly into the gutter.

Without a word, he turned and shot me a deadpan stare.

"What?" I asked innocently as I picked up my ball. We exchanged places, and I took a deep breath before rolling my ball down the alley… to get a strike.

"Loser buys dinner," I tossed over my shoulder.

"I think I was the one getting hustled," he muttered, just loud enough for me to hear.

Thanks to my strike, I won by a comfortable margin. After we returned our rented shoes, we left and headed toward the waterfront.

"So, what did you think?" he asked.

"It was really fun. But more importantly, where are we eating?"

He rolled his eyes. "One-track mind."

"What? I'm hungry."

"Trust me, I'm aware. There are a bunch of places down by the harbor. I'm sure we'll find something."

The closer we got to Thames Street, the stone-paved road that ran along the water, the livelier things got. People were everywhere, spilling out of bars and restaurants, walking along in big crowds, or just hanging out in the square.

We ended up in a crowded bar where we both ordered burgers and fries.

"Just so you know," Kyreh shouted over the music while we were waiting, "I want a rematch. I think I could have won if you hadn't distracted me on the last ball."

"You were on your third ball. There's no way you could have won with my strike."

"Fuck your logic. I still demand a rematch. I need to reclaim my title."

"Oh, so now you have a title?"

"Just admit it, you're scared to play me again."

I sighed dramatically. "Fine, you can get your rematch. But only if you're sure you really want to get beat again that badly."

"Oh, it's like that, huh?"

"I mean, how else is it gonna be? I just don't want to embarrass you again."

"Damn."

Before he could come up with a snappy comeback, our food arrived. "This isn't over," he warned, a sparkle in his eyes.

"I'm counting on it," I shot back. Were we flirting or just being friends? I'd be having a similar conversation if I were there with Haniah, but this felt different somehow—electric and exciting.

I pushed those thoughts from my mind to concentrate on my burger.

After we'd finished and paid—I didn't make Kyreh pay for my dinner even though he tried—we walked outside. The moon was bright in the sky, and the air was crisp. The reflection from the Domino's Sugar Factory glistened on the water.

"Man, that's gorgeous," I said. "I really need to come down here more often."

"Do you have class in the morning?" Kyreh asked.

"Yeah. What about you?"

"I do, but I'm not ready to go home."

I checked the time on my phone. "It's not that late. Want to take a walk?"

"Sure."

We strolled toward the pier, but suddenly Kyreh veered off.

"Where are you going?" I asked.

"I just remembered this really good gelato place. My treat."

"Ice cream last time and gelato this time? I'm going to get spoiled."

"That's not such a bad thing. Come on."

I followed him across the square to a small storefront selling gelato. I got dark chocolate and raspberry, while Kyreh picked out chocolate-hazelnut and *fior di latte*, a rich creamy flavor.

We ate as we walked down to the end of the pier, where it was less crowded. We found a bench and sat down, a little closer than necessary. The warmth of his thigh against mine made me realize that the night was turning out to be very much like a date.

That thought led to Mason, and suddenly the delicious gelato lost its appeal. Enjoying myself with Kyreh felt like I was betraying Mason, especially since his ghost had been standing in my bedroom just a couple of nights ago and he thought we were still dating.

But he was dead. And he'd been gone for over a year. Maybe it was time to move on.

"Penny for your thoughts," Kyreh said after a few minutes of silence.

I glanced down at my melting gelato and tried to shake off my mood. I couldn't very well tell Kyreh I was thinking about my late boyfriend whom I'd recently summoned from the dead.

I forced a laugh. "When did you suddenly become a senior citizen? Penny for your thoughts?"

He smiled, but I could tell he wasn't fooled. "My grandma always said that."

"Well, with inflation, I think you should raise the offer to at least a dollar."

"I dunno. That seems like a lot for your thoughts."

"Hey!" I shoved him playfully, which then turned into an impromptu wrestling match as we each tried to push the other off the bench. Our playful tussle ended in a draw, and we settled back to finish our frozen treats.

"All done?" he asked after a few minutes of companionable silence, during which I tried not to let my thoughts go back to Mason.

"Yep. It was really good. Thanks."

"My pleasure." He grabbed my empty cup and jumped up to toss them in a nearby trash can.

He returned and put his hand out to pull me up. Once I was on my feet, we were standing almost chest-to-chest. There was a moment when I thought for sure he was going to kiss me, but then he stepped back. "I'm getting chilly," he said. "Maybe we should head back."

"Yeah, I should get home soon too." I turned sharply and started toward the car. Did I want him to kiss me? Was I interested in him like that? What did I want from him? I wasn't sure, and that left me unsettled.

The drive back was quiet. My thoughts had left me unexpectedly melancholy, and Kyreh seemed preoccupied as well.

When I pulled onto the campus, he gave me a smile that didn't quite reach his eyes. "Thanks for driving," he said.

"Of course. It was fun. And I owe you a rematch."

"Yeah. Right. Good night."

He was out of the car so fast, I barely had time to say good night back. I watched as he walked away, wondering if I'd said or done something wrong.

Chapter 9

THE NEXT afternoon, I drove to the office after my classes. Jordan was at his desk, but before I could say hello, Walker appeared. "Let's chat," he said. "In my office."

"Oh. Okay, I'll just drop off my stuff...." I petered out. He was already gone. With a wry smile, I turned back to Jordan. "Why do I feel like I'm getting called to the principal's office?"

"Because you are," he said with a grin as I filed past. "Cav is in trouble," he sang as I headed down the hall.

I threw my stuff on my desk, then continued on to Walker's office. He was already sitting behind his huge midcentury maple desk by the time I joined him.

I settled into one of the two wooden chairs facing his desk and waited.

"Well?" Walker said after a few moments where we just stared at each other.

"Well what?"

"You said you'd finish filling me in about the case today?"

I sighed and shifted uncomfortably. I was convinced Walker had chosen these chairs on purpose, to discourage visitors from lingering longer than necessary. "To be fair, you said that."

He gave me a look.

"Okay, but there's not much more to tell you besides that abandoned neighborhood thing I asked you about yesterday. Otherwise, nada."

"And the police?"

"They know as much as I do."

"Okay, well, I know even less, so fill me in on what you do know."

I quickly brought him up to date on my investigation so far, leaving out my more supernatural concerns. "So now I'm about to do some research, see if I can find any ghost towns or abandoned neighborhoods," I finished up. "If that doesn't pan out, I don't know what to do next."

He frowned. "This is a very odd case."

I snorted. "You're telling me."

"How does nobody know what these kids were up to? How has no one found their car? How did none of their phones have tracking turned on?"

"The last one is the only one I really have a solid guess for. Kids are tech savvy. They probably know more about their phones than their parents do. I'm sure they turned off the tracking feature. There's tons of videos and stuff floating around about how dangerous it is to have it on—corporate and government spying and all—and maybe they didn't want their parents snooping. As for the first bit, everyone keeps saying they were good kids. I think they took for granted that they'd stay away from trouble."

Walker shook his head. "Sounds like trouble found them."

"Now *I* just have to figure out how to find them."

"Just take it one lead at a time. All you need is one break."

"I'm working on it." I stood up and headed for my office.

I opened my laptop and searched for abandoned towns in Maryland. A few results came up. I clicked on the first one and found it was just a listicle of creepy places in the state, most of which were completely gone. I tried a few more links, but they were more of the same. One listed some so-called ghost towns, but the majority were in the far west counties, hours away. After combing through several of the lists, I managed to find a couple of places that seemed promising.

The first was a forgotten town called Lapidum in what's now the Susquehanna State Park in Harford County. I'd grown up near there and never heard of it. According to Wikipedia, it was a port town on the Susquehanna River in the 1800s, but it died out when the railroads came through. The last buildings were torn down in the sixties, although there were some foundations left in the park. It wasn't the most promising prospect but worth checking out.

The second was Warren, a small town in Baltimore County that was flooded when the Loch Raven Reservoir was formed in the 1920s. The town itself was underwater, but there was still a cemetery nearby that was associated with the lost town.

Then I found an old newspaper article about forgotten towns in
Maryland. It was well-written and interesting, and I almost forgot why I'd
looked it up in the first place. I only found one more possibility there, a
small village called Dunham.

It wasn't exactly a ghost town since people still lived there, but it
had dwindled to the point that most of what had once been a thriving
small town was abandoned. Dunham had been a mining town in the early
nineteenth century but had slowly died out after the iron supply ran dry.
There wasn't much to keep folks around, so they moved on. The post
office burned down in the early twentieth century, and that seemed to be
the final nail in the coffin. It wasn't even on modern maps. I found a map
from the 1850s that placed it in the northern part of Carroll County, not
too far from the Mason-Dixon line. I overlaid a modern map over the
antique one to get a general sense of its location. It was a good hour's
drive from my office, if not more.

Only three places, and none of them close to where Gareth was
found.

I checked the time and decided Dunham and Lapidum would have
to wait until the next day when I'd have more daylight. Loch Raven
Reservoir was in Baltimore County, however, and fairly close to our
office, so I could probably squeeze in a quick visit to the cemetery if I left
right away.

I closed my laptop and grabbed my phone and keys. I stuck my head
in Walker's office. "I'm going to follow up on a lead."

He raised an eyebrow. "A lead?"

"A very weak one, but it's better than nothing."

I entered the coordinates I'd gotten off the internet into my GPS
and drove out. I parked in a small lot and found the trail that supposedly
led to the cemetery. The walk was beautiful, and if I wasn't so distracted,
I would have enjoyed the hike. Eventually I came to a fork in the trail.
I wasn't sure which way to go, so I pulled out my phone to do some
quick research. I was having trouble finding decent directions, but finally
I found a comment under a YouTube video that helped. A short while later,
I stumbled across the cemetery, all alone in the woods. I could just make
out glimpses of the reservoir through the trees in the distance.

A slightly dilapidated park sign declared that I'd found the Merryman
Cemetery and implored me not to disturb. Disturb who, I wasn't sure. The
long-dead souls of the Merryman family?

The cemetery itself was in sad shape, enclosed in a dingy concrete wall and overgrown with weeds. An iron gate served as the entrance, with about two dozen gravestones inside, some toppled or leaning drunkenly. As I'd expected, there was no sign of the boys.

The YouTube video had shown an old cellar and well nearby, though, and since I was already there, it seemed worth checking. I poked around and found a faint, worn path leading into the trees not far from the cemetery. I followed the path, and sure enough, I soon found the cellar, which was really just some stone stairs leading down into the ground.

I pulled out my phone to use as a flashlight and cautiously made my way down the stairs. At the bottom was a small stone room, empty aside from two plastic lawn chairs and some beer cans. Again, no sign of the boys.

I emerged back aboveground and searched for the well. I found it nearby, but it was mostly filled in, its bottom covered with leaves and more beer cans.

With a sigh, I turned and started back toward my car. I'd known it was a long shot, but I was still disappointed.

I didn't bother going back to the office. I didn't have anything to report, and I was in a rotten mood. I had a bad feeling about the other two towns as well. This entire case was like being mired in quicksand; I was getting nowhere fast and sinking in over my head.

As soon as my class was over the next morning, I set off for Lapidum and Dunham. I would head up to Dunham first and swing by Lapidum on the way back. I figured since Lapidum was relatively close to Jason and Eli's farm, I could stop and say hi if I had time. I cranked up the music to keep my brain from overthinking either the case or my love life on the hour-long drive.

When I reached the general area the map had indicated was Dunham, there was little to suggest there was ever a community there. No signs, no retail-type buildings, not even a church—at least at first. There were a couple of run-down farmhouses set well back from the road, but that was about it. Then I noticed a small cemetery near a pile of rubble that I figured was a church at some point. Just beyond that, near the road, stood two or three boarded-up or partially collapsed two-story buildings. I had found what was left of Dunham.

I pulled my car onto the shoulder and got out to look around. The buildings were in terrible shape. If the boys had ever found this place, I hoped they had enough sense to stay out of the death traps.

My gut was telling me this wasn't the place, but I had to be sure, so I walked around back. I didn't see the boys' car.

I looked over the buildings again. The more collapsed structures I wrote off, but I took a closer look at the most intact one. A quick circuit of the building showed that the first floor was completely boarded up, every window and door covered. I couldn't see any way in. I surveyed the surrounding area but didn't see anything else that could conceivably be considered a neighborhood. Even this little cluster of ruins was a stretch.

I was on my way back to my car when a rusty pickup that was probably older than I was came into view. The truck pulled in behind my car, much closer than I would have liked. An older man glared at me from behind the wheel, making me a little nervous. Some of the older rural folks didn't appreciate people on their turf. He threw open the door and slid out, still eyeing me suspiciously. He wore a grubby green trucker hat advertising a tractor brand and faded overalls over a short-sleeved plaid shirt.

I gave him a friendly wave and a big smile. He didn't return either.

"This is private property," he growled as I got closer.

"Sorry about that," I said cheerily. "I didn't see any signs. I'm not trying to bother anything. I'm a private investigator looking for the boys who went missing a few weeks ago."

His frown deepened. "Why would they be out here?"

"We understand they were exploring abandoned buildings."

He shook his head. "They haven't been out this way. I'd notice."

I believed him. He'd shown up awfully fast.

"Okay, well, thanks for your help. You don't know anywhere else they might have gone, do you?"

"Nope."

"No other abandoned buildings around here?"

He spat in the grass. "I said nope."

"All right," I replied with another wave. "I'll be heading out, then."

He nodded once, then said, "I hope you find them. Sad story."

I gave him a small smile. "Yeah, very sad."

I got into my car and drove away. I found a driveway where I could turn around, then headed back. That had been a complete waste of time.

I didn't have a good feeling about Lapidum either, but I set my GPS for the area of Susquehanna State Park. I was fairly familiar with it, since it was just north of the town where I'd grown up.

I parked and walked along the river for a bit, then started spotting historical markers. I'd seen them a million times but never really paid attention. When I veered closer, sure enough, they were all about the history of the lost town of Lapidum.

I stopped and looked around. You could see the dried-up remains of a canal and a pile of rocks that was presumably a foundation at some point, but that was about it. Nothing here suggested a neighborhood or even anything to explore. I could cross Lapidum off the list as well.

With a heavy sigh, I started back for my car. Hopefully Jason and Eli were home or this would be a totally wasted trip. So much for my lead.

I was halfway back to my car when I remembered Walker's idea about calling the historical society.

A quick Google search showed every county had its own historical society. I was already in Harford County, so as soon as I got back to my car, I called their office. Ben, the man who answered, suggested Lapidum right away, but when I told him I'd already been there, he hemmed and hawed for a bit, then suggested an area north of Jarrettsville.

"I wouldn't even call it a town, and don't think it ever was, but there's a cluster of houses. Maybe it was a little hamlet at some point. Don't even have a name, far as I know. Most of the buildings are in some stage of fallin' down."

He gave me directions, I thanked him and ended the call, then moved on. Next, I figured I'd try the counties closest to where Gareth was found, so I picked Frederick County.

Linda, the woman who answered, went silent after I explained why I was calling. She was so quiet that I thought the call had dropped.

"Hello?" I said after what felt like an eternity.

"Oh, sorry," she said with a chuckle. "I was thinking. I'm here alone on Tuesdays, so I'm racking my brain. There are a few communities around here that might qualify, towns that have seen better days, but a lot more in Garrett County."

Garrett County was the most western county in Maryland and very mountainous. It was also one of the poorest counties in the state.

"Have you tried Dunham in Carroll County?"

"Yes, I was there today."

"Nothing, huh?"

"No, ma'am."

"Hmm." And then she went quiet again.

"Okay, I have a couple of ideas," she said finally.

I got my pad and pen ready.

"Okay, first off, neither of these places have names anymore, if they ever did, so I can't just tell you to go to such-and-such and look around. I'll have to give you directions, and even then, you'll probably have to put your detective skills to use. The first one I can think of is a little easier. It's on Green Vale Road, north of Thurmont, just after you go over the bridge. If you're coming from the south, it'll be on your right-hand side, close to the road. Should be two houses in a row followed by an old general store. The folks that lived there are long gone, either dead or moved to a town. As far as I know, the houses are still there. I haven't been out that way in ages, though, so who knows.

"The second one is actually in Washington County on Licking Creek Road. You'll pass a little white country church, and then there'll be woods on both sides of the road. After maybe a quarter mile, it'll still be wooded on one side, but it'll open up with fields on the other side. If you look back across the fields, along the tree line, you should see a house in the woods—the roof, anyway. You might have to look real hard for it. If you spot that house, what you can't see is a few more just beyond it back in the woods. It's a neighborhood that got abandoned back in the 1960s or '70s. Not sure why, maybe just too remote. The dirt road that went back to the houses is long gone, so it might be hard to spot. That's the second one. You getting this?"

"Yes, I'm taking notes."

"You need me to go over any of that again?"

"No, no, you're good. Thank you."

"Great. That's all I can think of right now, but that ought to get you started."

"Thank you so much. I really appreciate your help."

I gave her my contact info, and she promised to keep thinking. Then I thanked her again and ended the call.

No one answered at the Carroll County office, so I called Howard County next. Howard was less rural than the other counties, so I didn't expect much. Much to my surprise, Bethany had a couple of places at the ready.

"There are a few," she said without hesitation. "They're pretty well-known with urban explorers. Of course, the most famous is probably the Enchanted Forest. That's an abandoned amusement park, but it's mostly gone now. I think they moved that last of the stuff off the site a few years ago."

That wasn't exactly what I was looking for anyway.

"Then there's Daniels. It was a mill town in the 1800s, but when the mill closed in the sixties, the town was shut down too. All that's left is some ruins. It's quite a hike out to the ruins, but you can park on the corner of Dogwood Alberton Road and follow the footpath. And then there's St. Mary's College. It was a big draw for a long time, but I'm pretty sure that's all been torn down now too."

Daniels sounded promising, but I figured I could cross the other two off the list.

Finally I called the Baltimore County Historical Society. I definitely wasn't expecting much from them since it was much more populated, and sure enough, their only suggestions were two abandoned forts—Fort Carroll, an abandoned Civil War era island fort, and Fort Armistead, which was popular with urban explorers. Both seemed like unlikely candidates for an abandoned town or neighborhood.

I did some quick Googling of the locations I'd gathered, just to get a feel for where they were. It was still early afternoon, so I had a few hours of daylight left. If I skipped a visit with Jason and Eli and made good time, maybe I could cross a few off my list. I made a mental map and headed to the closest one first, the area north of Jarrettsville.

Linda's directions turned out to be excellent. I found the abandoned houses right where she said they would be. A two-story house stood near the road, with a small cottage set far back with trees grown up all around it. I pulled as far onto the shoulder as possible and got out to look around. I didn't see anywhere the boys could have hidden their car, so I didn't expect to find anything, and I wasn't even sure two houses counted as a neighborhood, but I was there, so I might as well do a search.

The house near the road was thoroughly trashed. There was graffiti on almost every wall, broken glass and beer cans everywhere, and smashed furniture. In one of the upstairs bedrooms, I found a grungy mattress on the floor. I didn't even want to think about what happened on it. I didn't find any sign of the boys.

The house in the trees, despite being more isolated, looked untouched, maybe because the front door was intact and locked. As I walked around to the back of the house, I noticed most of the windows were unbroken as well. The back door was locked too. I was about to give up when I noticed an open window. Vines had grown through, giving me a handy way in.

Inside, the vines had grown up the wall and halfway across the ceiling of what was once the kitchen. Several cabinets stood open, glasses and mugs still sitting on the shelves. A shiver ran up my spine and the hair stood up on the back of my neck. I was starting to guess why this house was unmolested.

I started into the next room, but it was a lot darker. I pulled out my phone and turned on the flashlight.

The house was basically fully furnished. I was looking into the dining room. A huge china cabinet stood against the far wall, still stocked with knickknacks and what I guessed were the former occupants' good dishes.

There was a musty smell, like damp carpet, and something earthier, sharper—maybe animal urine? I moved on.

Sunlight filtered into the front room, so I turned off the flashlight and slipped my phone back into my pocket. There was a lot less furniture. An old console TV, the kind in a wooden cabinet, stood against one wall, and cheap framed art prints hung in painted gold frames, but there were no couches or chairs.

A moldy upright piano stood along another wall, a few framed photos on top of it, and I walked over. They were formal posed pictures from what looked like the sixties and seventies, the kind often taken at church. The couple both wore large-framed glasses and looked to be in their sixties or so. I picked one up for a closer look. A woman in a floral dress with a wide white collar was sitting. A man in a pale blue suit stood behind her, his hand on her shoulder.

I set the photo down and turned to the staircase. It was narrow and dark. The deep stillness in the house creeped me out, and that uneasy feeling had never gone away. There were no signs that the boys had ever been here, but I knew I had to follow through.

I climbed the stairs, passing more framed photos as I went. At the top, a narrow dark hallway ran the length of the second story. I peeked into the first room I came to. It was small, with a sloping ceiling and a simple wooden-framed single bed lit only by a dormer window. The plaster ceiling had crumbled, leaving a layer of white debris on the faded quilt that covered the bed and the area rug under it. A small dresser sat off to one side with a mirror over it. I caught my reflection. I looked as spooked as I felt.

I moved down the hall to the next room. It was dark, so I pulled out my phone again. The bright white flashlight revealed a bathroom, complete with pink tiled walls, a pink toilet, and a pink shower and tub. A rusted can of shaving cream still sat on the sink.

I moved on to the last door at the end of the hall—the only closed door. A weird sense of foreboding filled me as I stood before it. I had to force myself to reach out and grasp the round brass knob. I turned it slowly until the latch clicked, then pushed gently.

It was dark inside—vines had grown over the windows—so I flashed the phone light still in my hands into the gloom. The beam caught the body hanging in the middle of the room. I cried out as the phone flew out of my hand. It bounced off the floor once before settling with the light shining down, plunging the room into darkness again.

Chapter 10

My heart pounded against my ribs. Was there really a body hanging from the light fixture, or had it been some weird trick of the light? Maybe it was my reflection in another mirror. I wished I hadn't dropped my phone. I very much did not want to go into that room. But if I had seen a body, I needed to contact the police.

I took a deep breath and forced myself to step inside and grab the faintly glowing phone. I quickly shone the light at the place I thought I'd seen the body, but there was nothing there.

I released a shaky sigh of relief and looked around. There was a double bed with a splotchy bedspread that looked like it had once been white. The large dresser next to it still had a crocheted runner along its top, along with a small milk-glass lamp and a wooden box. A chair sat nearby, its seat chewed up by some forest animal, its stuffing spilling out like innards. There was nothing else.

Suddenly the hair on the back of my neck stood up again and a chill chased its way down my spine once more. I slowly turned and almost dropped my phone again.

A woman stood in the doorway. I recognized her from the photos downstairs. She made no acknowledgment of me, seemingly unaware of my presence. Her mournful gaze was locked onto the light fixture where I'd thought I'd seen a hanging body.

She stood there a moment. Then I blinked, and she was gone.

It was time to get out of that house. Something had happened there, but it didn't involve the missing boys. I went back downstairs and climbed out of the window, then dropped the short distance to the ground. I dusted myself off and headed back to the car.

I wasn't particularly surprised to find someone waiting for me there, a second car pulled up behind mine with, presumably, its owner leaning on the hood. The guy was maybe in his thirties, with a short reddish well-trimmed beard, a trucker hat pulled low over his eyes, a faded tee, and jeans.

"Hello," he said as I approached. He didn't sound particularly welcoming, but he didn't sound too threatening either.

"Hi there," I said in what I hoped was a friendly and professional tone. "Hope I wasn't trespassing. I'm a private investigator, and I've been hired to look into those missing boys from Baltimore County."

He didn't react much one way or the other. "Out here on my family's property?"

"We got a tip that they were exploring abandoned houses, and someone suggested this area."

"If you're looking for abandoned houses, you found 'em." He nodded toward the one closest to the road. "Teenagers in there all the time, tearing it up and partying. 'T be fair, I used to do it when I was a kid too. Ain't seen nobody that wasn't local, though, 'cept for you."

I nodded. "I saw the graffiti and beer cans and stuff. Well, not in that one." I gestured toward the house set back in the woods.

His lips tightened as he glanced in that direction. "That was my great-grandparents' house. Nobody bothers it. They say it's haunted."

"Oh. Yeah. It… was eerie. Did someone—" I was about to ask if someone had hanged themselves but stopped myself, remembering it was his great-grandparents' house and that a family suicide might be a touchy subject.

He was still staring at the house, though, and didn't seem to even be listening to me. "I heard my great-granddad hung himself. He was diagnosed with lung cancer, real bad, and didn't want to put my great-grandma through that. She found him and had a heart attack. Died a few days later."

"Jesus," I said under my breath.

He shook his head and shrugged, straightening up. "I don't even remember them. I was too little. Gives me the creeps, though."

It seemed best to not mention what I'd seen.

"Anyway," he said, his eyes meeting mine, "good luck with your search. Hope you find them boys."

"Thanks," I said as he climbed into his car and drove off.

I looked back at the house in the trees, then got into my car. I didn't start it right away, though. My mind was still on the apparitions I'd seen inside—if that was even what they were. They felt different from other ghosts I'd encountered, more like emotional imprints left in the fabric of the house.

But there was no mystery there, I reminded myself. It was a sad story, and that was all. I still had a case to focus on. A case that was going nowhere.

I shook off my melancholy and started the car. I had a few more places I wanted to hit before it got dark, and they were pretty far away.

The second place Linda had described was a lot harder to find, just like she'd warned. The fields were huge. I drove slowly, scanning the tree line for all I was worth, and I still had to turn around and cruise past twice before I spotted what I thought might be a house. I couldn't tell the condition from the road, and I certainly couldn't see the other houses she'd mentioned. There was also no shoulder to pull off onto. The trees came right up to the edge on one side, and there was a ditch on the other.

At the edge of the woods, I finally found an overgrown dirt path that led into the trees. It was just wide enough to pull off the road. As I nudged the front end of my car into the low-hanging branches, I noticed a car was already parked there.

My heart jumped into my throat. Had I found Gareth's missing vehicle?

I cut my engine and jumped out. The car matched the description. With my heart racing, I pulled out my cell phone and was relieved to see I had a signal. You never knew on these back roads.

I called Mead.

"I found Gareth's car," I said as soon as he answered.

"What? Where are you?"

I gave him directions and said I'd wait by the side of the road.

I didn't have to wait too long before Mead arrived in an unmarked black sedan. A squad car was right behind him. Both had their lights flashing.

Mead was in full investigation mode from the second he stepped out of his car. "You didn't touch anything, did you?" he barked before his door even closed.

"No. I know better."

He looked at my car, then at me. "Where is it?"

I pointed into the trees. "Just in front of my car."

He shook his head in amazement. "How'd you even find it?"

"I was scouting possible locations the boys might have been exploring, and this is the only place to pull off the road for miles. It was pure luck."

"You're going to have to move your car."

"Of course." I hopped in and backed out, then parked on the road in front of the official vehicles.

As I was getting out, another squad car pulled up. Detective Gibson climbed out and gave me a dirty look. "What are you doing here?"

I was starting to get the impression that Gibson didn't take rejection well. He'd been an asshole to me ever since I'd turned him down.

"I found the car," I said simply. "I called Mead right away."

He cocked his head to one side. "Mead, huh? This is still technically my case."

Mead rolled his eyes. "This isn't a pissing match, Gibson. And if it was, I'd win."

Just then, an officer emerged from the trees. "Plates and description match, sir."

"As expected," Mead said. "But what I don't understand is how—if the car is here, and presumably the boys were nearby—how did the Miller kid get all the way over to where we found him in Frederick County? That's miles away. He was covered in blood and totally out of it. It's not like he hitchhiked."

"Could there have been someone else involved?" I suggested. "Like a kidnapping or something? And Gareth got away?" I was speaking almost exclusively to Mead, pointedly ignoring Gibson.

"Seems unlikely." Mead said. "I suppose the car could have been moved. The kid didn't have the keys on him when we picked him up."

"That would be pretty bizarre if I just happened to find the car in some random location," I said.

"This entire case is bizarre. Well, let's get to it. Search the car," Mead barked to the officers, then paused and threw a look in my direction. "You wait out here."

Gibson glared at me as they disappeared into the tree line.

I sat on my trunk while one of the uniformed troopers unlocked Gareth's car using a device and then rummaged through the interior.

After a few minutes, Mead emerged, followed by the others.

I hopped off my car at their approach. "Did you find anything?" I asked.

"Nothing," Mead said. "At least nothing suspicious. The car looks like it's been here a while, most likely since the kids vanished. So if it was moved, it happened right around the time they disappeared."

"What's next?"

"We call in a search team."

"How long will that take?"

"Hard to say. An hour? Maybe half an hour, if we're lucky."

"Do you mind if I look around a bit while you're waiting for the search party?" Gibson looked like he was about to protest, so I rushed on. "I promise not to interfere with evidence, and if I find anything, I'll call you right away."

Mead thought for a moment, then nodded. "I can't argue with your results so far. Go ahead. Just don't mess anything up."

I turned and strolled off down the road toward the fields, trying my best to not look smug.

The house I had spotted earlier was way across the field. Luckily the corn crop had been harvested or I never would have seen it. All that was left was the short brown stubs of the corn stalks.

As I trudged across the field, my mind wandered. I was sure the car hadn't been moved. That just didn't make sense. Nothing drew me here, and it would be too much of a coincidence if I just stumbled across Gareth's car.

I was so lost in thought that I tripped over a broken corn stalk and almost face-planted. Fortunately nobody was around to see my clumsy recovery.

I was only halfway to the house, but I was close enough to see that it was in bad shape. The walls of the two-story structure were weathered gray wood. Any hint of paint was long gone. The windows gaped, empty and dark, making it look like a classic haunted house. The back section looked like it might have caved in, but I wasn't close enough to be sure.

As I drew closer, I could see that the roof on the one-story section at the back of the house had indeed fallen in. This made me wonder, once again, if the boys really had just gone too far in their explorations and gotten hurt or trapped in a collapse. If that were the case, they would almost certainly be dead by now, and it still didn't explain how Gareth had made it so far, weak and on foot.

When I finally reached the house, I could make out the remains of what must have been a dirt road running in front of it. Trees and underbrush had grown up over the years, but they were smaller, and it looked different, more open, than the forest surrounding it.

As the woman at the historical society had indicated, now that I was closer, I could see at least two more houses farther along the "road." They looked to be in slightly better shape than the first one. The second still retained most of its pale green paint, and all the windows and doors on the first floor looked to be boarded up. Neither the first nor third houses were boarded up.

The porch on the first house had collapsed, leaving a pile of rotted, nail-spiked timbers. I carefully picked my way across the debris, balancing on the joists like I was in a circus high-wire act. The door hung crooked on one hinge. I pushed it in with a loud scrape, stepped into the doorway, and glanced inside.

The entire back of the house had collapsed. I could see right out of the back wall into the trees. Large sections of the ceiling had also collapsed in places, and vines and small trees had sprouted through gaping black holes in the floor. It definitely didn't look safe to explore, so I retreated.

I made my way back to the remains of the dirt road and moved to the next building. I stood in front of it for a moment. An odd sense of foreboding washed over me as I studied the house—nothing specific, just a sense that something about this place wasn't right. There was something almost familiar about the feeling.

From a distance, it had appeared to be completely boarded up, but closer, I could see that someone had pried some of the boards away from across the front door, enough that someone relatively small could squeeze through—someone like a teenage ghost hunter. Or me.

I climbed the stairs and took in the porch. It looked fairly solid aside from a hole here and there, certainly in better shape than the first house. I took a few steps, and suddenly my foot crashed through a rotted board, throwing me forward. I caught myself before I could fall, but it startled me. I stood still a moment, trying to catch my breath, then extricated my foot and flexed my ankle, checking for damage. No harm, but I was lucky. That could have been bad.

With a healthy dose of caution, I continued forward until I reached the entrance. The door was partly ajar. Taking a deep breath, I ducked under the boards and clambered inside.

It was dark. The only light filtered in from the stairwell leading to the second floor. A small round window about halfway up allowed a shaft of leaf-diffused light to slice through the gloom, dust particles dancing through the ray. None of that light made its way past the main entry hall. A dark hallway stretched away in front of me to the left of the staircase, and a doorway opened into a pitch-black room on my left.

I pulled out my phone, turned on the flashlight, and entered the room off to the left. The house appeared to have been abandoned mostly furnished, but it looked as if some kids had trashed the place. Glass and debris littered the floor, a recliner was flipped over onto its back, a large old-fashioned console TV had its screen shattered, and the sofa was ripped open, its stuffing strewn about, its springs left exposed.

I backed out and started down the hall, which led into a small kitchen that had also been heavily vandalized. Shards of smashed dishes covered the floor; doors had been ripped off the cabinets. A small wall calendar hung by the back door, and I made my way over to it for a closer look, the ceramic rubble crackling under foot with each step.

The calendar was open to August of 1973, compliments of Tawes Home and Life Insurance.

I slowly turned and took in the destroyed room, trying to imagine what it must have been like when people lived here. Who were they? What were their lives like? Did anyone remember them now? Were they happy?

I had a feeling that something had happened here. Something bad. Not necessarily in this room, but in this house.

A third door opened off the kitchen, and I shined my light inside. It was, I surmised from the table and chairs, the dining room. A china cabinet against the far wall had also received the vandalization treatment.

I made my way back down the hall and stared up the staircase. Whatever had happened in this house, it happened up there. I couldn't say why I was so sure, but I was. I was equal parts drawn and repelled.

I steeled myself, squared my shoulders, and started slowly up the stairs. I tested each step before placing my full weight on it, but things seemed solid inside. As I became more confident in the structural integrity, I picked up speed, ready to be out of this unsettling house.

When I reached the top step, I ran into a wall that stopped me fully in my tracks. Not a physical wall, though just as effective. It was almost like a wave of ill intent crashed into me. Immediately an overwhelming sense of panic hit me, closing my throat and making every hair on my body stand at attention.

I tried to control my emotions, separate the external stimuli from my thoughts, but I could barely think through the primal sense of fear.

There was something—someone?—there, something with a sense of malice.

Evil was a word I tried not to use much. It had been overused to the point of losing its meaning. But that was the only word I could think of to describe what I felt.

I tried to fight through it, but the feeling only grew until the intensity was too much. I spun around and half fell, half ran back down the stairs. I didn't stop when I reached the bottom, I just threw myself through the door, leaped across the porch and down the steps—where I collided full force with a solid body.

Chapter 11

A PAIR of strong arms wrapped around me, but I quickly pushed away, still in panic mode. They caught me by the shoulders as I focused on the person's face. I tensed up even more when I realized it was Detective Gibson.

He looked annoyed again. Or maybe that was just his usual expression, at least where I was concerned. "What's going on? Why were you in the house?"

I pulled away from his grasp. "Nothing is going on. I was just looking around and… got spooked."

He glanced toward the house. "Did you touch anything?"

"No. I just looked around the first floor," I said. "I didn't even make it to the second floor." I realized we weren't alone. There were several other officers, along with Mead, who was looking at me with narrowed eyes.

Gibson nodded and turned toward the other officers. "Okay, let's go in. Be careful. Watch your step."

He led the way, and the others followed. The bigger officers pried off a few more of the boards over the door to enlarge the opening, then ducked in.

Mead didn't follow them. He had crossed his arms over his chest and was regarding me suspiciously. As soon as everyone had moved inside, he shook his head.

"Spooked?" he asked in a low voice.

I shrugged and looked away from his steady gaze.

"What happened in there?" he pressed.

"Nothing," I replied shortly.

He raised one eyebrow. "You were in a full panic when you burst out of that door."

"Nothing happened," I insisted. "I just… had a bad feeling."

"Must have been one hell of a bad feeling." He looked up at the house. "You think something happened here."

It wasn't a question, but I nodded anyway. "But I don't know if it had anything to do with the boys. The house…." I almost said the house felt evil, but I stopped myself. "Something feels off," I finished lamely.

Mead didn't look like he was buying what I was selling, but he turned to face me. "Shall we join them inside?"

"I'll just wait here," I said quickly, and Mead gave me another searching look.

I was saved further poking when his radio crackled and a voice said, "I found what looks like dried blood in a bedroom on the second floor."

Without another word, Mead ducked inside.

I paced back and forth, uneasily taking in the house, then got an idea. I pulled out my phone and took a few photos.

I waited outside for what felt like forever but was probably only half an hour or so. Then Mead reappeared.

"Did you find anything?" I asked.

"Definitely looks like dried blood upstairs. And quite a bit of it. We're waiting on forensics now. I volunteered to wait outside for them. Just between you and me, I'd rather be out here."

I glanced over at him. "Why?"

He chuckled. "No bad juju. It's just dark and musty in there."

"You found just blood? No bodies?"

He shook his head. "No bodies so far. But we did find some equipment in the same room as the blood. Probably ghost-hunting stuff."

"You think they're dead."

"Like I said, a lot of blood."

"And you think Gareth killed them."

"In my experience, the most obvious answer is usually the right one. Number one, he had opportunity. Number two, he admits he was with them even though he claims not to remember anything. Number three, he was the only one of them we found. And finally, and most damning in my mind, he tried to run away."

"He's still the only one you've found. If he killed the others, where are they?"

"It's an ongoing investigation. Are you saying you don't think he did it?"

"I… don't know. Something doesn't add up. Why would he kill them? What's his motive?"

"It's not my job to figure out why people do what they do. I leave that up to the prosecutors."

"So does that mean this is your case now?"

"Sure does. Effective immediately."

We were quiet for a minute. Then Mead glanced toward the house and took a step closer to me. "Look," he said in a low voice, "I know it's none of my business, but I thought I noticed something off between you and Gibson earlier. Feel free to tell me to buzz off—"

"Buzz off," I said quickly.

Mead studied me carefully for a few seconds, then sighed. "Sure thing. Just… something about his behavior toward you concerns me."

I frowned. "It's nothing."

"You sure?"

"Positive."

Mead didn't look convinced, but he let it drop.

It was a while longer before the forensics team showed up, and they took their time in the house. While they were working, Mead and Gibson joined me outside with a handful of officers.

"We've searched the entire house," Mead told me. "No sign of the bodies."

"What next?"

"We're going to do a quick visual inspection of the surrounding area. Care to join us?"

"I've got nothing else to do."

He called everyone over and gave quick instructions. We'd be walking in ever-expanding circles around the house, looking for anything suspicious or out of place. He stressed not to touch or disturb anything, and that we were to call him over if we found something. We walked around for about an hour before giving up. Gibson left at that point since Mead had taken over the case. I wasn't sorry to see him go.

It was starting to get dark by the time the forensic team wrapped up. I'd stayed around just in case something came up, but nothing did.

As I walked back to my car, accompanied by Mead, I asked, "What happens now? Is it officially a homicide case?"

"Not until we get the results back from the forensic team. Officially, at least," he said.

"But you took over the case."

"That's because the tests are just a formality. There's way too much blood up there for those kids to still be alive."

"Okay, well, I took some pictures of the house, and I was thinking it might be interesting to show them to Gareth and get his reaction. I suspect you might want to be there for that."

Mead nodded. "You're right about that. That's a good idea. Meet you at the hospital?"

I agreed and climbed into my car and set off.

I found Mead waiting by the main entrance after I parked.

"What's the game plan?" he asked as I approached.

I shrugged. "I don't really have a plan. I was just going to show him the photos and see what he said, watch his reaction."

"Don't tell him about the blood. In fact, let me do most of the talking. I don't want to give away too much just in case he slips up and reveals something."

I nodded my agreement, and we went inside and took the elevator up to Gareth's floor.

Mr. and Mrs. Miller were both in the room with Gareth when we arrived. All three seemed surprised to see us.

"Cav," Mrs. Miller said as she and her husband stood up. "We didn't expect to see you today." She turned to Mead and eyed his name badge. "And... Officer Mead?"

"Detective Sergeant Zeb Mead," he said with a smile. "I've taken over the case from Detective Gibson. We wanted to stop by and let you know that we made some progress on the case today, thanks to Cav here."

All eyes focused on me, Gareth's with a look I couldn't quite name. I smiled awkwardly. "I think Detective Sergeant Mead should probably take the lead."

"Why is Detective Gibson no longer in charge of the case?" Mrs. Miller asked.

"Detective Gibson is in missing persons. I'm a homicide detective."

A chorus of gasps arose from the Millers.

"You... you think the boys are dead?" Mr. Miller asked, his voice suddenly hoarse.

"We're still hopeful they'll be found alive, but we have to consider the alternatives. But let's focus on the positive." He turned his attention to Gareth. "Cav found your car today, Gareth."

"Where?" Mr. Miller asked.

"I'm sorry?"

"Where did Cav find the car?"

"On a back road in Washington County. It was pulled off the road and was hidden by some trees, which is why no one had spotted it."

"How did you know to look there?" Mrs. Miller asked me.

"I was following up on some leads about an abandoned neighborhood," I said, then gestured for Mead to continue.

"After Cav found the car, he did indeed find a few abandoned houses. In one of them, we found some evidence that the boys had been there."

"But you didn't find the boys?" Mrs. Miller asked, her voice tight.

Mead hesitated a second. "No, we haven't found the other boys yet."

"But you found something that made you think the boys might be dead," she pressed.

"Mrs. Miller, I can only say so much since this is an active investigation, but I can tell you we found some equipment that we believe was their ghost-hunting equipment."

"But that was all?"

"As I said, we haven't found the other boys yet, but we are still looking."

While he was talking, I was watching Gareth. He hadn't shown much emotion when Mead mentioned that we'd found his car, but he visibly deflated when the detective said they hadn't found the others. That wasn't the reaction I would have expected if Gareth had killed his friends.

"Cav, could you show Gareth the photo you took?" Mead asked.

I pulled out my phone and brought up the picture of the house, then showed it to Gareth. He looked at the photo for a second. His eyes darted to mine for the briefest moment before settling back on Mead.

"Do you recognize that house, Gareth?" Mead asked.

He shook his head. "Should I?" His voice quavered ever so slightly.

"We have reason to believe you were there."

Gareth's expression darkened. "I… I don't remember."

"Try hard," Mead pushed. "Something happened there the day you and your friends disappeared. This would be a lot easier if you just told us what that was."

"I told you I don't remember!" Gareth's voice rose. "If I could, I would tell you. I hate this. I hate not knowing what happened to them, what happened to me. I want to help my friends. Why won't you believe me?" His voice cracked on the last sentence, and he started to cry.

His mother rushed to his side and placed a comforting hand on his shoulder, then turned flashing eyes toward Mead.

"Is this really necessary?"

"Ma'am, we're trying to find three missing boys who may have been murdered. I'm afraid it is necessary."

At the mention of murder, Gareth let out a strangled sob.

"Detective Sergeant Mead," Mr. Miller said firmly, "we understand the gravity of the situation, but you've upset Gareth. With all due respect, I think it would be best if you leave now."

Mead nodded. "No problem. Sorry to have upset you, Gareth."

"And I think it would be best if Gareth only talks to you with his lawyer present in the future," Mrs. Miller added sharply.

Mead nodded again. "Of course. Perhaps we could have a word in private before I go," he said, giving me a meaningful glance.

"I'll stay with Gareth," I said, picking up on his not-so-subtle hint.

Mr. and Mrs. Miller exchanged looks of their own and then agreed, following Mead into the hall.

They were barely out of the room before Gareth stopped crying. He turned toward me, and a chill went down my spine.

"You should stay away from that house," he said calmly.

Every hair on my arms stood up. "Why?"

He blinked once and his eyes rolled up in his head, just like the time in the police barracks. Then he slumped back on the pillow.

"Gareth?" My voice was louder than I intended.

His eyelids fluttered.

"Gareth, can you hear me?"

His eyes opened but remained unfocused. I said his name again, and this time he locked in on me with a slightly panicked look.

"Gareth, why should I stay away from the house?"

"What are you talking about?"

"You told me I should stay away from that house."

"No, I didn't."

"Yes, you did. Just now."

"I.... No. My parents left the room with that detective guy and then... I must have closed my eyes, because the next thing I knew, you were calling my name." He was getting upset again.

"You don't remember saying that to me?"

He shook his head, his face filled with fear. "What…. What's happening to me?"

I reached for his hand, but he snatched it back. I rested mine on the edge of the bed instead. "I don't know, Gareth."

"Please help me."

"I'll do my best."

Tears spilled over onto his cheeks.

I STAYED with Gareth until his parents returned to the room. Then I quickly made my excuses and left. I caught up with Mead at the elevator.

"What do you think?" he asked me as soon as the doors closed.

"Has a therapist or psychiatrist seen Gareth yet?"

"I don't think so. I haven't seen a report, so I'm guessing no. Why?"

"Something weird is going on with that kid. Either he's the world's best actor or… something is wrong."

"You still thinking it could be split personalities?"

"I think they call it dissociative identity disorder now, and that's one possibility. The better option."

Mead gave me a sharp look. "What's the other option?"

"You won't like it."

"Try me."

"Possession."

"You're right. I don't like it."

"Told you."

"You don't really believe in that mumbo-jumbo religious shit, do you?"

I sighed as the elevator doors opened. "I don't know what to believe. I just know something is wrong, and I'm not so arrogant as to think I know everything about this universe we live in."

He raised an eyebrow. "Did you just call me arrogant?"

"I would never be so bold, sir."

He snorted. "You might be more trouble than you're worth, Crawford."

"You wouldn't be the first person to tell me that. But I did hand you Gareth's car on a silver platter *and* led you to the house."

"You have a point."

"You'll see about getting someone in to see Gareth?"

He shook his head. "Do you ever stop working?"

I gave him a sheepish grin. "Occasionally I sleep."

"And even then, you probably dream about your cases."

I couldn't deny it, so I shrugged again.

"Take a break, kid," he said as he started across the parking lot. He stopped a few feet away and turned back. "All joking aside, good work today."

"Thanks," I said as I watched him head toward his car.

I sighed as I headed to my car. If I'd done such a good job, why did it feel so crappy? We still didn't know where the boys were—or even if they were alive or dead.

"THERE YOU are!" Haniah said as I entered our apartment.

"Here I am," I replied. "We had a break on the case today, so I got held up with that. Why? Were you looking for me?"

"Not really. I was just a little worried."

"Sorry, I didn't mean to worry you. I should have texted you."

"It's okay. What's this big break?"

"Eh, I really don't feel like talking about it," I said as she followed me down the hall and into the kitchen. I opened the refrigerator, but it was mostly empty. "We need to go grocery shopping," I commented.

"We do. But how about if I treat you to dinner and you can tell me more about your day."

"I'll buy *you* dinner just so I don't have to talk about my day."

She laughed. "Okay, we don't have to talk about your case. But dinner is still on me. Roommate date."

"Fine, but let me call Walker first. I should update him."

I retreated to my bedroom and dialed Walker. "You have a minute?" I asked when he answered.

"For you, always," he replied.

"Always, huh?"

"That's my job as your mentor. What's going on? You rarely call me in the evening."

"Am I really that obvious?"

"Yes."

"Okay, well, you're right."

"As usual. Go on."

"We had a break in the case today."

"You don't sound as happy about that as I would have expected."

"It was a big break, but things are still as muddy as ever."

"What happened?"

I quickly filled him in about finding the car, what the police found in the house, and my strange encounter with Gareth.

"What's your gut telling you?" he asked when I had wrapped up my account of the day.

"That something is wrong."

"Then listen and pay attention. Do you think he did it?"

I leaned against the wall and let out a long breath. "I don't know. If the other three are dead, where are they? Why did he kill them? What did he do with their bodies? And where was he for all that time before he showed up on the side of the road an entire county away? Nothing makes sense."

"That's because you don't have all the information yet."

"Okay, sure, but how do I get that information if he says he doesn't remember anything?"

"Good old-fashioned detective work. You already found Gareth's car and the house. That's progress. All you can do is keep plugging away."

"I was afraid you were going to say that."

Walker chuckled.

"So, what do you think?" I asked.

"About what?"

"All of it. What are your impressions as someone who's been doing this a lot longer than I have?"

"You know my mantra. It's almost always the most obvious answer. I think either Gareth killed his friends or he knows who did and he's protecting them. The majority of murders are committed by someone known to the victim."

"Why would he protect the killer?"

"Loyalty? Fear? People lie for any number of reasons."

"I don't feel like he's lying."

"Then I guess it's your job to figure out what really happened."

"Gee, thanks for the pep talk, boss."

"What did you think I was going to say? If this was easy, we'd be out of jobs."

"It's usually easier than this! Besides, there will always be cheaters and frauds."

He sighed. "Don't remind me. That's my entire caseload right now. At least you have something fun and interesting to chew over."

I made a face. "Missing—likely dead—teenage boys aren't fun and interesting."

"You're right. That was in poor taste. My years in the CIA are telling on me. You get desensitized."

"I keep thinking about their parents. They're all so worried. Well, almost all."

"Someone wasn't worried?"

"One of the dads seemed like he couldn't care less. His wife, the missing boy's stepmother, seemed more worried than his actual father."

"Hmm. Any chance he could be involved?"

I hadn't thought about that. "I don't know. It hadn't even occurred to me. I can't really see him getting his hands dirty."

"Might be worth digging into a little more. Here's my advice. Be suspicious of everyone and trust no one."

"Sounds like a fun time to me. Well, thanks for all the encouragement. On that note, I'd better go. Haniah is taking me to dinner."

"Good. Let go of the case for a while and enjoy dinner."

"I'll try." That seemed easier said than done.

Chapter 12

"WANT TO just go to the Nest?" Haniah asked when I emerged from my room.

The Nest was short for the Wasp's Nest, the school café. The name was inspired by our mascot, the Waring Wasp.

"That's fine." The café was surprisingly good, at least as long as you stuck to the basics. "You ready?"

"When you are," she shot back. "Want me to drive?"

"That would be great. It was a long day with a lot of driving."

"Okay, let's go." She grabbed her keys, and I followed her out.

"Where did you go today?" she asked once we were in the car. "You said it was a lot of driving."

"I was all over central Maryland," I told her. "Carroll County, Harford County, Washington County."

"For the case you're working on?"

"Yes, but we're not talking about that per our deal."

"You're right," she said and let it drop. She might pry into my personal life, but she knew I couldn't always talk about my cases.

When we finally arrived at the Nest, it was fairly crowded for a Tuesday night. We scanned the room looking for an empty table.

"There's one." Haniah pointed to an unoccupied booth in the corner. "Why don't you grab the table and I'll order for both of us? What do you want?"

I asked for a burger and fries with a chocolate milkshake, and she headed for the counter to order. The line was long, so I had a little time for my mind to wander back to the case before she slid into the booth across from me. "Just so you know, I may have called this a roommate date, but it does not let you off the hook for finding a real date."

"Do you ever give up?"

"No. Never. I just want to see you happy."

"I am happy."

"Are you?"

"Happy enough."

"But you could be happier."

"And I could be richer. And taller. And a movie star. But I'm not any of those things, and that's okay. I do the best with what I've got."

She rolled her eyes. "You know what I mean."

"Getting back into the dating scene wouldn't necessarily make me happier. Dating sucks." She started to protest, but I rushed on. "Not for you maybe, but for most of us mere mortals, it sucks. Just the other day, this cop asked me out, but he turned out to be married."

"Well, he's a cop," she said, as if that explained everything. "You just need to keep looking. You need to… how do you say, ride the horse."

"Ride the horse?"

"Isn't that the saying?"

"Do you mean get back on the horse?"

"Sure."

I burst into laughter. Haniah's lips twitched; then she joined me.

"Look," I said when we finally stopped laughing, "I know you mean well, but I swear, between you and my grandmother, I'm going to lose my mind. Everybody thinks they know best about my love life."

"So you're saying your grandmother agrees with me."

"Haniah…."

Just then our names were called, and I took the opportunity to escape and grab our food. My burger looked greasy and delicious. Haniah's chicken Caesar salad looked sad in comparison. When I arrived back at the table, she eyed my sandwich enviously. I pushed the fries toward her, and she snagged one.

We each took large bites. Haniah continued to study me while we chewed.

"What?" I asked after I swallowed.

Before she could answer, the door opened and Kyreh came in alone. I saw an opportunity to distract Haniah and called out to him. His face lit up when he looked over, and he approached our table.

"Hey!" Then he noticed Haniah. "Oh, I'm not interrupting anything, am I?"

"No, this is my roommate, Haniah. Haniah, this is Kyreh." They said hi to each other; then I turned back to Kyreh. "Why don't you join us after you order?"

"I can't stay. I have a paper I need to finish tonight. But I'll sit with you while I wait for my order, if that's okay."

"Of course."

"Cool. I'll be right back."

As soon as he left to go to the counter, Haniah spun back to me. "He's cute! How do you know him?"

"He's in my World Religions class. We've been hanging out a little."

She nodded and went back to her salad, but I could tell the gears were turning.

Kyreh rejoined us quickly, and I scooted over so he could sit.

"What are you guys up to?" he asked as he slid into the booth next to me. Then he added to me, "I've never seen you here before."

"Yeah, I don't eat on campus much. But it's close to where we live, and pretty decent."

"If you know what to order." He indicated my burger, then gave Haniah's salad a dubious look.

"Do you live here on campus?" Haniah asked, ignoring his silent judgement.

"Yeah. I lucked out. I have a great roommate who is almost never around on weekends."

"Lucky you. I had the roommate from hell."

"Hey, I'm sitting right here," I inserted, and they both laughed.

"That was my freshman year," Haniah said. "Cav is a big improvement."

"Why was your freshman year roommate so bad?" Kyreh asked.

"She was a racist bitch," Haniah said matter-of-factly as she stuffed a forkful of lettuce into her mouth.

Kyreh snorted. "That'll do it."

She swallowed and fixed Kyreh with a curious stare. "So, tell me more about you."

Was she trying to flirt with him? My hackles started to rise, but I told myself to relax.

"What do you want to know?"

Wait. Was he flirting back? I was sitting right there!

"Do you have a girlfriend?" She paused, then deliberately added, "Or a boyfriend?"

Kyreh gave her a charming smile. "I'm as free as a bird."

Haniah raised one eyebrow and glanced over at me. It hit me what she was up to. Time to change the subject.

"What's this paper you're writing?" I blurted out, and they both gave me strange looks.

"It's for my philosophy class. Nothing exciting," Kyreh answered.

"Do you like boys or girls or both?" Haniah continued as if my interruption hadn't happened.

Kyreh laughed. "You don't beat around the bush, do you?"

Haniah looked at me. "What's that mean?"

"It means you get straight to the point," I said.

She nodded as if she'd been complimented and turned her attention back to Kyreh. "Yes. I do. So?"

"I like both," he said.

Her smile grew wider.

Just then, someone at the counter called Kyreh's name. "Guess that's me. It was good running into you. Nice to meet you, Haniah. Let's hang out soon, Cav. Bye, guys."

We said bye, and he grabbed his bag of food and left.

Haniah was eyeing me the entire time. Finally I couldn't take it anymore and, against my better judgment, asked, "What?"

"You should date Kyreh."

"He's just a friend."

"He likes you."

"What? No, he doesn't."

"He does. And I think you like him too."

"Haniah."

"I like him."

"Great, then maybe you should date him." I regretted the words as soon as they left my mouth, but Haniah just scoffed.

"He isn't interested in me. He only has eyes for you."

"You're only seeing what you want to see."

"I know what I saw. Maybe you should open your eyes."

"And maybe you should stay out of my private life."

"No. Get used to it."

"Now who has the roommate from hell?"

"You love me."

We continued our banter as we finished up our meals, but my mind was spinning. Could Haniah be right? Did Kyreh like me? I was certainly attracted to him, and I'd had fun each time we'd hung out, but I hadn't picked up on any signs that he was into me. Or was I just not looking for the right signs? He was just being friendly, right?

We cleaned up after ourselves and headed back to the apartment, but I knew I'd be thinking about what Haniah had said all night.

BACK IN my room later, I was straightening up a bit. I moved a sweatshirt I'd tossed on my desk, and it uncovered the candle I'd used to summon Mason. I dropped the shirt and picked up the candle.

"Oh, Mason," I sighed.

Where was he now? What happened to him after I summoned him, now that he knew he was dead?

I placed the candle back on the desk and finished cleaning up.

As I was dozing off, someone whispered my name. I sat up to find a figure standing by the window, illuminated softly by the moonlight. Somehow, I wasn't surprised.

"Hi, Mason. You came back."

He took a step closer. "I didn't know where else to go. Cav, why did you—what did you call it? Summon me? Why did you call me back?"

"I don't know. I didn't really think it through. I just missed you so much. And I wanted to know you were… okay. I wanted to know what happened to you. But wait. Where were you before I called you?"

"Darkness. Nothingness. It was like I was asleep, a deep dreamless sleep. Then you were calling me. Or I felt it. It's hard to explain. And then I woke up here in your room."

I scooted up so my back was against my headboard and turned on the lamp on my bedside table. He looked so solid, even in the light. Every fiber of my being wanted to leap out of bed and throw my arms around him. But I couldn't. How could something that appeared so substantial just vanish? Where did he go? "Okay. What… what happens when you're not… here? Where did you go the other night?"

"I wandered around for a while, but I keep feeling drawn back here, to you. I fought it, though, and I thought a lot. I went by my old place. Someone else lives there now. It was weird. Then I went to my parents'.

They seemed older, sadder. But they're okay, I think. Or as okay as they can be. They have some things of mine on the mantel. There was a… there was an urn. I guess that's… me?"

"You're here. That's just… ashes."

"Ashes to ashes, dust to dust," he muttered, then sighed. "I guess I'm really dead."

"I'm sorry," I whispered.

"Did you kill me?"

"What? No!"

"Then you shouldn't be apologizing."

"I just… I hate it. I hate everything about this. I hate that you're gone. I hate that I can't give you a hug even though it's all I want to do. I hate that I'm the reason you're here now."

He paced a bit while I talked, then stopped to stare out the window again. "That's a lot of hate. Not to say it's not justified and all, but I feel like if anyone should be filled with hate and anger, it should be me."

"Yeah, uh, you do seem a lot calmer now."

"Like I said, I've done a lot of thinking. It's all I've done, really, since I left. I guess I don't sleep anymore."

"So you're just awake all the time?"

"No. Not exactly. Sometimes it's like I drift back into that darkness."

I pulled my knees up and hugged them. "That sounds scary."

"It's not bad, really. It's kind of comforting. Especially since when I'm… awake, for lack of a better word, all I can do is think about how I'm dead."

"Oh. Yeah. That, uh, does sounds worse. But you seem to be at peace with it?"

He started pacing again. "Well, if I am dead, and that's pretty hard to argue at this point, I guess I have to accept it. I thought maybe a bright light would appear once I did and I could just walk into it or something. I don't really know how this works. But no such luck. When nothing happened, I didn't know what to do, so I came back here." He stopped and turned to face me. "What happens now?"

"I don't know," I admitted. "What do you want to happen? Do you want to go into the light? Or move on or whatever?"

He ran a hand through his hair, and my heart skipped a beat at the familiar gesture. It was something he always did when he was frustrated.

"I have no idea. I've never felt so alone and adrift. But there's something pulling me back to you."

A shiver ran down my spine. That was the second time he'd said something like that. I remembered Nana saying his untethered spirit might attach itself to me. Was that what he was describing now?

"What do you mean?"

"I can't explain it. I know it's a cliché, but maybe I have unfinished business or something. Maybe I need you to help me."

Or maybe you're just attached to me because I'm the one who summoned you. But I didn't want to say that out loud.

"Help you how?"

"How did I die?"

I sucked in a breath. "There's a lot we don't know. Can you remember anything?"

"About how I died? No. It's just a blank. Everything from that last day is blank. You said they found me in a park? Which one?"

"Leakin Park."

"No wonder it took so long to find me."

Leakin Park was huge, one of the largest urban parks in America. It was over a thousand acres of wooded trails.

"Why were you even there? Were you meeting someone? Did someone take you there?"

He frowned. "I don't know. I wish I could remember. I used to go there sometimes to clear my mind, but I haven't—*hadn't* been there in months, maybe even years."

"If you can't remember anything, what do you want me to do?"

"Investigate my death. Find out what happened."

"The police tried. They couldn't even definitively say if there was foul play."

"Yeah, but you're a private investigator. You can find things maybe they couldn't."

"I wouldn't even know where to start…."

"Cav. Please."

I looked away. "Walker won't let me."

"What?"

"I wanted to investigate. After you disappeared. Especially after they… found you. He said I was too close and that the police would handle it."

"But they haven't handled it."

"They ruled it an accidental death."

"Okay, but is that what you think?"

"I don't know what to think. There's no reason to believe it was anything else."

"But you suspect something."

"I don't. I mean, not really. It's just…. It's the not knowing. Not understanding. That's the worst part. Do you suspect something?"

He rubbed his face. "Something feels wrong." I opened my mouth, but he cut me off before I could get a word out. "And before you ask, that's all I know. Maybe it's just not knowing, like you said, but I just have this nagging feeling that something bad happened."

"Well, yeah…."

"I mean besides just me dying. Something doesn't feel right. I wish I could remember. But I can't. And I don't know why. That's why I need your help."

"But Walker…."

"He doesn't have to know."

"You want me to go behind my boss's back?"

"Is it any of his business? It's not like I'm hiring you. What am I going to pay you with? Ghost dollars? It doesn't have to be anything official."

"Where would I even start?"

"How would I know? You're the investigator."

"I'm in the middle of this case—"

"Then I can wait. It's been a year already. What's a few more weeks?"

"I… but…."

"But what?" He stared at me intently. "Cav, if you don't want to do it, you can just say that. I… I would understand. I just don't know who else to turn to. I need your help. Please."

I was torn. Part of me wanted to agree. I couldn't say I hadn't thought about it. A lot. But I didn't want to betray Walker's trust in me. Maybe he'd feel differently about it now, with a little distance.

"Maybe I could talk to Walker again, see if he'd give his approval, you know, since it's been a while."

His face lit up with hope.

"But I can't promise anything," I rushed on. "He might say no. And it won't be until after I wrap up this case. And even if he says yes, it's been so long. All the leads might have dried up, assuming there ever were any leads. Maybe you just went on a hike and fell and hit your head on a rock, like the police believe."

"Maybe so, but at least I'd know. At least *we'd* know. Just say you'll try."

I sighed. "Yeah. I'll try."

He broke into a wide smile. "Thank you. You have no idea what this means to me."

"I think I have an idea."

"Oh, hey, watch this," he said, sounding so much like the old Mason I remembered that tears welled up in my eyes.

He walked over to my desk chair and reached out, an intense look of concentration on his face. He placed his hand on the back of the chair and slowly swiveled it around to face me, then sat down.

I watched all of this in amazement.

He grinned at the look on my face. "I've been practicing."

"But how…?"

"I just have to really focus. I can't really pick something up, at least not yet, but I can push things around. And I can sit."

I shook my head in disbelief.

He reached out again, his brows creased, and pushed against the candle. It slid about an inch, and he gave me a look filled with pride. "I guess I'm starting to get the hang of this whole ghost thing."

"That's amazing. I've seen ghosts all my life, and I don't think I've ever seen any of them do that before."

He beamed. "Guess I'm just special."

I blinked rapidly. "I always knew you were," I said softly, and the smile faltered a bit.

"Hey, uh, we've been talking a lot about me. Which, you know, makes sense since I'm the ghost and all, but… how have you been?"

I quickly looked away. "It's… been hard."

"But you're okay?"

"I wasn't. For a long time. I was devastated. I suppose I'm doing a little better. It's a process. That's what everyone keeps saying. 'Everyone grieves differently.' Or 'Give yourself time.' And then after a while, it becomes, 'You need to move on eventually.' And 'You need to get back out there and start dating.' But I haven't felt ready, you know?"

He looked surprised. "Hold up. You haven't dated anyone since me? At all?"

Kyreh entered my mind like an intrusive thought. "No. Someone asked me out recently, but he turned out to be married, so I declined. Just not what I'm looking for, you know?"

"Sure. But you haven't even been interested in anyone?"

"No. Or...."

"What?"

"Not until recently."

"Oh." He blinked at me.

"Mason, I—"

"No. It makes sense. I died. It's been over a year. And you just said it. You have to move on at some point."

"I mean, that's what everyone keeps telling me. But I'm not sure I'm ready."

"You won't know until you get back out there, right?" He looked down at his hands. "What's he like?"

"He, uh.... This is really weird, right?"

"What, discussing your new boyfriend with your dead boyfriend?"

"He's not my boyfriend! He may not even be into me."

"He'd be crazy to not be into you. Tell me about him."

"He's nice."

"Nice? You can do better than that."

"I don't really know him that well yet."

"Oh, come on. How'd you meet him?"

"He's in one of my classes. We're working on a paper together."

"What's the paper about?"

"Whether or not ghosts—" I cut myself off.

"You can say ghosts, Cav. I promise I won't freak out again. No more indoor storms."

"How did you do that, anyway?"

"No clue. I couldn't exactly control it. Now stop trying to change the subject."

"I'm just saying. If you can't control it, you can't guarantee it won't happen again."

"Cav," he said patiently. "You're trying to change the subject. What the paper about?"

"Whether or not ghosts are real."

He gestured at himself. "Paper finished."

I laughed. "I wish it was that easy."

"What's his name?"

"Kyreh."

"Is he hot?"

"Um...."

He laughed again. "I can tell by your blush that he's hot."

"Mason...."

"Okay. Maybe you're right. Maybe this is a bit weird."

"Just a bit."

He looked around the room, as if just realizing where he was. "What time is it, anyway?"

I shrugged. "Late?"

"Do you have class in the morning?"

"Yeah."

He stood up. "Then I should let you get to bed. I've haunted you enough for one night."

"Where are you going?"

He looked toward the window. "I don't know."

"Maybe...," I started, then stopped.

"Maybe what?"

"If you can sit, do you think you can lay?"

He tipped his head to one side and gave me a confused look.

I slid over in my bed and smoothed the blankets next to me. "Maybe you could just, like, lay here for a little while."

He swallowed and stared at the spot on the bed I'd indicated, looking like I'd just punched him. "I... I'd like that." His eyes found mine. "But are you sure?"

I nodded.

He took a few steps toward the bed. "I haven't tried laying down yet."

"Was sitting hard?"

"No. I just did it."

"Then just... do it."

He walked around my bed to the far side and stopped to stare at me again. "You're sure?"

"Just lay down. Damn."

He gave me a small smile, then sat gingerly on the edge of the bed. The mattress didn't move. He slowly leaned back as he swung his feet onto the bed, his arms rigid at his sides. The pillow depressed ever so slightly as his head settled into it. He stared up at the ceiling.

I leaned over and turned the lamp off, then slid back down under the covers. We lay next to each other, both of us staring up at the ceiling. Somehow it was both familiar and foreign, comforting and confusing, all at the same time.

I rolled onto my side facing him, and he turned his head and met my gaze. I wanted to snuggle into him so badly, the way we used to. That wasn't possible, though. Nothing was the same. Instead we just lay there, eyes locked in the darkness.

"You should get some sleep," he said softly.

"I just don't want this moment to end," I whispered back as tears threatened to spill over again.

He reached out a hand as if to touch my cheek, but then pulled it back. "Me either."

I don't know how long we lay there, just staring into each other's eyes, but his face was the last thing I saw before my eyelids got too heavy and I faded into sleep.

Chapter 13

WHEN MY alarm went off the next morning, the first thing I did was look for Mason, but he was gone. I sat up and looked around. No sign of him. I finally reached for my phone and turned off the alarm.

Had last night really happened? Maybe it was all just a dream.

My desk chair was out in the middle of the floor, turned to face my bed, right where I remembered Mason leaving it. I touched the bed where he'd lain the night before, but of course it told me nothing.

If it was real, I'd agreed to look into his death. Assuming Walker cleared it.

What was I thinking?

And what was I thinking, asking him to lie next to me in bed while I fell asleep? I had to admit it was nice, though. And maybe a little like closure.

Finding out what happened to him would be actual closure.

I shook my head to clear it. "One case at a time, Cav,"

I made a mental list for the day as I showered. I wanted to talk to Gareth, if possible, and I wanted to go back out to the house for a closer look. I regretted getting chased out of the house by a bad feeling. I needed to see the second floor for myself.

After classes, I drove directly to the hospital. As I approached Gareth's hospital room, a woman was coming out. She wore a gray pantsuit and had a very professional look about her, her hair in a neat bun. She nodded at me and kept going.

I knew something was wrong as soon as I entered the room. Gareth's eyes were red, and both of his parents were visibly upset.

Mrs. Miller looked up as I knocked on the doorframe. "Cav, we weren't expecting you."

"Sorry. I didn't mean to interrupt. I was just hoping to talk to Gareth."

"It's been a bit of a rough day," she said. "This might not be the best time."

I looked between her and Gareth, who was avoiding my gaze, and nodded. "Sure. Then, could I speak to you privately before I go?"

She hesitated for a second, but Mr. Miller touched her arm and spoke softly to her. She nodded. "Of course."

She followed me into the hall.

"Is everything okay?" I asked. "Who was the woman leaving as I was coming in?"

"She was a psychiatrist sent over by the police. She asked a lot of very personal questions. It was hard on Gareth."

"I'm sure, but it needed to be done."

That seemed to surprise her. "What do you mean?"

"Well, has Gareth ever shown any signs of mental illness?"

"No."

"None at all? Not even depression or anxiety or anything like that?"

"Nothing out of the ordinary for a shy teenage boy."

"Have you ever heard of dissociative identity disorder?"

"I.... Maybe? I'm not exactly sure what it means, though."

"It used to be called split personalities."

"Oh!" She looked surprised. "What does that have to do— Oh! You don't think Gareth has that, do you?"

"I wanted to rule it out."

"Does that mean you think he's guilty? You think he killed his friends because he's crazy?"

"No. First of all, even if he does have the disorder, it doesn't mean he's crazy. It's a defense mechanism that the brain sometimes resorts to after extreme trauma. Like, it compartmentalizes itself in order to protect you. But it's very rare, so I wanted someone to check for it specifically."

"What even made you think of something like that?"

"Some of the things he's experiencing, like his amnesia and fugue states. And there have been a few times when I'm talking to him that it almost feels like I'm not talking to him anymore, like someone else has taken over or something. It's hard to explain."

She frowned deeply. "I know what you're talking about. Sometimes it's like he's not my son anymore. Do you really think it could be that disorder?"

"I don't know. That's why I wanted a psychiatrist to examine him. I'm sorry it was difficult for him."

"You should have let us know."

"I don't know if that would have been a good idea, necessarily. At least not for Gareth to know ahead of time."

"Why?"

"I didn't want him—or whatever part of him that is in control—to have time to prepare and maybe try to hide it if he was warned."

"I see. Will you let us know what they say?"

"If the police allow it."

"What do they have to do with this?"

"Well, they arranged to have the psychiatrist see him, after all."

"Are you working with them?" She sounded upset.

"In a sense, yes. That's the only way I can get access to information I otherwise couldn't get. Remember when they let me into the interrogation room at the police barracks to talk to Gareth? They'd never allow that if I weren't cooperating with them. But my first allegiance is always to my client."

"What would happen if you uncovered evidence that implicated Gareth?"

I gave her a hard look. "If Gareth killed those boys, I would have to tell the police, obviously. Why? Do you have any reason to think he did?"

"No! I can't even imagine that. I just.... I'm not sure how I feel about that."

"I'll never cover up for a serious crime, and no legitimate private investigator would. Now, something minor… that's different."

"What would you consider minor?"

"Let's say I learned something along the lines of the boys were just using the ghost-hunting story as an excuse to go hang out in an abandoned building and smoke weed. I wouldn't turn them in for that."

Her eyes widened. "Is that what they were doing?"

"No, no! Sorry. That was just a random example."

"Oh. Well, then in that case, I suppose tell us what you can when you can." She didn't seem happy about that compromise, but I couldn't offer her much more.

"Of course."

"What's next for the investigation?"

"I'll check in with the police after we talk, see if they've heard back from the psychiatrist yet. After that, I might go back to the house where we found Gareth's car. I didn't really get to finish looking around yesterday."

She nodded. "Be careful. I bet there was a homeless person or a lunatic living in that house and he attacked the boys."

"That's... a possibility." It occurred to me that the Millers were already trying out a defense just in case it became a homicide case. "Thanks for taking a few minutes to talk to me. And again, I'm sorry the psychiatrist upset Gareth."

"He just seems so... fragile these days."

"Hopefully it'll all be over soon."

"God, I hope so."

She returned to Gareth's room, and I went out to the parking lot. I called Mead from my car.

"Detective Sergeant Mead here," he answered.

"It's Cav," I replied.

"Crawford! Good timing. I just heard from Dr. Sewell, the psychiatrist who agreed to see Gareth for us. She went to see him today."

"I know. I'm at the hospital now. I was coming to see Gareth and his parents just as she was leaving. They were pretty upset."

"The good doctor said it wasn't an ideal scenario."

"What else did she say?"

"She said she doesn't think he has dissociative identity disorder, but that she couldn't really definitively diagnose him off of just one emotionally fraught and somewhat combative visit."

I sighed. "Not exactly the conclusive answer I was hoping for."

"What exactly *were* you hoping for, anyway?"

"I don't know. Just some answers for his weird behavior, I guess."

"To be honest, I'm glad we don't have to deal with an insanity plea if this does turn into a homicide case. I was a little worried about that when you asked for the shrink."

"It's best to know all the facts, though, right?"

"In theory, sure."

I wasn't thrilled with that response but figured there was no point pressing the issue. Before I hung up, I asked, "Hey, do you mind if I go back out to the house? I didn't really get a good look yesterday."

He thought for a moment, then said, "We finished our initial investigation yesterday, so I don't see any harm in you taking a look around. But if you find anything, let me know right away."

I agreed, and we hung up.

As I left the hospital, instead of heading directly to the house, I had a sudden flash of inspiration. Or maybe it was just common sense. After my unsettling experience the day before, it might be prudent to be a little more prepared this time. Maybe another visit to Nana was in order.

She was quite surprised when I appeared in her doorway for the third time in a week. She was in her wheelchair again today, which I was glad to see. She hated when she couldn't get out of bed for days at a time, whether it was due to her health or because the facility was short-staffed. She set down the book she was reading as her eyes narrowed suspiciously. "What did you do now?"

"Can't your favorite grandson just drop in for a visit?" I said with what I hoped was my most charming smile.

"You're my only grandson, and you can and do drop in for visits, but rarely so many in such a short amount of time. Something is up."

I moved into the room and sat on the edge of her bed. "Well, I did have a few things I wanted to talk to you about."

"Did you summon Mason again?"

"No! He, uh, showed up on his own this time."

"Cavanaugh!"

"I swear, I didn't call him. He wanted to talk. And he wants my help."

"Of course he does. He's attached to you."

"Yeah, I have to admit that crossed my mind. What does that mean, exactly, though? Is it bad, necessarily?"

"I don't know. Is it bad that the ghost of your ex-boyfriend is hanging around asking for favors?"

"Is he technically my ex when we never broke up?"

"Dying is usually the end of a relationship, technically and legally."

"Fair enough."

"What does he want?"

"He wants me to find out how he died."

"He doesn't know?"

"He says that entire last day is blank. He can't remember anything. He said he can't move on until he knows."

She sighed. "And he might not move on then. Once a spirit is attached, it's hard to break that attachment."

I shrugged. "It's not so bad, really. It's kind of nice to have him around again, even if I can't touch him. He is getting the hang of moving things around, though."

Nana frowned. "There are two things wrong with that. First, I know how tempting it must be to want to keep him around. I know how much you cared about him. But it's not healthy for either of you. You can't be in a relationship with a ghost, and he can't stay here forever."

"I know that! We even talked about me dating. He was very supportive."

Her eyes narrowed again. "Do you know how insane that sounds?" I snorted a laugh, but she wasn't amused. "This isn't funny!"

"I mean, it kind of is, if you stop and think about it. But I hear what you're saying, and I understand. I'll be careful. What was number two?"

"Number two?"

"You said there were two things wrong with what I said."

"I did? What did you say?"

"I think it was in reference to how it was nice to have him around even if I couldn't touch him."

"Oh. Yes. You'll have to excuse an old lady. I think my mind is starting to catch up with my body."

"Yeah, right. You're still plenty sharp."

"I'm sharp enough to know you shouldn't summon spirits, that's for sure. Especially when you don't know what you're doing. If your dead boyfriend is already able to interact with the physical world, it implies that he could end up being very powerful."

I straightened up. "What do you mean?"

"Just that spirits aren't meant to remain on this plane after their bodies expire. It takes a lot of energy for them to exist as an incorporeal shade. Some will fade away eventually, but others seem to be able to draw energy from somewhere—or someone—and stay for longer, maybe even indefinitely. Some of those who manage to hang on will become twisted and dark."

"Could that happen to Mason?"

"I don't know. Who knows what causes anyone, alive or dead, to become corrupted? It's a danger, though."

"I don't think Mason would do that."

"I hope not, for your sake. Are you going to look into his death?"

"I promised him I would, but only after I wrapped up this case I'm working on now. That's actually why I came to see you."

"This is the case about the missing boys?"

"Yes. Yesterday I found the house the boys were going to the day they vanished. The police found blood inside, so it's not looking good. But when I was in the house, I got this overwhelming feeling of… terror. I guess that's the best way to describe it. Nothing happened. I didn't see or hear anything. I was just suddenly filled with this sense of horror. Nana, it really scared me. I couldn't get out of there fast enough."

"I'm glad you listened to your intuition, at least. Do you think it was a presence, something in the house?"

"No clue. I've never experienced anything like it."

"Maybe you were simply reacting to the negative emotions left by so much trauma in one place. I once visited the battlefields at Antietam with your grandfather, years before you were born, and I was completely overwhelmed with emotions. There was so much pain left in the fabric of that place."

"That could be it. It just felt so… evil."

"Evil is a strong word. If it's just leftover psychic energy from the bad things that have happened there, it can't physically hurt you. If it is some sort of supernatural entity, something truly evil, then that's a different story."

"I want to go back. I wasn't even able to explore the crime scene. Is there anything I can do to make it safer? Any way to drive out any negative energy or, like, purify the space? Isn't there something with, like, sage or something?"

"Sage would be smudging, which is an American Indigenous custom. The Celtic version is saining, though, and that's traditionally done with juniper, so unless you have a juniper branch lying around, you're out of luck. That doesn't mean we can't find something to protect you, though."

"What do you mean?"

She gestured toward the narrow closet in the corner of her room. "Look on the top shelf. There should be a wooden box. Can you get it for me?"

I opened the closet, but the top shelf was above my head. I had to stand on my tiptoes just to reach it, and even then, I had to blindly feel around for a box until my hand bumped against it. Then it took a little more maneuvering to get the box close enough to the edge that I could grab it. Sometimes I hated being short.

"How are you supposed to reach anything up there from your chair?" I grumbled as I brought Nana the box and set it on the bed next to her chair. The simple rectangle of polished wood had a prominent grain, silver mountings on each corner, and a lock with a keyhole in the center of the front face. In the center of the top of the lid was an inlaid Celtic symbol, also in silver.

"I haven't opened this box in ages." She lovingly caressed the symbol on the lid. "But if I did need it, I'd ask one of the nurses. Also, keeping it up there keeps it safe. I also keep it locked. People steal here."

"Steal?" I was shocked.

She chuckled. "Not everyone here is in their right mind, you know. Some can't help it. And for the most part, the people who work here are lovely, but there's always a bad apple." She pulled open the drawer of her bedside table and dug around for a moment before pulling out a small silver key. "My father gave me this box when I turned sixteen. I've had it all these years, and I still have the key."

"Does the design on top mean anything?"

"It's a Dara knot. It symbolizes the oak tree and represents strength and wisdom."

She slid the key into the little keyhole and turned it. The lock clicked softly, and she lifted the lid. Inside was an assortment of small items: jewelry boxes, several yellowed letters tied in a ribbon, cards, tickets stubs—a lifetime of mementos, each undoubtedly with a cherished memory attached. She rummaged through the contents until she found what was she was looking for. She produced an emerald-green velvet jewelry box and held it out to me.

I accepted the box and opened it. Inside, on a little cushion of more green velvet, was a carved wooden pendant about the size of a silver dollar on a silver chain. The design reminded me of the Dara knot on the lid of the box, but it wasn't quite the same.

"That's a shield knot," Nana said before I could ask. "It's carved from rowan wood, a sacred tree to the Irish, along with the oak. It's a protection charm. Soldiers put them on their shields or wore them in battle. Mothers sewed the design on their babies' clothes. It supposedly wards off evil spirits. It was your grandfather's. You should have it."

"Nana, I can't—"

"Nonsense. Of course you can. Who else am I going to give it to? You'll get it when I die anyway. Might as well have it now when it can do you some good. Now, put it on for me."

I carefully lifted the necklace from the box, undid the clasp, and fastened it around my neck. The pendant nestled just below the hollow of my throat.

Nana stared at it for a moment, then reached out and touched it softly. Her eyes were unfocused, as if she was remembering something far in the past. Then she blinked and focused on me again with a small smile as her hand dropped to her lap. "I should have given this to you years ago. It looks so good on you."

I reached up and touched it as well. "Is it real?"

She arched her eyebrows. "It's hanging around your neck and you're touching it. What do you mean is it real?"

"Can it really protect me?"

"That's the idea. The thing about charms, though, is that they're imbued with the power your belief gives them. I believed when I gave it to your grandfather. He always said it was too beautiful to wear, but I think he was just too macho to wear a necklace."

I laughed. "Well, that's not a problem for me." Nana swatted me playfully, but I grew serious again. "But you're talking about charms and power. That's, like, magic. You're saying magic is real?"

"It certainly is."

"But…."

"But what?"

"I thought magic was just… fantasy stuff."

"Cavanaugh Patrick Crawford, you've seen ghosts as far back as you can remember and just summoned the spirit of your dead boyfriend and you don't believe in magic?"

"That's different, though."

"Different how?"

"Seeing ghosts, that's just a talent I have. A gift. What you're talking about is more like… spells. It's creating something, making something happen through supernatural ways."

"It's all part of the same thing. It's a connection to the Otherworld, the supernatural plane. You have it. I have it. Our ancestors before us had it."

"This connection, it's... inherited?"

"The Sight can be passed down generation by generation, but the rest of it is taught. Traditionally, it would be mother to daughter or a hand-selected apprentice." She sighed. "Of course, your mother didn't get the gift. And she was our only child."

"But I got the gift."

Her face creased into a smile. "You did."

"You just said it was passed mother to daughter."

"I meant the traditions, not the inherent gift. And that was really only after the English conquest, when things like healing and hearth magic were thought of as women's work. Before that, the men were also magicians and bards, and even farther back, in ancient times, both men and women were druids, fili and vates."

"So why haven't you taught me?"

Her smile faded. "Your mother didn't want me to. I'm not sure she really believed, at least not until you started talking to all your imaginary friends. Even then, I think she hoped you'd grow out of it. I told her then that I should teach you, but she wanted you to have a normal life. It's the only fight we ever had."

"What's normal about seeing dead people everywhere? And why didn't you start teaching me when she died?"

"I promised her I would wait until you came to me. It just took you longer than I expected."

"Oh. Okay. Well, I'd like to learn about—" I paused, hardly believing what I was about to say. "—about magic."

She grinned. "Then I'll teach you, grandson. But not all at once. It'll take time. Understand, it'll only be our Gaelic folk magic tradition. I don't know much about other traditions."

"There's more than one?"

"Oh yes. Almost every culture has their own system of magic."

"Ah. Got it. I think. And this…." I touched the necklace again. "This has some sort of spell on it? That can protect me?"

"Not a spell as you'd think of it. It's more that the symbol and wood are a sort of sigil that guards against evil and ill will. There are other actual protection spells I could teach you if I had the ingredients, but things like eye of newt and toe of frog are surprisingly hard to come by in a nursing home."

My eyes widened. "Really?"

"No, not really. I'm pulling your leg. Although eye of newt was really just witch's code for mustard seed. And toe of frog referred to buttercup. Not nearly as exotic as it sounds. But if I was actually going to create a protection ward, I'd need things like rowan berries, hazel, vervain, yarrow, foxglove, et cetera, and those things are just about as hard to come by in here as an actual eye of a newt."

"How does it work?"

"It's not as crazy as you think. You'd just combine them all in a little bag to make a charm."

"And that's it?"

"That's folk magic. It's really just a lot of common sense and herbs, with a little supernatural thrown in for good measure."

"So you're sort of an herbalist?"

"Yes. Or I was when I was more able-bodied. And so was your great-grandmother. And her mother before her. You've got a lot to learn. And I'll teach you, I promise. Just, maybe not right now. All this excitement has given me a bit of a headache."

"I'm sorry!"

"Nonsense. You didn't do anything wrong." She closed the box and locked it, then dropped the key back into the drawer. "Could you put this old box back so this old lady can rest?"

I returned the box to its spot on the shelf and closed the closet door. When I turned back, Nana looked as tired as I'd ever seen her.

She tried to perk up when she realized I was studying her. "It's a relief to finally tell you these things. But I have to admit, I haven't thought about a lot of this in a long time. I think I need to sit with my memories for a bit. We'll have another lesson soon."

I went over and gave her a hug. "There's no rush, Nana. Thank you for telling me."

She patted my hand on her shoulder. "We never know how much time we have, as we both know all too well. I love you."

"I love you too, Nana." I bent down and gave her a kiss on the cheek, and we said our goodbyes. Just as I was leaving the room, she called out to me.

"Cavanaugh… be careful. At the house, but also with Mason. There's so much you still don't know."

"I will. I promise."

She nodded. "Will you tell the nurses' station that I'd like to get back in bed now?"

I said I would and went to find someone.

IT WOULD be an understatement if I said I had a lot on my mind as I drove out to the house. My mind was aswirl with everything Nana had told me. It was a lot to process, and I still wasn't sure what I thought about a lot of it. I kept reaching up to touch the pendant, but it just felt like plain old wood to me. I couldn't sense anything mystical about it, no aura of power. But Nana said magic was real and that we came from a long line of... what? Witches? Magicians? The first conjured images of crones in tall pointy hats and the latter a guy in a cape and top hat with an overly dramatic flair. Neither made sense.

As I neared the house, I gave myself a mental shake and tried to push all that aside. My magical heritage could wait until later. For now, I needed to focus on the case.

I parked in the same place as yesterday, but Gareth's car was gone. No doubt the police had towed it to the impound lot to be thoroughly searched. As I hiked across the field to the house, I kept touching the pendant, almost subconsciously.

As I approached the house, I grew increasingly nervous. That feeling had really spooked me, even more so because I didn't know the source. The blind panic was unlike anything I'd experienced before. The police tape across the door almost made me chicken out, but instead, I took a deep grounding breath, ducked under the tape, and stepped through the door.

The downstairs looked just as I remembered, but of course, it was the upstairs that remained unexplored—for me, at least. I started up the stairs, my sense of dread growing with each step. About halfway up, I realized that I was tightly gripping the shield knot. I relaxed my grip—I didn't want to break it—but I kept my hand on it for comfort.

As I reached the top of the stairs, the sense of panic hit me again. I reminded myself that the police officers seemed to be completely unaware—aside from some mild feelings of discomfort, according to Mead—and they'd all come and gone without harm. Whatever was causing the feeling was unlikely to hurt me, especially if I kept my cool.

Most likely, the emotion was just leftover energy from whatever had happened here.

Either my internal pep talk helped or the necklace was doing its job, because I was able to steel myself enough to take the final step. I found myself in a long, narrow hall with several doors opening off it. As I neared the first door, the panicky sensation almost became overwhelming, so I bypassed it for the moment and continued down the hall.

The next door opened to a bathroom. It looked like something had made a nest in the large claw-foot tub. Out of curiosity, I opened the mirror-fronted medicine cabinet. There were a few water-damaged cardboard boxes that looked like their contents had crystalized and grown out of them like a cancer. There were also several glass bottles and a brush with a wooden handle. I closed the cabinet and noticed the spooked look on my face in the mirror: eyes wide, lips pressed tightly together. I took a deep breath and tried to relax while maintaining eye contact with myself.

I returned to the hall. The next room was a bedroom and, like the rest of the house, fully furnished. A stained, bare mattress sat on a very corroded brass bed frame. The stains were a dark rusty color and mostly centered near the head of the bed. There was a small vanity next to a dresser against the wall by the window, and a rusted tin can filled with pencils sat on top. The closet door stood open, showing moth-eaten clothing hanging inside. I walked over and looked closer. It was mostly dresses, skirts, and blouses in small sizes. This had obviously been a little girl's room.

The far bedroom at the end of the hall had another bare mattress, also stained, but only on one side. There were two dressers, one large low one and one narrow and higher. The lower one had a jewelry box and several perfume bottles on it. I was surprised the upstairs rooms were so untouched after the havoc downstairs. I pulled open the top drawer of the tall dresser to find it stuffed with yellowed Fruit of the Loom underwear and undershirts. Something had made a nest in one corner, and the acrid smell of rodent urine gave me a clue as to what might have made it. I closed the drawer with a grimace.

I found the closet neatly divided between dresses, blouses, and skirts and men's dress shirts and pants. Several pairs of badly deteriorated shoes lined the floor, though most of the leather ones looked like they'd been chewed on, and a mouse or something had made another nest in one of them.

It seemed like whoever had lived here left suddenly.

I took a deep breath and knew I couldn't avoid the last room any longer. I walked slowly back down the hall and stopped in the doorway, taking in the room without stepping over the threshold.

A twin bed stood against one wall, again stripped bare, but this one didn't have any stains. The small table next to it held a lamp that was tipped over. A bookshelf filled with moldy books sat under the window next to a small desk. A dresser sat next to the open closet door. Button-up shirts hung in the closet, so probably a boy's room.

It was impossible to miss the blood Mead had mentioned. The stain covered almost the entire exposed part of the floor.

"Jesus," I mumbled out loud.

I backed away. The police had been over the room with a fine-toothed comb. I couldn't see any reason I had to go in there.

With a huge sense of relief, I trotted back down the stairs. Mixed in with the relief, though, was a sense of pride that I'd overcome the bad energy.

But something was bothering me too. I couldn't shake the odd sense that something had happened here years ago. What had made an entire family just up and leave, abandoning their house, their belongings, even their clothes? From the contents of the closets, it seemed like a mother and father and two kids: a son and a daughter. How could I find out what had happened?

Maybe they'd know some of the history at the historical society. They were the ones who told me about the neighborhood in the first place, after all.

I looked up the number again and dialed. A woman answered. I thought it was the same woman I talked to last time. What was her name? Linda?

"Hello, Linda?" I said, trying it out. "I believe we spoke earlier this week. I'm Cav Crawford, a private investigator."

"Of course! Were we helpful?"

"You were very helpful. I actually had some follow-up questions and was hoping you had more information about that neighborhood in Washington County, the one on Licking Creek Road."

"Oh, I don't think I do."

"You don't know the history or why it was abandoned?"

"I'm afraid I don't. There are lots of abandoned neighborhoods and houses around. Usually the owners are elderly, and when they pass away, they either don't have children who want to take over the house or the house is just in such bad shape."

"One of the houses was fully furnished and was clearly owned by a family, and all their things were just left."

"That is intriguing. There must have been some sort of tragedy. Have you tried the Washington County Historical Society? They might know more."

"I haven't. I thought I'd start with you, since you told me about them. I'll give them a call now. Thank you again for your help!"

"Of course. It was a bit of excitement, really livened up the week."

I ended the call and searched for the number for Washington County's historical society. An older-sounding man answered. "Barry here," he barked.

"Is this the Washington County Historical Society?" I asked, wondering if I'd somehow dialed the wrong number.

"Sure is. How can I help you?"

"My name is Cav Crawford. I'm a private investigator working on a case that has led me to an abandoned neighborhood in Washington County."

"An abandoned neighborhood, ya say? Whereabouts?"

"Out on Licking Creek Road, just past the little white church and through—"

"Oh, way out there."

"Yes, sir."

"My mother's people are from out that way, but I grew up in Hagerstown. Don't know too much 'bout that area, to be honest with you. What d'ya need to know?"

"Do you know the neighborhood I'm talking about? It's several old houses back in the woods behind a field. Looks like there used to be a dirt road back to them, maybe?"

"Hmm. You know, that does sound familiar. Hang on while I access my files. That's my memory, by the way. When you get my age, it takes a little longer to pull up those files in my mental computer. Sometimes I think maybe my files are corrupted. Know what I mean?"

"Not really, sir."

"How old are you? What did you say your name was? Cam?"

"Cav, sir. Cav Crawford. I'm twenty-one."

"And you're a detective?"

"A private investigator."

"At twenty-one? I was still getting drunk and chasing the ladies at that age."

"About that neighborhood…."

"Right. Let me think. I believe I remember hearing something about a murder out that way back in the sixties or seventies. I have a vague recollection of a family gettin' killed, but I can't recall the details. Big hubbub at the time, but I was just a teenager, so I didn't pay it much mind."

"Do you remember the name of the family?"

"Afraid not."

"Ah. Okay," I said, trying to keep the disappointment out of my voice. "Well, thanks for your help."

"Now hang on. Just because I can't remember doesn't mean it's a lost cause. Have you tried searching the newspaper archives at the library?"

"I haven't."

"I'd try that next. They have an archive at the free library. Goes back over a hundred years. Comes in real handy when you're researching local history."

"Okay. That's very helpful. Thank you."

I ended the call, then tried a quick Google search for murders on Licking Creek Road. Sorting through piles of dusty old newspapers in a library sounded so old-fashioned.

A recent stabbing came up in my search, but that was about it. I tried searching for *murdered family* and several more search terms but found nothing more. Looked like I was off to the library after all.

I searched for the Washington County library system. The closest branch was in a town called Clear Spring, but they weren't open on Wednesdays. The next closest was the main branch in Hagerstown, which was about a twenty-five-minute drive.

I don't what I was expecting, but I was surprised when I pulled into the parking lot to find a modern multi-floor glass-and-red-brick building. I parked and went inside, where I went directly to the information desk.

"Hello," I said to the young woman behind the desk. She didn't look too much older than me, with at least a dozen visible piercings and bright green hair with blue streaks. Her eyes were a pale blue behind stylish cat-eye frame glasses. She wore a brightly patterned blouse under a mustard yellow cardigan, and a long teal skirt. According to her name tag, her name was Alysia. "I'm hoping you can help me."

She gave me a bright smile. "I'll sure try! What do you need?"

"I'm a private investigator, and I'm trying to find information about a murder that happened here in Washington County in the 1970s. Barry from the historical society suggested I might find something in your newspaper archives?"

Her face lit up. "We love Barry! He's the best. He does history talks here. That's so cool that you're a private investigator. You look so young! Is that really exciting?"

I tried not to grimace at the age comment. "It has its moments. It's mostly kind of boring. Like searching through old newspapers."

She laughed. "Right. We might be able to make it easier for you. Do you know what year the murder happened? That'll make the search a lot quicker."

"No, I—" I stopped, remembering the calendar I'd found on my first trip. What was the year? "1973. August. We can start there."

"Great! A lot of our newspapers have been digitized, so you can technically search them from anywhere. They're available on our website. But since you're here, you can use one of our computers. Then if you find something, you can print it if you want. Follow me." As she led me across the room toward rows of computers, she asked, "Is this a cold case you're working on? I love true-crime stuff."

"Not exactly," I told her. "Something just came up on another case I'm working. I'm not even sure it's important."

"Gotcha," she said, in a tone that indicated she didn't. "Okay, do you have a library card?"

"Just for Harford County and Pratt in Baltimore City."

"That's fine. Just sign in here and the program will assign you a computer. You have one hour."

I signed in, and it gave me a station number. We went to the computer, and I sat in the chair while my new librarian friend hovered over me. "Just click on Local History and then choose Digital Newspapers from the dropdown. Great. What area was the murder in?"

"I don't really know what it's called. It's on Licking Creek Road."

"Ah, so it's rural? A paper for this area would probably be best, and one that was in print in the 1970s. Try the *Daily Mail*. That should get you started. If you can't find anything there, there's also the *Morning Herald*. If you need any help, just give me a holler."

"Thank you."

I scrolled down the page to the newspaper she'd mentioned. I could choose the year and the month. This was going to be a lot easier than I thought.

I clicked on August 1973 and quickly realized I'd spoken too soon. It brought up scanned images of the newspaper with no way to search within that I could see. This could take a while.

It did take a while. I had to scan each page for any mention of a family being murdered, and it took forever for each page to finish loading. I figured it would be front-page news in a small community in the seventies, but I still scanned the inside pages as well, just in case. Mostly, I learned that groceries were a whole lot cheaper in 1973 and that not much happened in Washington County. There were articles about people returning from vacation, other people getting promotions, and a lot about high school sports.

My hour was almost up when I finally found what I was looking for. To be fair, I found more than I'd bargained for.

TEEN SON KILLS FAMILY IN SATANIC RITUAL, the headline screamed. The hair on my arms stood up.

> Police made a gruesome discovery over the weekend after being called to a home on Back Creek Lane in Washington County. Victor Handy (16) was found dead in his bedroom of a self-inflicted gun wound. After a search, Ralph Handy (36), Ellen Handy (35), and Pam Handy (8) were found dead in a well in the backyard. They had all been stabbed to death. Police believe the family had been dead for several days.
>
> Police said they found evidence of a bizarre ritual in the teenage boy's bedroom, along with books on the occult. There was no evidence of drugs.
>
> Benston Fuller, a concerned neighbor, called the police after his daughter noticed she hadn't seen her friend or any of the Handy family for several days.
>
> While the investigation is ongoing, police state they are certain that Victor Handy acted alone in the murder/

suicide. Evidence indicates that Pam Handy was killed in her bed, as was Ralph Handy. Police believe Ellen Handy attempted to escape and was killed at the top of the stairs. It appears that the entire family was then dragged down the stairs and into the backyard, where they were thrown into the disused well.

Victor Handy then returned to his room, where he conducted what police described as a satanic ritual before shooting himself in the head.

No motive is known.

Ralph Handy had worked for Tawes Home and Life Insurance for less than a year, while Mrs. Handy was a housewife, and their daughter Pam attended Clear Spring Elementary School. Victor Handy was a sophomore at Clear Spring High School.

Teachers and students at Clear Spring High describe Victor Handy as quiet and aloof, an average student. The general reaction seems to be shock. Clear Spring High Principal Ed Reed said there was no evidence that anything was seriously amiss and no hint of satanic activity at school.

The Handy family bought and moved into the house on Back Creek Lane off Licking Creek Road just a year before the tragedy. They moved from Woodland, New Jersey. Others in the small community on Back Creek Lane said the family had always been ideal neighbors.

A funeral service will be held for the family on Saturday at 2 p.m. at Parkhead Methodist Church, where the family attended.

There are no surviving family.

I sat back with a growing sense of dread. What were the chances that two horrific murders had occurred in the same house, almost fifty years apart? Satanic rituals? What did that even mean? What was I dealing with?

Chapter 14

I NEEDED to know more about the murder/suicide. The article was light on information. First, though, I needed to print the story. Alysia the librarian helped me figure out how to send the article to the printer—which I had to pay for, but it wasn't much—then I scanned the next few issues of the paper, looking for more information. There was a brief mention that said the police considered the case closed, but that was it.

A satanic ritual killing seemed like it would be bigger news, especially in a quiet rural community in the seventies. Then again, the family wasn't local and didn't seem to have many connections in the area. Perhaps a closed case was just case closed. After all, the killer was dead, and any perceived threat was gone with him.

Great for the neighbors. Bad for my investigation.

I sighed in frustration, then thanked Alysia again and headed out to my car.

I called the historical society to ask if there was any chance Barry knew anyone who'd lived in the area back then. It took me another twenty minutes to find out Barry didn't know anyone who lived in the area at the time. Actually, it took me about two minutes to find that out, and another eighteen to get off the phone. Barry really was a talker. I didn't know anything more about the Handy family, but I did know when Barry was getting his next colonoscopy.

After I ended the call, I sat in my car to think. How could I find more about this story? Would the police have records dating back that far? Probably not if it was a closed case. Maybe worth asking, though.

Then I remembered a neighbor's name mentioned in the article. I grabbed the story I'd printed and found the name: Benston Fuller. It was a long shot, but maybe he was still alive and I could find him. It was an unusual name.

I googled and found an obituary from 1998. Mr. Fuller had died of cancer, leaving behind his wife, Mildred Fuller, and daughter, Carol Fuller Tull. A search for Mildred showed that she'd passed two years ago, but Carol Tull was still listed as her survivor.

That search was more fruitful. I found an address and a phone number for Ms. Tull. She was still in the area. I dialed her number and waited while it rang. I was mentally preparing myself to leave a message when someone answered.

"Hello, I'm calling for Carol Tull," I said after her greeting.

"Speaking. Who is this?" She had the gravelly voice of a heavy smoker.

"Ms. Tull, my name is Cav Crawford. I'm a private investigator. Have you heard about the missing boys in Baltimore County?"

"Yes, of course. It's all over the news. What's that got to do with me?"

"My investigation led me to the house they were exploring when they disappeared. It was the house next door to where you used to live as a child, off Licking Creek Road. The house where the Handy family was murdered in the seventies."

That was met with dead silence that went on for so long, I checked my phone to see if she'd hung up on me or I'd lost the signal.

"Ms. Tull?"

"I haven't thought about the Handys in a very long time," she said at last, her voice so soft I could barely make it out. "The daughter, Pam, was my best friend. She was eight. Just a child. It changed me."

"I'm sorry to bring up painful memories, but I have a feeling that the two incidents are connected somehow."

"How could they be? That was decades ago. And the police said it was that psycho brother of hers."

"I don't know, but I have a hunch. I need to learn more about what happened. The news story I found didn't have much detail."

"It wouldn't. It was a big scandal for back then, especially with the weird circumstances. I think they were afraid other kids would be inspired by it or something."

"Would you be willing to talk to me about it?"

"In for a penny, in for a pound. Sure, why not."

"Are you free now? I'm in Hagerstown, so if you still live in Clear Spring, it's not that far."

"You know my address? You really are a detective."

"It was just a simple Google search."

"Well, I guess I'm free. I'm just babysitting my granddaughter, but she's down for a nap, so come on over."

"Thank you. I appreciate it. I should be there in about half an hour."

I arrived sooner than that, but Ms. Tull didn't seem to mind. She ushered me into her slightly run-down ranch with a gruff welcome. She was several inches shorter than me, and plump. Her gray hair was permed and curled around her face, which was weathered and tanned from years spent in the sun. Her grayish-blue eyes peered at me suspiciously behind thick glasses. She was wearing a floral-patterned shirt, faded jeans, and scuffed white sneakers.

She led me into a small, stuffy, dimly lit living room whose worn furnishings showed the evidence of much use. Family photos covered the dark wood-paneled walls. There was a slight hint of stale cigarette smoke in the air. Ms. Tull indicated I should take a seat in the overstuffed recliner as she dropped onto the couch, still eyeing me warily.

"Thank you for seeing me," I started.

She nodded curtly. "Still not sure how it can help."

"I need to understand what happened back then. It seems odd that two tragedies should happen in the same house."

"Are... are the boys dead? 'Sides that one they found, I mean?"

"We don't know yet, but it's not looking good."

She raised a hand to her chest and looked sad. "That's awful. Those poor parents." She paused and thought for a moment, then said, "Okay. What do you want to know?"

"Anything you can tell me about what happened. Let's start with the Handys. The article I found said they'd moved in a year before the murders?"

"Yes. I remember the day they moved in. I was so excited when I saw they had a little girl. Turned out Pam was the same age as me, and we were in the same grade. That area was just as remote then as it is now, so it was a big deal to have someone my age nearby. We became friends right away."

"They moved from New Jersey?"

"If you say so. I don't remember."

"What was the family like?"

"They seemed like nice people, for the most part. Mr. and Mrs. Handy were always very nice to me. I stayed over sometimes, though Pam stayed at my house more, especially after…." She trailed off. "Victor, Pam's brother, was an odd one."

"Odd how?"

"Quiet, sulky, mean."

"Mean?"

"He could be cruel. He liked to tease Pam, make her cry. Their parents almost seemed wary of him."

"What do you mean by wary?"

"I don't know. I was a kid, but I remember wondering why they didn't correct Victor more. He was real disrespectful, talked back a lot. My daddy would have whooped his ass. His parents almost seemed… scared of him. I guess it turned out they had reason to be. Maybe something happened where they used to live. Like I said, I don't know much about that."

"Was there anything else odd about him? The article mentioned a satanic ritual or something?"

"Psh," she scoffed. "Who knows. Everything was satanic back then. They even called it satanic panic, though that got a lot worse later, in the eighties, I guess. But it was starting back then. He was certainly a strange kid. Twisted. He liked to torture and kill small animals. Sometimes he painted designs with the blood."

"Do you remember what the designs he painted looked like?"

"No. I stayed away from him as much as possible. He gave me the heebie-jeebies." She paused. "He got into some weird stuff. I remember my parents talking about it once, that he'd stopped going to church and his parents were worried because he was fascinated by the occult—we were all Methodist—but they didn't know what to do. They'd asked the church to pray for him. I wasn't allowed to go over there much after that. Mighta saved my life, now that I think about it."

"The article mentioned that you were the one that noticed something was wrong next door."

She took a deep breath. "Yes. I waited and waited for Pam to come out and play. I even went over and knocked a few times, but there was no answer, of course. It was unusual. The family car was there—they only had the one—so they hadn't gone anywhere. At first, Mama and Daddy just thought they were sick or something, but then they weren't answering their phone, and we hadn't seen hide nor hair of them for days. Daddy finally called the police. And… well, you know what they found."

"How many people lived in the neighborhood?"

"I don't even know if you could call it a neighborhood. It was just a few houses on a dirt road. There was us, the Handys on one side and my grandparents on the other, and Old Man Banks on the other side of the Handys."

"Your grandparents lived next door?"

"Yes, the whole area was in my family for generations, going back to before the Civil War. I don't really know the ins and outs. My grandma used to refer to the old homestead that was long gone. When she married my granddad, he didn't want any part of running a big farm. He worked at a bank in Frederick. When they inherited the farm, Granddad started selling it off, piece by piece. By the seventies, all he still owned was the houses on Back Creek Lane, and even those he started selling. The house Mr. Handy bought belonged to my great-aunt and uncle before they got too old to keep it up and moved in with my cousin, their daughter. I think Mr. Banks was related in some way, but don't ask me how. Maybe a distant cousin. My parents always called him Mr. Banks. Us kids called him Old Man Banks."

"What was the reaction after the family was found dead?"

"Horror. Disbelief." She shook her head. "It was awful. I remember that. I was never the same after that. None of us were, I reckon. But for an innocent little girl, it was life-changing. I lost my best friend, my neighbors… and her own brother did it. I couldn't even comprehend it. I had nightmares for months. We moved a few months later. We just didn't want to be there anymore. It felt tainted. The nightmares got better after we moved. Eventually they went away."

"What about the other neighbors?"

"My grandparents moved in with one of my aunts and her husband. They were the first to leave. Mr. Banks stayed until he died, a few years later, I believe. After he died, there was nobody left, so they plowed under the road. I haven't been out that way in ages, but the woods was all grown up last time I drove past."

"Yeah, it's hard to even tell there were houses back there from the road. If I hadn't gotten a tip from the historical society, I never would have found it."

"So how can any of that be connected to those missing boys?"

"I don't know. Maybe it isn't. The boys thought of themselves as ghost hunters, so it's possible they'd learned about this story somehow and went there just for that reason. Or maybe it's all just a coincidence. I don't really believe in coincidences, though. I mean, there are some eerie similarities. Three people were killed by a teenage boy back in 1973. Now three boys are missing, and the only survivor is another teenage boy."

"But Victor didn't survive. He killed himself."

"Yes, and to be honest, that's the part that still confuses me. I mean, first of all, why did he kill his family? But then, after he did all that, he didn't try to go anywhere or escape. He went to his room, did some ritual, and then killed himself? That doesn't make sense. I'm intrigued by the ritual the police mention, but I don't know what it means."

"I'm afraid I can't help you there."

I figured I'd gotten all I was going to get from her, so I thanked her for her time and left.

Back in the car, I called Mead.

"I didn't expect to hear from you so soon," he said when I identified myself. "Does that mean you found something?"

"Sort of, but it's not what you think."

"I don't like the sound of that."

"Did you know there was a murder/suicide in that house decades ago?"

"The house we were in yesterday?"

"Yes. An entire family was stabbed to death by the teenage son, and then he killed himself."

"I did not know that. How on earth do you know that?"

"Good old-fashioned detective work."

"Meaning what?"

"I got curious about what happened in the house, why it was just abandoned like that. Someone told me they had a vague memory of a murder there, and a little research turned up a news story from 1973."

"Interesting, but what does that have to do with this case?"

"Look, I know it's a stretch, but something is telling me that murder is connected somehow to the boys. The article I found mentioned that the killer, Victor Handy, performed some kind of ritual after he stabbed his family. I want to know more about that ritual. Any chance some of the cops who worked that case would still be around?"

"You said it was 1973?"

"Yes."

"They might be alive, but they'd almost definitely be retired by now. They'd be in their seventies or older."

"What about records? Case files?"

"If it was a closed case, most agencies only hold on to files for twenty years."

"It was a closed case. Is there any way you can look into it?"

"Look into what? A fifty-year-old closed case in another county?"

"Yes."

"You're not asking for much, Crawford."

"I led you to the house and handed it to you on a silver platter. You owe me."

"I don't owe you anything."

"Please? It can't hurt to just ask around, right?"

He heaved a beleaguered sigh. "Okay. I'll see what I can do. But send me that article you found. And don't expect much."

"Thank you!" I started to gush, but Mead had already hung up.

I started the car and headed back to Baltimore. I wanted to write up my notes while things were still fresh on my mind. While I was there, I'd scan the article and send it to Mead before I forgot.

Before I left town, it occurred to me that maybe, based on what I'd learned that afternoon, just maybe I should have taken a closer look at Victor's bedroom. I didn't really relish going back to the house as the afternoon wore on, considering how early it was getting dark these days, but if I made it a quick trip, I should be in and out well before dusk. I really should have pushed through the negative energy on my last trip.

Twenty minutes later, I parked in my now-usual spot and approached the house. I ducked through the door and started up the stairs. This time, when the terror hit, I paused and examined the feeling.

Often, when something horrible happens in a particular place, the powerful emotions leave a sort of psychic stain. The stronger the emotions, the darker the stain. I could sometimes sense those emotions in much the same way I could see ghosts.

Whatever was happening in the Handys' old home, it wasn't that. The feeling of dread and terror was pervasive, but it wasn't focused enough to be an emotional echo. The entire second floor felt... wrong, as if there was something evil lurking there. Or something evil had been lurking there for so long that it had left its stench permanently embedded in the physical space. Or I had an overactive imagination.

I touched the pendant again and headed for Victor Handy's bedroom—or at least the room I presumed to be his.

Once again, I paused in the doorway. This room definitely held some recent trauma. It practically vibrated with it. But layered beneath that was something older, darker. I wished I'd taken the time to find a juniper branch or some of the other things Nana had mentioned, although I didn't know if that would even work here. Was it effective on evil residue? Was that even what this was?

I steeled myself and stepped into the room, avoiding the massive bloodstain as much as possible. I looked around, trying to decide where to start. If only the article had explained more about this ritual the boy was supposed to have performed. Was it the sort of thing that would leave evidence decades later? Either way, I had a strong feeling that Victor Handy was important.

I squatted in front of the bookshelf, scanning the titles that I could still make out. Nothing caught my attention. I pulled a few out to peek behind them but didn't find anything. On the second shelf, there were several gaps, which implied to me that some books had been taken. Since I hadn't seen any of the occult books mentioned in the article, I wondered if they were what was missing. If so, where had they gone? Would the police take them for evidence?

I moved on to the desk. There was only one shallow drawer, so I pulled it open. Inside, I found a very old calculator, a small penknife, some pencils, a stack of yellowed lined paper, and an assortment of loose coins and small bones. The bones gave me a moment's pause. Then I pushed the drawer closed.

I wasn't turning up much. Then again, chances were the police would have taken anything of interest. Between that and the great amount of time that had passed, I don't know what I was even looking for.

I walked over to the closet and peered in. A pungent odor that I thought was most likely animal in origin emanated from inside. I didn't want to touch anything in there for fear of tangling with a raccoon or a possum or who knew what else. I turned to face the foot of the bed and crouched down to peek under. Nothing. But from my new, lower vantage point, I noticed something I'd missed earlier. Something was scratched into the floor. Maybe carved was more like it. The lines were deep, at least a quarter inch, and jagged.

I stood up and tried to trace it. The bed covered part of it, and the blood and fifty years of dust, dirt, and chunks of collapsed ceiling plaster obscured the lines here and there, but it was obviously a large circle. It looked like something else might be carved in the center, but I couldn't make it out. There were other crude etchings here and there around the perimeter. The hair on the back of my neck stood up.

Not knowing what power the circle might hold, I was hesitant to step into it. Between avoiding the blood and the things I'd been examining being around the periphery of the room, I was pretty sure I hadn't veered into it yet. I still wasn't sure I believed in magic, but then, as Nana had pointed out, most people didn't believe in seeing and talking to ghosts. This, however, was far beyond my experience. It felt sinister.

Then again, the police officers and forensics team had undoubtedly been all over the room, and they were all fine. Maybe I was worrying over nothing.

Still, better safe than sorry.

I pulled out my phone and took a bunch of pictures, trying to angle it to catch the raking light from the window as much as possible, but the lines didn't show up very well. Maybe Jordan would be able to enhance them somehow. I'd ask when I got back to the office. The central part was what I really wanted to identify, and of course it was the area that was the most hidden.

I was feeling very much in over my head, but I had no idea who to turn to for help. Nana had said she didn't know much about other types of magic, and this didn't feel like Gaelic folk magic. It was certainly way beyond herbs.

Then I thought about Professor Lawson, my World Religions teacher. I remembered her mentioning once that she was a witch. I wasn't entirely sure what that meant, but she was a religions professor, so she might at least know someone who could help, even if she couldn't.

Of course, I wasn't exactly the teacher's pet in that class.

I glanced out the window at the sun getting low in the sky. I didn't want to be in the house when it set, so it was time to head out.

On the way home, my brain was going a hundred miles an hour, turning over everything I'd discovered that day. I was just entering the city when it occurred to me that a trip to see Gareth could be useful. I drove past our office and headed to the hospital.

On the elevator up to his floor, I thought about how often I was visiting the hospital these days. I hoped it didn't become a habit.

I checked in with the uniformed trooper by the door before knocking on the doorframe. "Come in," Gareth called out.

He was watching TV alone in his room. I was pleased. I didn't really want to have this conversation in front of his parents. He looked up with surprise as I entered.

"Have you found them?" he asked hopefully.

I shook my head. "I'm sorry. Not yet."

He slumped back into the pillow, his eyes avoiding mine once again. "Then why are you here?"

"I had some questions for you."

"More things I don't know the answer to."

"You never know when something will jog your memory."

He shrugged.

"Is it okay if I sit down?" I was still standing in the doorway.

Gareth made a halfhearted motion toward the chair next to his bed. I dropped into it and looked him over. His color was a little better.

"Nothing more has come back to you?" I said after a few awkward moments of silence.

He shook his head no.

"How are you feeling?"

"Better, I guess. Maybe they'll let me go home soon."

I doubted he'd be going home any time in the near future, especially if he became a murder suspect.

"You didn't recognize the house I showed you yesterday, right?" I purposefully left out the fact that he'd warned me against going back to the house the last time I was there.

He shook his head again.

"I found out some stuff about it."

He darted a glance my way. "Like what?"

"There was a murder there back in the seventies. A family was killed."

His eyes grew wide. "The whole family?"

"Well, a mother, father, and sister."

"Do they know who killed them?"

"Yes. The brother. He killed himself after."

"That's crazy."

"You didn't know?"

He shot me a perturbed look. "No."

"Do you think it's possible the other boys knew? Do you think that's why they picked that house?"

"I don't know! Like I've told you and the cops over and over, I don't remember anything. It's all just... blank. Maybe Kyle knew. He was always doing research to find new places. He'd even study satellite images and stuff on, like, Google, looking for places that might be abandoned, but that wouldn't show up in a normal search. He was really good at that kind of stuff."

I leaned back. Perhaps Kyle had found the neighborhood randomly while studying satellite images. Maybe it was all just a big coincidence and I was chasing a red herring, digging into a fifty-year-old closed case. I sighed.

"I guess you've never heard of Victor Handy, then," I said.

The words had no sooner left my mouth than Gareth's entire body stiffened. His eyes rolled back into his head and he started convulsing again, just like that day at the police barracks.

I leaped up and rushed into the hall. "Help!" I called. "I need a nurse! He's having a seizure!"

The trooper on duty rushed into the room as a nearby woman in scrubs spun in my direction. "Who's having a seizure?"

"Gareth Miller. In here." I pointed to his room.

She ran past me into Gareth's room.

I stayed in the hall, out of the way. Another nurse rushed into the room. I could hear one of the nurses talking calmly to Gareth, telling him he was going to be okay. The other asked the trooper to stay out of the way in a terse, no-nonsense tone.

It was several minutes before the second nurse came out without giving me so much as a glance. I waited a few more seconds, then poked my head into the room. The first nurse was taking Gareth's pulse as the trooper stood stiffly against the wall nearby. Gareth was lying back on the pillow, his eyes closed, his face pale and sweaty. I stayed quiet until the nurse laid his hand back down at his side on the bed. She typed into a tablet, then turned to the door. She stopped when she saw me there.

"Are you family?"

I shook my head no. "Just... a friend."

She pursed her lips. "He needs to rest."

I nodded. "Sure. Of course. Do you know what caused his seizure? I know he's had one before."

"No. And I'm not a doctor, so I'm not going to make any guesses."

"But you'll let his doctor know it happened again?"

She gave me a look as if I were stupid, but her only response was a curt "Yes."

I guess it was a dumb question. "Sorry. Of course."

She brushed past me and went back to work.

I watched Gareth from the doorway for a few more minutes, then sighed and walked away.

JORDAN WAS at his desk when I entered the office. He took one look at me and frowned. "Long day?"

"You could say that. Do I look that bad?"

"No, you just look worried."

"I guess I am. I just came from the hospital. That kid Gareth had another seizure while I was there. It's really unsettling to witness. Can't imagine what it's like for him."

He nodded. "My cousin had epilepsy when we were kids. He outgrew it, thankfully, but I remember how scary it was when he'd have a seizure."

"Yeah. Definitely scary. I need to talk to you about something, but I'd rather only have to go through the story once. Is Walker in?"

Jordan picked up the phone and hit a button.

"Yes?" Walker said. He was on speaker.

"You have a minute, boss?" Jordan asked.

"Yes," Walker responded. "But only if you stop calling me boss."

Jordan winked at me and got out of his desk chair, then gave it a shove back toward his desk. "After you," he said, making a grand gesture for me to go first.

He followed me down the hall and into Walker's office, where we dropped into the two chairs in front of Walker's desk.

Walker raised his eyebrows. "Both of you? To what do I owe this pleasure?"

"Cav has something he wants to tell us."

Walker gave me a questioning look. "You're not leaving us, are you?"

"What? No! I just learned some things today that may or may not play into my case."

"Like what?"

"And what does it have to do with me?" Jordan asked.

"So, I went back to the house today—the house where we found the boys' ghost-hunting equipment and the blood. I wanted to do a better search on the second floor. But it really struck me as odd that everything was still there. Belongings, clothes in the closet, medicine in the bathroom. Either the family had left suddenly or something had happened to them. I did some digging, and I found an article from 1973. The entire family died, the mother, father, and a sister murdered by their own son and brother, a teenager with all the classic signs—quiet, loner, cruel tendencies, animal torture. He killed himself in his bedroom after murdering his family. The article said that police claimed he'd performed a satanic ritual before he shot himself."

Walker's brows shot up again. "A satanic ritual?"

"That's all it said. I went back to the house and could see something had been carved into the floor of his bedroom, like a big circle with something inside it."

"You said this happened in 1973?"

"Yes."

"Okay, that's all really interesting and would probably make for a great episode of one of those true-crime shows, but it sounds like a closed case that happened fifty years ago. What does it have to do with your case now?"

"I don't know. I suspect the boys—or at least one of them—learned about it somehow, and maybe that's why they went to the house."

Walker shook his head. "Even if they did, how does that affect your case?"

He had a point. Obviously, whatever was drawing me to the murder/suicide, it wasn't that.

"I don't know. I just know it feels important for some reason. There are weird parallels. Three people being murdered by a teenage boy."

"Wait." Walker leaned in. "Have the other boys been confirmed dead?"

I realized what I'd said. "Oh God. No."

"But you're obviously starting to think they're dead, even if just on a subconscious level."

"Yeah," I admitted. "If you saw how much blood there is in that bedroom…."

"And you think Gareth did it?"

"That's just it. I know what I just said, but I'm not sure. There's something going on with him, and I can't figure out what."

"What do you mean, something is going on with him?"

"He's acting so strange. I was thinking dissociative identity disorder, but the psychiatrists who examined him say no."

"And you don't think he's faking it?"

"No. I don't think he's faking anything. He had a seizure when I stopped by the hospital on my way back here. I don't think anyone could fake that. It was terrifying. And he had it when I mentioned the name Victor Handy."

"Who the hell is Victor Handy?"

"He's the kid who killed his parents and sister back in 1973."

Walker's eyes narrowed. "Do you think he knew about him?"

I shook my head. "I don't know. He says he didn't, and I tend to believe him."

"Then what— You're not thinking he's possessed or something?"

I shrugged.

"You do." Walker sat back and stared at me. "I don't know how much I believe in stuff like that." I opened my mouth to argue, but he held up a hand. "I wasn't finished. While I guess I would say I'm a skeptic, I'm also open-minded enough to recognize that there are things beyond my understanding. The CIA made that crystal clear. Is that what you think? You think Gareth is possessed?"

I threw my hands up. "I don't know how else to explain the feeling that there's constantly someone else in the room with us, even when we're alone. Or how sometimes it feels like there's somebody else looking at me through his eyes. Or how the last time I was there before today, it was like there was someone else speaking through him, and then immediately after, he had no idea what I was talking about."

"So, we've got satanic rituals and a possible possession. I gotta tell you, kid, this is way outside my comfort zone. I can't help you much."

I sighed again. "I know. It's helpful to just bounce stuff off you guys, but I wasn't expecting experts in occult matters."

"Sounds like you might need to find an expert, though."

"I know. I'm going to talk to my World Religions professor."

"Your professor?"

"She's a witch. Maybe she can help or knows someone who can."

"It's worth a shot, I suppose."

"What about me?" Jordan asked. "Why did you want me here?"

"I took some photos today of that carving on the bedroom floor, but the lines don't show up that well. Do you think you could, like, enhance them or something?"

He raised an eyebrow. "I appreciate your faith in my abilities, but I'm not exactly *CSI: Baltimore*. Enhance them how?"

My face fell. "I don't know. Like with Photoshop or something. You can't?"

"I don't know. I'm hardly an expert. Send them to me and I'll see what I can do. I'll do some research."

"Thanks."

Jordan and I stood up and headed for the door.

"Oh, and Cav?" Walker said just before I closed his door. "Be careful with this stuff, okay?"

I gave him a nod and went to my office. I sent the photos to Jordan, then started typing up my notes. I was about halfway finished when Jordan yelled good night. About half an hour later, I was finished. I started getting ready to head home for a much-needed shower—or maybe a long soak in the claw-foot tub—when my phone buzzed. It was a text from Kyreh.

Hey! What are you up to?

Just finishing up at work. About to head home. Why? What's up?

Have you had dinner yet?

Was he asking me out? I snorted but decided not to read too much into it. *Not yet.*

Me either. Want to grab something?

Sure. I just to need to run home and take a quick shower first. Give me like half an hour?

Sounds good. See you soon.

I shoved my phone in my pocket and rushed out so fast, I almost forgot to arm the alarm and lock up.

Chapter 15

I WAS half hoping Haniah wouldn't be home when I got there so I wouldn't have to explain myself, but no such luck.

"I don't feel like cooking," she said as soon as I cleared the door. "Want to go out for dinner?"

"Hello to you too, and sorry but I can't," I said as I sailed past, making a beeline for my room to get some clean clothes.

Haniah followed me. "Why not? Did you eat already?"

"Uh, no... I just have plans." I opened the top drawer of my dresser and grabbed clean underwear, then thought twice and put them back to choose a cuter pair.

I could feel her presence in the doorway even though I didn't dare make eye contact. "You have dinner plans? Are you going out to the farm?"

"No." I slammed that drawer shut and opened the next, then chanced a glance in her direction.

She was giving me a suspicious look. "Are you going out with a boy?"

"It's not like that," I said a bit too quickly as I rummaged through my T-shirts. Did I even want to wear a T-shirt? Would a button-up be better?

Haniah's lips twitched. "Oh really? Then who are you having dinner with?"

I chose a plain black tee. It was a classic for a reason. "It's just Kyreh."

Her eyes lit up and she broke into a grin. "Aha! Dinner with Kyreh, huh?"

"Yes, he texted and asked if I wanted to grab something with him. It's not a big deal, so please don't make it one."

"I told you he liked you."

"Calm down. It's just dinner."

She gave me a knowing look.

"What?" I asked.

"Nothing. I just think that little smile you can't hide when you talk about him is very interesting."

"I didn't smile!"

"You did. And I think you like him too."

"Haniah, butt out."

"I'll want all the details when you get back."

"There won't be any details to tell."

"Uh-huh." She gave me one last look, then turned and started to sashay away. "Enjoy dinner."

"I will."

"Good. I won't wait up."

I let her have the last word as I turned and headed for the bathroom. This would have to be the world's fastest shower.

Kyreh was waiting for me when I pulled into the parking lot. He seemed distracted and didn't see me at first, giving me a chance to observe him. He was wearing an oversize hoodie over shorts that barely showed under the hem of the sweatshirt and low-top Converse sneakers with no socks. The hood was up, so I couldn't see his face, but his shoulders were hunched, and his hands were shoved deep in the pockets of the hoodie.

I honked the horn, and he looked up and spotted my car. He broke into a smile as he jogged over. "Hey," he said as he jumped into the passenger seat. "Thanks for coming out. I know it's late. I just didn't feel like eating alone tonight."

"It's not that late." We both sat there awkwardly for a few seconds. "So, where did you want to go?"

He shrugged. "I don't know. What are you in the mood for? I hadn't planned that far ahead. I just couldn't study for another minute, so I took a break and then realized I still hadn't eaten."

I glanced over. His head was resting against the seat. He looked tired. "Everything okay?" I asked.

He nodded and rolled his head in my direction. "Yeah. Just a little stressed about a few of my classes. Guess I needed a distraction."

"Anything I can help with?"

"You are helping."

I smiled. "You know what I mean."

"This is what I need—just hanging out with a friend. And a good meal."

"Then let's get you fed." I put the car into reverse and backed out of the space.

"Where are we going?"

"I know this little spot that serves amazing homestyle cooking. Real comfort food."

He gave me a soft smile. "That's just what I need."

"Thought so."

We made small talk on our way to the restaurant. Once we arrived, I parked on the street, and we entered.

Peg's Place was an unpretentious hole-in-the-wall run by a husband and wife. Peg cooked, Barry served. It was small—only four or five tables—but cute and clean. I figured most of their business had to be takeout and delivery since they never seemed busy, despite the food being delicious. That night, there was only one other couple at a table in the corner.

Barry seated us and handed us menus then disappeared into the kitchen.

"How'd you find this place?" Kyreh asked.

"Just, um, stumbled across it." Mason had taken me here on a date once, but I didn't really want to get into that.

Kyreh looked around. "It would be a great little date spot."

"Oh! Yeah," I said, as if the thought had never occurred to me. "I just like it because the food is great and it's pretty cheap."

Kyreh laughed, "Like I said, a good date spot."

"Yeah, I guess I haven't been doing much dating lately. You know, dead boyfriend and all."

Kyreh lowered his menu, a look of horror on his face. "Oh my God. I'm so sorry, Cav. I forgot…."

"It's fine."

He still looked aghast. "I'm such an ass."

I laughed. "It's really okay. I promise."

I went back to my menu but realized Kyreh was still studying me. I glanced up to meet his gaze.

"Do you mind if I ask what happened?" he said softly. "I know it's none of my business—"

"No, it's cool. I understand. I'd be curious too. He just disappeared one day. It was our anniversary actually. We had dinner plans… and he just didn't show up. Nobody knew where he was or what happened.

Months later, they found his body in a park. He, uh, wasn't in good shape, so they couldn't say for sure what happened to him. The police declared it an accident and closed the case."

"Jesus H. Christ."

"Sorry. This isn't exactly dinner conversation."

"Hey, I asked. Did you investigate?"

"No, I wasn't allowed."

"You weren't allowed?"

"Yeah, my boss said I was too close and too emotionally raw. He was probably right, but it's haunted me ever since." I realized my poor choice of words as soon as they left my mouth. "But yeah, that's why I haven't been dating. I just haven't felt ready yet."

"I can't even begin to imagine what that was like."

"I had a lot of support—my dads, my grandmother, and Haniah. And a lot of therapy. It was rough at first, but I'm doing better these days."

"That's good."

Just then, Barry returned to our table, and we realized we hadn't even looked at the menus yet. We asked for a few more minutes and focused on our dinner selections.

"Will it gross you out if I order liver and onions?" I asked.

Kyreh shook his head. "No, but now you're the one who sounds like my grandmother."

I laughed.

When Barry came back, I ordered the liver and onions with mashed potatoes and gravy, and Kyreh got the chicken-fried steak with mac and cheese and Brussels sprouts.

"You weren't kidding about this place being comfort food," he said when we were alone again.

"Told ya."

"So, you haven't dated at all for a year?"

"Nope. Someone did ask me out recently, though."

One eyebrow jumped up, but he quickly brought it back in line with the other one. "Oh really? Did you accept?"

"No. Turns out he was married."

"So?"

It was my turn to raise an eyebrow.

"Were they, like, open, or was he trying to cheat?"

"He said they were open, although I only have his word for that. Either way, it's just not what I'm looking for. He was also really pushy, and it made me uncomfortable."

"That's fair. So what are you looking for?"

"Right now?"

"Or just in general?"

"I guess I'm a romantic. I want what my dads, Jason and Eli, have."

"And what's that?"

"Mutual respect. Cooperation. Support. Deep love."

"Damn. Yeah. That does sound good. You could have all those things in an open relationship too, you know. But I get it. That's just not what you're looking for. Your dads sound amazing. You're lucky to have them as role models."

"I'm pretty lucky in a lot of ways, but yeah, they're great guys, and they complement each other so well. That's what I want."

He nodded and looked down at the table. "Me too, I think. I mean, I've been with my share of married guys—and women—but I think those days are behind me."

I was a little surprised by his admission but tried to cover it. I must not have done a good job, because Kyreh smirked. "What?"

"Nothing," I said a bit too quickly.

"Uh-huh. Now you think I'm a big old ho bag."

"I don't. Really. No slut-shaming here, I promise."

He let out a bark of laughter. "So now you're calling me a slut."

"That's not—"

"Cav, I'm just teasing you. It's all good. I'm not ashamed or anything. I was figuring stuff out. It's how you learn what you like and what you want, right?"

"Right. Exactly." I knew he'd been teasing me, but I still felt like I'd put my foot in it. I didn't know what to say next.

Luckily, Kyreh changed the subject to safer topics of conversation, and by the time the food arrived, the awkwardness was forgotten.

After dinner, I drove Kyreh back to campus. When we pulled into the parking lot, he reached for the door handle, but hesitated. "I know we both have work to do, but want to put it off a little longer?"

I laughed. "Doing what?"

"Just hanging out. A walk, maybe?"

I shrugged. "Sure. Why not?"

I turned off the car, and we got out. We ambled along in companionable silence for a bit. We were coming up on the quad, where we'd had our ice cream the first time we'd hung out. My mind wandered back to that night, so I wasn't fully present when Kyreh spoke up again, snapping me out of my thoughts.

"Tell me something about you that most people don't know."

"Huh?" I responded brilliantly.

"Tell me something about you that most people don't know," he repeated. "Just trying to get to know you better."

"Oh, um…." The only thing I could think of was that I could see dead people, and I wasn't sure I was ready to go there with him. Not even Haniah knew about my abilities. In fact, Nana, Jason, and Eli were pretty much the only people alive who knew. Mom had known, and I'd told Mason. To his credit, he'd simply taken me at my word and never questioned it. Now he knew firsthand.

"You there?" Kyreh asked, and I realized I'd gone quiet for a while.

"Sorry, I'm, uh, having trouble thinking of something."

He bumped me with his shoulder. "You mean having trouble of thinking of something you're willing to tell me."

I laughed. "Maybe."

"What? Are you a cold-blooded killer? No. A top-secret spy? Wait! I've got it! You're a furry and you're deeply ashamed."

I threw back my head and laughed. "Your wild guesses make my actual deep dark secret seem pretty tame."

"Oh, so you do have a deep dark secret. I knew you were hiding something behind that cute, charming façade."

"Cute and charming, huh?" I batted my eyes at him.

"Don't try to distract me. I want to know the dirt."

"There is no dirt. Really. It's not that serious."

"So what is it?"

I debated for a few more seconds. For some reason I trusted Kyreh. "I, uh, see ghosts," I blurted out.

He laughed, then realized I wasn't joining in. "Wait, like, for real?"

"Yeah."

He stopped walking and looked around nervously. "Do you see them now?"

I couldn't resist messing with him. I stepped back, staring over his shoulder with the most horrified expression I could manage, and screamed, "Watch out!"

He yelped and spun around while ducking as I started cackling hysterically.

He froze and gave me a dirty look, but I couldn't stop laughing. Suddenly he pounced, tackling me and sending us tumbling backward into the soft grass.

That only made me laugh harder, and soon he joined in.

We ended up lying on our backs next to each other, our arms not quite touching, as we calmed down.

"Okay, so really, what's your secret?"

"That was it. I really do see ghosts. I guess it kind of runs in my family. As far back as I can remember, I could see and talk to dead people."

He turned his head to look at me. "So you're serious? And you can talk to them too?"

"Yeah."

"So… you're, like, a psychic?"

"No. I mean, not really. At least I don't think of it that way. In my family, we call it the Sight. Or just our gifts. We don't really make a big deal out of it. Or my mom didn't, anyway. My grandmother says the gifts sometimes skip a generation, and I guess it skipped my mom. I'm still learning about it. Nana knows a lot more than I do."

"What's it like?"

"What do you mean?"

"What's it like to see and talk to ghosts?"

"Mostly just like talking to you. They're usually pretty excited to talk to somebody."

"Oh. Yeah. I can see that. Being dead must be pretty lonely. But aren't they scary?"

"No. It's not like a horror movie." Mason's reaction when I told him he was dead popped into my mind. That had certainly been terrifying, but I wasn't about to tell Kyreh that I could see my deceased boyfriend. "When I was a little kid, I couldn't really tell dead people apart from living people, so I'd talk to them anywhere I saw them—at home, at school, in public. My mom told people I had imaginary friends, but until I figured things out, a lot of people just thought I was a weirdo. Eventually I was able to distinguish the dead from the living, and after that I learned to sort of… tune them out when I need to."

"But how do you tune them out? Are there a lot of them? Just thousands upon thousands of dead people walking around?"

"You know how you don't really pay attention to the people you pass on a busy street? It's just like that. I see them, but I don't really notice them, if that makes sense. And it's not uncommon to see them, but there aren't, like, tons of them. Most people don't become ghosts, and if they do, they don't last that long. My grandmother says it takes a lot of energy to stay on this plane after you die. The ones that linger usually have something holding them here, either a connection to a person or place or thing they don't know how to break, or something left unfinished."

"I have so many questions."

I laughed. "Enough about ghosts. What about you? What's your big secret?"

"I was just going to say I play the drums, but that feels really lame after your big confession."

"No way! Everybody thinks drummers are really sexy. Nobody ever says that about seeing ghosts."

He rolled toward me. "So are you saying I'm sexy?"

"I mean, I didn't say that. Just, you know, people. Like, in general." My heart was racing, but I tried to play it cool.

"Uh-huh. Just admit you think I'm hot."

"Maybe if you were in a band…."

"So all I have to do is form a band and then you'll think I'm hot."

"I'd take it into consideration. No promises."

He laughed and rolled onto his back again, and my heart began to return to its normal pace.

We talked for another hour, lying in the grass, before lightning flickered across the horizon. A few seconds later, thunder rumbled in the distance.

I sighed. "I guess that's my sign that I should get home. I have classes tomorrow anyway."

"Me too, and I still have work to finish up tonight. Thanks for coming out, though. This was just what I needed."

I gave him a half smile as I sat up. "They do say laughter is the best medicine."

He snorted but stayed on the ground. "I think you were laughing a lot harder than I was. I thought I was about to be murdered by a ghost."

"I dunno, you were laughing pretty hard after you tackled me."

He smiled up at me, then said, "I'm glad we've been hanging out."

"Me too," I said, and I meant it. I jumped up to offer him a hand for a change. He took it, and I pulled him to his feet. He left his hand in mine just a second longer than he had to, then pulled me into a quick, tight hug.

"Thanks again," he whispered into my ear, then dropped his arms and pulled back. "Good night, Cav."

"Good night, Ky," I said, already missing his body against mine. "I mean, Kyreh."

He tipped his head to one side and smiled. "You can call me Ky." He started backing away as his smile turned into a grin. "I kind of like it." Then he turned and trotted off toward his dorm.

I thought about Kyreh all the way home. I was fairly certain he was flirting with me now, but I wasn't sure what to do about it. I really enjoyed hanging out with him. It was nice to have another friend. But I didn't want to risk losing him or things getting weird if we didn't work out.

I also couldn't deny that I liked him. He was fun to be around, thoughtful, and smart. I was attracted to him. Despite my denial, I definitely thought he was sexy. Just thinking about his body as he'd lain next to me on the ground, his hoodie riding up to show off his abs, made me tingle.

I shook my head to clear it. There was no reason to get too far down that road just yet. Maybe Kyreh was just flirty and it didn't mean anything. Maybe I was reading too much into it.

Besides, I still had Mason to deal with. If Nana was right and he'd attached himself to me, what did that mean? Would he really leave if I found out how he died? Did I want him to leave? And what if it was too late?

I arrived home just before the storm hit. True to her word, Haniah didn't wait up for me. Her bedroom door was closed, and I didn't see her as I brushed my teeth and got ready for bed. All the while, the storm raged outside.

It took a while to fall asleep. Besides the almost constant lightning and earsplitting cracks of thunder, my mind kept returning to Kyreh. If I tried to push those thoughts away, Mason took over. And if I tried to think about something else, Victor and Gareth rushed in to fill the void. None of them were conducive to a peaceful rest.

Eventually, after much tossing and turning, I drifted off.

I WAS approaching the Handys' old home. It was nighttime and so, so dark. The only illumination came from the lightning that still flickered through the heavy cloud cover.

I was almost to the front door when I noticed movement off to one side. A slender figure stood by the corner of the house. I could just make them out in the gloom. They held a finger to their mouth and then gestured for me to follow them. I hesitated a moment but then did as they bid.

They moved silently and furtively toward the back of the house, with me following a few feet behind. As we emerged into the backyard, two more figures stood with their backs to me, looking down at something at their feet. The first person slid in next to them and looked down also.

I stopped a few feet away. Was I supposed to join them?

The first figure turned slightly and waved me over.

I approached cautiously, but none of them moved or even looked in my direction. I made it to the side of the one I'd followed. Now that I was closer, I could see it was a young man. I looked down to see what they were staring at, but it was just a pitch-black hole in the ground, two or three feet across.

I looked to my guide for clarity, but his gaze was locked on the gaping pit.

Just then, the clouds broke and the full moon cast its light over the four of us, impossibly bright after the pervasive darkness.

I gasped and recoiled, stumbling back as I recognized my companions now that I could see them clearly. I was looking at Kyle Itoh, DJ Juarez, and Wade Smith, the three missing boys. But they were covered in blood, and their throats had been sliced open.

They didn't react, just continued to stare down into the hole. Slowly, ever so slowly, I crept back up next to Kyle, staying on guard in case they made any sudden movements. I screwed up my nerve and peeked into the abyss. The moonlight just reached the bottom, and I gasped again.

I was looking down at the tangled bodies of the three boys standing next to me.

But that was impossible. I stared, frozen in horror, until suddenly two hands shoved me roughly between my shoulder blades. I tripped forward with a scream and fell. It seemed as if I was falling for much longer than the depth of the hole, but eventually I hit the bottom with a jolt. I could feel the dead boys under me, and I had to fight down a wave of nausea. I scrambled around and looked up as the moon slid back behind the clouds, leaving four silhouettes staring down at me.

I SAT up with a shout, feeling clammy and damp. I was in my own bed, in my room. I wasn't at the bottom of a chasm with three dead bodies. My heart was still pounding as I tried to calm my breathing. I lowered myself back down on my pillow, staring up at the ceiling.

I had a terrible feeling that I knew where to find the boys.

Chapter 16

I DIDN'T sleep well after my dream, but I still had to get up early for class. I was tempted to skip since I couldn't stop thinking about my dream, but I kept telling myself it would wait. Still, I might as well have skipped for as much attention as I paid. As soon as my last class ended, I made a beeline for my car and headed directly to the house.

The field was muddy after the storm the night before, and as I trudged across it, I found myself wishing I'd taken time to run home and change. My shoes were going to be ruined.

When I reached the house, I skirted around the corner instead of going inside, just like in my dream the night before when I'd followed Dead Kyle.

I reached the backyard and tried to figure out where DJ and Wade had been standing. I had a vague idea, but there was no hole in sight—which made sense. If there'd been a giant gaping hole in the backyard, we'd have found it when we searched the area.

I walked over to the general area where I thought the boys had been in my dream. There was only overgrown grass and thorn bushes everywhere I looked. No sign of an old well. Not that I was sure of what I was looking for. In my dream, it was just a hole in the ground. There was certainly nothing like that anywhere.

I started kicking around, which had the benefit of knocking off a little of the mud that caked my shoes. Then again, I still had to return to my car, so any gain would be lost.

I was stomping around when suddenly my foot produced a hollow thunk instead of the solid thud of the earth. My heart started thumping as I did it again with the same result. I crouched down and dug my fingers into the ground. Just a few inches under the surface, I hit something solid.

I dug around until I found the edge of whatever I'd discovered. A little more digging and I realized it was a flat slab of concrete. Further excavation revealed that it was a very large, circular slab of concrete. If it was the top of a well, there was no way I'd be able to move it on my own.

I looked down at my muddy hands and, with a sigh, wiped them on my pants so I could extract my phone from my pocket. Might as well ruin my entire outfit. Maybe when I was done, I could wallow around in the mud like a pig.

I dialed Mead and waited while his line rang. Much to my relief, he picked up.

"What are you up to now?" he asked as a greeting.

"I had a hunch," I said.

"Oh boy. What about?"

"The missing boys. I have an idea of where they might be."

"Where?" His voice was suddenly all business.

"In the article about the Handy case, they mentioned a well in the backyard where the bodies of the mother, father, and daughter were found. I think that's where the boys are."

"I don't remember seeing a well in the backyard. We searched. They probably filled that in years ago."

"No, I think it was just sealed off. I'm at the house now, and I think I found it. But it's covered with a big concrete slab, and I can't lift it by myself."

"Okay, but that leads to the question of if you can't lift it, how would that scrawny Miller kid lift it?"

I looked down. He had a point. But I was so sure.

"And even if he suddenly developed superpowers and could lift it by himself, why didn't we notice a disturbed area when we searched?"

Another excellent point.

Then I noticed something sticking up through the grass, maybe only four inches high: a handle shape made of rebar.

"Leverage," I breathed.

"What?"

I looked around. "He used leverage to open it, leaving the soil and grass on top so when it was replaced, you'd never notice unless you knew exactly where to look. And by the time we got here almost two weeks later, you'd probably not notice, even if you knew where to look. Ah-ha! I bet he used that metal rod leaning against the back of the house."

"Okay, smarty-pants. Don't touch anything. I'm on my way. We'll see if your theory holds up."

"It will."

If I was right, and I was certain I was, that meant the boys had been dead all along. My heart broke for their parents, still holding on to their last shred of hope. I thought of the Itohs and how fragile they'd seemed. I didn't envy whoever ended up telling them—or any of the parents, really.

Waiting for Mead to arrive was torture. I just wanted to get this over with. I returned to the front of the house to watch for him.

Finally I spotted him crossing the field. There were several uniformed officers with him.

"It's around back," I said when they were close enough. "Follow me."

I led the group to the backyard and pointed out what I'd found.

Mead stared down at the exposed bit of concrete I'd unearthed.

"How?"

"What?"

"How in the name of all that is holy did you find that?"

I had an answer prepared. "I guess my subconscious was working on it, because last night I had a dream that the boys were in the well."

"And you saw the well... here?"

I shrugged. "No. I stomped around until I heard a hollow sound, then dug down. If I hadn't read about the well in the news article I found, it would have never occurred to me to look for it."

Mead shook his head. "Okay. Where's that metal pole you mentioned?"

I pointed it out where it stood against the house. Mead walked over to inspect it, and I followed.

The pole was about four feet long and two inches in diameter. One end was blunt, but the other was flat, almost like a giant screwdriver.

Mead shook his head. "I was hoping we might be able to get some prints, but it's rusty as hell and it's been out in the elements. Not a chance. But you're right that this is a tool to open things, like the well or a septic tank." He grabbed it and started back to the well, where he tossed the pole to one of the uniformed cops.

"Okay, let's pop it open," Mead said grimly.

The two uniforms wedged the rod under the rebar handle and lifted the lid. The slab wasn't as thick as I'd first thought, maybe two inches and about two to three feet across.

Then the smell hit me, and my stomach lurched. Mead grunted but didn't say anything as I tried my best not to embarrass myself by gagging. I pulled my shirt over my nose, but it didn't help.

The troopers set the slab aside, and we all stepped forward. As we stared down into the black hole, I was reminded of my dream again.

It was too dark to see to the bottom, but one of the cops produced a high-powered flashlight, flicked it on, and aimed the beam into the well. The light caught the unmistakable form of a crumpled body.

Even though I was expecting it, my stomach jolted again. I turned and walked a few feet away, fighting down a sudden wave of tears welling up in my eyes. Maybe the parents hadn't been the only ones holding out a sliver of hope.

Mead was on his phone, talking to someone about bringing out a crew to extract the bodies, but I'd mostly zoned out. I jumped a little when he suddenly shouted my name. I looked up and realized his conversation was over and he must have called me several times.

He gave me a searching look. "You okay?"

"Peachy."

"I'm serious. Seeing dead kids is hard even for a veteran like me. Never gets easier."

"I'm fine. What's next?"

"We get them out of there, see what the score is, then see where we go from there."

"I guess Gareth is officially a murder suspect now, huh?"

"Without question."

"What happens with that?"

"We'll take him into custody."

"Will he leave the hospital?"

"He's been ready to leave for a few days now, technically. They've only been keeping him there because we asked them to. We'll take him in."

"What about the seizures?"

"They can't find any medical reason for the seizures. We think he's faking it. They seem to happen at very convenient times."

I wasn't so sure about that, but I couldn't very well tell him my theories.

He stared toward the well. "Poor bastards."

"Yeah." I sighed. "If you don't need me, I think I'll head out. Let me know what you find out, will you?"

He looked over, surprised. "You're not hanging around?"

I shook my head no. "I've seen enough. I don't really want to stick around for the... extraction."

Mead nodded. "Okay. Yeah. I'll give you a call later once things settle down."

"Thanks."

"I think, technically, I should be thanking you."

I shrugged and started back to my car with a halfhearted wave.

I WENT back to the office, where I found Jordan at his desk.

"Hey!" he said as soon as I opened the door. "I've been—" He broke off as he took in my muddy and melancholy appearance. "What happened?"

I nodded. "I found the boys."

His face fell. My tone of voice gave it away. "Dead?" he asked.

"Yep."

He looked me up and down. "Were they... buried? And did you dig them up?" He almost sounded like he didn't want to know.

"Sort of. They were in a well in the backyard of the house where they were killed. It was sealed up with, like, a lid... thing. I dug that up, then called in the professionals." I shrugged. "They're doing the real dirty part. I didn't stick around. Didn't want to see...." My voice faded out.

Jordan nodded sympathetically. "I don't blame you. Well, if you're up for it, I have some news for you."

"Give it to me."

"I've been working on those photos. Come around behind my desk and I'll show you."

I did, being sure not to shed any dried mud anywhere.

He pulled up an image on his monitor. "Okay, I spliced your photos together as well as I could. Then I increased the contrast. When I did that, I was able to highlight the carving. It's easy to see the outline of the circle now, and a few of the border glyphs are clear. I just wish you could have gotten better photos of whatever is in the center."

I leaned forward and stared at the image on his screen. He'd done a really good job piecing my photos together like a puzzle. You could see the entire circle now, except for the part covered by the bed and, as he'd said, the center portion. He'd outlined the circle and the visible glyphs in bright yellow, making them jump out.

"Well," I said, straightening up after a moment's study. "I guess I can't blame the cops for saying it looks like a satanic ritual."

Jordan gave a snort of laughter. "Yeah, it honestly creeped me out when I was outlining it. I was like, am I casting some sort of digital spell right now? But there are enough things missing that I didn't worry about it too much."

"Yeah, not sure it works like that."

He laughed again. "I'm mostly kidding. I don't think I believe in this stuff." He paused. "Do you?"

I shrugged. "Not sure what I believe at this point."

He frowned and glanced back at the screen.

"Anyway," I continued, "I'll try to go back out tomorrow and see if I can clear it off, get the missing parts photographed."

"Sounds good." He looked me over again. "Do you have a change of clothes?"

"No. I keep meaning to bring a change of clothes to keep at the office. I'll have to run home. For the first time I can see the point of having a shower here, and I still can't use it."

Jordan laughed as I headed for the door. Walker had installed a shower in the bathroom and insisted it would come in handy, though I had yet to have a reason to use it—until now. It was a bit of an ongoing joke.

I drove home to change, then headed back to the office to type up my notes and wait anxiously to hear from Mead. I was destined to be disappointed, though, since I still hadn't heard from him by the time it was time to close up and go home.

I WAS in class the next day when my phone vibrated in my pocket. I slid it out to find a missed call and a voicemail from Mead. I desperately wanted to check it right then and there, but I forced myself to wait until after class.

Turned out, Mead wanted me to swing by his office when I was free. I skipped my last class and head directly to the station. The professor relied heavily on his written material and posted all his lectures online, so I could catch up if I missed anything important.

At the barracks, I didn't have to wait long before the inner door opened and Mead waved me in and led me to his office.

I settled into the chair in front of his desk as he slid behind it and collapsed into his desk chair with a weary sigh.

"What's up?" I asked.

"Oh, you know, not much. Unless you count the three dead teenagers we've got in the morgue."

I frowned. "How did they die?"

"Stabbed and throats cut. At least one of them—" He glanced down at a paper on his desk. "—Wade Smith—was probably knocked out first. No defensive wounds. He was the lucky one."

I drew a shaky breath. It sounded remarkably like the Handy murders, too similar for mere coincidence.

"And Gareth?"

"Currently in custody, but the parents have hired a very good lawyer who is demanding we release him to his parents' custody for medical reasons. Based on the evidence we have—or, more importantly, what we don't have—we might have to let him walk, at least until there's a trial."

"What do you mean?"

"Almost all our evidence is circumstantial. It's pretty damning, but it's nothing solid. We found him miles away, covered in their blood, but we don't really have any proof it was him who killed them and hid them in a well we didn't even know existed. We've got no proof that he knew about those 1970s murders you turned up. We even requested library records. We've checked his search history, what books he checked out, what databases he may have requested, everything. Nothing indicates he knew."

"Maybe he didn't," I said hesitantly.

"You think he just happened to kill them in the same house, using the same techniques, and then stumbled across the well to hide the bodies?"

"No...."

"Then maybe you agree with his lawyer, who thinks there's a deranged lunatic living in the woods kidnapping and killing people, and that Gareth was somehow spared and was released or managed to escape and subsequently blocked the trauma from his memory."

"No," I said more firmly. "I don't buy that."

"Neither do I, but unless you've got another theory, I'm pretty sure we'll have to release him."

"Can you give me more time?"

He shook his head. "We can maybe get away with holding him over the weekend. It's Friday, and we can reasonably put off a hearing until Monday. Is that enough time for whatever you have up your sleeve?"

"I'm not even sure I have anything up my sleeve. I'm just following up on a few loose threads. Maybe one of them will unravel this whole messy case."

"You're not giving me much to go on."

I shrugged. "I don't have anything else to offer."

He rubbed his bloodshot eyes, then stared at me for a moment. I wondered if he'd been up all night.

"I'll see what I can do," he said finally. "I appreciate any help you can offer."

I nodded. "What about their parents? Do they know?"

He sighed again. "They were notified last night."

"God," I muttered under my breath.

"Yeah. I went to all of them. It wasn't exactly a picnic."

"I can't even imagine."

"All part of the job."

"At least my theory about the Handy case being connected seems to be confirmed."

"Speaking of that, I've got something for you." He shuffled things around on his desk until he found a sticky pad with a note scrawled on the top sheet. He peeled it off and handed it to me. "That's the contact info for a retired Washington County deputy named Buddy Dreisch. He worked the Handy case back in… whenever it was."

"1973."

"Right, well, there you go. I haven't talked to him, but someone at the sheriff's office was able to look it up for me. Let me know if you turn up anything useful."

"Of course."

Mead eyed me for a few more seconds, then sat back in his chair. "Okay, that's it for me. Unless you've got something else for me, I guess we're done."

I stood up. "Thanks for filling me in, and for the tip." I waved the sticky note in my hand.

"That was the deal."

I shook his hand and started for the door before I paused. "Oh wait. Don't you have to walk me out?"

He looked confused. "Nope. You know where the exit is."

"Got it. I must be mistaken," I said and left his office.

I guess Gibson had lied to get me alone long enough to ask me out.

Chapter 17

I SAT in the parking lot for a moment to work out a plan of attack. What did I need to do next? I wanted to talk to the retired deputy Mead found for me, and I wanted to go back out to the house to fully photograph the carving.

Speaking of the carving, I also needed to find someone knowledgeable about spells and rituals. I could ask Nana, but it probably meant talking to my professor.

But first I'd call Mr. Dreisch. I pulled out my phone and dialed the number Mead had given me.

It rang several times before a woman answered.

"Hello, I'm looking for Mr. Dreisch," I told her.

"Bobby or Buddy?" she asked.

"Oh, uh." I glanced at the note in Mead's scrawl. "Buddy."

"May I ask who's calling?"

"My name is Cav Crawford. I'm a private investigator. A case I'm working may be related to a case Mr. Dreisch was involved in back in the seventies."

"Oh, then he'll love talking to you. He's sharp as a tack, and he loves to talk about his old law-enforcement days. Hang on a sec."

The line went quiet for about a minute. Then a tremulous older male voice came on. "Hello, this is Buddy."

"Hello, Mr. Dreisch," I said and started my introduction all over again.

"Please call me Buddy," he said when I'd finished. "And my memory ain't what it used to be, but I reckon I'm not too bad for an old eighty-four-year-old coot."

I laughed. "Well, anything you remember will be helpful, I'm sure."

"What case is it you're asking about?"

"Do you remember the Handy case? A father, mother, and daughter murdered by the son, who then killed himself. It would have been 1973."

He was quiet for a second, then said, "I remember it well. Probably the most disturbing case I ever worked on. I was the first on the scene, and I'd never seen anything like it. Never saw anything like it again, for that matter. There was blood everywhere up on the second floor. Every room, just about. I'd heard the term bloodbath but never related it to real life, but that's what it was. I almost quit after that day. Something like that, it changes you."

"The article was light on details. I'm sorry to bring up such unpleasant memories, but is there anything else you can tell me?"

"I could tell you loads. A lot of it was kept from the press at the time. A whole family murdered like that with the weird ritual stuff, it had the potential to be pretty sensational, and we were worried about copycat crimes. We were all sworn to secrecy."

"The case was closed, right?"

"Oh yeah. There was no doubt who did it."

"Then it's been so long, and with the entire family dead, there's no one to be upset about the truth coming out, right? Besides, it could really assist me with the current case I'm working. If it helps, I'm cooperating with the police. In fact, that's how I got your name."

"You don't say. What's the case? Anything I might know about?"

"Have you heard about the missing boys in Baltimore County?"

"Sure have. Sad thing. They still ain't been found, right?"

"Well, it's not public yet, but we found them yesterday. They were killed in the Handys' house in the same manner as the family was killed fifty years ago."

He went quiet again.

"Mr. Dreisch? I mean, Buddy?"

"I'm still here. I s'pose it won't hurt to tell you about it. I can't believe there's a copycat all these years later. I wonder how much they know."

"I won't know until I know more about the original murders."

He started talking, his voice somewhat distant, as if he were reliving the memories as he told me the story. "As soon as I hit the top step of that stairs, I knew it was bad. There was so much blood. It had started running down the stairs at some point, but it was dried by the time I arrived. There was blood splattered all down the hallway, a handprint here and there. Footprints everywhere. It was a nightmare to try and untangle. We think he killed the sister first, probably in her sleep. There was no sign of struggle." He paused. "She was such a little thing. Still haunts me, how somebody could hurt a child. Then it looked like he killed his pa and attacked his ma. The father must have woken up, because he had some defensive wounds. That must have woken up the mother, because she got away somehow, even though she must have been hurt pretty bad, judging by the trail of blood. It looked like he caught her and finished her off at the top of the stairs. She was in the worst shape. She must have put up a hell of a fight, bless her heart."

I was furiously taking notes. So far it lined up with the few details in the article, which at least made me feel better about Mr. Dreisch's memory.

He continued, "At some point, we think he dragged them into his bedroom."

"What? Why would he do that?"

"Don't rightly know unless it had something to do with that carving on his floor. At first we thought he might have some... unsavory reasons, but there was no sign of that on their bodies."

"Do you mean, like, sexual abuse?"

"Yes, but like I said, there was no sign of that."

"Then what?"

"Whenever he was done with whatever he was doing in the bedroom, he dragged them all outside and threw them down the old well, then covered it back up. Then he went back inside to his room and died."

"You mean he killed himself?"

"Nope. I mean he dropped dead. I'll be damned if we could figure out why or how. He'd been dead for a few days by the time I showed up, but the toxicology reports didn't indicate anything in his blood. He had a few small cuts, probably from the struggle with his parents, but nothing that was life-threatening. It was like his heart just stopped, but he was a healthy fifteen-year-old kid."

"The article I found said he shot himself."

"Yeah, like I told you, we kept some details back when we talked to the reporters. All we said at the time was he killed himself. Someone wrote that he shot himself, and that became the story. We didn't really care, so we never bothered to correct it."

"He just... dropped dead?"

"That's what it looked like. He was sprawled out in the center of that circle he'd carved into his floor, eyes wide open, covered in blood but none of it his."

I shuddered. The parallels between Victor and Gareth just kept coming.

"The article mentioned a satanic ritual. Can you tell me anything more about that?"

"Not really. He had a bunch of books about demons and satanic stuff. The neighbors said he was a disturbed kid. He'd carved some sort of big circle on the floor of his bedroom. It had all sorts of symbols inside it, but of course none of it meant anything to us."

"I've seen the carving."

"Then you know what I mean."

"I do. Is there anything else you can tell me?"

"Well, one of the oddest things about the case was that we never found the murder weapon. That's the one thing that always bothered me. Couldn't let it go for years. You'd think with all the other crazy stuff going on, finding the knife he used would be the least of our worries, but it bugged me. It wasn't in the well, it wasn't in his room—we searched the entire house and didn't find it anywhere. Even had all the knives in the kitchen tested. Nothing. The experts said it was probably a dagger of some kind, a double-edged blade. Didn't see anything like it anywhere."

"Why would he get rid of the murder weapon?"

"That's a good question."

"Do you think he hid it?"

"That's all we could figure. We discussed every possible solution back then. Even briefly considered an accomplice, but there were no footprints unaccounted for, no fingerprints that weren't family."

"So you're confident that Victor acted alone."

"As confident as we could be. Just a lot of questions left unanswered, and with the boy dead, I guess they'll never be answered."

I thanked him for his help, and we ended the call. I stared at my notes, trying to make sense of them. I had more questions now than I did before the call. How did Victor die? What happened to the knife he used to kill his family? What was Victor trying to accomplish? And did any of it even matter? Maybe this was all just a wild goose chase and I was wasting my time.

But it did raise one question that I could answer immediately. I called Mead.

"Did you find the murder weapon?" I asked as soon as he answered.

"The knife used to kill the boys? As a matter of fact, no, we haven't."

"One more similarity," I muttered under my breath.

"What's that?"

"I just got off the phone with that retired deputy. He said they never found the original murder weapon either."

"Let me guess, was it a double-sided blade?"

"You got it."

"I'm starting to come around to your theory that these killings are somehow connected, although I can't fathom how. Copycat crime?"

"Possibly. But you'd have to prove that Gareth knew about the Handy case."

He sighed. "I'm working on it."

"Me too. I'll keep you informed if I learn anything else."

I hung up and checked the time. It was still early afternoon. I shot off a quick email to my professor asking if she had time to talk today or tomorrow, then headed to Nana's.

She didn't even look surprised when I showed up this time. She was in her bed, still in her nightgown with the blankets pulled up past her waist, but in a sitting position.

"I wondered if you'd be by today," she said when I appeared in the door.

"Why was that?"

"I had a dream last night. Didn't sleep well. That's why I stayed in bed today."

I came in and sat down on the edge of the bed to give her a kiss on the cheek. "What was the dream about?"

"It was a muddled mess. All I could tell for sure was that you were in danger. You were surrounded by dead boys."

A shiver ran up my spine. "Dead boys?"

"Yes. Mason was one of them, but I didn't recognize any of the rest of them."

"How many were there?"

"Five altogether, in the shape of a pentagram, one at each point of the star. You were in the center."

"Mason, the three boys, and... Victor?" I counted off softly.

"Who is Victor?"

"He's a boy who died back in the seventies. He killed his family and then died mysteriously in the middle of some sort of circle he'd carved into the floor."

"Why would he be there?"

"I don't know. I'm just guessing. Maybe it wasn't even him."

"Do you have a picture of him?"

"No."

"Ah well. Maybe it doesn't matter. The main point of the dream seemed to be that you're in over your head. What's going on? What brought you here today?"

I took a deep breath. "What do you know about possession?"

She frowned; her brows knit. "Are we back to that? Like I told you before, I know next to nothing about possession, but I know you should stay far away from anything to do with it."

"What if I can't avoid it?"

"Then you need to tread very carefully."

"I'm doing the best I can. You said you know next to nothing, but that implies you know a little, at least."

"Very little. Our family was Catholic back in Ireland, and for at least a generation or two after we moved to America. My parents were practicing Catholics. I left the church when I was young and haven't looked back since. But possession and exorcism are as much a part of Catholic beliefs as Mother Mary and the sacrament. A lot of those beliefs have become intertwined with Celtic Gaelic beliefs over the centuries. It's hard to know much about what they believed in ancient times. The Church took great care to stamp out most of the traditional ways, though some managed to survive. But why are you asking? Is this about Mason?"

"No. Nothing to do with him. But it's looking more and more like Gareth, the boy who was found and whose parents hired me, might be possessed. By what, I don't know."

"What makes you think it's possession?"

"Just a feeling I have. Sometimes it seems like someone else is looking at me through his eyes, or there's a sense that someone else is in the room with us. Once, it was like someone else took over his body and warned me to stay away from the house where we found the boys' bodies and where the boy Victor killed his family."

She shook her head. "I don't like any of this. I guess it's useless to tell you stay out of it."

"I think it's too late for that."

"And what do you plan to do if it is possession? Exorcise it?"

"I hadn't thought that far ahead, to be honest. I guess that would be the ultimate goal if something really has taken over this kid. I have to do something. Maybe I can still save him."

"And if you're wrong? What if it's not possession?"

"Then I have to stop him."

"How?"

"I don't know yet. One step at a time. I don't even know where to begin with an exorcism. I don't suppose a Bible and some incense would work for this?"

"I wouldn't recommend trying it. Like I said, a lot of exorcism concepts that we're familiar with come from the Catholic faith. But you might run into a problem if you go into this with any preconceived ideas based on movies or TV shows. So many of these rituals rely on everyone believing in the same faith or belief system. Whether you burn juniper, sage, or incense, chant or pray to God and the saints, what's to guarantee that whatever is in this boy, if indeed there is anything in him, believes the same things you do? Would a Christian exhortation affect a Jewish or Hindu spirit? Would an Ojibwe ritual even register with a Christian?"

"So you're saying I'd have to know what the… thing believes before I can find an effective solution?"

"I'm not saying anything. I'm the farthest thing from an expert. But it's not as simple as reciting some Bible verses and lighting some incense or burning juniper."

"I don't even know if he is possessed, let alone what is possessing him. It's just that there are so many parallels to a murder that happened fifty years ago—too many to be a coincidence at this point."

"Like what?"

"Like the same house, same number of victims, same sort of murder weapon—maybe even the same exact murder weapon, for all we know, since they're both missing—and it's looking more and more like both killers were teen boys. And then there's the whole magical ritual thing…."

"That *is* an awful lot of similarities. Tell me more about the ritual?"

"Well, the article from the time called it a satanic ritual. The kid who killed his family back in the seventies had carved something into his bedroom floor, a large circle with symbols all around the edge and something carved into the middle."

"Sigil magic."

"What?"

"That's what that sort of spell is sometimes called."

"Do you know much about it?"

"No. Only what it's called. And that I stay far away from it."

"Is it always bad?"

"No. There are those who practice it who say they only use it for good."

"Is it real?"

"As real as any magic. I told you there are different traditions of magic. Who's to say what's real and what isn't? Does that shield knot you're still wearing have any real power? What about prayer? There have been studies that suggest that praying does help, but putting positive thoughts into the world seems to be just as powerful. That leads me to think it's all about belief and intent. The power of an object, a prayer, or a spell all come from the intention and conviction you imbue into it. Does that make sense?"

"Yes, but it sounds like what you're saying is I need to understand more about what the, for lack of a better word, spirit that has possessed Gareth believed. Or believes, I guess."

"I think that would be useful. And if these killings are so similar, it implies that the same being—or spirit, as you put it—is most likely involved in both."

"How is that possible?"

"Can you kill a supernatural being?"

"I have no idea."

"Since I don't know what you're dealing with, neither do I. But it seems to me you can draw a few conclusions. The boy clearly believed in sigil magic, or he wouldn't have gone to all the trouble of carving a casting circle into his floor."

"A casting circle? Is that what it's called?"

"I believe so, yes. Don't quote me. As I said, this is pretty far outside our traditions. Do you know what the sigil in the center is?"

"No, it was mostly covered, and I was afraid to enter the circle to clear it. I didn't know what I was dealing with."

"Caution when dealing with things you don't understand is the epitome of wisdom. It would probably be helpful to know what he was trying to accomplish when he carved it. Or what he did accomplish." Nana frowned. "But I fear we've reached the limits of what I can do to assist you. I think you need more help than I can provide."

"I've reached out to my professor, the one who's a practicing witch, so maybe she'll have some ideas."

"That sounds promising. Let's hope your professor can help."

PROFESSOR LAWSON hadn't responded to my email by the time I left Nana, so I headed back out to the house for more photos.

I parked in my usual spot, then trudged across the field. I was more prepared with an old pair of shoes today, but it was much less muddy than my last hike.

When I reached the house, I didn't waste any time ducking under the police tape and starting up the stairs. The feeling was still there, still making the hair on my arm stand up, but I ignored it and pushed through. It got easier each time.

I hesitated in the door of the room. The carved circle made me even more uncomfortable now that I had more of an idea of what it might be. I took a deep breath and eased into the room. I stared at the circle in dismay. There was no way to clear off the center without stepping into the circle, and until I understood more about its purpose, I wasn't about to do that. It belatedly occurred to me that I should have brought a broom. Then again, maybe there was one somewhere in the house, or something else I could use as a tool.

I went back downstairs and headed back toward the kitchen. That seemed a likely place to store a broom.

A quick glance around didn't reveal anything, but then I noticed a narrow door in the corner of the room near the back door. I crunched my way across the layer of broken glass and pottery and swung open the door.

Eureka!

No, literally, there was a rusty antique Eureka canister vacuum in front me. I'd found the cleaning supplies, and sure enough, propped in the corner was an old broom. Its bristles were doubtlessly brittle and might turn to dust as soon as I touched it, but it should do the job.

I grabbed it and headed back upstairs. I used the broom to push the bulk of the big chunks of debris outside the circle and up against the wall. Then, as best I could from outside the border, I brushed away the rest of the blood-crusted dust and dirt to reveal a crude image carved clumsily into the stained wood.

I took a bunch of photos from various angles; then I cleared the few symbols around the edges to get clearer photos of them as well. Part of the circle was still hidden by the bed, so I dragged it away from the wall and flipped it onto its side, uncovering the entire circumference.

For some reason, seeing the whole of the circle sent a chill down my spine. What was it for? Was it a casting circle, as Nana suggested? If so, what sort of spell was Victor trying to cast? What was he trying to do?

And where was the dagger he'd used to kill his family? Or, for that matter, where was the one used to kill DJ, Kyle, and Wade?

I filed those questions away for later and got back to work. I took photos from all angles, paying special attention to each symbol around the border and the larger design in the center. When I was finished, I attached the photos to an email and sent it off to Jordan.

That finished, my mind returned to the dagger. If the information Mr. Dreisch had given me about the Handy case was right, it didn't seem as if Victor left the house before he mysteriously died, except to throw his family in the well.

But if Victor hadn't left, that meant the dagger had to be somewhere in the house or yard. Mr. Dreisch said they'd searched the house and the well and they hadn't found the dagger anywhere. And Mead's troopers had also searched. But maybe they hadn't searched thoroughly enough. Or maybe they weren't thinking like a teenage boy.

I would do my own search, and I'd start with the most logical place for Victor to hide something—his own room.

I pulled out each drawer in the desk and dresser, testing for false bottoms as I went and checking for things taped to the back or underside. I slid the bookcase out and looked behind that. I even took advantage of the bed being tipped on its side to check inside the box spring and under the mattress. I searched the bedside table as well. Nothing.

That only left the smelly closet. The bed was partially blocking the door, so I rotated it up on its end, clearing the closet. I closed the closet door and kicked it a few times, hoping to scare off any critters that might be living in there.

Then I steeled my nerves and opened the door. Much to my relief, no furry friends leaped out into my face.

I pulled out my phone and turned on the flashlight. The musty smell was even stronger up close. I realized that while some animal urine smell was present, it mostly smelled sour, like mildewed laundry. I looked up and noticed the ceiling had caved in. There must have been a leak in the roof right above us. Water had clearly been running into this area for some time.

I pulled my shirt over my nose and tried to breathe shallowly through my mouth as I began my search. I checked the shelf first. It was filled with chewed-up, mildewed sweaters. Then I spotted a decaying shoebox at the far end. I carefully slid it out and sat it on the desk, where it practically disintegrated when I tried to open it. Inside was a brick of what used to be comic books before years of water, mildew, and heat had fused them together.

I returned to the closet. I sifted quickly through the clothes that were hanging, then knelt to check the floor. Nothing there either.

I was just about to give up and crawl out when I noticed the thin outline of a rectangle on the wall in the far corner of the closet. It faced the bathroom. "What is this?" I said aloud as I pushed the clothes out of the way.

Looked like a pretty ideal hiding place to me. I knelt down to study it closer. I ran a finger along the line. The center panel was perfectly flush with the wall, all painted the same color. Had Victor made this, or was it just some feature of the house?

I studied the panel closely but couldn't see a way to open it. I rapped on it with my knuckles, then pushed on it, but it didn't move at all.

Maybe I could pry it open, but I'd need something very thin. Then I remembered seeing a penknife in the desk drawer. I scrambled back up and scooted around the bed, avoiding the circle, and opened the drawer. Sure enough, there was a small folding knife with a yellowed bone handle.

I grabbed the knife and tried to pull out the blade, but it was stuck after decades of disuse. I fiddled with it for a few minutes but accomplished nothing more than chipping my fingernail, so I finally gave up.

It occurred to me, perhaps belatedly, that there were almost certainly knives in the kitchen. So back downstairs I went. I found a thin-bladed paring knife—rusty, but it would do the job.

Back in the closet, I slid the blade into the crack at the top. A little leverage and the panel popped right out.

I directed the phone light into the opening. At first I only saw pipes, which implied all I'd found was a plumbing access panel. Disappointment washed over me, but then the beam caught something wedged under the pipes and between the studs—a wooden cigar box.

"Ah-ha!" I crowed.

I reached in and carefully extracted the box, then backed out of the closet. I carried the box to the desk, shoved the remnants of the old shoebox and its moldy contents aside, and replaced them with the cigar box, feeling a bit like Indiana Jones.

The moment seemed significant. Whatever was inside this box hadn't been seen since 1973. It could hold the key to my case. Or, at the very least, the key to the Handy case.

I took a deep breath and tried to lift the lid. It stuck. Then I noticed the little corroded brass latch on the front. I snapped it up and the lid lifted easily.

Inside was a small glass bottle, a black leather-bound book, and a thick wad of folded paper. There was a lot of water damage. Much like the comic books, the paper had almost fused together, though not quite to the same extent, and the book was warped, its pages wavy and moldy.

But no dagger.

I left the box and went back for another look in the wall, but I didn't see anything else in the cavity.

With a sigh, I returned to the cigar box. Might as well see what was so important to Victor that he stashed it inside the wall of his bedroom closet.

I gingerly slid the book out from under the paper wad. There was no title on the front cover or spine, so I gently opened the cover and flipped to the title page. *Wards, Spells and Sigils*, it read. So, some sort of spell book?

I sat it on the desk and picked up the bottle. The dried remains of something black coated the inside of its back where it had been lying. I sat the bottle next to the book, then picked up the wad of paper. It looked like loose ruled paper that had been folded in half to make a simple booklet. I slid my finger carefully between the first two sheets and started working the top one loose. The stained, yellowed paper was brittle from getting soaked and drying out repeatedly for several decades. Several times, the paper tore, but I kept working until I managed to free the page.

Inside, I found lines of faint, tiny handwriting in pencil. I struggled to make out the first line.

"*Nobody lakes*— No. *Nobody takes me… seriously,*" I read out loud to the empty room. The second line was "*I'll show them.*"

The wad of papers appeared to be a sort of journal. Somewhere for a maladjusted kid to vent his feelings. He sounded like a bad movie villain, but knowing what he ended up doing gave a lot more gravity to his melodramatic writings.

So, I had a book of spells, a bottle containing an unknown substance that dried up ages ago, and a journal. But what to do with it? I definitely wanted to read the rest of the journal, but dusk was rapidly approaching, and I did not want to be in this house after dark.

"Guess you're coming home with me," I muttered.

But first, I probably needed to check with Mead to make sure it was okay if I took it. It was technically evidence. Granted, evidence from a fifty-year-old closed case, so I doubted he would care.

I pulled out my phone and called Mead.

"Find something?" he barked as a greeting.

"Yes and no. Meaning yes, I found something, but it's only evidence in the Handy murders, not your current case. I came back out to the house to… uh, see if I could find the missing murder weapon."

"But you didn't find the weapon?"

"No."

"What did you find?

"A cigar box. Inside it, there's a book of spells, an empty bottle, and a journal."

"Does it have any bearing on these dead boys?"

"I don't think so."

"Then, Crawford," he said with exaggerated patience, "why are you telling me this?"

"I mean, I didn't want to take something from a crime scene without checking with you first."

"If it doesn't have anything to do with the current case, then I don't give a shit. Sounds like you've got some bedtime reading materials."

"Yeah, sure does."

"You have my blessing to take it. Goodbye."

Before I could say bye, he'd already hung up.

I slid my phone back in my pocket, repacked everything into the box, and tucked it under my arm.

I headed to my office. I could have gone back to the apartment, but I was hesitant to take this stuff into my home.

Since it was after hours, I had the office to myself. As I sat the box on my desk, my stomach growled. It was dinnertime, and I'd skipped lunch in my rush to get to the police barracks.

I ran to the Mexican place next door to our office and got an order of tacos, then returned to my desk to decipher Victor's cramped scribbles.

The work went slowly, and it took several hours before I managed to transcribe as much as I could. Some of the pages were so ruined I couldn't make anything out, some I couldn't get unstuck without destroying, and a large chunk of the pages were just Victor drawing the same symbol over and over—obviously practice before he carved it on his bedroom floor. There was no rhyme or reason that I could find, and no dates. Just odd snippets of rants and random thoughts. Finally, though, I had a transcription of everything I could puzzle out.

Nobody takes me seriously. I'll show them.

I was so mad when they made me move after they found out about me and R, but now I'm going to show them they made a mistake. I'll make them pay. And all the kids at school who make fun of me too. They'll all be sorry.

[unreadable section]

suffer.

[unreadable section]

though lucky for me nobody looked at my books when we moved so I still have all the ones R gave

[unreadable section]

I've been studying and I think I'm almost ready. R said I have to be confident, or it won't work. I memorized the name he gave me. I carved the ritual circle into the floor. I made it the exact same size as my rug so nobody can see it unless the rug is rolled up.

The dagger R gave me is hidden and waiting. I wake up at night sometimes and I can hear it calling me. It is almost

[unreadable section]

Nobody understands. They caught me trying to call R. I knew I'd get in trouble eventually but figured I had until the long-distance bill showed up at least. I think the brat snitched on me. They say R is too old, that it's wrong, that I'm sinning and R is a bad man. If only they knew the truth. He's the only person who ever understood me. He's the one who told me what I was destined for and started training me. Someday, I'll be a high priest just like him. I know it. He told me the prophecy. They can't keep us apart forever.

Bobby and Doug cornered me after school again today. I hate them so much. I can't wait until they are dead.

[several pages of sigils]

Almost ready.

[stuck together pages]

Talked to R today. I skipped class and called him from a pay phone. I reversed charges but he accepted. He told me he could feel my power growing even from there.

He thinks I'm ready. He said it would require a blood sacrifice to

[unreadable section]

and see if it works. I've been practicing painting the sigil in blood.

Tried the ritual for the first time today. I killed Old Man Banks's cat and used the blood. I hate him so I didn't even feel bad. I followed the steps exactly but nothing happened. Maybe I did it wrong. Or maybe it won't work with a dumb cat.

[unreadable section]

didn't work either. Starting to think it needs to be human blood. I'll try my own to

[unreadable section]

filled a bottle with my blood. I have it hidden until I can use it. I have so many cuts and bruises from getting beat on at school nobody even noticed. I'll try the ritual tonight.

Nothing happened.

My mother searched my room today. She said she did it because she thought I was doing dope. She found the books on my shelf, but she didn't find the circle under the rug or my hiding places. She said they were worried about me. She said they thought I'd left that stuff behind me when we moved. She said they did it for me. I told her I never asked to move. I wanted to stay with R. She said R was a pervert. I told her she was a bitch. Now I'm grounded. Not that it matters. I never go anywhere anyway.

It's been weeks since I talked to R. They never let me out of their sight. I have to do something soon. I thought about using the stupid girl next door to complete the

[unreadable section]

right here in my own house. I originally wanted them to suffer before they died but as long as their deaths serve my purpose it will do.

[unreadable section]

tonight. I'll be with R soon.

That was the final entry. While there was a lot missing, I could make some guesses. I assumed R was someone he met while living in New Jersey, most likely an adult who groomed him with grand talk of prophecies, feeding on the kid's insecurities by telling him he was special. It seemed like the guy was into the occult. Victor called him a high priest. In what, though? He'd given Victor the books and a dagger, and it sounded like he was teaching him. I wondered if there was more to the story, based on the tone Victor used when writing about him and his mother calling him a pervert. I didn't know much about the occult, but I knew that sex—both gay and straight—played a big role in some magical belief systems.

He'd said his mother hadn't found his hiding places, plural. That meant I hadn't found all of them either, since I'd only found the one in the closet. The dagger must be in one of his other hidey-holes.

I also had a sneaking suspicion that the dried black crust in the bottle was Victor's blood. I was thoroughly creeped out. I eyed the bottle where it sat on my desk, then put it back in the cigar box so I wouldn't have to look at it.

It seemed that he thought the spell would do something to give him power or somehow punish people he thought had wronged him. The readable parts of his journal didn't say exactly what he was trying to do.

That reminded me of the spell book. Maybe it could shed some light on the subject. I set the journal aside and slid the slim book over. As I did, I noticed a thin slip of paper sticking out of the top. I flipped open to that page and immediately noticed the symbol in the illustration on the marked page was the same as the one Victor had drawn over and over in his journal and then carved into the floor of his room.

The top of the page read *Summoning Sigils*. What—or who—was Victor trying to summon? And did he succeed? Was that what killed him?

I started reading the text on the next page. One section, in particular, jumped out to me.

Once you have chosen the power you wish to summon and know its true name, you are ready to begin. Prepare the space with all the elements represented as described above. Be sure that your mind is calm and clear, your intentions true. Cast the circle and perform the full ritual, and when you are ready, write its name in blood.

Then, speaking loudly and clearly and using the power's true name, speak aloud these words. "Name, by my will, I invoke thee. Name, by my will, I bid thee come. Name, by my will, I call upon you."

Now that you have its attention, it is time to make your request or command. This is where will comes in; you must desire the outcome with all your heart, mind, and soul. You are convincing the power that what you are asking it to do is important, and that you are worthy to ask/make the demand. This must be as specific and limiting as possible to prevent undesired side effects, and it must, of course, be within the scope of the capabilities of the power you invoked.

A word of warning: The spell caster must be willing to accept all of the consequences of the working of the spell not just without reservation but with gratitude. There may also be a price to be paid for such workings. You must be prepared to pay that price willingly, be it incense, a physical gift, a blood sacrifice, a promise to do a favor in return, or your ongoing worship of the power. Many "spirits" have no concept of time, so you may have to pay up front. Note that a sacrifice of someone or something else's blood may not be the only sacrifice you have to make.

Finally, the spell must be closed; all agency must be given over to the power that was invoked, usually by using its name again.

Once you have dismissed the power to do your bidding, undo the casting circle by moving backward through the steps you used to prepare the space.

With a shudder, I sat back. What exactly was Victor trying to summon, and what price did it demand? Did he pay with his life? If so, how did that explain whatever was going on with Gareth? Was the summoned spirit somehow trapped? Was that what was possessing Gareth?

I really wished Victor had said who or what he was trying to summon. He'd only mentioned in passing that "R" had given him the name to use. Maybe he got the name wrong and summoned the wrong thing?

Reading about all this summoning also made me think of my own unintentional summoning. I hadn't gone through anything remotely like what the book described, and yet I'd somehow called Mason back to me. The book said the summoning spell had to be closed, whatever that meant. It specifically said you had to use the name of the entity you'd summoned again. Would that work on Mason? And did I want it to? I'd feel guilty if I… what? Banished him? I couldn't send him away without at least helping him first. I knew I couldn't live with myself if I did that.

Lost in thought, I absentmindedly flipped through the spell book. Several pages past the section Victor had marked, I noticed another sigil that looked almost identical to the one he'd drawn. I flipped back and forth, comparing the two sigils. It reminded me of those games I used to play as a kid where you had to spot the slight differences between two images. It took me a while, but finally I noticed that in the first sigil, the summoning spell, the vertical line that ran through the center reached all the way to the point of the inverted triangle near the bottom, while in the second sigil, the line stopped before it reached the point. It was an incredibly subtle difference.

I got out my phone and pulled up a clear image of the carving. I zoomed in and realized that Victor's carved line didn't quite connect to the point of the triangle, which meant that if these spells were real, he'd possibly cast the wrong one.

I turned the page to see what he might have cast instead of his summoning, and my eyes widened.

It was a spell to release a person's consciousness from their body so they could enter a new willing vessel.

Chapter 18

I SLUMPED back in my desk chair as things started falling into place. But with every question answered, several more bubbled to the surface.

Victor hadn't summoned some spirit of vengeance, as he'd intended. He'd forced his own consciousness—his soul, for lack of a better word—out of his body. And with no "willing vessel" at the ready, what? Was his spirit trapped in the house until someone open to him came along? And was that willing vessel Gareth? If so, what made him willing? And did that mean it was Victor who was watching me through Gareth's eyes, who had spoken to me with Gareth's voice? I shuddered.

More importantly, was Gareth truly willing, or was he somehow tricked into accepting Victor's possession? Was he innocent or complicit?

My mind was racing, but I thought maybe there was something else in the book that might be helpful, some way to undo what Victor had done. I flipped through it again, but nothing stood out to me. There were no reversal spells or anything of the sort. But then something caught my eye—a binding spell. Maybe I couldn't reverse Victor's spell, but perhaps I could still stop him somehow.

I started reading more about the binding spell, but I wasn't sure I understood. For starters, the book wasn't written for beginners. The author was clearly writing from the assumption that his readers would already know what a binding spell did. I could guess, judging by the name, but I didn't know anything about magic, and at least from what I had gathered, it seemed like a rather exact practice, one best not left to guesses and assumptions.

To make matters worse, this section was rather esoteric compared to the relatively straightforward spell casting of summoning.

The enchanted accoutrements of Apuleius's witch and Martina, who attacked Germanicus, included tablets inscribed with the victim's name. Archaeologists have found hundreds of the tablets. The Greeks called them "curses that bind tight," and the late Latin term for them meant "curses that fix or fasten someone." To make such a binding spell, one would inscribe the victim's name and a spell on a thin lead tablet, fold it up, pierce it with a nail, and deposit it in a grave, well, or fountain, placing it in the domain of ghosts or the gods of the underworld who might be entreated to enforce the spell.

What did all of that even mean? Who were Apuleius and Martina? Or Germanicus? Was I supposed to just know them on a first-name basis? Were they mentioned earlier in the book? I didn't really want to read this thing cover to cover like a novel. This wasn't the kind of knowledge I necessarily wanted to take up real estate in my head.

Speaking of my head, I was definitely in over it. I needed to talk to someone who knew more about this sort of magic, and soon.

I checked my email again and was very relieved to see Professor Lawson had replied. She said she had open office hours Monday and I could drop in between noon and two.

It was only Friday night. I didn't want to wait all weekend with this looming over me.

I emailed back, thanking her but explaining that it wasn't class-related and asking if she had any time over the weekend to chat with me about my case. Then I packed all of Victor's hoard carefully away and locked it in my desk before heading home.

I WOKE up entirely too early the next morning thinking about spells, rituals, and sacrifices. I tried to fall back asleep, but my brain was having none of it, so eventually I found myself thinking about Victor and how I could help Gareth.

I was staring up at the ceiling when I sensed someone next to me. I glanced over and somehow wasn't surprised to find Mason sitting cross-legged on my bed.

"Are you just going to randomly appear in my bedroom whenever you feel like it?" I asked.

"Maybe."

"What if I had a guy here? That would be... awkward."

"For you or for me?"

"Why not both?" I pushed myself up into a sitting position, and the blankets slid down to my waist, revealing that I was naked under the covers.

Mason's eyes roved down my chest, and he gave me a lopsided smile. "I see you still sleep naked."

"Don't be a perv."

"Hey, I might be dead but I'm not blind. You're more beautiful than ever. And... there are things I really miss. Like eating. And touching you."

I started to blush at his compliment, but his last words left me blinking away unexpected tears.

I cleared my throat. Time for a change of subject. "That reminds me. I know you've told me before, but when I accidentally summoned you, what was it like?"

"It was like hearing someone calling your name from far away and waking up from a dreamless sleep. Why?"

"This case I'm working on, I think a kid named Victor was trying to perform a much more formal summoning spell."

"What was he trying to summon?"

"I'm not sure. Something supernatural and powerful, I think."

He frowned. "That sounds dangerous."

"Yeah, especially since I think he cast the wrong spell. I don't know."

"The wrong spell?"

"Yeah, instead of summoning something, I think he managed to separate his consciousness from his body."

"So... he accidentally killed himself and became a ghost? Like me?"

I gave Mason a sheepish look. "I think maybe it was more than that. I don't think he was a ghost exactly. I think he was more like... a disembodied soul without a host to move into."

"I feel like we're really splitting hairs here."

"Not really. You exist as this sort of incorporeal energy. I think Victor needed another body to fully exist. I think he was trapped in the house until a willing host came along."

He fell silent, his brow creased in thought. Then, "Wait, did you use a spell to summon me?"

"No. At least I don't think so. I lit a candle and said a prayer, but then I kind of thought about you and spoke your name—your full name."

"I think that's basically a spell."

"What do you mean?"

"What are prayers if not spells?"

"Oh. Yeah. I guess you're right."

"What kind of spell did the kid cast?"

"A very different sort of spell. I think it required some sort of blood sacrifice."

"Jesus. That's intense. So what happened to the kid's spirit? Did a willing host ever come along?"

"I think he might be possessing another kid, who in turn killed all his friends."

"Cav, what are you involved in?"

"I wish I knew."

He was frowning now. "I don't like this."

"Can't say I'm exactly loving it either, but it's my case, and I'm going to see it through the best I can. The first kid killed his entire family fifty years ago, and now three more kids are dead, killed in the exact same way in the exact same house. It's too much to be a coincidence. I'm worried that another kid's life is in danger. Or that he's a danger to others. Or maybe both. I have to find out what happened before more people die."

Mason shook his head. "Promise me you'll be careful."

"I'll do my best." My stomach growled just then. We both smiled. "I think that's my cue to get my ass up and eat."

His eyes roamed back down to my exposed hip. "Don't let me stop you."

I threw back the blankets with a sigh and jumped up, turning away as I pulled on the pair of underwear I'd left on the floor next to the bed. I turned back to face him with my arms held out at my side. "There. Happy now?"

His eyes hadn't left me. He gave me a sad smile. "I'd be happier if you hadn't put on the underwear, even if they are awfully cute on you."

I dropped my arms. "I, uh… I miss touching you too, by the way."

He shook his head and looked away. "Maybe you're right. Maybe I shouldn't just pop in whenever I feel like it."

I cocked my head to the side. "Where do you go when you're not here?"

"Not far. It's getting harder and harder to be far from you. When you leave, I feel… drained. I usually just… go back to sleep, for lack of a better explanation."

"What's that like?" I asked as I pulled on some shorts.

"Kind of how I imagine it would be like in a sensory deprivation tank. It's just dark and nothingness. It's not unpleasant. I can think if I try hard enough, but it's easier to just… be. I can feel when you're nearby. If I want to resurface, I can."

"So if I wanted to talk to you, I could call you and you'd hear me?"

"I think so?"

"Even without the candle?"

He shrugged, and I reminded myself that this was all just as new to him as it was to me. "This is so wild. Is that what you're going to do now? Go to sleep?"

"Maybe I'll come with you to the kitchen."

"Sure. Just don't, you know, move anything around if Haniah shows up."

He laughed. "But can you imagine her face if I did?"

I laughed too as I pulled a sweatshirt over my head. Then another thought occurred to me. "Hey, have you tried through walls yet?"

He rolled his eyes. "Duh. That was one of the first things I did once I calmed down."

"Show me!"

"What is this? Party tricks with Ghost Mason? If you've seen ghosts all your life, you've seen it before."

I waggled my eyebrows. "But not you doing it."

Mason got up with an exaggerated sigh and came around the bed. Then, with a pointed look in my direction, he just faded through the door.

I was still watching with a delighted grin when he reemerged. "I've always wanted to ask, what does it feel like when you do that? Can you even feel it?"

He screwed up his face. "Yeah, but it's hard to explain. Things that are physical have a sort of… resistance to them. I can feel that, but I can just move through it if I want. But that's also how I can move things or sit or whatever. When I feel that resistance, instead of passing through, I just sort of… focus my energy. Does that make sense?"

"Not really, but it's very cool."

"Glad you think so. Does that mean you're satisfied?"

"For now." Then, since I did not possess such powers, I opened the door and headed for the kitchen with Mason following.

I was trying to decide what to make when I got the idea to surprise Haniah with breakfast. I grabbed a loaf of bread and got out eggs, milk, sugar, cinnamon, and vanilla.

"What are you making?" Mason asked.

"French toast," I answered.

He made a little moaning sound. "Oh God, I miss your french toast."

It was one of the few things I could make really well. I started preparing the custard. "It's really Jason's recipe," I said as I worked. "He taught me how to make it. I haven't made it since—" I hadn't made it since Mason died. "I haven't made it in a while," I finished lamely. I could tell Mason knew what I'd left unsaid.

I soaked the bread slices and set them aside while I melted some butter in a pan. That done, I fried each slice until it was golden brown. Mason didn't say much, just stayed out of the way and watched me cook.

I was finishing up when Haniah appeared in the kitchen doorway, bleary-eyed, barefoot, and in a long oversize tee. I glanced up at her, then over to where Mason stood by the fireplace. I was nervous she'd somehow sense him or something, but she didn't react at all, even when her eyes followed my gaze.

She eyed me suspiciously. "What are you doing?"

"Making us breakfast. What's it look like?"

"Why do you look guilty?"

"I don't."

"You do."

"I was just going to surprise you with a delicious feast, but you, uh, ruined the surprise." Mason snorted from behind me, but I didn't acknowledge him.

Haniah gave me a look. "Fine, I'm surprised. What are you making?"

"My special french toast."

"What makes it special?"

"Love."

"Ew."

I laughed. "It's Jason's recipe. It's very good, I promise."

She sniffed. "We'll see. Did you make enough for three?"

For a moment I panicked, thinking she meant Mason, but then she glanced down the hall toward her room. "I… guess? Do we, uh, have a guest?"

She gave a nonchalant shrug. "Maybe. Is it okay if she stays for breakfast?"

I fought the urge to sigh with relief. Instead I just raised an eyebrow. "Sure." I rarely met any of Haniah's nocturnal guests unless it was in passing as they were arriving or leaving. She'd never invited one to stay for a meal. "Should I make some eggs too?"

"Scrambled, please, with cheese." And with that, she turned and padded off down the hall.

"If three's a crowd, what is four?" Mason asked as soon as she was gone.

"At this point, I think it's a séance," I said in a soft, dry voice.

Mason snorted again. "Fine, I can take a hint. I'm going back to your bedroom." He started to leave but paused in the doorway. "Maybe you should get a TV or something for your room and you could just leave it on now and then."

I rolled my eyes and made a shooing motion. "Go haunt someone else for a while."

He narrowed his eyes. "You haven't even seen a haunting yet, Cav Crawford. Don't piss me off." Then he spun and exited the kitchen dramatically.

I chuckled and turned on the oven, then got the eggs back out. As I cracked eggs into a bowl and started whisking, I could hear movement and low voices coming from the hallway. Then the bathroom door closed and the shower turned on, followed a few minutes later by giggles.

I smiled to myself as I continued to prepare the eggs. I stacked the french toast on a cookie sheet and slid it into the oven to stay warm, then put a clean pan on the burner, turned it on, and thew some butter in.

I was plating the fluffy eggs and sprinkling some extra cheese on top when Haniah reappeared in the kitchen, followed by a pretty girl around my height. She was Black, with close-cropped hair and big brown eyes. She gave me a smile, which I returned.

"Cav, this is Ayanna. Ayanna, this is my roommate, Cav."

I waved. "Hi! Hope you're hungry."

"I'm ravenous!" Ayanna said with a giggle. "It smells so good. Thank you for cooking."

"My pleasure," I said. Then I added to Haniah, "Just don't get too used to it."

"Too late," she said, and we all laughed.

I pulled the french toast out of the oven and served up breakfast with maple syrup on the side. We chatted while we ate. Ayanna was really sweet and very funny. I could see why Haniah liked her.

After we finished eating, I cleaned up while Haniah and Ayanna retreated to Haniah's room. When the last dish was in the dishwasher, I checked my email. Much to my surprise, Professor Lawson had replied already. She gave me her cell phone number and asked me to call her.

I checked the time. It was a little after ten, which seemed late enough to call your professor on a Saturday morning, so I went to my room and closed the door. There was no sign of Mason. I dialed the number.

"Ah, yes. Good morning, Cav," Professor Lawson said after I introduced myself. "I see I finally have your attention, just still not in class."

I gave a nervous laugh. "Hey! I've been better. And this isn't totally unrelated."

"You are, and I assumed not. Why else would you want to talk to me? So what's this about?"

"The case I'm working on has some possible… occult aspects?" I wasn't sure how to explain it. "I remembered that at the beginning of the semester, when you were introducing yourself, you said you were a…." I faded out.

"A witch?" she finished for me. I could hear her smile over the line. "Yes. Among other things. You can say it, you know. It's not a dirty word."

I chuckled sheepishly. "Right. I was hoping I could show you some things and ask you some questions."

"What kinds of things?"

"Some photos I took at a murder scene of what I think is some sort of casting circle, or maybe a summoning circle. Definitely something intended for a ritual of some sort. And a spell book I found that the person who made the circle might have used. Except I think they may have cast the wrong spell. And maybe separated their soul from their body. And might be possessing someone else now. And maybe used that body to kill more people."

That was met with dead silence. Finally she said, "Is this a joke?"

"No, I promise you. I… I'm very much out of my depth."

"Most people would be."

"Do you think you can help me?"

She sighed heavily. "I don't know if I can help or not. This isn't exactly something to handle over the phone, though."

"I know this is an imposition, but is there any way we could meet this weekend? It's kind of urgent."

"On one condition."

"What's that?"

"That you give that paper you're writing just a fraction of the energy you're giving your case."

"I, uh…."

"Look, I know my class isn't a matter of life and death, but if you find me a valuable enough resource for your case, then maybe, just maybe, I'm teaching something equally valuable."

"You're right. And I'm sorry."

"Let's call it a lesson learned. Let's see, it's a little after ten. I can probably make some time for you this afternoon. Would that work?"

"Yes, that's great. Thank you so much."

"How about one o'clock, then?" She gave me her address, and I said I'd text her when I parked.

As soon as we hung up, I called Jordan on his cell. "Hey! Did you get a chance to work on those photos I sent you yesterday?" I asked as soon as he answered.

"Cav. It's Saturday."

"I know, but it's urgent."

"Then lucky for you I finished it and just hadn't sent it to you yet."

"Is there any way you can send it to me now? I'm going to meet with an expert on all things occult this afternoon."

"That sounds fascinating. I'll have to run by the office to send it to you."

"Is your computer locked? I need to go in to get something from my office anyway. If you tell me how to find it, I can send it to myself."

"I guess I trust you," he said teasingly, then gave me his password and told me where he'd saved the file. I hung up, took a shower, and dressed. I was about to head to the office when I remembered Mason's request. I didn't have a TV, but I did have a laptop. I booted it up, then opened Netflix and turned on a movie.

"Hey, Mason?" I called softly.

He popped into view. I smiled and gestured to the computer screen.

He looked over with a grin that quickly twisted into an eye-rolling grimace. "*Ghostbusters*? Really? You're so hilarious."

I laughed. "What would you like to watch? I'll set something up before I leave."

He shook his head. "Nah, this is fine. It's a classic. Uh, thanks."

"No problem." I waved and headed out, closing my bedroom door before I left.

I swung by the office, found the file where Jordan said it would be, and sent it to my email. Then I grabbed the cigar box and its contents from my desk, locked up, and left.

I had some time to kill before I went to Professor Lawson's house. It hit me that I was going to my professor's house, and that was kind of weird, right? I guess it didn't have to be. I just hadn't done it before. Rationally, I knew my professors had lives outside of school, but I hadn't thought too much about it. What would her house be like?

I'd find out soon enough.

In the meantime, I sent Kyreh a text asking what he was up to. He responded within seconds saying he was free and bored. I asked if he wanted to hang out for a few hours, and in response, he told me to meet him at his dorm room.

I pulled out of the parking lot and headed toward school. When I arrived at Kyreh's dorm, I realized my ID didn't have access to this building. I was about to text him to let me in when a clique of girls spilled out, and I slipped in before the door closed behind them. I made my way up to the fourth floor and knocked on Kyreh's door.

He looked surprised when he opened up. "How did you get in?" he asked.

For a moment I forgot how to speak. Kyreh was shirtless with his hair down, only wearing a tiny pair of silky, worn soccer shorts that looked like he'd had them since high school. His chest was every bit as chiseled as I'd pictured. I had a desperate urge to reach out and run my hands across his pecs, but I somehow resisted. Instead, I gathered my wits and managed to reply. "I'm a private investigator. I, uh, have my ways."

He shook his head and laughed. "Sorry, I thought I had a few more minutes. Come on in so I can get dressed."

I stepped into his room, and he shut the door behind me. I tried not to stare as he started rummaging for something to put on. I distracted myself by looking around his room. It was a pretty typical dorm room shared by two guys. It wasn't messy per se, but it also wasn't exactly neat, and there was a decided lack of décor.

"Where's your roommate?" I asked.

He pulled a T-shirt out of a pile of clothes on the floor and sniffed it. "He's out of town until Monday. He's actually gone a lot on weekends. His folks live a few hours away, and he has a girlfriend at home. It's nice. Means I get the room to myself for a few nights."

"For all your hookups?"

He glanced up, but I couldn't quite read his expression. "Would that bother you?"

I shrugged and wished I hadn't made such a dumb joke. "No. Why should it? I was just kidding."

He smirked and pulled the shirt over his head. Guess it had passed inspection. "Yeah, I know," he said as he started looking for pants. "I'm just giving you a hard time. But to answer your question, it's been a while since I had anyone over."

"Oh," I said, sounding dumb even to myself.

He shot me another sideways glance as he shook out a rumpled pair of jeans. "You might say I have my sights set on someone."

I blinked. Was there somebody else? Maybe he just wanted to be friends after all. If so, that was probably for the best. I was still so mixed up over Mason. But damn. Had I just been imagining our chemistry?

Suddenly I realized he was standing there waiting for me to say something. "Oh yeah? Do I know him?"

He shrugged and then, without warning, shucked off his shorts. He stood there a moment as I desperately tried to not drop my eyes to the bulge I could see in my peripheral vision. "Maybe," he finally said as he pulled on the pants with a little hop that made his package bounce. He buttoned and zippered them while watching me. "But I can't figure him out."

"What do you mean?" I hoped I sounded as casual as he did, because I felt anything but.

"I don't know if he's interested or not. I'm getting mixed signals."

"Then maybe you should just ask him."

He tilted his head and looked me over. "Maybe so." Then he turned and grabbed a balled-up pair of socks and sat on his bed to pull them on. "So what did you want to do? You said you only have a few hours?"

"Uh, yeah. I didn't have anything in mind, but I have a meeting at one."

He frowned. "That's not much time, then. Have you eaten?"

"Yeah, but I'll go with you if you're hungry."

"I'm starving." He stood up and slid on a pair of shoes. "Let's hit the Nest." And with that, he pulled open the door and gestured for me to go first.

We made small talk as we crossed the campus to the Wasp's Nest, but there was an odd tension between us that wasn't usually there. Or maybe it was just me.

Once at the café, he ordered a bacon, egg, and cheese breakfast sandwich with avocado and a coffee milkshake. I just got a coffee.

We grabbed a table and waited for his order to be called. He fiddled with the sugar packets I'd grabbed for my coffee, seemingly lost in thought.

"Hey," I said softly after watching him for a minute. "You okay?"

He looked up and gave me a distracted smile. "Sorry. Just in my head today."

"Yeah, you seem to be in a mood. Anything you want to talk about? I'm here for you. Is it just the guy you were talking about in your room?"

He studied me for a moment. "You know, for such a smart guy, you can be kind of dense sometimes."

"What? Oh!" My eyes widened. "Were you... were you talking about me?"

He laughed. "Yes, Cav, I was talking about you."

"I've been giving you mixed signals?"

"The most mixededed."

"That's not a word."

"That's not the point."

"How have I been sending mixed signals?"

"One minute you're all flirty or you look at me in a certain way that makes me think you're interested, and the next you say things like you're not ready for a relationship. I get that maybe you're not really over your last boyfriend or whatever, and I'm cool with just being friends, but then you eye-bang me like a piece of meat."

My heart was racing. I opened my mouth to deny "eye-banging" him, but he cut me off before I could get a word out.

"If you are into me, it would be nice to know. I don't mind waiting while you figure things out. I can be patient if something is worth waiting for, but I need to know if there's even any point in waiting. I need to know how you feel. About me, I mean."

"How do you feel about me?" I tried turning the question back around on him.

"I asked you first."

I couldn't argue with that ironclad logic, but before I could come up with a response, they called his name.

"Hold that thought," he said as he stood up. "I expect an answer when I get back."

He went to grab his food while I sat there, head spinning, trying to decide what to say. He was back long before I was ready, sliding into his side of the booth.

"So," he said as he unwrapped his sandwich, "where were we?" He took a big bite, his eyes never leaving mine.

I inhaled deeply. "I've really liked hanging out with you these last few weeks, getting to know you. I've had a lot of fun."

He swallowed. "Me too. Go on."

I glanced around. "Is this really the best place for this conversation?"

He raised one eyebrow. "Are you worried about someone overhearing us, or are you avoiding my question?"

I stuck my tongue out at him. "You've been taking too many psych classes."

He laughed. "So which is it?"

"Okay, fine, I guess you could say I'm into you. I mean, I'm attracted to you. Very attracted to you. You're funny, smart, really fun to be around, and sexy as all get-out."

He looked surprised my sudden confession. He set his sandwich down, his lips twitching. "Sexy, huh?"

I rolled my eyes. "Duh. You knew what you were doing with your little show back in your room. Was that planned?"

He broke into a grin. "I wouldn't say it was planned. I just saw an opportunity and took it."

"And by taking an opportunity you mean you did a strip show."

"You should have seen your face. You looked like you didn't know if you should run or tackle me."

"Those were the two options warring in my head. *But*...." I emphasized the word. "You're also right that I'm kind of mixed up still. I'm not sure what I'm really looking for. There's a lot going on in my life right now, and things are, let's just say, not really settled with Mason."

"What do you mean by not settled? He died, right?"

I shook my head. "Yes, but it's not that simple."

"I didn't mean to imply it was, but—" He broke off and his eyes widened. "Wait. Does this have anything to do with what you told me about seeing ghosts? Is your dead boyfriend, like, haunting you?"

I stared at him aghast and looked around to make sure no one had heard him. "Shh!" I admonished. Then in a lower voice, "Haunting is a strong word. And it's kind of my fault."

"How is it your fault?"

"I may have accidentally summoned him."

"Accidentally?"

I shrugged. "Well, it wasn't on purpose. At least not the first time. And now I think I'm kind of stuck with him. For now, at least."

Kyreh sat for a minute, then picked up his sandwich and took another bite. He chewed, then swallowed and took a sip of his milkshake. "Okay. So I guess I can see how that might complicate things. Are you guys still, like... dating?"

I frowned. "How would I date a ghost?"

He threw his hands up, still holding his sandwich and sending a little piece of avocado arcing through the air. "I don't know. How do you summon a ghost?"

"Right. Sorry."

"Then you're not dating?"

"No!"

"But you have the ghost of your dead boyfriend hanging around all the time."

"Not all the time. He just sort of... pops up now and then. And I can call him when I want."

"So you have a pet ghost."

"I.... What? No!"

"I'm kidding. But it's definitely weird, right?"

I nodded.

Kyreh looked around, as if expecting Mason to materialize at our table. "So where is he right now?"

"I left him in my bedroom. Watching a movie."

"Watching a...." He scrunched up his face. "What movie does a ghost like to watch?"

"*Ghostbusters*," I admitted in a small voice.

He threw back his head and laughed. "Now I know you're fucking with me," he said when he got himself under control.

"I'm not, actually. I put it on as a joke, but then he actually wanted to watch it. He said it's a classic."

Kyreh stared at me in disbelief. "Well, this officially tops our last late-night chat as the strangest conversation I've ever had."

"Go me!" I said with sarcasm. "I guess I've scared you off now, huh? Oh hey, you never said how you felt about me."

"Obviously I like you, you big dummy. We wouldn't be having this bizarre conversation in the first place if I didn't. And no, you haven't scared me off."

"So... what does that mean, then?"

"What do you want it to mean?"

"I don't know. You're the one who started this."

"Fair enough. I don't want to rush you or make you feel uncomfortable, but I guess I'd like to see where this"—he gestured to the two of us—"might go. We don't have to put a label on it right now, and I don't have any expectations other than getting to know you better. Does that sound reasonable?"

I nodded. "Yeah. That sounds really good."

"Great. Then maybe we could go on a real date."

"As opposed to a fake date?"

"As opposed to the friend dates we've been going on."

"What's the difference?"

"I don't know. Intention? It doesn't have to be anything crazy. I can't afford to take you to a fancy restaurant or anything."

"That's fine. I'm not really into the whole fancy restaurant thing. Just doing something with you is enough. I don't care if we just watch a movie together."

"With or without Mason?"

"Definitely without."

"Good answer. How about tonight?"

"Tonight?"

"Too soon?"

"No. I just don't know how the rest of my day is going to shake out after this meeting." I checked the time on my phone. "Which, speaking of the meeting, I need to leave soon to make it on time. Can I let you know about tonight after my meeting?"

"Sure."

"Cool. Then I'll talk to you soon." I said and started to slide out of the booth.

Kyreh caught my hand as I stood up. "Hey, Cav, I'm glad we had this conversation."

I gave him a big smile. "Me too."

Chapter 19

I ARRIVED at the address Professor Lawson had given me to find it was in Charles Village in the middle of a block of two-story brick rowhouses with colorful front porches. I found a parking spot and got to practice my parallel parking, something I didn't have to do much on campus or at my apartment, which had a driveway. It took me three tries, but I finally managed to squeeze my car into a spot.

I shot off a quick text to Professor Lawson, tucked the box under my arm, found the right house, and rang the bell.

"Are you a good witch or a bad witch?" I mumbled under my breath while I waited for her to answer the door.

A few moments later, Professor Lawson opened the door. She looked very different from how I was used to seeing her in class. She usually wore pantsuits or professional outfits to teach, but today she was barefoot in a loose embroidered blouse and a pair of faded jeans. It made her a little less intimidating.

She gave me an appraising look and stepped back. "Come on in, Cav."

"Thank you for agreeing to see me," I said as I stepped into her house. I found myself in her living room, a comfortable space with an exposed brick wall running the length of the house. The walls were painted warm colors—rusty oranges and red ochres—and the furniture looked comfortable and inviting. Abstract oil paintings hung on the walls, and a bookshelf held equal parts books and knickknacks.

Professor Lawson watched me look around. "My cauldron is out for cleaning, sorry," she said with a little smirk.

I chuckled. "Your home is beautiful."

"Thank you. Have a seat and let's see what you've brought me."

I took a seat on the couch and sat the cigar box on the coffee table.

"Actually," she said as she took a nearby chair, "before we get to that, maybe you should tell me the whole story so I have a better idea of the context."

I quickly filled her in on the case, about the missing boys and how Gareth's parents hired me, and how that case led me to the Handy murders and what I'd found in Victor's room. She listened with narrowed eyes as I caught up to the present.

"I can see how this might distract you in class," she said when I finished. "I'll be honest with you: this is a lot. You're definitely in over your head, and I may be too."

"Do you think you can help me?"

"Maybe. I'm not sure. This sort of thing isn't exactly in my wheelhouse. I'm not sure what I can do except maybe help you understand better what you're dealing with."

"So it's definitely all real?"

"What do you mean?"

"This kind of magic, spells and rituals."

"That depends on what you mean by real. What makes one supernatural belief more real than another? Because you've grown up surrounded by Christian theology in a decidedly theocratic nation, you probably accept the rituals surrounding that particular brand of ecclesiastical pomp as valid. But what's the difference between a Catholic crossing themselves and the hamsa of the Middle East? Or drinking wine and eating bread that represent—or, depending on your particular religious sect, actually magically transform into—the blood and body of a deity and performing a sacrifice? Everyone thinks their god or gods are the right ones, and everyone else somehow got it wrong. It's all just humans trying to make sense of the universe. None of it is more nor less real than anything else.

"Now, if you're asking can someone really summon a spirit or transfer their consciousness into another body, that's another matter altogether. If you accept the existence of beings that move on another plane—whether that's ghosts, angels, demons, whatever—then it's reasonable to infer that contact or influence might be possible. Even if you're coming from a strictly Christian point of view, those things are described quite frequently in the Christian Bible.

"Magic can be defined as the art of controlling or channeling various kinds of invisible forces, often thought of as intelligent spirits. Pretty much everything we think of as magic is all about belief and intent. Are you following?"

I nodded. "I'm with you."

"Good. I hate explaining myself twice." She gave me a grin.

"For the record," I said, "I'm not Christian. I guess you could say I'm an atheist, or maybe… pagan? My family is Irish, and we do believe in the Sight, but I wasn't raised with any particular religious beliefs. My grandmother is just now starting to teach me some of our family's more traditional beliefs."

"Interesting! I'd love to talk to you more about that some time, but let's not get distracted. You mentioned traditional beliefs, though, and that's a good starting point. An awful lot of modern Christianity is directly borrowed from, and in some cases outright stolen from, other belief systems. There's a lot of pagan traditions with some saint or sacrament copied and pasted over it. But that's not why you're here, and that's a much longer conversation than we have time for today—just pay attention in class. So, let's see your spell."

I took out my phone and pulled up the email I'd sent myself from Jordan's account, then opened the photo. I passed my phone to Professor Lawson.

She pushed her glasses down her nose and peered at the photo over the top. She frowned and zoomed in. Then she handed me my phone back. "This isn't my tradition, so I can't tell you much about that sigil except it's ugly business."

I opened the box and pulled out the spell book. "Well, I found this hidden in his closet." I held it out to her. She hesitated a moment, then took it.

"What is it?"

"A spell book. Victor marked the page of the sigil I think he was trying to use. It's the first slip of paper."

She opened the book and scanned the page, her frown deepening as she flipped the page. I let her read until she looked at me.

"The second marker, the sticky note, I added. It's a sigil that looks an awful lot like the one you just read about."

I waited while she flipped to that one and read.

"They do look similar, and actually, the spells aren't as different as they might seem. They're both asking for assistance from something very powerful. One is summoning the power to do your bidding, and the other is summoning it for a very specific bidding."

"So the power is what separates your consciousness from your body?"

"Yes. The first sigil leaves the bidding a little more open-ended so you can ask or demand what you want. The second is more tightly controlled, but they are variations on the same spell. Why do you think it was the second one Victor cast?"

I pulled the photo back up, zoomed in on the sigil, and handed the phone back to her. "The line isn't complete at the bottom," I said.

She studied it closely for a moment, then nodded. "You're right. And that's the sort of oversight that matters when dealing with these powers. From my understanding, they follow the letter of the law very closely, regardless of intent. That's why we have all those stories about phrasing your wishes very carefully when confronted by the jinn or faeries."

"Jinn?"

"Genies."

"Are they real too?"

She looked at me as if I were a particularly disappointing student. "Do I need to give that whole speech again?"

"I thought they were just fairy tales."

"It's dangerous to dismiss fairy tales, the stories told around the fire or in the dark. Those stories survived and were passed down for a reason, and it's not just because they're good tales. They are prescriptive and protective, warnings for those who remained, memories of the Thing that Must Not Be Forgotten. The jinn are every bit as plausibly real as angels. Whatever form they may take in our reality, however, would be far different from a Disney movie. In fact, what the Arabic tradition calls a jinn is quite possibly the same sort of being that is being conjured by these spells. Different cultures may have different takes on the same entities."

"Okay, but does that mean it's possible Victor accidentally separated his consciousness from his body?"

"Very possible."

"And what would happen if he did that without a…. What's it called in the book? A willing vessel?"

"A willing vessel, yes. I think—and again, I preface this by saying this is not my area of expertise—his consciousness would be bound to the place where he performed the ritual until such a time as he found a suitable vessel or his spirit was released."

"Released?"

"Yes. If the circle was destroyed, he'd have been free to roam until he found a vessel."

I shuddered. "And what would constitute a willing vessel? If what I suspect is correct and Victor is, for lack of a better word, possessing Gareth, did Gareth have to agree to the possession?"

"In my understanding, yes. He would have had to consent in some way. You said they were ghost hunting, right?"

"Yes."

"Then it could be as simple as him saying 'if there's anything here, come to us now,' or something to that effect. That would be enough of an invitation for an angry disembodied spirit."

"Fuck. Oh, uh, sorry."

"Fuck doesn't offend me," she said dryly.

"That poor kid. He says he doesn't remember anything that happened between his disappearance and when he was found a week later, and he keeps losing chunks of time. Would the possession affect his memory?"

"Possibly, at least when Victor takes control. To keep Gareth from fighting him, he probably has to force Gareth into what amounts to sleep or a temporary coma."

"He keeps having seizures too."

"That's probably Gareth fighting for control on a subconscious level."

"Is there a way to free Gareth?"

"That's hard to say. It would depend on how much control Victor has wrested from Gareth or exactly how willing a vessel Gareth was. A deal is a deal…."

"What do you mean?"

"If Gareth deliberately and knowingly invited Victor in, that's essentially a contract, and that would be much harder to break. If it was more of a technicality, like I described before, then you might have a loophole big enough to free him."

"This all sounds like a legal fight."

"That's basically what it is, except depending on what you're dealing with, it may not think the same way you do."

"What I'm dealing with?"

"You're assuming at this point that it is Victor, but you don't know that for sure. You have to be prepared for the possibility that it's another entity altogether, perhaps not human in origin."

"What would that mean?"

"It would affect how you deal with it. A timeless otherworldly power is going to take a lot more force, wits, and strategy than a disembodied teenager."

"Which is worse?"

"They're both dangerous, but in different ways. The spirit is potentially powerful and unpredictable, but they aren't necessarily inherently evil any more than people are. The spirit world likely has a very different moral code than we do. They may not see us any differently than we see, say, an ant or a mosquito. If you step on an ant hill or swat a mosquito, you don't give it a second thought. It's not what we would consider evil.

"Humans, on the other hand, well, we know they are capable of great evil. If it is Victor, he's already killed his entire family and probably influenced Gareth to kill his friends or killed them through him."

"Assuming it is Victor, is it possible to get him out of Gareth? Like an exorcism?"

"Exorcism is not my area of study. In America, our primary frame of reference for exorcism is Catholicism, and even that is mostly from popular culture. Most other cultures have their own methods and beliefs surrounding casting out spirits that may be possessing someone or something, but I'm far from an expert."

"My grandmother said that we'd probably have to know Victor's beliefs for an exorcism to be effective anyway."

She looked impressed. "Your grandmother sounds like a smart lady. I think knowing Victor's belief system would certainly help. But even more important would be understanding what he was trying to accomplish. If this kid was an actual Satanist—and not in the modern Satanic Temple sort of way—that's often the opposite side of the coin from Catholicism, so who knows. But this isn't the sort of thing you want to go into unprepared."

"Right. Victor was raised Methodist. The article mentioned he had occult books, though."

"Either way, I don't think an exorcism is what you need here. Even if you free—or destroy—his current vessel, Victor's consciousness will still have to be dealt with or he'll just move on looking for his next vessel now that he's been freed from the circle. You'll need to trap or bind him somehow."

That reminded me of something. I grabbed the book and started flipping through it. "What about a binding spell?"

She thought for a moment. "That could work."

I found the page I was looking for and held it out to her. "What about this one?"

She read over it with a look of concentration, then handed me the book. "That one is a little simple. I'm not sure it would be strong enough to physically bind him."

"I only have a vague idea of what a binding spell is. Why wouldn't this one work?"

"A binding spell is intended to keep an entity from doing harm to themselves or others. It binds their will. In some cases, depending on the spell, it could even bind someone or something to a specific location. The spell in this book may not work because it isn't specific enough."

"Do you know of a stronger one?"

She frowned. "I'm a lightworker. I wasn't always, but as I've grown older, my views and feelings have changed. Binding spells are no longer a part of my practice."

"Why is that?"

"Many magic practitioners believe in the power of three, meaning whatever energy a person puts out into the world, be it positive or negative, will be returned to that person threefold. I also believe there's enough negativity in this world. I don't want to contribute to it. But most importantly, I don't believe in casting a spell that impinges on another being's free will."

"Even if that person is a murderer?"

I could tell that hit her, so I pressed on. "Please. I don't know how to stop him. I need your help, even if you just tell me what to do and I do it myself. Or maybe you know someone else who would be willing to help. It could save lives. Surely that's a net positive for the world."

She sighed. "I'll help you. I know a very powerful binding spell. It's a Kolossos, or an ancient Greek poppet."

"Poppet?"

"A poppet is basically a doll. You've seen voodoo dolls, right?" I nodded yes. "Those are a type of poppet. They're an effigy representing a person. Many traditions use poppets, and there are many regional differences. They're used for healing, which is the only way I've used them for a very long time, but they can also be used defensively or even to destroy. A Kolossos is primarily defensive. It can be used to contain a hostile force. It's… as far as I'm willing to go."

"Okay. Containing Victor would be a good start."

"You're still acting as if you're sure you're dealing with Victor. I caution you again that you can't be sure of that."

"Then what do you recommend?"

"I'll make you a poppet for Victor, but if it turns out to be something other than him, you can't use it. It will be ineffective and quite possibly cause more harm than good, especially to you."

"If it's not Victor, what do I do? Could I bind whatever it is?"

"That would be a lot more difficult. You'd need to know its true name, at the very least."

"How would I find that out?"

"You probably won't be able to. It would never tell you willingly, and since I don't know what else you could be dealing with, I don't have any advice for you."

"Then we'd better hope it's Victor. What do you need to make the poppet?"

"For starters, the spell will be a lot more effective if you have something from the person you are attempting to bind, like a hair, fingernail clippings, or even a piece of their clothes."

"I wish I'd known that. There's an entire dresser and closet filled with his clothes back at the house." I thought for a second, then remembered the bottle. "What about his blood?"

Her eyes widened. "Why do you have his blood?"

"He collected it in a bottle when he was trying to get the spell to work." I grabbed the bottle from the box and held it up. "It's dry now, but we could probably scrape some out…."

Her face paled. "That is dark magic, but very, very powerful. It would unquestionably work. Now, I just need to think…. What should we use to stuff it?"

"Stuff it?"

"As I said, it's a doll. There are different methods, but I make mine out of fabric. I may have one already made, but it's not stuffed because what you stuff it with depends on the purpose of the poppet. For instance, a poppet intended to heal may contain medicinal herbs or crystals."

"What about his journal?" I showed her the wad of paper. "We could shred it. I've already transcribed it."

"That could work. It would make the connection even stronger since the journal was written in his own hand. I could write the binding spell on the paper as well. Many poppets have a spell inside." She stood up and pulled out a drawer from a small table, then produced a notebook and a pen. "What is Victor's full name?"

"Victor Handy," I said.

"Do you know his mother's name?"

"Um, hang on. I can check my notes."

I pulled up my notes on my phone. "Ellen."

"Excellent. I'll also include a combination of binding herbs."

"My grandmother was an herbalist before she was paralyzed. She's told me a little about the power of herbs just recently. She said if she was going to make a protection ward, she'd need certain herbs, but I can't remember what she said. Maybe… rowan berries? Foxglove? There were more."

She looked intrigued. "I'd love to meet your grandmother sometime."

"She'd probably love to meet you too. What would you use for a binding spell?"

"I'm not an herbalist, but I have some general knowledge. Sage and cedar are certainly two herbs I would consider for this. Rue, mandrake, thistle, wolfsbane, and yarrow would all work."

"Yarrow was another herb my grandmother mentioned. You have all of those on hand?"

"Not all, no, but enough."

"Okay. What do I need to do?"

"Right now? Nothing. I'll explain what to do with the poppet when you get back."

"Get back?"

"This could take a while. I'm not sure where everything is, so I'm going to have to do a lot of digging through things I don't use very often."

"This is kind of urgent. How long do you think it will take?"

"Only an hour or two. I'm not talking about days."

"Oh, okay. In that case, is there somewhere I can go nearby to kill some time?"

"There are several cafés over by the Hopkins campus." She gave me directions to a nearby café and reluctantly held out her hand for the bottle and journal, and I handed them over, but she just sat there staring down at them. She seemed especially disturbed by the bottle and its crusty contents, not that I could blame her.

"I'm sorry," I said suddenly.

She looked up at me in surprise. "For what?"

"For asking you to do this. I know it's against your beliefs. If there was any other way.... Maybe you could just tell me what to do and I could do it with your supervision. You could even give me more extra credit!"

She was shaking her head before I'd even finished. "While I appreciate the sentiment, and you could definitely use all the extra credit you can get, this is powerful magic. To have any chance of working, it needs to be done exactly right. We can't risk you making a mistake that could put your life—and the lives of others—at risk. No, I'll do it. Come back in an hour."

She stood up and showed me out.

The first thing I did when I got to the café was look up more information about poppets and binding spells. Information on the internet was extremely limited, however, and I wasn't sure how much of it was accurate. When I ran out of questionable resources to read, I played on my phone and sipped a latte until I got bored. I was too antsy to sit still any longer, so I took a walk. I wandered onto the campus of Johns Hopkins along the brick paths until I finished my latte and it was time to head back to Professor Lawson's.

I rang the doorbell again and waited a bit longer for her to answer this time. "Come on in," she said as she swung the door open. "I'm almost done. Just wait here and I'll be back in a few."

I returned to my seat on the couch and waited. About ten minutes later, she returned looking grim and carrying a plastic bag and a crude doll made from black fabric.

"Here." She held the doll and bag out to me.

I took them both and then peeked into the bag. There was a length of red string and a handful of odd-looking nails. "What's all this?"

"That's everything you'll need to perform the ritual."

"I have to perform a ritual?"

"Yes. Otherwise you just have a very ugly, gross doll stuffed with moldy paper and blood powder."

I regarded the doll with distaste. "What do I do?"

"I'll explain, don't worry." She pulled the notebook from earlier out of her back pocket, ripped out two pages, and handed those to me as well. "Okay, to start off, this is all from the traditions of my practice. It's all I know. Chances are, if you asked your grandmother, she'd have different methods."

"Maybe, but I don't intend to even tell my grandmother I'm doing this. It would only worry her."

"I understand where you're coming from, but maybe you should reconsider that."

"What? Why?"

"For one, this is very dangerous. Maybe she can talk you out of it."

"No way."

"In that case, you never know what she may have up her sleeve that could increase your chances of survival."

"Oh. It's… that dangerous?"

"I can't stress enough to you how dangerous this is. You're messing with incredibly powerful forces. Now that I've had a little time to think about it, I can't even believe I agreed to help. I had some serious second thoughts while you were gone."

"Then why *are* you helping me?"

"Mainly because I think you'd do something stupid with or without my help and you might as well be as prepared as you possibly can be."

"Oh. Okay." I looked down at the doll. "So how do I do this?"

"When you're ready to perform the ritual, you'll want to prepare the space. Some people like to draw a chalk circle, but you don't have to do anything that elaborate. You said you're not particularly religious, right?"

"Right."

"Okay, then praying to the Christian god won't cut it, but you may want to ask the elements or the ancestors for protection. You should probably have the four elements represented, though—air, fire, water, and earth. It doesn't have to be especially deep. A feather for air, a cup of water, a little dirt, and a lit candle will suffice. Arrange them around you in a sort of circle pattern. After you do that, read the spell on the first sheet of paper I gave you."

I glanced down at it, but Professor Lawson kept going, so I focused on her. I could read the spell later.

"As you call on each element, take a second to envision what you are calling and try to make a connection. Picture wind blowing for air, the heat of a flame for fire, the coolness of a stream flowing around you for water, and the smell of the dirt after a rain for earth. Or whatever works for you. Really focus on the grounding aspects of earth. Be aware of your feet, or your bottom if you're sitting, and imagine sending down roots or a column of light into the core of the Earth. Visualize drawing that energy from the core up through yourself to create a circle of protection.

"After you've done that, you'll take the red cord and tie the poppet's hands and feet behind its back, then wrap and secure the rest of the cord tightly around the body. That's the ceremonial binding. As you do that, read the second spell I wrote for you."

I flipped to the other sheet of paper. It read, *I hereby bind Victor Handy, son of Ellen. As the dead are powerless and still, just so powerless and still will Victor Handy be, his feet and hands and mind and body! I bind thee, Victor Handy, with my will. You will harm no others.*

"You'll notice it uses his name three times, just like the spell he was using to summon whatever power he was attempting to call. After the poppet is bound, pierce it with the nails. Traditionally, the ancients pierced the mouth, eyes, feet, arms, buttocks, and groin, but I don't think it really matters all that much. There are thirteen of them. Use them all."

"And when should I do all this? Is there a time that's best?"

"Not really. You can cast a spell any time, although some witches believe in working at dusk or under a full moon or equinoxes or on a high holy day. They believe it strengthens the spell. And certain holy days might be more appropriate, depending on what you're trying to accomplish."

"Like Samhain?"

"Undoubtedly. Samhain would be especially effective for this spell since, if it is indeed Victor, the boundary between this world and the spirit world will be blurred on Samhain, creating a liminal time when contacting spirits is easier. Any spell dealing with the dead will be especially powerful then."

"But that's a week away. I don't know if we can wait that long. And if it is Victor, his consciousness survived somehow, so does he really count as dead?"

"Talk to your grandmother about it, see what she thinks. As for Victor being dead, I believe he is, at least as we understand death. Or at least a kind of death. His consciousness, as you put it, was separated from his body, and then his body expired. So even if some part of him survived, it now exists only on a purely spiritual level."

"Got it. I think. So that's the whole spell? That's all I do?"

"That's just the binding ritual. Once he's bound, you need to dispose of the poppet. Sometimes the poppet is ceremonially destroyed, perhaps burned, melted, or beheaded. But for a binding, especially of a ghost or spirit, it's more common for it to be confined and buried."

"Confined?"

"Usually in a lead coffin or box, but those aren't exactly easy to come by. You could also use copper or bronze, or even just a sheet of papyrus."

"I don't have any of those things."

"Hmm. Hold on. I have an idea." She left the room again, then returned a few minutes later with a small wooden box. She opened the lid of the box and showed me the inside. It was copper-lined. "This is an old humidor," she said. "This should work."

"I can't take that!"

"Consider it a gift for a worthy cause. Besides, it was just something I picked up on a whim at a flea market. I didn't pay much for it."

"Still! It's just going to get destroyed."

"And it's just gathering dust here. Take it. If you're going to do this, you need to do it right."

I took the box. "Well, thank you, I guess. What do I do with it?"

"Place the poppet inside, then seal it somehow. A length of string or chain should suffice, even tape, for that matter. After it's sealed, there are several ways to dispose of it. You can throw it into deep water, such as a well or the ocean, or bury it, for example, in a graveyard, a sanctuary, or uncultivated land."

My ears had perked up at the mention of a well. That seemed like a poetic end, considering that was where he'd dumped the bodies of his family and the boys. I already knew where the box would end up.

"Okay. I think I've got it."

"Great. Then I think we're just about done here."

"What do I owe you?"

"Absolutely nothing."

"Are you sure? I'd pass the cost on to my clients—"

"I won't accept any payment."

"Oh, okay. Then, thank you."

"Don't thank me. I don't want any credit for this. Once you're gone, I'll probably spend the rest of the day performing purification rituals. From here, it's all on you. Just remember what your book mentioned. You must be prepared to accept any consequences of working the spell."

Something in her tone worried me. "What kind of consequences?"

"If the spell fails, you will have alerted Victor to your intentions. You can be sure he'll not be pleased. And that's assuming it is Victor. If it's not, this spell will likely do nothing, so that's in your favor. And don't forget what I told you about the power of three."

"Could this spell reverse back on me?"

"Not in a one-to-one sense of you being bound, but it could draw some negative attention to you. That's why I recommend you ask for protection. This isn't a game. You need to take it very seriously."

"I will."

She studied me for a few seconds. "You'd better. Your life could depend in it."

"Well, uh…." I wasn't sure what to say after that. "I guess I'll see you in class tomorrow."

She saw me to the door, and then I was on my way back home, the elements of a powerful spell in my passenger seat. What had my life become?

I TOOK Victor's cigar box and the binding spell accoutrements back to the office and locked it all in my desk drawer again. I was heading out when Walker let himself in the front door.

"What are you doing here?" I asked.

"I could ask you the same thing," he said. "I got an alert that someone turned off the alarm, so naturally I checked the cameras, and who do I see skulking around with shopping bags but my young padawan."

"I wasn't skulking!" I said indignantly.

"It's Sunday," he replied.

"So?"

"Would you care to tell me what you're doing in the office on a beautiful Sunday afternoon? Didn't we just talk about this last weekend?"

"Well, yeah, but—"

"But what?"

I sighed. "Maybe we should sit down. This could take a while. Your office or mine?"

"Mine. Always mine."

I followed him down the hall and waited while he unlocked his office and flipped on the lights. To my surprise, however, he didn't sit behind his desk. He took one of the chairs in front and gestured toward to the other one for me. I sat, and he gave me an expectant look.

"A lot has happened since we talked last."

"I'm aware. I watch the news. The boys were found dead, and the Miller boy is the prime suspect."

I nodded and rubbed my face. "Yeah. That's all accurate."

"I'm surprised I didn't hear from you. I've given you a lot of leeway on this case, but I still expect regular updates. Finding the missing boys seems like an obvious chance for an update."

"You're right. I've just been so distracted."

"By what, exactly?"

"By… by the case."

"The case? The case is over. You were hired to find out what happened to the boys. We know now. Good job."

"But it's not over. I mean, yes, we know the boys are dead, but not… not how."

Walker raised an eyebrow. "That's not what you were hired to do. Have you spoken to the Millers? Have they changed the scope of your work?"

"Well, no…."

He made an exaggerated expression of surprise. "Then what?"

"I…." How did I explain that I suspected that a kid who died fifty years ago after murdering his family in some sort of bizarre ritual had possessed the body of a sixteen-year-old who in turn murdered his friends?

"Cav?"

"There's still things I need to do, to figure out. It might help Gareth Miller."

"If he killed those boys, why would you want to help him? Or do you have any reason to think he didn't kill them?"

"No, I think he did kill them."

"Then what?"

"I don't think he was… in control when he killed them. I don't think he was himself."

"So you still think it could be possession."

"I'm more convinced than ever. Look, I'll explain everything, but I know it sounds batshit. Just hear me out." I quickly outlined what I'd found in Victor's bedroom, my suspicions about Victor possessing Gareth, my conversation with Professor Lawson, and my plan. When I finished, I sat back and waited for Walker to explode and forbid me from following through with my admittedly absurd idea.

But he didn't do either of those things. Instead, he calmly leaned forward.

"It sounds like Gareth killed his friends. Or, if your theory is correct, Victor killed them using Gareth's body, but try convincing a jury of that. Either way, Gareth—and by extension, Victor—will be in prison, right? Won't that keep Victor out of trouble?"

"That's assuming they can convict him. He's just a kid showing a lot of signs of mental illness, so even if they do convict, he'd probably get out eventually. Even if he gets life in prison with no parole, am I just supposed to ignore the fact that I know he's possessed? Besides, if my understanding is correct, when Gareth dies, Victor will be free to move on to a new host. I need to stop Victor now. And if I can help Gareth in the process, shouldn't I at least try?"

"Rescuing people isn't your job, Cav."

"But it's the right thing to do."

"Maybe so." He looked thoughtful for a few moments, then nodded. "I'm going to level with you. This is all very much outside my experience. It sounds really dangerous, but you present a solid case, and I pride myself on being a fair person. If this is what you think you need to do, I'm going to go out on a limb and trust you on this."

"You are?"

"Yes. I'm going to give you the space to follow this through. If Gareth is possessed by Victor Handy, then you're right. He has to be stopped."

"So… you believe me?"

He stood up and walked around his desk to the window. "A few years ago, the CIA made available about thirteen million declassified files concerning decades of studies in various metaphysical phenomena—everything from remote viewing to psychics to UFOs. Now, some of those things were debunked, but a lot was left unexplained. As I said before, I fully admit there are things beyond my understanding. I could pull rank and order you not to do this... ritual, but I have a feeling you'd do it anyway. If it's all nonsense, then nothing will come of it. If you're right, then maybe you can stop Victor Handy once and for all."

I didn't know what to say. I was moved by his display of confidence in me, but I also felt the weight of that trust. It was a significant moment in our relationship, and it demanded some sort of acknowledgment. I stood up and awkwardly held out my hand.

Walker gave me a quizzical look but reached across the desk and shook my hand.

"Thank you," I said sincerely.

"For what?"

"For your trust. I'll try not to let you down."

Walker shook his head. "You take yourself far too seriously sometimes, Cav Crawford," he said with a note of amusement. "For what it's worth, you haven't let me down yet. Now, let's lock up and go home to enjoy what's left of our Sunday."

Chapter 20

I TOOK Walker's advice. Since I was waiting to do the ritual at least until I talked to Nana and it was a little too late to swing by the home, that meant I had my evening free. I had to admit, a night off sounded like a good idea. The case had become so intense that I knew I needed to take a step back and refocus. And I knew just what to do.

I sent Kyreh a text. *Still want to hang out tonight?*

He texted back within seconds. *Yes! What do you want to do?*

I'm down for anything.

We could get dinner. Or watch a movie?

What's out right now?

Doesn't have to be at a theater. We could just stay in, order some food and watch something.

Sounds good to me. My place or yours?

My roommate is probably getting back tonight. Could we do your place?

Sure. Haniah will probably be around, but we can hang out in my room.

Sounds good. Seven work?

Yep. See you then.

I sent him my address and headed home to shower and change. I fully understood that we were just hanging out at my place, but that didn't stop me from changing numerous times. I wanted to be cute without looking like I was trying too hard. I finally chose a dark green henley and a pair of faded jeans.

That settled, I commenced pacing until Haniah couldn't stand it anymore.

"What is going on with you? You're as nervous as goat at a cookout."

"A goat at what now? No, never mind. I'm nervous because Kyreh is coming over to hang out tonight."

"Oooh!" she cooed. "Like a date?"

"Sort of. But we're just keeping things casual for now."

"Is he spending the night?"

"No. Nothing like that." I didn't think. We hadn't discussed a sleepover, but maybe he was expecting to. I had invited him over to hang out in my bedroom, after all. Then again, he did say we could take it slow.

Great. Something else to overthink.

I suddenly noticed Haniah was watching me intently. "What?" I asked.

"Nothing. It's just obvious that you really like him."

I started to deny it, but there was no point. "Maybe," I admitted.

She smiled. "Good. I like him. And don't worry about me. I'll give you space."

"I, uh, figured we'd mostly hang out in my room," I said.

She arched an eyebrow. "Oh really now?"

"We're taking it slow," I insisted.

She just gave me a knowing look and exited the room, leaving me to my nervous breakdown.

I got a text from Kyreh at seven o'clock sharp. *Hey, I think I'm here, but there are three mailboxes. Do I knock on the door or what?*

Oh sorry, I sent back. *Come around to the back of the house and take the stairs to the second floor.*

I went to the door and opened it, then stepped out onto the small deck to wait for Kyreh to come around the corner. He waved when he saw me waiting and took the stairs two at a time until he reached me. He swooped in for a hug, then stepped back quickly.

"Thanks for having me over," he said with a warm smile.

"Of course! Come on in. I'll give you the grand tour. It'll only take a few seconds."

I showed him the living room, kitchen, and my room; then we returned to the living room, where we sat awkwardly on the couch.

"So, uh, what do you want to eat?" I asked.

"I don't know. You craving anything?"

"Not really. I'm down for whatever."

"Me too."

"Well, one of us is going to have to make some decisions or we're going to go hungry."

"I nominate you."

I laughed. "Fine. How do you feel about Thai?"

"Love it."

"Decision made."

I pulled up the app, and we scrolled through the menu together. I chose drunken noodles, and Kyreh picked pad thai.

We chatted about our classes while we waited. When I got the text that our food was almost there, I went down to meet the driver.

We moved to the kitchen for dinner. Haniah made an appearance while we were eating—so much for staying out of our way, but then I never expected her to be able to resist—but she didn't hang around long. Just said hi, grabbed the bottle of water that was her excuse, and then retreated to her room.

When we finished, we cleaned up, put our leftovers in the fridge, and retired to my room to watch a movie.

After a repeat of our food selection process but for movies, we settled on a recent thriller neither of us had seen, and I set it up on my laptop and angled it on my desk so we could see the screen from my bed.

At first we sat stiffly next to each other, backs against my headboard, but about fifteen minutes in, we both shifted into more comfortable positions, and somehow his arm made its way around me until my head was nestled against his shoulder.

The movie turned out to not be that great, and about halfway through, I noticed that he was watching me more than the screen.

"What?" I finally asked.

"This is nice."

"The movie?"

"Oh God no. That's garbage. I mean being here with you, like this."

"Yeah," I agreed. "That part is nice. I feel really comfortable with you."

He looked delighted. "I feel comfortable with you too."

"I'm kind of glad we were just hanging out with, like, no pressure or anything. Just getting to know each other a little better without the expectations of it being a big elaborate date or something."

"I hate to break it to you, but we're on a date."

I laughed. "You know what I mean."

"I do. I just like giving you a hard time."

"I've noticed."

He grinned, then looked around the room. "Hey, uh, your ex isn't here now, is he?"

Miraculously, I hadn't even thought about my dead boyfriend up until that moment. "Mason? No," I answered, but I was suddenly concerned.

"Good. Because that would be a little weird."

"Just a little."

He stared into my eyes, and for a moment I thought he was going to kiss me. But then someone screamed on screen and the moment passed. Our attention returned to the shitty movie.

When it was over, he slid his arm out from under my head, sat up, and stretched. "Thanks for having me over. I should probably get back. Class in the morning."

"Yeah, me too," I said, feeling a pang of disappointment that he was leaving, but I'd been the one to say I wanted to take things slow. He was only respecting my wishes.

I got up and followed him to the door, where he slipped his shoes back on. Then I walked him to his car. When we reached the driver's side door, he turned and pulled me into another hug. "Thanks again for having me over."

"You're welcome," I mumbled into his neck. "We'll have to do it again, only with a better movie."

He laughed and pulled back. "What are you doing for Halloween?"

"Oh, uh, nothing special." I didn't want to tell him that I might be casting a dangerous spell to trap a murderous ghost.

"We should do something. Maybe a horror movie marathon. Or we could find a party to crash. I think I saw that the LGBTQ+ group is having a dance."

"I might have to work."

He frowned. "On Halloween night? It's a Saturday."

"I know. It's complicated." He looked so disappointed that I felt bad. "I'm sorry. I'll try to figure it out tomorrow. If I don't have to work, I'll spend it with you. And if I do have to work, then we'll do something Friday night. Okay?"

He pulled me back in close. "Okay. I swear I'm not trying to be a brat. I just want to see you."

"And you will, I promise."

"I guess a promise will do. Good night, Cav."

"Good night, Ky."

I watched him get into his car and drive off with one last wave, then practically floated back to my room.

As I shut the bedroom door, a voice came from behind me, making me practically jump out of my skin.

"I like him."

I spun around. "Jesus, Mason." My heart was trying to beat out of my chest. "Were you watching us the whole time?"

"Nah. You said my name, and I guess that was enough to pull me back. I arrived to find you two staring deeply into each other's eyes. It was very sweet."

"Oh my God." I sat on the edge of my bed with my face in my hands.

"I didn't hang around. I swear. Once I realized what was going on, I peaced out. Is this the guy you told me about?"

"Yes," I answered from behind my hands.

"What's his name again?"

"Kyreh."

"You looked very cozy. Was this a date?"

"Yes, our first, but we're taking things slow. I'm… not sure I'm ready for a relationship."

"Oh. Because of me?"

"Yeeeah…." I drew out the word.

He had the grace to look sheepish. "Right. Well, do you like him?"

I nodded. "Yeah, I do."

"Good. I want you to be happy."

"Uh, thanks."

"Not that you need my permission," he rushed to say.

I waved him off. "It's fine. I knew what you meant." I stood up to shut down my laptop.

"Right. So, uh, what's going on with your other ghost kid? The murdery one."

"Victor."

"Is that his name?"

"Yeah, and Gareth is the kid he's possessing. I think. I hope."

"Why do you hope?"

"Because if I'm wrong and it's not Victor, then that means I'm dealing with something potentially far worse. And I don't have a plan for dealing with whatever that might be."

"But you do have a plan to deal with Victor?"

"I think so. I went to see my professor today. She's a witch. She really helped a lot. She made a binding spell for me."

While we talked, I started getting ready for bed, pulling back the covers.

"Maybe it should be obvious, but what's a binding spell do?"

"Yeah, it's pretty much all there in the name. It binds someone or something from doing harm. I'm using something called a poppet. It's sort of like a voodoo doll."

"Then what do you do with the doll?"

"I'm going to seal it in a box and then throw it down a well."

"Can he get out?"

"I don't think he's actually in the box." Although, having said that, I had to admit I wasn't 100 percent sure about that. I was still a little unclear how the whole thing worked.

"Well, can he break the binding?"

"I don't think so. Not unless someone found the box and opened it and then unbound the poppet."

"But they could, right?"

"I mean, it seems unlikely, but I guess so."

"What happens when the box rots?"

"I… don't know."

"Isn't there any way to just, you know, help him to, like… move on?"

I was sitting on the edge of my bed in the middle of pulling off my socks but stopped to look at Mason. He wouldn't meet my gaze.

"Are we still just talking about Victor?" I asked softly.

He shrugged. "Mostly. Kind of."

"Are you worried about moving on?"

He glanced over at me. "Aren't you worried about me moving on?"

"Not right now. We made a deal."

"What about after that?"

"We'll figure that out when the time comes."

He nodded but didn't look convinced.

"Mason, I'm not going to bind you or anything like that. You're not running around murdering people. At worst, you're a bit of a peeping tom."

He cracked a small smile at that. I pulled my last sock off, followed by my shirt. I stood up to unbutton my pants but paused.

"Are you, uh, spending the night here again?"

He looked surprised by the question. "No. I think I should leave you be. I don't think Kyler would like me being in your bed, if he even knew I existed, anyway."

"It's Kyreh, and he does know you exist."

He looked surprised. "You told him?"

"Yeah. It was the right thing to do."

"Oh, well, still. Unless you guys also agreed to be polyamorous with a dead guy, I should go."

"Okay. Uh, good night?"

He laughed a little. "I guess that works. Good night, Cav. Oh, and I know I keep saying this, but be careful. This stuff with Victor and the spells and all, it sounds really scary."

"Yeah. It does."

IMMEDIATELY AFTER my last class the next day, I drove to Nana's facility. She was up in her chair today, reading a book by her window, a blanket across her legs.

"Hi, Nana," I said softly from her door so I wouldn't startle her.

She glanced up and smiled. "Cavanaugh. I could get used to all these visits."

I laughed as I came into the room. "I'll try to keep it up even when I'm not in crisis."

Her smile faded. "Are you in crisis?"

"No," I said quickly. "Poor choice of words. I just came by for some advice."

"About what?" She looked concerned. "Is this about those boys you were telling me about?"

"Yes, but also a different boy."

"What do you mean?"

"We'll get to that. First, let me get this hard part out of the way." I pulled a chair over to the window and sat down in front of her. "I went to see my professor, the witch. She wants to meet you sometime."

"Meet me? Why?"

"She was very interested in learning more about your—our—beliefs. She was especially excited that you were an herbalist."

"I'd be happy to talk to her."

"I'll let her know."

"Did she help with this mess with the boys?"

"Yes. At least, I think so. She made me a binding spell."

Nana looked surprised. "How?"

"It looks kind of like a cloth voodoo doll, but she stuffed it with Victor's journal that she shredded up, some binding herbs, some of his dried-up blood, and a spell that she wrote for me where I bind it with red string and pierce it with iron nails."

Nana looked horrified. "Where on earth did you get his blood?"

"He'd put some in a bottle to use in his spells. I found it with his journal and spell book."

She shook her head. "This is some dark magic. Blood magic is very powerful."

"That's what Professor Lawson said. She almost refused to do it. She's a lightworker, and this goes against her beliefs. She only helped me because she said it might be the only way to stop Victor from killing more people."

"Then she's sure it's Victor."

"Not sure, no. She said the spell will only work if it is Victor."

"And if it's not?"

"Then we're back to the drawing board."

"If it is Victor, what happens to the boy he's possessing?"

"His name is Gareth, and I'm not sure. I'm hoping it will separate them."

"You're hoping? That means you don't know."

"Right."

"And if it does separate them, then what? What happens to Gareth?"

"You mean with the police?"

"I meant with his mind, his psyche, but yes, he'll still have to deal with the police as well."

"I don't know. I mean, whatever happens, at least he won't be possessed by a homicidal ghost."

"True enough, I suppose. And what about whatever Victor summoned?"

"What do you mean?"

"Don't forget that Victor was calling on something when he cast his spell. We don't know if it showed up or not, but Victor was separated from his body, so it certainly seems as if it did. Did it stay around? Did it go back through whatever portal Victor opened once it did his bidding?

Is the portal still open? Does the connection still exist? Did anything else come through?"

"That's a lot of questions," I said after a few seconds. I felt abashed that none of that had occurred to me.

"They're questions you should be concerned about. Maybe the entity he summoned is long gone and it won't be an issue, but you should at least be prepared that it could still be lurking somewhere on our plane."

"And if it is?"

"If you're lucky, it won't notice you."

"What if I'm not lucky?"

"We'd just better hope the luck of the Irish is with you."

I shuddered. "Okay, but what about the spell? Do you think it'll work?"

"I don't know a whole lot about that sort of magic. What did your professor think?"

"Professor Lawson seemed pretty sure it would work as long as I followed her instructions exactly."

"Sounds about right," Nana said with a sniff.

"What do you mean?"

"The problem with an academic view is that you think just because you think you have established the rules, the supernatural beings you're dealing with will follow them."

"So you don't think it'll work?"

"I didn't say that. From what little I do know, it should work, as long as it is Victor. It's just very dangerous."

"That's what she said too. Is there anything I can do to make it safer? She said I should ask you."

"She did?"

"Yes. She was very respectful of your traditions. She said you could maybe help."

"Wear the pendant I gave you."

"I haven't taken it off since you gave it to me. Anything else?"

"Start with a prayer of protection. I'll teach it to you. It's similar to the ancestor prayer for Samhain that you used to summon Mason. 'Tonight, I call upon my ancestors for protection. Spirits of my fathers and mothers, loved ones who have gone before, I call to you and beseech you to encircle me. Your blood runs in my veins, your spirit is in my heart, your memories are in my soul. May you shield me this night from hate, from harm, from act, from ill. Circle me and keep love within, keep hatred out. Keep joy within, keep fear out. Keep peace within, keep worry out. Keep light within, keep darkness out.'"

The room remained silent for a few moments as she finished the prayer.

"That's beautiful. Can you, uh, maybe write that down?"

She laughed and gestured to her bedside table. "There should be a notepad and a pen in the drawer there."

I fetched the items for her, and she wrote down the invocation in her spidery handwriting, then tore off the page and handed it to me. I read it over again.

"Professor Lawson said I should ask the four elements for protection. She gave me a spell for that as well. Does this make that unnecessary?"

"I think you should ask for and gratefully accept any protection available."

"Okay, then how would I do that?"

"Just perform her spell first, then say the prayer I gave you."

"Okay." I read over her prayer again, folded it in half, and slid it into my pocket. "And that's it?"

She stared out the window for a second. "You need to be very sure of what you're doing. Have a plan, have a plan B, and have an escape plan."

"Professor Lawson suggested I perform the ritual during Samhain. What do you think?"

"Without question," she said without hesitation. "Do it after sundown, as close to midnight as possible. That's when the veil is the thinnest."

"But that's a whole week away. Do you think it's wise to wait?"

"I think it would be foolish not to wait. If you have any chance of making this work, then you'll need all the help you can get."

I sighed. "That's what Professor Lawson said too."

"She sounds like a wise lady. I think I would like to meet her."

"I'll arrange it after this is all over. But only if she'll give me class credit for it."

Nana laughed. "Maybe you should just write an essay about me."

"No more essays," I groaned.

Just then, my phone buzzed in my pocket. I slipped it out and checked to see who was calling. It was Mead.

"I should take this," I told Nana. "I'll be right back."

I stepped out into the hall and hit Answer. "Hello?"

"Crawford, tell me you've got this case figured out."

"Not exactly. Why? Is there an issue?"

"Possibly. As I expected, we're going to have to release Gareth Miller today unless you've come up with something we can use to hold him."

"I got nothing," I said with a sigh.

"Then he'll be out soon. I've pushed it back as much as I can."

"Okay. Well, thanks for the heads-up."

I ended the call and stared at my phone. I was convinced Victor was a threat. I didn't like the idea of him being out on the street. I didn't know if—or when—he might kill again. His motives were too hazy.

I briefly considered moving the binding spell up, but both Professor Lawson and Nana had suggested I wait until Samhain. Besides, I had to admit, I wouldn't mind a few more days to mentally prepare.

It was going to be a long week.

MUCH TO my surprise, Mead called again the next afternoon. I was in my room working on a school project. My stomach clenched when I saw his name come up on my phone. Gareth had only been released the night before. Had something already happened?

"What's going on?" I asked as soon as I answered.

"Not sure. A coincidence, possibly. Now that this is a homicide case, it's caught the attention of neighboring law-enforcement agencies. A detective in Washington County called me today about a man named Douglas Frank. He lived alone on his farm. His family hadn't heard from him for a few weeks, which apparently isn't that unusual—he's got a bit of a drinking problem—but when his kids couldn't get a hold of him after a while, they called it in. The responding officers found him in his yard, stabbed to death."

"Okay. Why are you telling me this?"

"This all happened about a week ago, right before we picked up Gareth Miller. The guy lived less than a mile from where we picked up the kid. Like I said, it might be a weird coincidence, but I thought I'd check with you to see if you could think of any connection. Right now, we don't have any real reason to suspect the kid was involved, but you know I don't like coincidences."

"What was his name again?"

"Douglas Frank. Went by Doug."

That rang a bell for some reason, but I couldn't figure out why. "I can't think of anything right now, but if something comes to me, I'll let you know."

"I knew it was a long shot. Thanks anyway."

I ended the call but couldn't stop thinking about it. Why was that name familiar?

Then I made the connection. I pulled up my transcription of Victor's journal. Sure enough, there it was. Someone named Doug had been one of Victor's tormentors at school, one of the people he vowed vengeance upon.

I knew it could be a fluke, but the timing and the fact that Gareth was found nearby seemed too much. I had an uneasy feeling that Victor might be a believer in the old saying that revenge is a dish best served cold. I couldn't very well call Mead back and tell him that it wasn't Gareth but a dead teenager with a fifty-year-old grudge. But that did make me wonder if there were more people on Victor's hit list. He'd mentioned at least one other bully by name—though just by his first name—but most of the journal had been unreadable.

I once again wondered if I should go ahead and perform the spell now, but deep down, I knew I was going to wait until Halloween.

The thought of Halloween reminded me that I still needed to tell Kyreh I wasn't free that night, and that caused a pang of disappointment. Then it occurred to me that if I waited and did the spell at midnight, maybe I could hang out with Kyreh earlier in the evening. It might even help keep my mind off what was to come. I texted him and asked him to call me when he got a chance.

My phone rang before I could even set it down.

"That was fast," I said with a laugh.

"I was afraid something was wrong," he said. I could hear the concern in his voice.

"Oh, no, sorry! I mean, kind of, but not like that. It turns out I do have to work on Halloween."

"What? No horror movie marathon?"

"Well, maybe an early one?"

"Early?"

"The thing I have to do for work isn't until, like, midnight. So I could hang out for a while. I'd just have to leave by eleven or so." I was being purposefully vague, but at least I wasn't lying. It was work-related, even if it wasn't something I was actually getting paid for, as Walker had pointed out.

"Midnight? On Halloween night?"

"Yeah. It's complicated."

"Are you digging up graves?"

"Ha. No."

"Casting a spell?"

I forced another laugh, though it sounded fake even to me. "I told you, it's just a work thing."

"A work thing? Well, can I go with you?"

"No!" It came a little more forcefully than I intended.

"Oh. Cool." He sounded a little hurt.

"It's just that it's really dangerous. I don't want to put you in harm's way."

"How dangerous? Is anybody going to be with you?"

"Don't worry about it. I'll be fine." At least, I hoped so.

Another pause. "Okay," he said. "Can you tell me what's going on or is that, like, classified?"

"Can I tell you afterward? I don't want you to worry too much."

"Too late for that. Cav, I don't like the sound of this."

"I know. I'm sorry. Look, I don't want to ruin your Halloween night, so maybe we should just do something on Friday instead."

"Oh yeah, don't ruin my night of sitting alone in my dorm room. We can hang out on Saturday. But you definitely owe me." His tone was teasing now.

"I know. I'll make it up to you."

"Promise?"

"I promise."

"I'm holding you to that."

We hung up, and I breathed a sigh of relief.

I THOUGHT the week would drag on, but between school and talking to Kyreh, the days flew by. I didn't hear any more from Mead, which I took as a good sign. I also didn't hear from the Millers, and I was less sure what that might mean. Mason only showed up once, complaining that he was bored. I put more movies on for him to watch while I did schoolwork.

Friday morning, Professor Lawson caught me after class to ask if I was going to perform the ritual the following night. I told her I was, and she asked me to call her on Sunday to let her know how it went. I agreed.

Saturday finally arrived, and with it, a bad case of nerves. During the week, I'd mostly been able to ignore the fact that I'd be casting a dangerous spell to try to bind the spirit of a bloodthirsty ghost, and that was the best-case scenario. I tried not to consider the alternatives. I had to go into this expecting it to work—*believing* it would work. Both Nana and my professor had stressed that much of magic depended on intent and will, and while they hadn't said so specifically, I got the feeling that going into this with a lot of doubt might jeopardize the whole thing.

By that evening, I was especially glad I'd made plans with Kyreh. We were meeting at his dorm this time since his roommate was going to a Halloween party. Haniah was staying home to hand out candy with our landlord.

Before I left for Kyreh's, I gathered some things I'd need for the ritual and stuffed them in a backpack. Then I swung by my office to get everything else for the spell and locked all of it in my trunk.

I wasn't lucky enough to catch anyone coming out of Kyreh's building when I arrived this time, so I had to text him to let me in. He arrived at the door in a werewolf mask, gray sweatpants, and a ripped T-shirt that barely hung on his torso. He threw open the door and let loose with a howl.

"Trick or treat?" I asked when he'd finished.

He pulled off the mask. "I'll be the trick and you can be my treat," he said with a leer.

"Was this supposed to be a costume thing?" I said, looking down at my black jeans with matching hoodie ensemble. "Because I guess I didn't get the memo."

Kyreh laughed and grabbed me by the arm to drag me inside. "Nah, just thought it would be fun. I think I make a pretty sexy werewolf. You don't agree?"

"I didn't say that. But in the interest of authenticity, I have to point out that it's not even a full moon."

He rolled his eyes. "Close enough. It's a waxing gibbous."

"Well at least somebody is waxing. You're looking a little hairy."

He snorted and took off up the stairs, leaving me to chase after him. In his room, he shut the door, yanked off the shredded shirt, and quickly pulled on a less tattered one.

"I didn't mean to ruin your fun," I said. "You can keep your costume on if you want."

"I only put it on to greet you. Let's get comfy. What should we watch? A slasher? A ghost story? A monster flick?"

"Um, actually, I know we said we'd do a horror marathon, but do you think we could watch something a little less… tense? My nerves are a bit on edge."

He quickly grew serious. "We can watch whatever you want. Why are you on edge? Is this about that mysterious dangerous thing you have to do later?"

"Yeah. I'm just a little anxious. It's no big deal."

He eyed me for a minute but just nodded. "No problem. What would you like to watch?"

"I dunno."

"Like, are we talking Disney, here?"

I laughed. "I don't necessarily need a princess movie."

"Oh! That gave me an idea. Have you ever seen *Princess Mononoke*?"

"I've never even heard of it."

"What? Studio Ghibli? Miyazaki?"

"I don't know any of those words."

"*Spirited Away*? *Howl's Moving Castle*? *My Neighbor Totoro*?"

"Okay, those are movies, right? I think I've heard of them."

"Oh wow. You're a Ghibli virgin. I have so much to teach you."

I narrowed my eyes. "Why do I feel like I've been insulted?"

"No! It's exciting, I swear. I get to introduce you to some of the best movies I've ever seen. Studio Ghibli is kind of like the Japanese Disney, except better."

"You're really selling it."

"You'll see. You'll love it. Now get on the bed. I'll get it set up."

"Yes, sir," I said as I kicked my shoes off and jumped onto his bed.

I had to admit, he was right. The movie he put on was excellent. I was engrossed all the way through. Even Kyreh's snuggles couldn't fully distract me. When it ended, he put on another movie called *Kiki's Delivery Service*. It was very different in tone but just as good.

The mini film fest did the trick and kept me distracted, but by the time the second movie was over, it was about time for me to head out to the Handy house.

"I guess I should get going," I said when I checked the time. My reluctance was clear in my voice. I stood up, and Kyreh jumped to his feet and pulled me into an embrace.

"Do you really have to go?" he asked.

"Yeah. Afraid so."

"I still don't get why you have to work so late on a Saturday night."

I pulled away a little. "All part of the job," I said as lightly as I could manage.

"You said it was dangerous."

"Also part of the job, sometimes."

"And is it always so top-secret too?"

I sighed. "No. This isn't, like, super confidential or anything. I just don't want to worry you more than I have to."

"You see how that's not comforting in the least, right?"

I laughed a little and leaned back into his body, resting my forehead against his shoulder.

He gently rubbed my back. "I've never seen you like this. What's going on?"

After a brief internal debate, I made up my mind. I stepped back, and his hands dropped to his sides.

"So you know this case I've been working on?"

"Yeah, the missing kids. I saw on the news that they'd found them dead, but no arrests have been made yet."

"Right. I found them."

"Holy shit, Cav! No wonder you're so upset."

"Yeah, hang on. It gets so much worse. I think they were killed by the ghost of a boy who killed his entire family back in the seventies, and now he's possessing the boy who was found a couple of weeks ago—the only one who survived."

"Possessing him?" he repeated in disbelief.

"That's my theory."

"Okay, but wait." He blinked at me for a few seconds. I could see the wheels turning. "I have about a million questions, but the biggest one is what does all that have to do with what you have to do tonight?"

"I, uh, have to cast something called a binding spell to try and stop him."

"You have to cast a spell? Like… a magic spell?"

"Yeah. Just like that."

"So, I know you said you see ghosts, but are you, like, a witch? Should I call you Kiki? Or wait. Would you be a warlock? A wizard?"

I couldn't help laughing. "It's not like that. But if I was anything, I'd just be a witch. But I'm not. I'm just reading a spell an actual witch gave me and performing a ritual and hoping like hell it works."

"Oh, is that all? Just reading a spell and performing a ritual at midnight on fucking Halloween?"

"Uh, yeah. I think that covers it."

He nodded. "Okay. Okay. Right. Got it."

Then he spun around, yanked open a dresser drawer, and hauled out a black sweatshirt.

"What are you doing?" I asked as he started pulling the sweatshirt on.

His head popped out. "I'm going with you."

"No, you're absolutely not."

"Don't argue with me. There's no way I'm letting you do this alone."

"This is why I didn't want to tell you."

"This is why I'm glad you did." I started to argue, but he cut me off. "What if something goes wrong? Where are you even performing this ritual? Is it in, like, some remote cemetery?"

"No…."

"Then where?"

"It doesn't matter."

"Cav."

"Um, the house where the boys and that family were killed."

"Are you fucking kidding me? You thought it was a good idea to go to a freakin' haunted house in the middle of nowhere in the middle of the night *by yourself*?"

"Well…." When he put it like that, I had to admit he had a point.

He could obviously sense my resolve weakening and went in for the kill. "Even without the danger of whatever spell you're spelling, traipsing around an abandoned house alone in the dark does not seem like a smart idea."

"I mean—"

"I'm going with you, and that's final."

I took a deep breath. "Okay."

"I'm serious. I won't.... Did you say okay?"

"Yeah. You can come." I had to admit, a little company would be nice.

He nodded decisively. "Good." He pulled on a pair of shoes. "You ready?"

"As I'll ever be."

Chapter 21

ONCE WE were in the car and headed to the Handy house, Kyreh asked, "So how does this work?"

I quickly went over the spell and what I had to do. It was actually good to review it.

"Okay," he said when I finished. "But why did it have to be tonight? This feels like some horror-movie white-people shit. No offense."

I laughed. "Halloween has its roots in an ancient Celtic holy day called Samhain." I was suddenly glad for Nana's lesson. "A lot of the traditions we associate with Halloween actually date back thousands of years. Samhain is the night when the boundary between the spirit world and the living world is at its thinnest. It makes spells particularly powerful, especially anything dealing with death."

"Okay, still creepy, but what sorts of traditions come from…. What did you call it? Sow… ween?"

"It's pronounced sow-in. Wearing costumes comes from the practice of wearing disguises during Samhain so they wouldn't be confused with the spirits roaming the Earth. Jack-o'-lanterns come from an Irish tradition of carving turnips to scare away the spirits. When the Irish came to America, they found pumpkins a hell of a lot easier to carve. Stuff like that."

"That's pretty cool. I'd heard some of that before, like about the jack-o'-lanterns, but I didn't know it was connected to Samhain."

"Yeah, that's also why ghosts are so associated with Halloween. That's even where the name Halloween comes from. Catholics have a habit of taking pagan or secular holy days and pasting a Christian holy day over it as a way of assimilating those older beliefs. So since Samhain was associated with the dead and ancestors, they created All Hallows' Day—or All Saints' Day—on November 1. Eventually, All Hallows' Eve became Halloween."

"Fascinating. And All Hallows' Eve fell on Samhain."

"Exactly."

"That's so cool."

"We're here," I said abruptly, my heart starting to pound. Our conversation about the history of Halloween had kept me somewhat distracted during the drive, but the reality of the situation was starting to hit me.

I pulled off the road and a little farther into the trees than usual. I didn't want anyone to notice my car and check on us or call the police. Nerves must have hit both of us, because we were both completely silent as we climbed out of the car.

I popped open the trunk and started unloading. I'd brought two battery-operated camp lanterns, one of which I handed to Kyreh. The other I gripped in one hand while I slung my backpack over my shoulder and hefted the bag full of spell materials in the other.

"Don't turn them on unless you have to," I said. "At least until we're at the house. I don't want to draw attention."

Fortunately, as Kyreh had pointed out earlier, the moon was nearly full, so there was enough light to see where we were going. I remembered Professor Lawson saying many people cast spells based on the moon cycles, and I wondered which carried more weight, Samhain or a full moon. Not that it mattered at this point. Everyone had pushed me to do it on Samhain, and here I was. The decision was made. I just wished I knew more about how this worked.

I took a deep breath. "Let's go."

We didn't talk much as we crossed the field. I could make out the first house's roofline, silver in the moonlight.

"That's it?" Kyreh asked in a raspy voice as we approached the first house. "It doesn't look very safe."

"No, there's more than one house. The one we want is the second house."

I turned my lantern on as we entered the trees, and Kyreh followed suit. When we reached the Handy house, I directed the beam over the front of the building. It looked a lot scarier at night.

"This is it," I said.

"How did those kids even find this place?" he asked.

"We don't really know. One of them looked for abandoned houses on satellite images, so that might be how. It's hard to see from the road, even in broad daylight. Let's get this over with."

I started for the door, and after a hesitation, Kyreh followed. I ducked under the police tape and stopped at the bottom of the staircase, shining the light up into the inky blackness.

"Are you sure this is a good idea?" Kyreh whispered when he caught up.

"No," I replied, but I started up the stairs anyway.

Once in Victor's bedroom, I paused again in the doorway.

"Don't step into the circle," I said to Kyreh.

"Circle?"

"The one carved into the floor. Also, try to avoid the blood."

"What? Blood?"

"It's a murder scene twice over. Just do your best to stay around the perimeter of the room."

I stepped in and edged around the circle, Kyreh so close on my heels that he actually caught the back of my shoe a few times. We placed the lanterns in strategic locations to light as much of the room as possible. Then I started unpacking the things I needed to perform the binding spell. I set up by the window, away from the circle. I still wasn't sure if it was active, and I wasn't about to risk transferring my consciousness out of my body.

Once I had everything laid out on the floor, I glanced up to see Kyreh watching me anxiously.

"What's all that?"

"These represent the four elements," I said, indicating the things I'd arranged around me. "This is a cup of water, this is a feather for air, this is soil for earth, and this"—I picked up the candle my mother had given me, the Samhain candle, and lit it—"is fire." I carefully set the candle down at the top of my circle. "They're for protection."

Then I drew out the poppet and the red string and, with shaking hands, set them down in front of me.

"That's the poppet, a doll used for the binding spell. The string is what I'll use to physically bind it. But before I start, I have to ask for protection."

I produced three pieces of paper from my pocket and found the first one Professor Lawson had written. I took a deep breath and began, focusing on each element as I called to it. "Element of air, I call on you. Element of fire, I call on you. Element of water, I call on you. Element of earth, I call on you. With these elements together, I cast a circle of protection above, below, within."

As I spoke, I did as Professor Lawson had instructed and visualized each element and the energy flowing from the center of the Earth to encircle the room.

Next, I moved on to the prayer Nana wrote. Just seeing her handwriting was comforting.

"Tonight I call upon my ancestors for protection. Spirits of my fathers and mothers, loved ones who have gone before, I call to you and beseech you to encircle me. Your blood runs in my veins, your spirit is in my heart, your memories are in my soul. May you shield me this night from hate, from harm, from act, from ill. Circle me and keep love within, keep hatred out. Keep joy within, keep fear out. Keep peace within, keep worry out. Keep light within, keep darkness out."

As I read the prayer, the candle flame flickered, and the energy in the room changed.

I looked up and gasped. Several indistinct figures had appeared in the room—sort of shimmering, smoky, vaguely human forms—and with them, Mason, looking as solid as ever.

"Mason?"

At the mention of my dead boyfriend, Kyreh looked around, but he didn't seem to be able to see anything. "What's going on?" he asked, a note of pinched panic in his voice.

I ignored him to focus on Mason and the figures. "What are you doing here?"

Mason gave me a lopsided smile and ran his hand through his hair. "You called. I came." He glanced around. "We came."

The hair stood up on my arms. "Who is with you?" I asked in a shaky voice.

"People who love you. People who want to protect you. Your father, your grandfather, other ancestors."

"Is… is my mom here?"

Mason glanced to his left, then back at me. "Yes. She's here."

A sob rose in my throat, but I quickly swallowed it. I didn't have time for this. I swallowed several more times and swiped at the tears that slipped out.

"Thank you," I whispered hoarsely.

"Get on with it," Mason said. "We'll do what we can to keep you safe."

I nodded and turned my attention back to the main attraction—the binding spell. I laid out the last sheet of paper so I could read it and picked up the poppet with the string. As I began the incantation, I pulled the poppet's arms behind its back and started to tie them. "I hereby bind Victor Handy, son of Ellen."

Once the arms were secured, I looped the cord around the feet, tying them together. "As the dead are powerless and still, just so powerless and still will Victor Handy be, his feet and hands and mind and body."

Then I wound the rest of the cord around the body until there was none left, and carefully knotted it so it wouldn't unwind. "I bind thee, Victor Handy, with my will. You will harm no others."

Then I picked up the nails and started piercing them into the doll: one for each eye, one for the mouth, one through each foot and arm, one through the buttocks, one through the groin, one through the throat, one through the forehead, and the last two through the abdomen. The doll wasn't very big, and it was starting to look a bit like a porcupine.

Then I had a flash of inspiration, or so I hoped.

"There should be a knife around here somewhere, like an old kitchen knife," I said to Kyreh. "Maybe on the desk? Or in the closet? I can't remember where I left it. Can you find it?"

He grabbed one of the lights and searched the desk, then moved to the closet. He quickly returned with the rusty knife.

I took it, dug the blade into the floor, and pried up a splinter of wood. I then stabbed it into the poppet as well.

"Victor Handy, I bind you to this place, this house, and its property, so you can do no more harm."

"Will that work?" Kyreh asked.

"I don't know, but it's worth a try, right?" I said, but inside I was desperately hoping I hadn't messed anything up with my last-minute addition.

Now that the ritual was finished, I placed the poppet in the box the professor had given me and closed the lid. I grabbed the bicycle chain

I'd brought to seal it up but then sat there just holding it and staring at the box.

"What's going on?" Kyreh asked. "What happens now?"

"I don't know," I admitted. "Professor Lawson said to seal the box and then bury it or toss it down a well. I was going to use the well in the backyard."

"So what are we waiting for?"

"How do we know it worked?"

"Oh. I guess... we don't?"

"I don't like that. I wish I sensed something, but it's just... nothing."

I looked to Mason, but he just shook his head. "We don't know either."

I turned back to Kyreh. "Maybe we should hang out a little while, see if anything happens."

Kyreh glanced around uneasily but just shrugged. "Hey, I don't have anywhere better to be. Why not hang out at a murder scene at midnight on Halloween?"

He came over and sat down next to me. We tried to make small talk, but neither of our hearts was in it. Eventually, we just fell silent.

Meanwhile, the sinking feeling in my chest was growing to Titanic proportions. "Maybe it isn't Victor inside Gareth," I finally said. My voice sounded unnaturally loud in the deep stillness of the house, and Kyreh jumped a little.

"Who else could it be?" he asked.

I wasn't sure he really wanted to know. "Victor was trying to summon something, and I think he did—just maybe not exactly what he thought he was getting. Maybe whatever he summoned killed him and then was somehow stuck here. Maybe it waited around until Gareth and the boys came along."

"Something like what, exactly? A demon?"

"I don't know."

"I didn't sign up for a fight with a demon."

"Neither did I. I was just so confident it was Victor. Both Professor Lawson and Nana warned me that it might not be. Or that it could be Victor plus something else."

"What happens if it's something else?"

"Well, the spell won't work. It was only written for Victor. Professor Lawson said that if it wasn't Victor, there's a small chance that the spell could somehow alert whatever is actually possessing Gareth. If that happens, I guess I become a target."

"What about me?"

"I cast the spell. I don't think it would target you."

"You don't think?"

"I'm sorry. Maybe you shouldn't have come."

"No, I wanted to. You told me it was dangerous. Whatever happens, I don't regret coming with you. But if it's not Victor, can't you just bind whatever it is?"

"Not without knowing its name."

"And I guess it won't just tell you if you ask nicely."

"I don't think that's how it works."

I stood up, dropping the chain, and walked over to the edge of the circle. "This is still bothering me too," I said.

"What do you mean?"

"What if it's still active?"

"Active?"

"Everything I've read and heard about casting circles suggests that you have to close these things after you perform your spell, but there's no way of knowing if Victor closed it before he died. He literally carved it into the floor, so it's not like we can just sweep it away."

"What do you think we should do?" Kyreh asked.

"No clue. Maybe we should destroy it."

"How?"

"Hell if I know. Cut it out with a saw? Chop it up with an ax? Burn the house down?"

"Well, I don't have my handy pocket ax on me, so I guess we get to have a Halloween bonfire. That's another tradition, right? Does that also have its origin in Samhain?"

"I think so." I was too distracted to worry about another history lesson. "Maybe we should throw the box down the well first, just in case."

"Probably. It might get a little warm in the backyard if the entire house is ablaze."

I turned back to Mason and the others. "We'll be back. Will you... wait?"

He nodded.

I gathered up the box, wrapped the chain around it, and secured the combination lock. I left everything else as it was.

We grabbed the lanterns and headed out.

"Mason is here?" Kyreh asked as we carefully made our way down the stairs.

"Uh, yeah. Along with some of my ancestors, apparently. They came when I called on them for protection."

"That's… comforting, I guess."

Once outside, we were about to head to the backyard when lights swept across the field.

I stopped in my tracks.

"What was that?" Kyreh asked softly.

"I think that was a car," I replied just as quietly. "Turn off your light and hide."

My mind raced. I didn't want to be trapped in the house, but I also didn't want to be caught out in the open. I looked around and spotted a thicket of brambles between the Handy house and the first house in the row. I pointed it out to Kyreh, and we crouched behind it. It wasn't perfect, but as long as our surprise guest didn't look directly at us, we'd be okay.

We waited for what felt like forever before a shadowy figure emerged from the gloom, approaching with a careful deliberateness. As they drew a little closer, the moonlight caught their face, and I recognized them. It was Gareth.

Maybe the spell had worked after all. Or were we just in the right place at the right time? Or was it the *wrong* place at the wrong time?

Then disappointment hit me. If Gareth was here, that meant he was still possessed by Victor. I'd hoped the spell would somehow separate them. Now what?

Gareth walked up to the porch and stopped. He looked around, almost as if he sensed our presence. The hair on the back of my neck stood up.

"I know you're here," he said suddenly. "What have you done? Why was I pulled here?"

There was something different about his voice, but I'd heard it before, when he warned me to stay away from the house. Victor was in control, at least for the moment.

I stayed where I was until Gareth/Victor walked up the steps and made his way inside.

"Stay here," I whispered to Kyreh as I stood.

He shook his head no and tensed to stand up as well, but I placed a hand on his shoulder.

"I need you out here. Call the state police barracks. Ask for Detective Sergeant Mead. Tell him Gareth is here and we need help fast."

He still didn't look convinced, so I crouched back down so we were eye to eye. "Please. I need to know you're safe."

He nodded reluctantly. I stood up, but before I could muster my nerve to follow Gareth/Victor, Kyreh grabbed my wrist.

"Wait!" he hissed.

He stood up as well and pulled me close.

"What—"

Before I could finish my question, his leaned in and pressed his lips to mine. The kiss completely took my breath. When he broke away, I blinked in shock.

"Promise you'll come back to me," he whispered.

I nodded dumbly, still speechless.

He went to crouch again, but this time I caught his wrist and pulled him in for another kiss, longer and deeper this time. Then, without another word, I spun away and started toward the house as quietly as I could.

When I reached the door, it occurred to me that Victor/Gareth could be waiting on the other side. I paused, but as I was trying to decide how to proceed, a heavy thump came from upstairs.

I ducked inside and started slowly up the stairs, taking them one at a time. I paused again about halfway up, listening to see if I could tell where he was. There was a faint scraping sound, then a muffled thud, followed by the floorboards creaking. He was in his old bedroom.

I didn't have a plan. The last thing I wanted to do was confront Victor, but all I could think to do was keep him busy and distracted until the police showed up. So, as silently as possible, I took the last few stairs. At the top, I turned the lantern on and stepped into the bedroom doorway.

"Hello, Victor," I said, hoping I sounded more confident than I felt.

He spun around and narrowed his eyes. "I should have known it was you. What did you do?"

"Oh, not much. I guess I'm just better at summoning spells than you are." I wasn't ready to tell him about the binding spell just yet. The box was still tucked under my arm. I discreetly scanned the room for Mason and the others. There was no sign of them. Had they left?

"How dare you!"

My attention snapped back to the seething boy in front of me.

"You don't know what you're dealing with," he snarled.

"I think I do. I know you're Victor Handy. I know you killed your family. You killed Gareth's friends. Hell, you probably killed Doug Frank too."

He cocked his head slightly, as if impressed.

"I can even understand why you killed Doug. You wanted revenge, and you waited a long time for it, but why the boys?"

"How do you know I wanted revenge?"

"I found your journal."

"You read my journal?" Outrage filled his voice as he glanced toward the closet.

"Yes. And I know that you did the summoning spell wrong."

"I did not."

"Yes, you did. You drew the sigil wrong. Why do you think the spell didn't work?"

He glanced over at the circle, but then his attention snapped back to me. "I could kill you now."

"Then you'll never leave this place."

"You can't stop me."

"You don't think so? Go ahead and try."

I actually had no idea if he could leave or not. I wasn't entirely sure how the spell worked. Were my improvisations with the sliver of floor enough?

His eyes narrowed. "You didn't just summon me here. What did you do?" His voice dripped with venom.

"You're bound to this place now."

"What? How?"

"You're also bound from harming others."

"A binding spell?"

"Maybe."

"What do you want?"

"I want you to stop killing people. And I want you to leave Gareth alone."

"Why should I?"

"Because he's just an innocent kid."

"Not so innocent."

"What do you mean?"

"He asked. He invited me in."

"You mean he said something that you twisted so you could violate him."

"He came in here with his little friends and asked me to come to him, to speak through him. So I did."

"That's not what he meant."

"Sure it is. Maybe he bit off more than he could chew, but what else was he doing if he wasn't inviting something in? That something just happened to be me."

"So you possessed him?"

"I like to think of it as sharing an apartment. We're sort of like roommates. Except he didn't really know I was here, and things would be a lot easier without him."

"Why did his friends have to die?"

Gareth/Victor made a face. "I was trying to make this stupid spell work. After all those years of being stuck in this stupid house, I finally had sacrifices available again. I still don't know why my spell wouldn't work. I did everything right, but just like before, nothing happened. It's just so hard to get good help these days." He tipped his head to one side and gave me a bone-chilling smile.

"What exactly were you trying to do?"

"Get power, of course. The power to punish everybody who'd made my life miserable and kept me apart from the one person who cared about me."

"But that didn't happen. Something else happened, though. Your consciousness was ripped from your body."

"You make it sound so dramatic. One second I was fine; the next I was staring at my own dead body. Our course, being a ghost in an abandoned house for decades wasn't all fun and games. You can't imagine how relieved I was when this idiot waltzed through the door and invited me in."

"A willing vessel," I muttered.

"Sure, if you want to be all poetic about it. Looks like we have a standoff. We both want Gareth. But I'm not giving him up."

"What if I promised to free you?"

"How?"

"I can break the binding spell."

"Why would you do that now that I'm trapped here again?"

"Because if you're trapped, so is Gareth."

"So? Why should you care? It was his body who killed his friends. Even if they can't connect him to Doug, they know he killed the others."

"If he goes to jail, what then? You'll be locked up with him."

"Then I'll have plenty of time to figure out how to get out of him. If I did it once, I can do it again."

"And what? Go on killing? What's the point in all this?"

"I have one more person to kill. After that, who knows?"

"The other boy who bullied you?"

"Bullied? They didn't just bully me. They raped me. Over and over. I thought you read my journal."

"Some of it wasn't... readable. Victor, I can understand why you're angry. That must have been horrible. The people who should have protected you didn't."

"Robert protected me."

"Robert? Oh. He must be R."

"Read that part, huh? Yes. He tried to protect me. And he tried to teach me how to protect myself. Then they ripped me away from him and forced me to move here, where the torture just started up again. Different town, same shit."

"You were raped back in New Jersey?"

"No. Just picked on there. The other stuff didn't start until we were here. My sister told some people about Robert, why we moved. Word spread that I was a homo. Doug and Bobby... they figured that if I was a queer, then I must like it up the butt. I hated it. At least when they did it."

"Victor, I'm sorry that happened. That's horrible, and you're right, those boys deserved to be punished. But Gareth didn't do any of that. He's innocent."

"Not anymore."

"What do you mean?"

"I finally let him see what he did. Or... what I did using his body. He's gone very quiet now. I'm in charge."

"Let me talk to him."

"No."

"Then I won't break the spell."

"Even if you do, and I leave Gareth, what's to stop you from just casting it again? I won't spend another fifty years trapped in this house without a body."

"What if I offer myself as a willing vessel?"

"What? Why would you do that?"

I had no intention of doing that. I just wanted to get him out of Gareth.

"Because Gareth is just a kid who got in over his head. He doesn't deserve this. Please free him."

"He'll never be free."

"He has a chance if you leave him alone."

Suddenly his eyes rolled up in his head. Maybe Gareth hadn't given up yet after all. Gareth/Victor stumbled back a few steps, then crumpled to the floor and convulsed.

I rushed into the room and knelt next to him. I set the box down and rolled Gareth onto his side the way I'd seen them do at the police barracks and in the hospital.

The seizure stopped as quickly as it had begun. His eyes shot open, and he pushed himself into a sitting position, his eyes never leaving mine.

"Gareth?" I asked hesitantly, my entire body tense.

"He's fighting me," he whispered. His face was a mask of fear and horror.

"Fight back."

"He'll win."

"Don't give up. I'm going to free you—"

His head snapped back, and when his eyes found me again, I knew Victor was back in control.

"Thanks for coming in," he said with a devilish smile and shoved me backward.

As I fell over, I realized I'd fallen for a trap. He was on his feet in a flash and quickly positioned himself between me and the door.

Victor/Gareth reached behind his back and produced a dark-colored dagger seemingly out of nowhere. It might have been silver once but looked almost black with tarnish… or dried blood. It had to be the same one Victor had used to kill his family and the three boys.

"Is that the dagger Robert gave you?" I asked, more to distract him than because it mattered. Every minute I kept him talking bought me time to think of a way out of this or for the police to arrive. I slowly slid backward toward the window, pushing the box behind me as I went.

"The very same."

"Where did you hide it?"

He looked smug. "You didn't find all of my hiding places."

"Then tell me. Doesn't matter now, does it?"

"Enough!" he snapped. "You're going to break the spell or I'll kill you."

"What's to stop you from killing me once I break the spell?"

"What's to stop me from killing you right now?"

Once again we were deadlocked—at least, he thought we were. If the spell had worked, he wouldn't be able to actually harm me. I wasn't sure I was willing to bet my life on that, however.

"If I agree to break the spell, I'll only do it from outside."

He seemed to consider it. "Fair enough. But show me what you're going to do. And move slowly."

I reached behind me and produced the box. "I performed the binding ritual on a poppet that's locked inside this box. All I have to do is remove everything in the exact order I did them," I said. I wasn't actually sure that was how it worked, but I hoped that if I spoke with enough authority, he'd buy it. I wasn't sure how much he knew about binding spells.

He looked from the box back to me.

"How do I know you'll actually do it if I let you leave?"

"Because I want to save Gareth."

He opened his mouth to reply, but no sound came out. Instead he started convulsing again. He fell to one knee and let out a strangled croak. The dagger clattered to the floor. Gareth was obviously fighting, but Victor wasn't ready to give up.

"Fight, Gareth! Fight!" I yelled.

Suddenly he slumped forward onto his hands and knees, his head dangling. When he looked up, the haunted look in his eyes told me Gareth was in control... for the moment.

"Gareth, what can I do to help?" I asked.

"Nothing. Get out. He's lying. He'll never let me go."

"We can figure something out—"

"No. It doesn't matter." His voice cracked. "I... I killed Kyle. My best friend. And DJ and Wade. I... I killed them." He retched as tears streamed down his face. "I saw it. I saw it happen." He broke down into sobs.

"Victor killed them. You weren't in control."

"No, but it was my body. Victor is right about one thing. I'm the one who will end up in prison."

"Gareth... I... I have to stop him."

"I know."

"I don't want to hurt you."

He dropped his head again. "You won't have to."

"Why? What do you mean?"

His hand shot out and grabbed the dagger, and I jumped back, thinking Victor was back in control. Instead, he scrabbled away from me, into the circle.

As his arm started moving, I realized what he was about to do.

"Gareth! No!" I screamed as I rushed toward him.

I was too slow. I'd only taken a couple of steps before he thrust the dagger into his own throat. His eyes were wide and locked on mine as he yanked the dagger back out with a nauseating gurgle. Blood spurted out, spattering warm across my face and splashing across the circle.

His eyes dulled and he fell forward, the dagger still gripped in his hand.

As his blood soaked into the circle, there was a change in the room. The air suddenly felt charged, and the hair on my arms stood up. I quickly backed away from the circle, which shimmered for a moment, and I realized that however quiet it might have been up until now, Gareth's death—or, more specifically, his blood—had reactivated the spell.

A pulse of energy blasted out, and in its wake, a teen boy stood in the center of the circle, his face twisted with fury. He was thin and short, with shaggy dirty blond hair that just brushed his narrow shoulders, and a pug nose. He appeared as solid as me or Gareth.

I didn't have to be told who it was. I was face-to-face with Victor at last.

Before either of us could speak, Kyreh appeared in the doorway with his lantern held high. He looked from me to Gareth's prone body, ignoring Victor completely. "Are you okay?" he asked. "You screamed."

"Get out," I rasped. "Go. Now."

"Cav, what's going on?"

"Just go."

He hesitated still, so I screamed, "*Go!*"

He reluctantly turned and left.

While I was distracted by Kyreh, Victor had moved closer. A twisted smile spread across his face as my attention returned to him. "I guess it's just you and me now," he said. "You got what you wanted. I freed Gareth. Time to keep your end of the bargain."

"You didn't free Gareth. He freed himself," I snarled.

He shrugged. "Same thing. What matters is that you promised to break the spell."

"Fuck you. You're never leaving this place again."

The smile fell from Victor's face. "You promised."

"I lied. Just like you lied."

Rage contorted his face as he took several more threatening steps toward me. "I may not have his body anymore, but I can still kill you."

"No you can't." I sounded unsure even to myself.

He continued to advance. "I can and I will. And I'll enjoy every second of it."

Was he telling the truth? I had no idea. Maybe he could attack me physically. Or maybe he could somehow forcibly take over my body. Did my offer to be a willing vessel count as an invitation? I didn't want to find out. For every step he took toward me, I backed away. Suddenly, the window frame pressed against my back. I was cornered with no place to go.

"If I'm stuck here forever, I might as well have a little fun first. Who knows? Maybe you'll be stuck here with me."

And with that, he lunged toward me.

I squeezed my eyes shut and heard the thud of two bodies colliding but didn't feel anything. I opened my eyes to find Mason and Victor grappling, stumbling back toward the circle.

"Mason!" I cried.

Victor was furious and had the strength to match, but Mason was quite a bit taller and was slowly gaining the advantage. Suddenly, the other hazy figures reappeared as well. They gathered in a tight circle around Mason and Victor, but I saw straight through them to the struggle within.

The two dead boys wrestled back and forth for several more seconds before Mason gained the upper hand and the two tumbled to the floor with Mason on top, pinning Victor's spirit to the floor.

"What's going on? What are you doing?" I asked, panic in my voice.

"Stopping him. Get out."

"And then what?"

"Do what you were planning to do. Bury the box. Burn down the house. I don't know. You just have to go. I'll hold him here until you're gone."

"He's tied to the house now. If we burn it down, it might free him."

"Then what's the box about?"

"I don't know. I... I changed the spell. I think I might have messed it up."

"Fuck," Mason said as Victor bucked wildly and almost broke free. "If we leave him here, the house will collapse eventually. Or the doll will rot. Or the spell will weaken in time. No matter what, something will free him."

"Then what do we do?"

Victor thrashed again, and I could see Mason's grip on him weakening.

"Cav, go. I... don't know how long I can hold him or even if I can maintain this form. I don't know how any of this works."

"But—"

Just then, the ancestral figures started moving, swaying as one, and a sort of vibration filled the air.

Victor went limp, and Mason looked up in surprise.

"What's going on?" I asked.

Mason looked as if he was listening intently for a moment. Then he refocused on me. "They say they can finish it."

"Finish it? How?"

"They say they can take him."

As soon as he said that, Victor started thrashing again, but Mason held on.

"Take him where?" I asked, already dreading the answer.

Mason looked up. "The Otherworld."

"What does that mean?"

"I don't know."

"And what about you?" I asked, my throat tightening. "Do you have to go too?"

Mason listened again, then shook his head, his eyes meeting mine. "They said I can stay."

Relief flooded through me. I wasn't sure where things stood with Mason, but I wasn't ready for him to go. I looked around at the smoky figures, wondering which one was my dad and which one was my mom. I wasn't ready for them to go either.

"Can they hear me?" I asked.

Mason nodded.

A sob rose up in my throat. "Mom and Dad, thank you for coming. Thank you for protecting me. I love you. I wish…. I wish we could have more time together."

One of the ancestors pulled away from the others, leaving tendrils of swirling mist behind them. It approached me, then seemed to materialize into a figure I'd recognize anywhere.

"Mom," I choked out.

She smiled, her eyes filled with a mixture of pride, sadness, and love. "You did good, Cav," she told me. "I guess I should have taken all this more seriously, huh? Turns out your nana was right all along. You take after her. Listen to her. She'll teach you everything you need to know."

"What will happen to him?" I asked, my eyes sliding back over to Victor.

"That's not for you to worry about. He's our responsibility now."

With that, she reached out a hand and stroked my cheek. My eyes grew wide. I could actually feel her touch.

"It's Samhain," she said, as if that explained everything. "But I can't maintain this form for long."

"Why? Why does Mason look so solid but you're like… this?"

"He has an energy source. We are deliberately not pulling any more energy from this plane than we have to."

I glanced over at Mason. "It's me, isn't it?" I whispered. "I'm his energy source."

She just smiled. "It's time for me to go."

"Wait! No… I…."

"You'll be okay." She gave me a little half smile.

"Will I see you again?"

"You never know," she replied, her eyes twinkling. "Halloween comes once a year."

With that, she stepped back, gave me one last smile, then turned and faded back into the other ancestors as they crowded in around Mason and Victor. They formed a pulsating cloud of iridescent haze that slowly started to swirl around them until I couldn't see them anymore. And then, just as suddenly as they'd appeared, they were gone—all of them, Victor, Mason, and the ancestors.

Gareth's lifeless body drew my attention, and I took an involuntary step toward him. "I'm so sorry," I whispered, and burst into tears.

Chapter 22

BY THE time I'd stopped crying and made my way downstairs, still clutching the box to my chest, I could hear people talking outside. As I drew closer, I recognized Kyreh and Mead's voices.

"I'm the one who called for help. We spoke on the phone," Kyreh was saying.

"Where are Gareth and Cav?" Mead barked.

"Still inside," Kyreh replied.

"I'm here," I said, stepping through the door.

Mead was in a standoff with Kyreh. Kyreh's hands were raised over his head, while Mead's hand was on the butt of the pistol at his waist. There were several other officers behind Mead, some training powerful flashlights on Kyreh, all with their guns drawn.

A few of the lights swung my way as Mead and Kyreh turned to me with varying degrees of relief. Mead also somehow managed to look annoyed. "Where's the Miller kid?" he asked. Then he took me in. "You're covered in blood."

I took a moment to gather my thoughts. "Gareth is upstairs. He's dead."

"Go find him," Mead ordered the officers, and several peeled off and brushed past me, guns still in hand.

Mead studied me closely. "Is any of that blood yours?"

"I don't think so."

"Mind telling me what in the name of all that's holy happened in there?"

Whatever happened, it definitely wasn't holy, I thought. But I couldn't very well say that out loud. "He stabbed himself. Right in front of me. I… I tried to stop him, but by the time I realized what he was doing, it was too late."

"Why the hell were you even here?"

I shook my head. I didn't have a good excuse lined up. I couldn't very well say we came to cast a spell and everything went sideways.

"We followed Gareth," Kyreh said softly, and Mead turned to look at him. I think he'd almost forgotten Kyreh was there.

"What's your name?" Mead asked Kyreh.

"Kyreh Chambers, sir."

"He's with me," I said.

Mead cut his eyes at me. "Yeah, I figured that out for myself." Then to Kyreh, "For God's sake, put your hands down." He turned back to me. "What's in the box?"

I hadn't realized I was still hugging the box. Not that it mattered anymore. If my ancestors had dragged Victor into some other dimension or plane, then the binding spell was moot. I didn't feel like explaining all that to Mead, though.

I shrugged. "It was my Hail Mary," I said, suddenly feeling very tired. I sat down on the top step of the porch. "Didn't work."

"Did he say anything to you before he killed himself?" Mead demanded.

"He confessed to killing the boys," I told him. "But can we continue this at the barracks? I'd like to do this on the record, if that's okay. I'm exhausted, and I don't want to have to tell this story more than once."

That was true, but the real reason for my request was that it would give me time to come up with a coherent story that left out Victor, Mason, and my ancestors. And maybe the part where I tried to cast a binding spell.

Just then, one of the officers emerged from the house. "He's dead," the officer confirmed.

"Shit," Mead muttered. Then louder, "Call the coroner's office. Better get them out here." He returned his attention to me. "Buckle up. It's going to be a long night."

Mead made Kyreh and I wait out of the way for hours with a trooper keeping watch over us while they secured the crime scene and removed Gareth in a black body bag. It was chilly now that my adrenaline was gone, but our guard was nice enough to give us a blanket at least.

Finally, Mead approached us with a deep frown creasing his face. He looked exhausted. "Having fun?" he asked.

"Not really," I replied.

"Me either. But we're just getting started. Time to get your statements, which we'll do in the relative comfort of the barracks. You're coming with me."

"Wouldn't it be easier if I take my car?" I really wanted to give Kyreh and I time to talk. We hadn't dared say too much with our guard hovering around. Kyreh would have to give a statement too, even though he'd missed most of the action, and we needed to make sure our stories matched.

"It would be easier if you just do what I say," Mead snapped.

"I'll need my car when you let us go."

"Who said I'm letting you go?"

"I didn't do anything!" I protested. "Am I under arrest?"

He clenched his jaw, closed his eyes for a moment, and pinched the bridge of his nose. "Relax, Crawford. You're not under arrest."

"Then why can't I drive?"

He opened his eyes. "Fine. You can drive, but I'm following you all the way there."

I breathed a sigh of relief.

Mead and another officer escorted us back to my car. Gareth had parked on the road behind me, partially blocking me in, so it took a little maneuvering to get past it, but then we were on our way, a marked car in front of us and Mead behind.

KYREH AND I spent the drive back to the police barracks concocting our cover story. We settled on letting Gareth take the blame. It was far too late to save his memory. We'd say Gareth had somehow stumbled across the story of the Handys' murders while working on a school project and became obsessed enough to recreate it by killing his friends, and then desperately tried to cover it up. He hid out for a week, but when hunger and dehydration overcame him, he became delirious and wandered off, which was when he was found on the side of the road. He only pretended to have amnesia.

I felt bad about throwing Gareth under the bus, but it was the only way, really. I could only hope that he would have seen it the same way. He and Victor were right. Gareth had killed his friends, in a way—at least, the only way the police would see it. But it still left a bad taste in my mouth.

He was just a kid who got caught up in something far more dangerous than he could possibly understand.

"What if they ask about the box again?" Kyreh asked.

I thought for a moment. "I'll tell them it was filled with Victor's things that I found in the closet. Mead already knows about them."

I instructed Kyreh to unlock the box and swap out the poppet for the spell book and bottle, which were still in my backpack.

"What do I do with this?" he asked, holding the poppet at arm's length using only his fingertips.

"Uh, put it in the glove compartment, I guess. I'll burn it tomorrow."

He made a face but did as I suggested.

When we arrived, Mead was kind enough to let me clean up—after getting several swabs of the blood on my face and clothes—before I sat down for the official interview. I could only hope we'd come up with a good enough story to pass. There was just enough truth in there that I hoped it would hold up, even if we were leaving out all the supernatural parts.

Luckily, Mead accepted my story with only a few questions.

"Why'd he kill himself? Why now?"

"I don't know. I think he was feeling remorse. And he was trapped. It... it happened really quickly."

"And the dagger he used? You think it's the one he used to kill the boys?"

"Yes, and probably the same one Victor Handy used to kill his family."

"Where did it come from?"

"No clue. He had it when I found him." That much was true, at least.

The interview took far longer than I would have liked. As it finally started winding down, Mead dismissed the other officer who'd been in the room with us. Once we were alone, he eyed me for a long moment, then sighed. "Look, I know you're not telling me everything."

"What do you mean?" I asked in alarm.

"Your story doesn't add up."

"I told you everything."

"Like hell you did. You have more holes in your statement than I have gray hairs, and I'm pretty sure I'm getting more by the minute. For instance, if you followed Gareth there, then why was he parked behind you?"

I opened my mouth but didn't have an excuse lined up. Before I could invent something, Mead held his hand up. "Whatever happened, though, I'm not sure it really matters."

"What?" That was about the last thing I expected him to say.

"We have a dead suspect and we have the murder weapon. We'll be checking the dagger for fingerprints. As long as Gareth's are the only prints on the handle, we have no reason to doubt the basic facts you gave us, even if I'm pretty sure you fudged some of the details. While I don't know why you would do that, I'm going to give you the benefit of the doubt here." He stared at me very hard. "If there was something important, something you left out that would change the outcome of this case, I trust you would tell me."

I nodded nervously.

"Good." He leaned back in his chair again. "Maybe you wanted to confront him alone at the scene of the crime. Maybe you thought going to a murder scene was a fun date night on Halloween and he just showed up by wild coincidence. Whatever it was, you made this case a lot easier to close, and quite frankly, I care more about that than finding out why you arrived at the house first. It doesn't hurt that your friend called as quickly as he did, although if you'd called a little sooner, maybe that boy would still be alive."

"Yes, sir. I know. Trust me, that will haunt me for a long time."

He studied me for a second. "Yeah, I imagine it will. That must have been a terrible thing to witness. Now let it be a lesson. You're a good investigator, Crawford. Impulsive, young, green—but you've got some impressive skills. Learn from your mistakes and don't repeat them in the future."

I nodded. "Yes, sir."

He eyed me a little longer, then jerked his head toward the door. "I think we're done. Get out of here."

I had to wait a while for Kyreh to give his statement before we were released. We were on our way out of the barracks when I spotted Iwan and Robin Miller sitting at a table. Mrs. Miller was sobbing on her husband's shoulder, but his eyes met mine for a second. His expression was dead, but I gave him a nod. I knew I'd have to talk to them at some point. This wasn't the time.

By the time I dropped Kyreh off and got home, the sun was just starting to creep above the horizon. Haniah was asleep when I got in, a fact I was very thankful for. I took a long, hot shower, then collapsed into my bed and cried myself to sleep.

I woke up later to a gentle knocking. "Cav?" Haniah called through the door.

I sat up and grabbed my phone. It was late morning. "Yeah?" I called back.

"Are you up? Your dads are here."

I rubbed the sleep from my eyes and tried to figure out why Jason and Eli were there. They never dropped in unannounced.

"I'll be right out."

I dressed and wandered out to the living room, still feeling a little bleary.

Jason and Eli sat next to each other on the couch with identical expressions of concern. Haniah was nowhere to be seen.

"Um, hi. What's up?"

"We heard on the news about what happened last night," Jason said.

"We're so sorry you had to witness that," Eli added.

I sighed. Oh well, at least I wouldn't have to tell them the story myself. "What are they saying on the news?"

"That the boy killed his friends in some sort of copycat crime," Jason said. "And then you figured it all out, and when you confronted him, he committed suicide."

I took a shaky breath. "Did they mention me by name?"

Jason and Eli exchanged looks.

Yes," Eli said. "They called you a hero."

I nodded and sat down. "Oh, great. Walker is going to love that." Then it occurred to me that if Jason and Eli had seen it on the news, it was only a matter of time until Nana saw it too.

I realized they were both staring expectantly at me. "Uh, if it's okay with you guys, I'd rather not talk about it. You know the basic facts. That's enough."

"Of course," Jason said quickly.

"Thank you. And if it's on the news, I should probably call Nana."

Jason nodded emphatically. "Yes. You're right. You want to give her a call now?"

I stood. "Yes. I'll keep it quick."

"Take as much time as you need," Eli said.

As I returned to my room, I could hear Haniah puttering around in the kitchen. I closed my bedroom door and dialed Nana's number.

"I'm okay," I said as soon as she answered.

"What happened?" she asked. "Did the spell work?"

"Kind of. Have you seen the news?"

"Not yet. It made the news?"

"So I've been told. The spell worked, but… I messed with it. I added something that didn't work out the way I expected. In the end, I don't think it really mattered. The binding spell was only a temporary fix. The ancestors had other ideas."

"The ancestors?"

"That protection spell you gave me. I called, they came. In the end, they took Victor away. To the Otherworld, whatever that means."

Nana was quiet for a moment. "And the boy? The other boy?"

"He…." My voice broke. "He didn't make it."

"Oh, Cavanaugh."

"There was nothing I could do."

"I'm sorry, sweet one. I'm glad the ancestors came when you called. Did you see them? The ancestors?"

"Not really. They were misty, more like phantoms that I couldn't see clearly. Except… Nana, Mom was there. And I got to talk to her." The tears returned, and my voice became thick. "She said you were right all along and that I should listen to you. That you'd teach me."

She was quiet for a few more seconds. "And I will. I'm glad you got to see her."

"Me too. I'll come see you later today and tell you everything."

I ended the call and took a moment to compose myself. While I was there, I shot Professor Lawson a text to let her know the spell had worked. That was enough for now. I was sure she'd want to know more, but I had to decide how much I wanted to tell her.

I returned to the living room, where Jason and Eli were talking quietly. They stopped when I entered the room.

"Everything okay?" Jason asked.

I nodded, and just then, Haniah bustled in with a tray of mugs. "I made tea," she said as she started distributing them. "Are you staying for breakfast? I can cook."

"You don't have to do that," Jason said quickly. "Besides, I think it's more like brunch at this point, and everybody knows the gays excel at brunch. Why don't we go out somewhere? Our treat."

"You don't have to do that," I protested, but Jason waved it away.

"You had a rough night. Let us do this. Haniah, you have to come too."

"Aw, thank you. I'd love to."

"Then, uh, in that case, could I invite one more person?"

They all three turned to look at me, Jason and Eli with confusion and Haniah with a knowing smile.

BRUNCH WENT surprisingly well. Jason and Eli were delighted to meet Kyreh, and Haniah couldn't stop gloating.

We mostly managed to avoid talking about Gareth or the case, but it was never far from my mind. I couldn't stop thinking about the Millers and what they were going through, thinking their son was a cold-blooded killer. Several times someone had to call my name more than once or repeat themselves, I was so distracted.

After we finished up and Jason and Eli paid the check, we walked out to the parking lot, where everyone thanked my dads profusely, and then we split up. I could tell Jason and Eli were still worried about me, but I assured them I was fine, although I wasn't really convinced myself.

I ran Haniah home first, then drove Kyreh back to campus.

"How are you really?" he asked when I pulled into a parking spot.

I gave him a smile. "I'll be okay. I just…. I wish I could have saved Gareth, but I think he was lost as soon as he walked into that house. At least I managed to stop Victor, even if it wasn't how I planned. I really fucked up that spell. If my ancestors weren't there…."

"But they were. And they were there because you called them. And they came."

"I know. You're right. It was just a lot."

"And that's the understatement of the year. But you've got your dads. They're great, by the way. Thank you for inviting me. And you've got Haniah. And your grandmother. And me."

I reached out and took his hand. "I'll have to take you to meet Nana soon."

He raised an eyebrow. "When you're ready." He laughed. "You said we should take it slow, and I've already met your dads."

"Yeah, well, there's nothing like bonding over a paranormal near-death experience for a second date."

Kyreh laughed again, then pulled me across the center console by the hand he was holding and planted a big kiss on me. "Dating you is never going to be boring, huh?"

"Not if I can help it."

He gave me another kiss, then released me. "Okay, I should let you get home. You look like you could use a little more sleep."

"You're not wrong there, but there's something I need to do before I go home."

ABOUT TWENTY minutes later, I pulled up in front of the Millers' house. I sat in the car for a few minutes, preparing myself. Finally I couldn't put it off any longer. I walked up to the door and rang the bell.

They took so long to answer, I was about to leave when it swung open. Mr. Miller seemed surprised—and not exactly pleased—to see me.

"What are you doing here?" he asked coldly.

"I came to see how you were doing," I said gently.

He glared at me from the doorway. Then Mrs. Miller walked up behind him. "Let him in, Iwan."

He stood there for another moment but then stepped back to allow me by.

"I won't stay long. I can't imagine how hard this all must be for you," I said as I entered.

Mrs. Miller looked pale, and her eyes were puffy and red-rimmed, as if she'd been crying all morning. We were all standing awkwardly in their entryway.

"I'm so sorry for your loss," I said, knowing it wasn't enough, that nothing could be enough.

"Our loss?" Mr. Miller said, his voice shaking with anger. "Our loss that you caused?"

I sucked in a breath. "I tried to stop him…."

"If you hadn't confronted him, maybe he'd still be alive," he said.

I sighed. I couldn't argue with his logic, at least from what he knew. "Maybe so," I agreed quietly.

"It's not his fault," Mrs. Miller said, her voice flat. "He had nothing to do with Gareth... with what Gareth did. He was only involved because we hired him."

"I guess you're just worried about getting paid," Mr. Miller growled. "What? No!"

"Don't mind him," Mrs. Miller said. "He's coping by staying angry. I'm coping by crying." She wiped at her eyes. "It's a lot to deal with."

I nodded.

"We believed he was innocent right up until the end, even though we knew something was wrong. There were times when it felt like he was somebody else. I just can't believe he'd... do that."

I so badly wanted to tell them the truth. "I... I don't think... he was in his right mind," I said, struggling with my words.

"What do you mean?" she asked, a note of desperate hope in her voice.

"He... wasn't himself. It was...." I took a deep breath. "It was like he was possessed."

"Possessed?" She sounded confused. Mr. Miller's frown deepened.

"I tried to help him...." A tear spilled over, and I quickly swiped it away. "He was horrified by what he'd done." That much was true, at least. "That's why he—"

"Enough," Mr. Miller shouted suddenly. "You'll get paid. You don't need to come here and concoct some insane story about our murderer son being possessed or seeking some kind of penance. He killed those boys, his own friends. Took them away from their families. And then he took the coward's way out."

There was nothing more I could say. My eyes locked with Mrs. Miller's, and she gave me a little nod. At least she seemed somewhat comforted by my words.

"I'll leave you alone," I said. "I'm sorry to have bothered you."

I turned to leave, and as I reached the door, I heard Mrs. Miller thank me. I just nodded and continued out.

WHEN I got back to the apartment, I was ready to lock myself in my bedroom for a month. I had no sooner shut the door than Mason appeared. I had to admit I was happy to see him. I so badly wanted to throw my arms around him and hug him.

"You're here," I said instead.

"I'm here," he agreed.

"Thank you." I didn't know what else to say. He'd probably saved my life.

He shrugged awkwardly. "I did what I had to do. You would have done the same for me."

"Yeah, I would have. But I'm glad you're still here."

"Hey, we made a deal. You didn't think I'd let you off that easily, did you?"

I laughed but then stopped as he took a step toward me.

"But maybe I should let you out of that agreement?"

"What? Why?"

"Because if your parents and ancestors weren't there, if I wasn't there, if it wasn't Halloween…."

"But they were. And you were. And it was. And I'm okay." I looked down. "Or as okay as you can be when someone stabs themselves in the throat right in front of you."

"I'm sorry. There wasn't much we could do until Victor was separated from Gareth."

"It's not your fault. You did what you could, and more than I expected. What does that have to do with our deal?"

"Just making sure you haven't changed your mind. Or, I guess, giving you the opportunity to change your mind if you want."

"I don't plan on reneging on our deal," I said, and he looked relieved. "But…." He tensed again, but I continued, "I might need a little space first. This case… it was rough. I need time to process. And the holidays will be here soon…."

He looked a little disappointed, but he nodded. "Of course. Take as much time as you need. Like I said before, I've waited this long. What's a few more weeks?"

"You're sure?"

"Completely." He didn't look sure, but I wasn't about to press it. My bed was calling me.

"Okay."

My phone started buzzing in my pocket, and I sighed. Bed would have to wait a little longer. I had a feeling I knew who it was without even looking. The only person I hadn't talked to yet today. I pulled out my phone, and sure enough, it was Walker. I glanced up to tell Mason that I needed to take the call, but he was already gone.

"Hey, boss," I started as soon as I answered, but he cut me off.

"Cavanaugh Crawford, what the hell happened last night?"

I sighed. "Long story. You have a minute?"

Keep reading for an excerpt from
The Silence Is a Lie
by Josh Aterovis

HANIAH WASN'T home when I got back to our apartment. She was probably squeezing in a few more dates this week before she headed back to Ghana. She was bisexual and enjoyed a vibrant dating life here in the States but would have to head back into the closet while she was home with her family. They definitely didn't know she liked girls.

We rented the second floor of an old Victorian house on the outskirts of Baltimore City. It was surprisingly affordable for as nice as it was, and we'd really lucked out with our landlord, which was good since she lived on the first floor. She loved Haniah and me. A guy named Lee lived on the top floor, but we rarely saw or even heard him.

I didn't turn any lights on as I moved through the apartment to my bedroom, which is why I was startled when a voice suddenly spoke up from the shadows of my bedroom.

"Can we talk?"

I jumped and clutched my chest. "Jesus, Mason. You scared the shit out of me."

I snapped the light on to reveal the ghost of my former boyfriend, looking as alive and solid as ever.

He chuckled. "Hey, scaring people is one of the few perks of being dead," he said. "That and walking through walls, and let me tell you, the excitement of being incorporeal wears off quick."

"You wanted to talk?"

"Yeah. You probably can guess what about."

"Yeah, I can guess."

Mason had mysteriously vanished a little over a year and a half before, on our anniversary, as a matter of fact. For months there was no sign of him. It had been a living hell. Then a hiker found some badly decomposed human remains off a trail in a huge local park. Those remains were identified as Mason. His cause of death was inconclusive due to the state of his body, but the police had ruled his death accidental thanks to a lack of evidence otherwise.

Then, a few months ago, I'd accidentally summoned his spirit, and he'd somehow never left. Well, the first time was an accident. The second summoning was very much on purpose. That was when we'd made a deal. I'd look into his death and then he'd move on—whatever that meant.

From the beginning, I'd felt like his death was suspicious, but Mason said he didn't remember anything from his last day, that it was all just black. He wanted me to look into it, though, you know, since I was a private investigator and all. He needed the closure, which I understood. I could use a little myself.

And yet… I'd been putting it off for months.

"You know, after the case with Gareth and Victor, you said you needed a little time, and I totally understood. But then it was the holidays. Then you needed to focus on your last semester of school. Then it was finals. Well, you're graduated now, and you don't have a big case currently, so I was thinking that it seems like the perfect time to investigate my death."

I sighed. He was right and I knew it. I had to admit, part of me liked having Mason around, even if he was dead. Would he move on once he had that closure?

Another part of me dreaded looking into his death. It was a painful time to revisit, and I knew it would be emotionally difficult. Plus, I would have to convince my boss, Sutton Walker, a retired CIA agent who had originally forbidden me to investigate when Mason's body was found. I didn't want to go behind his back.

Now I'd gone and complicated things even further by asking Kyreh to move in with me for the summer. Nothing like working a case about your dead boyfriend while living with your new boyfriend.

But that was just another excuse. Kyreh knew about Mason, and he'd be supportive.

If I was going to worry about anyone, it should probably be my nana. Like me, Nana had what our Irish family called the Sight, a supernatural heritage passed down from our ancestors. Nana had never been thrilled about me summoning Mason and had repeatedly warned me about him getting attached to me. Still, I knew she would ultimately, if maybe begrudgingly, be supportive as well.

"You're right," I finally conceded.

Mason looked surprised. "I am?"

"Yeah. I'll talk to Kyreh and Walker tomorrow."

"Walker I get, but why Kyreh?"

"Just out of respect. I know he'll be supportive, but I want him to be on board before I start a deep dive into the death of my former boyfriend, ya know? Besides, I just asked him to move in for the summer, so it will affect him even more directly if he's living here."

"Oh wow, you're moving in together?"

"Maybe. But just for the summer so he doesn't have to move home with his dad. They don't get along. And he'd be so far away without a car for months. It's not a big deal. And he hasn't even said yes yet."

"It's kind of a big deal, Cav."

"Okay, well, I don't want to make it a big deal."

Mason gave me a look.

"What?"

"You must like him a lot. We dated for a year and the subject of moving in together never came up once."

"We were both living in the dorms then. It wasn't even really an option. And it's not like we're getting married. It's just for a few months. Besides, Haniah will be gone all summer, so it would be nice to have someone around."

"I'd be around."

"Someone alive."

"Ouch."

"Sorry, but you know what I mean. You come and go."

"I'll probably be around more if you're investigating my death."

"Yeah, I guess so."

"Unless you don't want me around…."

"No! I mean, of course I do. But it's not the same."

"I know. I'm just giving you a hard time."

"But while we're on the subject, what happens after my investigation?"

"What do you mean?"

"Well, let's say I find out what happened. What then? Do you… move on?"

"Oh. Right. I mean, that was the original terms of our deal, right?"

"Yeah, but what does that mean, exactly?"

"I… I don't know."

"And what if it's not as easy as that?"

"What do you mean?"

"Nana said you've attached to me. I don't know exactly what that means, but when I saw my mom last Halloween, she also kind of implied that you draw your energy to stay on this plane from me."

Mason blinked. "I do?"

I shrugged. "Look, I don't even know what that means."

"Me either. I don't…. If I do, I don't even notice it. I'm not doing it on purpose."

"I know. And if you are drawing energy, it's not something I've noticed either. It's not like I feel any different."

"But Cav, what if it's hurting you somehow, on some level we just haven't noticed? You should have said something before now."

"This is why I didn't say anything. Like I said, I don't feel anything. If it was harming me in some way, I think I would have noticed. And if not me, then Nana surely would have."

"But still…."

"Look, I can't really start this investigation until I talk to Nana about it, so I'll ask her more then, okay?"

"The list keeps growing. Walker, Kyreh, your grandmother…."

"Yeah, it's going to be complicated. But Walker is the only one you really have to worry about."

"Why's that? Because he forbade you to investigate before?"

"Yeah. And he's my boss, so he actually has the most say. Plus, you're not exactly a paying client. If I'm devoting time—and possibly resources—to this, that's an actual gig I can't focus on."

"Oh. Yeah. I hadn't thought about that. I'm sorry, Cav. Maybe this isn't fair to ask of you."

"We made a deal. Let's just wait and see what Walker says."

He sighed. "Okay. You'll start tomorrow?"

"Yep. First thing in the morning. I promise."

A METAL ladder bolted to a stone wall led down through a yawning hole in the damp concrete floor and disappeared into the darkness. I hesitated a moment, but something was drawing me down. I tried to resist, but the unseen force was strong, and I finally gave in. I descended for what seemed like forever until I felt the floor beneath my feet and I was hit by an overwhelming musty scent.

I turned around, but the space before me was pitch black. The only light filtered through the opening above my head and didn't penetrate very far.

I pulled out my phone and turned on the flashlight to illuminate what turned out to be a cavernous subterranean space. It stretched on forever in front of me, or at least as far my flashlight could reach. It seemed to be completely open, punctuated only by brick columns here and there. The stone wall behind me was damp with condensation, and the polished concrete floors were slick. I could hear a dripping sound coming from somewhere.

Something drew me on. I stumbled forward as if being pulled through the shadows by a psychic thread.

At the far end of the room, a low structure materialized from the gloom. It looked like a table at first, but as I drew closer, I realized it was a large stone slab, about three feet high and at least seven feet long. It must have literally weighed tons.

As I got even closer, the dripping got louder, and I noticed something on top of the slab. I aimed the light from my phone and gasped as a horrible realization hit me. The stone slab was an altar, and the form on top was a person. The dripping sound was blood trickling over the edge into an alarmingly large puddle that had formed on the floor.

I desperately wanted to turn back, but I was still drawn ever forward. The person was nude and male. I was only a few feet away now. My eyes were drawn to the body's chest, which had been sliced open with surgical precision, leaving a gaping void where his heart used to beat.

A growing sense of terror filled me. I wanted to scream, but I stood frozen, staring at the corpse.

Suddenly I heard a loud metallic clang behind me, breaking me out of the macabre spell.

I spun around to see nothing but pitch black. Even the small shaft of light from the trapdoor was gone. Someone had locked me in with what I could only assume was some sort of horrible human sacrifice. I checked my phone only to find I had zero signal in the stone-lined room. I shouldn't have come alone.

I heard a gurgling, hissing sound behind me and spun back around to find the body slowly turning its head. For the first time, I focused on the face.

My knees buckled as a fresh wave of horror hit me. The body was Mason. His eyes were open, but they were an unseeing opaque white. His mouth was slack, as if he were as shocked to find himself there as I was. His dead eyes seemed to be searching for something.

Those milky eyes snapped to me, and that horrible gurgling sound returned. It came Mason. He reached toward me just as a viscous black substance vomited from his mouth.

I screamed and dropped my phone, which shattered as it hit the floor, plunging us both into the dark. I tried to scramble away, but my feet slipped on the smooth, damp floor, and I fell. I scrambled upright and ran in the direction I thought I'd come from. I could hear something behind me, a sort of wet slapping sound, like bare feet pursuing me. I ran on until I slammed into a rough stone wall.

I felt around, desperately trying to find the ladder. The squelching came ever closer.

Just then, my hand found a metal bar of the ladder. I grabbed it and started climbing as fast as I could. Just as I neared the top, the wet sole of my shoe slipped, and my hands ripped from the rungs. I was falling.

I screamed and, with a violent jerk, woke up.

I sat up, looking around my room, my heart pounding and my breath ragged. I could feel the chill of my sweat on my skin.

It was just a dream, I told myself. A nightmare. Almost certainly triggered by my conversation with Mason. It doesn't mean anything.

I repeated that like a mantra as I lay back down and stared at the ceiling.

JOSH ATEROVIS has been writing award-winning queer fiction for twenty years. He fell in love with mystery novels in the fourth grade when he discovered the Nancy Drew series in his school library. He soon moved on to Agatha Christie and other titans of the genre, which led to a lifelong love affair with whodunits. His books have won multiple awards from the StoneWall Society, and he is a former Lambda Literary Award finalist for Gay Mystery.

Aterovis lives in one of the quirkiest cities in America—Baltimore, Maryland—with his two birds, Edgar and Virginia Poe (Eddy and Ginny for short), where, besides writing, he is also a visual artist and immersive theater maker.

Website: joshaterovis.com
Facebook: facebook.com/JoshAterovis
Instagram: instagram.com/aterovis
Twitter: twitter.com/Aterovis
TikTok: tiktok.com/@aterovis

THERE IS NO CRIME WITHOUT WITNESSES

APIDAE

AN
ANDI HAYES
MYSTERY

XENIA MELZER

An Andi Hayes Mystery
By Xenia Melzer

No good deed—or good record of solving crimes—goes unpunished.

Detectives Andi Hayes and George Donovan of the Charleston PD are on vacation. Or at least they are until they are called back for an emergency: find Chief Norris's missing son.

Fortunately, Andi's insect spies lead him right to little Tyler Norris, who is safe and sound.

Unfortunately, along with the chief's son, they find twenty-five corpses, victims of a serial killer who's gone unnoticed for over a decade.

Chief Norris promptly cancels Andi and George's vacation and assigns them as lead detectives on the case. Physical evidence leads them to a mental health facility where some of the victims received treatment, but Andi's gift—his usual secret weapon—fails him. Promising leads and shady suspects all turn out to be dead ends, and they're running out of time. Because the killer isn't going to stop at twenty-five victims—and Tyler Norris has just gone missing again....

www.dsppublications.com